Praise for Cherise

Simon Says: Mine

"...both tender and sharply erotic"

– Shayna, *Joyfully Reviewed*

Welcome to the Dark Side

"Wow, such a terrific story!"

– *Long and Short Reviews*

My Liege of Dark Haven

A Recommended Read! "I found myself laughing and crying and laughing some more..."

– *TwoLips Reviews*

"...an awesome read, one I can recommend without hesitation..."

– *Guilty Pleasures Book Reviews*

"...well written, deeply enjoyable..."

– *Dear Author*

"...exceeded my expectations"

– *Under the Covers Book Blog*

"The best. The hottest. The most creative. That is all."

– *Fiction Vixen Book Reviews*

"I spent all day reading it—in fact, I practically DEVOURED it."

– *Sinfully Sexy Books*

Loose Id®

ISBN 13: 978-1-62300-125-4
MY LIEGE OF DARK HAVEN

Originally released in e-book format in August 2012

Cover Art by April Martinez
Cover Layout and Design by April Martinez

DISCLAIMER: Many of the acts described in our BDSM/fetish titles can be dangerous. Please do not try any new sexual practice, whether it be fire, rope, or whip play, without the guidance of an experienced practitioner. Neither Loose Id nor its authors will be responsible for any loss, harm, injury or death resulting from use of the information contained in any of its titles.

This book is an original publication of Loose Id. Each individual story herein was previously published in e-book format only by Loose Id and is a work of fiction. Any similarity to actual persons, events or existing locations is entirely coincidental.

Printed in the U.S.A. by
Lightning Source, Inc.
1246 Heil Quaker Blvd
La Vergne TN 37086
www.lightningsource.com

MY LIEGE OF DARK HAVEN

Cherise Sinclair

Acknowledgments

I'd like to thank all of you who have put yourselves in my hands, hoping to be taken to a different world for the next few hours. I'm honored by your trust, and I'll try not to let you down.

To those of you who demanded a book for Master Xavier (you know who you are), thank you! I hope I did him justice.

My Dark Haven characters and I thank my wonderful editor, G.G. Royale, who noticed I'd dressed them in chain-link rather than chain mail. They're quite relieved not to be wearing fencing material.

A big thank-you to Belinda McBride and Sierra Cartwright, who started the Dark Haven odyssey with me and generously said that I owned Master Xavier. (I explained that to him—it didn't go over well.)

Welcome to Leagh Christensen, my new personal assistant, who jumped right in and started overhauling my life. You're amazing!

To Bianca Sommerland, Fiona Archer, and Kathy Holtsclaw, who beta-read this book and made it far better than it would have been without them.

For those of you on my new street team—many, many hugs. Your LOL brattiness lightens my day, and your enthusiasm for new books forces me back to the desk. (Pain and pleasure, right?)

A shout-out to the San Francisco Citadel, especially Phil, August, and crew. Despite all the hardships, you've kept alive the dream of a home for lifestylers.

To my two fledglings who are ready to leave the nest—may your wings be strong and your flights long and glorious.

And, as always, my love and appreciation to my Dearheart. You truly do keep me sane.

Bless you all.

~Cherise

Author's Note

To my readers,

This book is fiction, not reality, and as in most romantic fiction, the romance is compressed into a very, very short time period.

You, my darlings, live in the real world, and I want you to take a little more time than the heroines you read about. Good Doms don't grow on trees, and there are some strange people out there. So while you're looking for that special Dom, please, be careful.

When you find him, realize he can't read your mind. Yes, frightening as it might be, you're going to have to open up and talk to him. And you listen to him in return. Share your hopes and fears, what you want from him, what scares you spitless. Okay, he may try to push your boundaries a little—he's a Dom, after all—but you have your safe word. You will have a safe word, am I clear? Use protection. Have a backup person. Communicate.

Remember: *safe, sane, and consensual.*

Know that I'm hoping you find that special, loving person who will understand your needs and hold you close. Let me know how you're doing. I worry, you know.

Meantime, come and hang out with the Doms of Dark Haven.

~Cherise

Chapter One

The thick fog swathed the streetlight, preventing the dim yellow glow from reaching the ground. On the dark San Francisco street, Professor Abigail Bern watched the red taillights of the taxi disappear into the mist. With the enthusiasm of a convict facing a firing squad, she turned toward the infamous Dark Haven BDSM club.

In contrast to the flashing display of the nightclub down the street, this place didn't exactly set out the welcome mat. To the right of the heavy black door, only a small, discreet sign proclaimed DARK HAVEN. She understood the lack of advertising. The BDSM community was in the same position as the gay population in the past. People weren't "out."

They certainly wouldn't like being studied.

She didn't plan to tell them. *Covert participant observation*, it was called, in which the subject never knew a sociologist was present. *And it makes me uncomfortable.* But she wouldn't gather anything that could identify a member. And really, her research on the culture might even help the community—it certainly couldn't do any harm.

She didn't have a choice. *Publish or perish* was no longer a cute phrase—not with the proposed cutbacks at her university.

It had been a ghastly week. She might lose her job, and she'd definitely lost Nathan. Although she would drive him to the airport tomorrow, he was already gone from her life. Her breathing hitched at the emptiness in her chest.

She hadn't been meeting his needs, he'd said. His need to tie her up, call her names, order her around. His need to have his precious BDSM in the bedroom. Hopefully, during her fieldwork, she'd grow to understand the appeal of such things. Maybe she'd even be able to indulge him by the time he returned in August. They could try again.

I don't want to lose him. Her attempt to take a deep, calming breath failed, and she realized she'd laced her corset far too tightly. Shaking her head, she looked down at herself, and her spirits lifted. *I look hot.* After researching BDSM styles, she'd bought a calf-length skirt, a fancy corset, and tall vinyl boots. All in black. The corset pushed up her ample breasts and yanked in her thick waist; the skirt hid her wide hips, creating a Barbie figure—well, if Barbie were a size sixteen and a Domme. The don't-mess-with-me effect was amazing.

Nathan called her a submissive—or maybe he simply hoped she was—but she wasn't convinced. Given the choice, she'd dress as a Dominant. Besides, going into a BDSM club looking like a…a victim would be stupid. *I might not be gorgeous, but smart? Oh yeah.*

She headed for the building, anxiety mingling with determination and…okay, maybe a little excitement as well. *Here goes.* She pulled the door open and—

A woman barged out, knocking Abby backward.

"Clarissa." A familiar-looking, gorgeous man followed her. "Are you certain you want to walk out like this?"

"I'm sure." Clarissa glared as she yanked on a coat over her skimpy bustier and thong. "Very, very sure, Simon."

Abby took a step back, her stomach unsettled at the woman's raised voice and open anger. *Don't yell. Don't scream. Please, please, please.*

"I thought being the receptionist meant I'd get some Xavier time, but nooo." Clarissa jerked her coat closed. "Instead he offered to find me someone to play with. Yeah, what the fuck good is that?"

As the woman edged back from uncontrollable rage, Abby relaxed enough to take mental notes. *Xavier time?* Was that a technique or a machine or what?

And she'd better go in before she got caught watching. She detoured around the man, entered the club, and faced a bulletin board with a huge calendar in the center. Various events were penciled into the squares with yarn running out to surrounding flyers. A tea for Dommes. A Master/slave event. A *furry* barbecue—which sounded just wrong. What did a party for *littles* involve? The busy calendar reminded her of the equally big one her mother had used to track Abby's debate-team nights, Grace's soccer games, and Janae's beauty-queen contests.

"Hi."

Abby turned at the greeting.

Like an ad for cuteness, a slender young man in bright-red running shorts and a matching red collar stood behind an L-shaped reception desk. He patted a device that resembled a credit card reader. "Ma'am. Swipe your membership card right here, please."

"I don't have a card." Membership? Wasn't the club a walk-in sort of place?

"That's okay. Show me your driver's license, and I'll find your number in the computer." He gave the monitor a dubious frown. "I think I can look it up."

"I mean, I'm not a member."

"Oh." He dropped into the wheeled chair, making it squeak in protest. "That's bad. See, you can't get in if you're not a member. Not anymore. You have to have a recommendation or take the classes. There's a bunch of hurdles to jump since Dark Haven turned all private and *ex-ca-loosive*."

Faint music and the hum of conversation came through the inner door as Abby stared at him in dismay. "Exclusive? But..." *I don't have time for this.* The club opened only on weekends, and her research had to start right now or she wouldn't get it done, peer-reviewed, and published in time to save her job. "Can I fill out an application?"

"I used the last one." He scowled at the computer. "I could print one. Maybe. There's a form somewhere."

She craned her neck and pointed to an icon on the desktop screen. "Try the APPLIC."

He clicked and an application appeared. "*Score.* Do you know how to send it to the printer? Last time I tried, I got awarded the blue screen of death."

After she guided him through the steps, the printer hummed to life. She grinned. Even after four years of being a professor, she still got a zing from teaching, no matter the subject.

"Here you go." He proudly handed her the form with several more from a folder. "You might as well fill out the waivers and consents too."

Off to one side, she started on the paperwork, sighing at the legalese. The usual disclaimers. The place wasn't responsible for any disaster that might befall her. *How reassuring*. She needed a physical and blood work? Jaw tight, she doggedly continued.

When the room had emptied of incoming people again, she handed the pile back to him. "How soon can you process this?"

"Hell, without Destiny here, probably forever," he said, turning glum. "Longer than that if my liege asks *me* to do the paperwork. I'm a lover, not a typist. But I can't afford the membership fees if I don't volunteer. Look at what it costs." He shoved a paper across the desk.

She scanned the monthly fees and winced. Joining would put more than a dent in her savings. Then again, getting laid off would hurt worse. "You lost your receptionist? Clarissa?"

"Man, talk about a diva. She hung on for a couple of weeks. One lady lasted almost a month. Destiny held the place together for years, but Xavier hasn't found a good replacement." He stared at the scattered papers.

Her fingers itched to clean up the mess. "It's not busy now. You could file a little at a time and then—"

He stared at her in horror. "Or not."

"Are you interested in volunteering?" a dark voice asked from behind her.

She jumped and turned to see the man who'd followed Clarissa out. "Volunteer?" Her hopes lifted. Would that let her skip the application delay? "Looks like you need someone." He really did seem familiar. She tilted her head. "Have we met?"

"A few months ago at the Harrises' wedding reception." He picked up the application she'd filled out, flipped through it, and gave her a keen look. "I believe you're Nathan's lady?"

"Well. No. We're only friends now." *Since we broke up yesterday.* She pushed the unhappiness away and held out her hand. "Abby Bern."

"Simon Demakis." His gaze focused on her paperwork again. "You're a professor?"

"Correct." She gave him a slight smile. "And those dues would force me to eat macaroni and cheese for the first time since I graduated. What does the receptionist do?" Would she get adequate time inside the club for her observations?

"Very simple. You man the desk from nine to midnight on Fridays and Saturdays. When Lindsey takes over, you're free to enjoy the club until closing at three." He grinned. "There's no point in joining if you never get to play."

Play? Do the BDSM stuff with strangers? She hadn't managed that even with someone she knew. "Of course." Her face heated. Obviously, because of Nathan's membership, Simon assumed she was familiar with BDSM. That was good, wasn't it?

If so, then why were clammy fingers sliding up her spine like they had before her chemistry final? The one exam she'd completely failed.

* * * *

Xavier Leduc stood in the downstairs dungeon, watching a younger Dom release his sobbing submissive. Rainier's session had gone badly. The younger Dom had asked for instructions on how to use nipple clamps correctly after the sub was settled.

A demonstration would be more effective than lecturing. Xavier looked around, half expecting his previous receptionist to hurry over with his toy bag and whatever else he might need. But no, Destiny had quit. He missed her efficiency.

Dixon, one of the Dark Haven staff submissives, stood nearby, obviously hoping to be used.

Xavier decided against using the young man for two reasons. Male subs often tried to disguise their pain, which would defeat the purpose of the lesson. And a woman's larger nipples made it easier to demonstrate clamps.

Besides, he enjoyed handling a woman's breasts.

"Dixon, run upstairs and get my toy bag from the bar." Which submissive to use? Hadn't the new staff member, Clarissa, been pushing for attention? "And bring the receptionist."

"Yes, my liege." Disappointment plain in his face, Dixon trotted away.

Rainier sat with his submissive on the couch, stroking her hair as she cried. Vivid red and purple bruising marked her right nipple. Nothing excessive, but this young woman wasn't into pain, and her Dom hadn't learned the difference between an erotic pinch and damage.

Turning away, Xavier surveyed the rest of his large dungeon. At almost midnight all the equipment was in use, from the Saint Andrew's crosses near the stairs to the spanking benches in the center. Lusty screams of at least two women came from the harem room. One of the evening dungeon monitors, deVries, in his usual ripped-up leathers, looked in the theme room's small window. Along with checking the participants' safety, the blond sadist was undoubtedly enjoying the show.

"Here's your bag, my liege." Followed by a young woman, Dixon handed over the leather bag.

"Quickly done. Thank you." Xavier glanced at the woman behind Dixon. Mid-to-late twenties. Medium height with pleasingly full curves, pale skin, and ear-length platinum hair. Dressed head to toe in black like a Domme, she stared around the room. His presence hadn't even registered.

Odd how refreshing that felt. But she wasn't the receptionist he'd requested. "You're not Clarissa."

She started, then smiled at him. "That's quite observant of you."

Dixon stared at her in alarm. "I... Um, my liege, she's—"

"Dixon." Xavier's warning tone silenced the young man. "Could I presume upon you to inform me who you are?" he asked the blonde politely. "And where Clarissa is?"

"Clarissa quit"—her man's digital watch was far too big for her delicate wrist—"about two hours ago. I'm filling in tonight." She held her hand out. "Abby."

His faucet of amusement cranked open. Straight-faced, he took her hand. "Xavier."

"Good to meet you." She gave a brief, no-nonsense shake and disengaged. "Now, can I help you with something? I'm new, but I'll do my best to figure out how to get you what you need."

Dixon looked terrified, clearly expecting Xavier to come down all Dom on Abby's head.

Had he been that bad tempered recently? Xavier smiled. "That's good to hear, Abby, since I need your breasts for a few minutes."

"Of course. I—" She took a hasty step back. "*What?*"

"Your breasts. I'm going to instruct Master Rainier on how to apply nipple clamps."

She retreated another foot before her chin rose. "I'm the receptionist, not a teaching assistant."

Teaching assistant? Interesting term. "The receptionist assists in demonstrations when needed."

She crossed her arms over her chest, and he almost grinned. She didn't realize how the posture pressed her pretty breasts upward. With her flawless pale skin, if he sandwiched her breast between his darkly tanned hands, the effect would be that of an Oreo cookie. The white center was his favorite part.

Her hair was wispy as a dandelion gone to fluffy seed. The downy hair on her arms was the same shade and indicated her mesmerizing coloring was natural.

"I'm not a submissive. I'm a Domme," she informed him in reasonable tones. "I'm the one putting clamps on, not receiving."

"The receptionists are always submissive." Before she got herself in trouble, he made a guess and asked, "Simon recruited you?"

She nodded.

"Despite your overly encompassing clothing, I doubt Simon made an error." Xavier took her pointed chin between his thumb and finger. As her smoky eyes widened and she tried to retreat, he let his voice slip into command mode. "Be still."

A shiver ran through her, and her pupils dilated. Even her breathing stopped.

"Very pretty," he murmured. Her surprise at her own reaction made his cock stir and brought his dominant instincts sliding to the fore. When she lifted her hand up to push him away, he captured her wrist. “No, little fluff, don’t move. I want to look at you.”

Her speeding pulse tapped a protest against his fingers. “I’m not submissive,” she whispered.

“Oh, I think you are,” he said. In fact, her Domme clothing looked so wrong on her that he was tempted to rip it off. “However, I might believe you lack experience. How familiar *are* you with BDSM? Have you been spanked?”

“No.” Her slight wiggle seemed to indicate possible interest.

“Toys?”

Her cheeks pinkened.

He’d bet the lady owned a vibrator. “Did your boyfriend use a vibrator on you?”

The flush started at the tops of her breasts and flowed upward. He’d never seen such a clear red color. Lovely. She gave a tiny shake of her head and realized she’d answered his intimate question. Her brows drew together.

“New to everything, then. Are you here because you want to know more?” But why would a newbie take a receptionist job? His eyes narrowed, and he took another guess. “You’re too impatient to wait through the screening process?”

She nodded, and her small upper lip pressed against the plump lower. “And the membership fees…”

Had gone high when he’d converted the club to exclusive. “I see.”

Should he let her stay without taking the class or being recommended? As the owner of a security firm, Simon had infallible instincts about people. A priority flag on her application would speed up her medical and background screening. And he did need someone on the desk. He tugged on a silky lock of her hair and caught a hint of a light springtime fragrance. "I'll make you a deal. You fill out the paperwork, do the physical, and stay as a receptionist for at least four months, performing *all* the receptionist duties, and I'll waive your first year's dues." He stepped back a pace to let her think.

Think she did. Her eyes turned unfocused in an expression oddly akin to that of subspace. Yet rather than relaxing, her entire body and brain seemed to jump into high gear. Unbelievably sexy. What would it take to shut off her brain?

Her attention returned to him. "Not that I doubt your word, but my reading indicated the lifestyle can attract unstable personalities. One, can you prove the manager will agree to your deal? Two, how do I know you won't ask something of me that I will refuse to do?"

Intelligent women were so fun to play with. He hardened as he imagined a chess game. Spanking her for every pawn he captured. Fucking her if he took her queen. If she lost the game, then... *Concentrate, Leduc.* "Those are valid concerns." Unable to resist, he ran a finger down her cheek. Her skin was as smooth as it looked. Smoother. "For question two—right now, I intend to use only breast clamps and bondage tape on your wrists. Do you have a problem with either?"

She swallowed. "I g-guess not."

He studied her. He was pushing, but he didn't think it was too much. Although he could overwhelm a compliant sub, this wasn't one. And the receptionist did need to be able to fill in as a submissive when needed.

Off to the side, Dixon was shifting his weight from leg to leg as if expecting Abby to get flattened. "Dixon, can you explain who I am?"

"Please, my liege, she didn't know. Don't—"

Ah, the fluff had made a friend. "I'm not offended. She simply needs confirmation of my position here."

Dixon turned to the young woman. "This is the owner of Dark Haven. Master Xavier. Call him 'my liege.'"

Xavier sighed. He had no idea who'd first given him that title, but the submissives took such delight in it, he'd allowed it to continue.

Taking a step forward, Dixon whispered all too clearly, "For fuck's sake, don't upset him or say no to him."

Don't smile.

Abby's lips curved into a provocative O. "Well. Forgive me, please, m-my liege."

Since she wasn't his, he tried not to think of the ways a submissive might demonstrate her penitence. "Now we have that straightened out, let's get on with the lesson."

Dixon motioned to Rainier's submissive. "I...uh...brought her an ice pack, sir."

Finished crying, the young woman had curled into a corner of the couch. "That was thoughtful of you. Ask Rainier if you may assist her while he joins me."

"Yes, my liege."

Xavier glanced at Rainier, who was leaning on the couch next to his submissive, and said, "I'm sorry for the delay."

"No problem. Destiny would be hard to replace."

"She has been." Xavier set his toy bag on the oversize coffee table and removed a roll of bondage tape. He preferred leather cuffs, but the tape was less intimidating. After stepping behind Abby, he grasped her right wrist. "Abby, since we've not played together before, you tell me if something is getting to be too much."

Chapter Two

It's already too much. Abby looked over her shoulder at the owner of the club. White dress shirt, black silk vest, black jeans, black boots. Definitely in the tall, dark, and handsome category, only the words seemed insipid compared to the reality. The wide, muscular shoulders turned *tall* into dangerous. His skin held the darkness of Native American ancestry, and the long black braid down his back was a definite statement. Very handsome, with chiseled European features that went well into hard-edged.

And scary. But she couldn't back out. She doubted the man had a benevolent bone in his body. Quite obviously if she didn't "assist," she'd be out the door. She sure hadn't thought her participant observation would include *real* participation. Unease tickled the back of her throat.

He glanced up, and the sun lines at the corners of his eyes crinkled with amusement. "Easy, Abby. The club safe word is *red,* and if you use it, play stops immediately. Say it loudly, and a dungeon monitor will show up to make sure you're all right." Holding her arm firmly, he wrapped what looked like wide packing tape around her right wrist a couple of times, and she realized the material wasn't sticky.

"Red. Got it."

"Abby," he said. "I daresay you know how to address a Dominant in this setting, especially the one working with you."

The uninflected reprimand made her flush as if she'd been caught cheating off someone's test paper. "Yes, my liege."

He didn't rant but nodded acceptance.

Despite her relief that he hadn't lost his temper, anxiety thrummed in her ears as he pulled her other arm behind her back and secured both wrists together. She closed her eyes and tried to pretend nothing was happening. She'd never been able to let Nathan put her in handcuffs. Why in the world was she allowing this stranger to restrain her arms?

But she needed this place for her fieldwork. Needed to keep her job. *Publish or perish.* If she ever met the academic who'd invented that phrase, she'd shove his papers down his throat until he choked.

"Abby."

She opened her eyes.

Xavier stood in front of her, looking down. Why did he have to be so tall? His warm hands massaged her bare shoulders. "Any strain in your joints?"

"No, sir."

He studied her silently.

She shifted her weight, trying not to think about her lack of mobility. If she didn't move, she wouldn't know—much like closing her eyes during gory movie scenes.

"Pull on the tape, Abby. How does it feel?"

Her arms jerked involuntarily, and just like that she knew she was restrained. Couldn't defend herself.

That her body was available to the impassive-faced Master. Alternating waves of heat and cold rushed over her as if she stood in front of a rotating fan. She pulled harder, and panic squeezed her throat.

"Easy, pet." He cupped her chin with one firm hand. His fingers curled around her arm, creating a warm place on her skin. His movements showed how easily he could touch her...yet the contact was comforting. Settling. "Eyes on me."

Panting, she looked up and into eyes the color of darkness, but the specks of golden brown made them warm, not cold.

"Good girl." He stroked his thumb along her jawline. "You know you can't escape, but I'm not going to do anything you won't enjoy. We're here in a public place, and you have a safe word that will summon every monitor in the dungeon. Now slow your breathing down before you hyperventilate."

Oops. His gaze never left hers as she pulled in a measured breath and let it out.

"Better. Another." His grip on her upper arm was unyielding but not painful. A man's hand.

Why did his touch seem different from Nathan's? Why didn't she get that horrible dread?

"Little fluff, I want you to remember how you're breathing now. When I tighten a clamp, it will hurt for a few seconds. I want you to inhale through the pain like you did with your fear."

"Pain? But—"

"Do you get flu shots?"

"Yes." When his eyebrows pulled together, she added a hasty, "My liege."

"This is the same level of pain, although people rarely get turned on by vaccinations. Whereas nipple clamps..." A crease appeared and disappeared in his cheek.

She nodded to say she could handle that much pain. But could she handle these disconcerting flares of heat? Her nipples actually tingled as if anticipating the touch of those powerful fingers.

Was this the kind of thing Nathan had wanted to do with her? Guilt pressed on her chest. Considering he had dumped her, she shouldn't feel as if she were betraying him. But she did. And she'd let a complete stranger restrain her. Alice had fallen down a hole into Wonderland; Abby had fallen into quicksand and was sinking fast. *What am I doing here?*

Xavier hadn't moved, was simply watching her. "What's the matter, Abby?"

"I don't know you at all. You're talking about..." *Nipple clamps.* "I don't *know* you."

"I see." His hand was still curved around her upper arm as he moved closer. With his fingers under her chin, he lifted her face and gave her a light kiss. His lips were firm but velvety. Gentle. How could someone with such a merciless face kiss so sweetly?

When he lifted his head, she whispered, "Why did you do that?"

His aftershave was totally masculine with a hint of the exotic, like a pirate who'd visited India. He rubbed his thumb in a circle over her cheek, his lips only an inch from hers. "Because I can," he whispered back. Then he smiled. "Because I'm going to be touching you much more intimately in a moment."

Heat roared through her at the thought of his hands...elsewhere.

"Think of this as an introduction. I'm Xavier." He covered her mouth with his, and it wasn't a gentle, sweet kiss any longer. He took her lips, demanding a response. When she pulled at the restraints and gasped, his tongue swept in. She couldn't move, couldn't escape, and...

He stepped back, grasping her arms to keep her steady. Ravished by only a kiss, she stared at him. Her lips felt swollen, and she ran her tongue over them.

A flicker of heat lit his eyes, followed by amusement. "Are we better acquainted now?"

Her voice came out sounding as if he'd strangled her instead of kissing her. "Yes, my liege." If he introduced himself like that at a faculty party, the floor would be littered with swooning academics.

"Very good." With far-too-competent hands, he undid the first hook on her corset. As he worked his way down, his long fingers brushed the skin between her full breasts. Each undone fastening exposed more of her body, and coolness wafted over her damp flesh. When he finished, he set the corset to one side, leaving her bare from the waist up.

She bit her lip. *Really, this is nothing.* In France, beaches were filled with women wearing no tops. Not that she had joined them, but... She took a mental step back. *Observe.* With a determined breath, she checked out a noisy spanking in the center of the room.

A warm hand cupped her breast.

She jumped, tried to pull away. "What are you doing?"

He grasped her arm with his other hand, holding her in place. "Did you think you could get clamps without being touched by the Dom?" Even as he spoke, he stroked her breasts, one then the other. His palm was calloused, slightly abrasive. His thumb circled the areola, and her nipple bunched hard enough to create an ache.

She tried to dissociate, to observe the other scene.

"Eyes on me, Abby." The softness of his voice didn't negate the command.

The intensity of his gaze sent a shudder up her spine. He tugged on her nipple, and she inhaled hard at the reverberating sensations—the rush of pleasure at his touch, echoed by another in her groin.

"You have beautiful breasts."

She blinked at the sweet compliment.

He didn't look away as he said, "Rainier, as with most play, you should warm up the skin first. Get the blood circulating. Especially with *your* submissive, you want her aroused first, or she'll only feel the pain." He rolled Abby's nipple between his fingertips, and the sensation almost sent her up on her toes.

"You can massage or suck nipples to long points. Be aware that with smaller breasts, wetness can cause clamps to slide. I prefer either tweezer clamps or adjustable alligator clamps, until I discover the sensitivity of the submissive's breasts and the amount of pain she enjoys." He picked up what looked like a metal spring clothespin with a screw in the center. The ends had a black coating.

When he chuckled, she realized she was staring at the device.

He put the clamp on her nipple.

Oh, that's not so bad.

Then he played with the screw, and the jaws closed more tightly. "If you know your submissive well, you can simply watch her for clues." Another slight turn and the sensation increased to a pinch. He brushed a finger over her compressed lips.

"However, at first, you should check verbally." He lifted her chin with a finger and held her gaze. "On a scale of one to ten, where ten is unendurable, how much does this hurt?"

The pinching sensation was easing. "Four, I guess."

"Very good." To her horror, he tightened the clamp, and she squeaked as the pinch turned to a bite. "Breathe through it, Abby."

She tried to get her hands around, to pull the damn thing off, only her arms were restrained behind her back. She couldn't do anything. Her breast hurt. Then the pain diminished. The pinch gradually changed to throbbing, and her nipple felt...bigger, tighter. Every movement made her more aware of the sensation—and the way her clitoris had begun to ache as well.

Xavier squeezed her shoulder in a comforting massage before glancing at Rainier. "Since you're not a sadist, this is far enough until you know what works for your submissive. You want her engaged in processing the sensations, unable to escape them, but not quite sure how much it hurts." He smiled at her. "Next one, Abby."

Owwwww. She'd braced for the pain, yet her eyes teared, making her contact lenses swim. But this time she worked her breathing, and it helped. As the pinch gentled to throbbing, she felt slickness between her legs. Thank heavens she'd worn a skirt and wasn't bare-bottomed like some women. No one needed to know this had turned her on.

A finger stroked over her cheek. “See the color here and on her lips? How her breathing is fast and shallow, even though the pain has decreased? The fondling aroused her. The clamps added to it.”

A tidal wave of heat rushed into her face.

His chuckle was low and dark. “She’s also easily embarrassed.”

The other Dom laughed.

“Once the clamps are on, you can play,” Xavier said. “Add a reminder of who is in charge.” His long fingers combed her hair. “Your hair is like dandelion silk, pet,” he murmured before his hand closed, trapping the strands. He firmly pulled her head back until she stared up at him, her throat exposed.

A sudden tug on one breast clamp sent a jolt of pain through her. She gasped, struggling instinctively to get her hands free. She couldn’t even move her head with Xavier fisting her hair.

“Helplessness is frightening to some women. Exciting to others.”

He tugged on her other nipple enough to hurt, yet as she struggled she realized that her panties were truly wet. That she wanted sex more than she ever had in her whole life.

“I think Abby finds it exciting.”

Oh sweet heavens, she was making an idiot of herself. Stiffening, she tried to step back and got nowhere.

Unmoving, Xavier watched her with an eagle’s predatory gaze. He glanced at the other Dom. “That enough to start with?”

“It is. Thank you, Xavier. I screwed up.”

"We all do," Xavier said. "Talk to her. An apology doesn't diminish your authority." He released Abby's hair and stroked the strands back down. "Remember to leave breast clamps on only a short time—fifteen minutes or less—until you assess her endurance. If on very long, they'll hurt more coming off than going on."

"Got it."

Trying to distance herself from the sensations flowing through her, Abby gritted her teeth. She couldn't let herself get diverted from making her observations. She turned her attention to a different scene where a man was restrained on a Saint Andrew's cross. But...why was an X-shaped piece of equipment called a cross? *Have to do some more research.* The female Domme had two floggers that swirled and slapped the man's shoulders in an amazing display of coordination.

A gawky person like Abby would probably hit herself in the face.

"Xavier, I had a question." A tall, stunning Domme approached.

"One second, Angela." His calloused hands closed on Abby's shoulders. "Kneel, pet, while I talk to Mistress Angela."

Kneel? She stared at him in outrage.

His expression didn't change, but he gave her a *look.*

The pit of her stomach dropped, and her knees bent like thin wire. Halfway to the floor, she lost her balance.

He caught her and lowered her easily.

Way to show how graceful you are, moron. Totally humiliated, she settled down with her bottom resting on her feet.

"That's right. Spine straight. Eyes down. Knees farther apart. We'll work more on your form later."

How could she straighten a spine that seemed to have disappeared?

"I've never seen one of your submissives with so many clothes," Angela remarked.

"Receptionist in training," Xavier said. "And new to the scene as well."

"Gorgeous skin."

"Yes."

Abby felt her gorgeous skin turning pink. As the two talked quietly, Abby waited, slowly becoming far too aware of how each breath made the clamps move, fixing her attention on her breasts. Of how aroused she was. She prayed she wasn't wet enough to soak her skirt.

"Thank you, Xavier."

Abby looked up, and Angela smiled at her before she walked away.

After setting Abby on her feet, Xavier glanced at his watch. "I'm going to release you. Then I'll answer your questions and give you the rules." He lifted her left breast, his warm palm supporting the weight.

She closed her eyes, acutely aware—again—of being half-naked. Of how nonchalantly he touched her. Need churned through her veins. *Please don't let him be able to tell.*

"This might hurt as the blood returns." He undid the clamp and put it in a container in his leather bag.

She had a second of thinking he'd exaggerated before blood surged into her nipple in an explosion of pain. After the first fist-inducing surprise, the sensation subsided. Pulling in a slow breath, she nodded that she was all right.

He had an interesting smile. Not slow, but…deliberate. The left corner of his mouth rose a little higher than the right, the crease on that side deeper. His approval warmed her to her toes.

After he removed the second clamp—and she breathed through the wave of pain—he ran a finger around each areola. The intense rush of sensation over the burning, tender skin curled her toes.

“Look how pretty your nipples are now. I’ve never seen this shade of pink before.”

Her gaze focused on his darkly tanned hand lifting her breast for her to see. Her nipples, normally just a blush of color, were now a hot pink. Her face heated—again. Honestly, she hadn’t wanted the reminder of her nudity.

“Beautiful.” His voice was almost as dark as his skin, low and resonant, with a hint of an accent too faint to identify. With a pair of blunt-ended scissors from his bag, he snipped the tape around her wrists.

Free, free, free. The trickle of disappointment was unsettling. Surely she hadn’t wanted him to continue.

“Move your arms slowly,” he cautioned. After she stretched for a minute, he massaged the last ache out of her joints.

It felt…nice. As if, since she’d done as he wanted, now he’d care for her in turn. “Thank you. Sir.”

“You’re very welcome, Abby.” He helped her into her corset, hooked up the front, then adjusted her breasts inside it.

What was wrong with her? Why did she let him handle her like a…a doll?

He picked up his bag. “Come. Stay one step behind and to the right of me.” As they headed upstairs to the reception area, the Dominants stopped Xavier every few feet, wanting to discuss a scene, ask questions, or just say hi. Submissives lowered their gazes, occasionally giving him a pleading look first. And everyone stared at her. Assessingly. She heard whispers, asking if she was replacing the estimable Destiny or if Xavier had actually brought his slave to the club.

AT THE FRONT desk, as Xavier showed his new receptionist the few things she hadn’t managed to figure out, he realized the woman was blindingly intelligent. But inexperienced. “I’d like you to attend the beginner’s classes, Abby. You’ll be more comfortable.”

After studying the schedule on the wall calendar, she shook her head. “I can’t. I teach reading that hour.”

“Ah.” A teacher. He assessed her in light of the new information, smiling slightly. Yes, he could see it. The keen look in her eyes, the way she listened with all her attention on what he was saying. Odd that she’d been singularly inattentive when he’d been playing with her body. Until the sensations overwhelmed that busy brain, she hadn’t stayed in the moment at all.

She noticed him watching and flushed, her gaze skittering away before she straightened and faced him directly.

She was a rather adorable little submissive. “You do want to learn more about BDSM, though?”

“I do,” she said firmly.

“Are you looking for a Dom?” Many of the club submissives requested that he introduce them to Doms he thought they’d suit.

"No. Just information." She absently straightened up the desk, filing papers as if she'd been born to the task.

"Ah." His eyes narrowed. "Do you have a Dom to play with here? Or a significant other? Anyone who will be upset if you are doing scenes?"

"No and no and no." Her lips pursed. "But really, I'd prefer to...observe. See what it all involves."

Observe? Did he have a watcher and not a participant? That fit what he'd seen of her so far. "I see. Well, as a staff member, you'll get called on for assistance and demonstrations. That's part of the job description." One most submissives enjoyed.

Despite the dismay in her eyes, a flush rose into her cheeks. She wanted to play, yet she didn't. Interesting.

"Watching scenes is part of the fun in a club, but complete voyeur-only types aren't welcome. BDSM is a participant sport." He walked over to the shelves behind her. "Speaking of which, are you allergic to anything? Food, fabric, medicine?"

"No. No, sir."

"Allergy to latex? Or rubber? Or leather?"

"No."

"Good." At the wall shelves, he pulled on a latex glove and smeared each fingertip with a different ointment from the sample case. "Hold your arm out."

The underside of her arm was the color of cream. He drew his fingers across her inner arm in four long lines, then dotted the lines with a marker. "These are the most common ointments used here. Since not every Dom tests beforehand, I prefer to know you're not going to react."

She stared at her arm with wide eyes. Never heard of chemical play, eh? The thought of doing a scene with her was almost too tempting.

After tossing the glove, he pulled a limits list from the form shelf. "Fill this out before you return. It shows what you won't permit a Dom to do. You'll of course negotiate beforehand, but I like to know your hard limits as well, so I can keep an eye on things."

"I don't plan—"

Lindsey sailed through the inner door and saw him. She bowed her head. Her brown hair, streaked with vivid blonde and red, brushed over her bare shoulders. "My liege." Her mild Texas drawl managed to turn *liege* into two syllables.

"Lindsey, this is Abby, who is taking Clarissa's place. She may have some questions for you." He glanced at Abby. "You signed the releases and forms, yes?"

"Yes. My liege." She had a pleasingly low voice, and he firmly put away any curiosity about what she'd sound like during a climax.

He pulled a pink leather collar from a drawer and crooked his finger at her. Her appalled expression had him smothering a laugh. The leather was engraved with double silver stripes on the top and bottom. The dangling tag stated: UNDER THE PROTECTION OF XAVIER. "This ensures that any Dom who wishes to play with you will obtain my permission first."

When she looked insulted, he ruffled her silky hair. "No, pet, I don't own you. This is for your protection."

"Oh." She considered and then bent her head so he could fasten the collar.

She had a delicate neck with tendrils of downy hair at her nape. He buckled the collar on, then widened her eyes by adding a tiny padlock. She didn't need to know they kept master keys everywhere in the building. "When you arrive at the club, put on your collar and lock it. Before you leave, find me so I can remove it."

Her swallow was obvious and delightful.

Yes, he liked this little submissive. "Abby?" he prompted. "Do you understand?"

"Yes, my liege."

"Very good." He let his gaze sweep down her body. "Tomorrow I expect you in suitable attire. The corset is beautiful. But not with a skirt and boots. A thong would work."

He chose to ignore her rebellious look. This time.

"Or a very short skirt. Naked is acceptable."

She ran her tongue over her plump lower lip. He had a momentary image of sitting on his bed with her kneeling in front of him, her lips around his cock and that small tongue swirling the head. To his surprise he hardened. *Receptionist, Leduc.* Her job was here. He carefully tucked her into the mental compartment labeled JOB. She wasn't for his home or for social dating.

Back in the main room, he swung by the bar to get a cup of coffee and looked around. On the stage, deVries was giving a flogging lesson. His student, a new Dom, swung wildly and missed the pillow completely.

Xavier spotted Simon at a table and walked over.

"Have a seat." Simon shoved a chair out with his foot.

As Xavier sat, he said, "That pretty little receptionist seems to take a messy desk as a personal insult. Where'd you find her?"

"Here. After she taught Dixon how to print out her application, she dared to suggest he do some filing."

Xavier snorted at the thought of Dixon's outrage. "A competent receptionist would be a nice change. I was getting desperate." He'd even asked his elderly accountant if she wanted to moonlight. "Unfortunately Mrs. Henderson refuses to set foot in the club."

"There's a shame." Simon's brows lifted. "Wouldn't she make a hell of a Domme?"

The image of the gray-haired Baptist grandmother wielding a flogger rather than her calculator made Xavier grin. "Competent or not, Abby seems appallingly new to BDSM, and she can't attend the beginner's classes." Xavier leaned back and stretched his legs out. "Would you keep an eye on her if I'm not around? Answer her questions?" The little fluff would be a temptation to any Dom.

"Not a problem. And Rona will undoubtedly adopt her."

"Excellent." Xavier winced as the new Dom on the stage hit the pillow with enough force to take out a kidney. Hopefully the man would stick with inanimate targets for a good while longer. He took a sip of his coffee and breathed in the fragrance of chicory.

Obviously catching a whiff, Simon made a sound of disgust. "You and your damn New Orleans coffee."

If the coffee wasn't thick, black, and strong enough to dissolve an unwary spoon, it wasn't worth drinking. "Any chance you want to teach the beginner's class next week?"

"Nope. I got a warm woman at home, and I don't see as much of her as I'd like."

"Ah." When Simon had found Rona, he'd plowed through every obstacle she'd put up to make her his. Probably one of the few battles the woman had lost. They were very much in love. Xavier's chest ached as he remembered how it felt to have a love like that—and then to lose it.

"You still dating that blonde?" Simon asked.

"Socially? One blonde, one brunette," Xavier said absently. Who could he get to teach that class? He might have been interested if the little receptionist were going to be in it.

"How about your latest slave? Did you manage to find her a Master?"

Xavier nodded. "Pedro Martinez. She's been there a week and sounds very happy."

"So you've lost your slave-at-home category and your business minion? You're down to just a girlfriend or two?" Simon had no patience with Xavier's inclination for keeping his women in slots. "Who's your next slave going to be?"

"I'm taking a hiatus from matchmaking." Sometimes being served was more exhausting than doing it himself.

"House a little lonely now?" Simon asked with a discerning look.

More than he'd ever admit.

Chapter Three

Standing on the richly colored Oriental carpet in her bedroom, Abby dragged on a pair of jeans and yawned so widely her jaw cracked. Her blood felt as if it had been turned into liquid lead, weighing her down until every movement was an effort. *Not even thirty, and I'm too old for late nights.*

Dark Haven hadn't closed until three a.m., and once home she'd stayed up to document her observations.

And forgot to set the alarm.

She hurriedly yanked her bra on and yelped. "Ouch!" Pulling the cups away from her tender nipples, she scowled. Wonderful. Every time she moved today, she'd be reminded of Xavier touching her. How it had felt when he'd circled his thumb over her nipple.

Her dreams had been more erotic than any porn movie, and Xavier had been in all of them.

I never dreamed about Nathan that way. Guilt welled up inside as she admitted she'd never let him restrain her like that either. Had she really let another man undress her and touch her? That was just wrong.

But no, it wasn't. She didn't have a relationship. Didn't have a lover. Everything she'd hoped to have with Nathan was gone.

And she was running late. The babies still had to be fed before he arrived.

The sound of whimpering puppies greeted her when she got downstairs. In between heating bottles, she started coffee. No time for a leisurely cup of tea today. From outside her duplex came the muted rumble of traffic, birds awakening, and morning frogs.

Juggling bottles, she crossed the living room to the plastic wading pool in the corner. A puppy resort, complete with a heating pad secured in one spot to battle the moist San Francisco air. At the sight of her, five roly-poly bodies, each the size of a pair of rolled-up socks, abandoned their pile of blankets, whining about imminent starvation.

"Honestly, guys, this is too darned early." And she was cold, grumpy, tired—and depressed. With a sigh of exasperation, she picked up the black ball of fur that was her favorite. So very, very soft. Blackie's puppy breath accompanied an adorable, tiny yawn.

Abby's smile broke free. Really, this was a fine way to start the day. She snuggled him on her lap, listened to the quiet sucking sounds, and hummed a lullaby.

Despite the extra work, she never tired of fostering puppies from the animal shelter.

By the time the fourth tummy was reaching a sweet roundness, contentment pulsed in her heart.

"You're next," she told the pup waiting in the pool. Freckles's floppy ears tried to prick up, but the anticipated food was far more important than listening to Abby. Sometimes she had the feeling her students felt the same way.

Just as she was hoping she'd finish on time, the doorbell rang. "Wonderful. I'm in trouble now." She pressed a quick kiss to the top of Tiny's furry head, set the puppy beside its tussling siblings, and hurried to open the door.

Dressed in a conservative button-up shirt and black slacks, Nathan looked wonderful.

Her heart gave a hard stab. *Not mine anymore.* "Come on in."

His mouth pressed thin when he noticed her bare feet. "You're not ready?"

Uh-oh, unhappy camper alert. Anxiety tried to rise, and she shoved it down. "I only have one more puppy to feed. There's coffee on for you."

"I told you seven o'clock."

"I know. I overslept—but we have plenty of time before your plane." After all, she was taking him right to the gate so he didn't have to find parking.

"Make it quick."

She poured him a cup and pushed the cream and sugar toward him before hurrying back to the dogs. Grabbing Freckles, she tried to smile. "When is your first class?"

"In two days," he said coldly.

At his tone her insides curled into a frozen ball. She'd hoped their last time together would be…easier, but now he was angry. Her hands went cold. As echoes of her father's uncontrolled yelling filled her head, she forced her voice to stay easy. "Will that give you time to get prepared and figure out where everything is?"

"I suppose." He glanced at his watch again. "Be nice to escape the bitching about slashed funding. Everett said they plan to increase class size and dump instructors at the bottom of the ladder."

"Like me. I know." Her stomach tightened. She'd already suffered the ordeal of being jobless. "This fall, they'll decide who gets laid off for the spring semester."

"Awards or not, with no recent publications, you'll be one of the first to go."

A professor could spend time on research, grants, and articles—or on teaching. Nathan insisted that making a class interesting wasn't as important as research. She'd thought differently, and last spring she'd won two awards. For teaching. "I'll have something published by then."

I hope. Unease stair-stepped cold fingers up her spine. Last fall, her small college had closed. She'd landed a position at the university, but with only a semester-to-semester contract. "A friend publishes an online ethnography journal which focuses on edgy sociological essays. Controversial topics. He promised to call in favors for an immediate peer review. My article will be in the fall issue if I get it to him before August."

"That doesn't leave time to do research." Nathan frowned.

"Not much, no. But it's adequate for the limited observations and analysis I plan."

"Controversial, eh? I hope you didn't think to do your study in my club. The owner would never let a sociologist in the door." He scowled, then relaxed. "It's private now anyway. You couldn't get in."

"So I heard."

His expression turned to stone. "You actually considered BDSM as a research topic, but not as something to do with your lover?" He didn't raise his voice. He never yelled.

Not like her father. "*Bitch. Slut. You're a whore.*" She closed her eyes. Why was Dad's voice so pervasive today? Because she was still unsettled from last night?

"Maybe if you'd been willing to be more adventurous, we wouldn't have broken up." Nathan took a sip from his cup and rose. This time when he looked at her, his control chilled her.

"I know." Their last date had been the final straw for him. Those ghastly handcuffs. She'd tried—she *had.* He'd cuffed one wrist, and she'd panicked. *Again.* The thought of being so helpless with him was just...just...*no.*

He was smart, charming, gorgeous, and polite. A renowned professor of anthropology respected enough to get invited to lecture at another university for the summer semester. They communicated well. Aside from his predilection for kink, the sex was pretty good—except for last time, when her refusal to be restrained had had a...deflating effect on him.

He'd gone so cold that she'd known she'd lost him, even before he said the words.

She turned her head away. So how in the world had she let Xavier restrain her and not Nathan? "I'm sorry. Some of that stuff makes me really uncomfortable."

"It wasn't all about you, Abby. Sometimes it needed to be about me and my needs. You pampered those mangy mutts more than you did your so-called lover."

That's not true. She bit back the retort. Her fingers were cold as she laced her other shoe, then crossed the room to get her purse and car keys.

Could she change enough to enjoy bondage and pain and stuff? If she was different when he returned in August, would he be interested again?

He held the door open, and as she walked through, he pulled her close. “I’m going to miss what we had, my pretty girl. My sweet slut. I’m sorry it didn’t work out.”

His sensual lips touched hers, but she’d stepped outside her body and was watching from a distance. Evaluating how he held her, how his voice sounded.

“I’m sorry too.” Ice formed on her skin, encasing her, buffering her from the pain.

Chapter Four

The second night at Dark Haven went much smoother. Abby enjoyed her time behind the desk, checking membership card photos, answering questions, handing out applications. Who knew a kinky place would be so popular?

Whenever she had a few quiet minutes, she filled out the limit list Xavier had given her. *Anal sex...hard beatings, soft beatings. Asphyxiation*—was that for real? *Face slapping...injections...piercings...mummification.* Each item had one check box beside it for *no*, indicating she absolutely wouldn't permit it.

Why didn't he have a list like the ones she'd seen online that offered a box for *maybe?* Or in her case, an option saying, *I might be willing after a lot of discussion and time and several margaritas.* She frowned at the paper. If she marked *no* to everything that made her uneasy, Xavier might kick her out of the club for being a fake.

Eventually she checked only the items that would make her run screaming for the police. *Asphyxiation.* No way in the world. And surely a smart woman would mark *no* to something called *orgasm denial.* What a horrible concept.

After the traumatic questionnaire, she found it a relief to file membership applications and straighten the desk. She labeled a paper tray with MY LIEGE for a place to put Xavier's messages. How did he get such a strange title? Although it did fit him well. His self-confidence seemed so integral to his nature he could well have been born a ruler.

As people came and went, she jotted down research observations in her own version of a code—shorthand Latin. She'd planned to compare the social network to a tribe or a family, but more complicated relationships kept appearing. Like the bisexual guy who told her he was submissive to a male Dom, but topped women when he visited the club. And smiled at her.

What was the proper response to that kind of flirtation?

A flurry of activity at the door grabbed her attention, and she checked in a lesbian couple, then a man with a human puppy on a leash. A minute later a blonde woman around forty walked in, followed by Simon.

Simon smiled. "Abby. You came back for another night. Excellent."

Did the man have to be so gorgeous? Maybe he had some silver in his hair, but like Xavier, he was even hotter than a younger guy.

He put his arm around the blonde. "This is my wife. Rona, this is Abby, Xavier's new receptionist, who will hopefully survive longer than the last one."

Rona held her hand out to shake. "Hi, Abby. Has Xavier terrified you yet?"

"Not...completely." *Kind of.* Unable to help herself, Abby gave a quick glance toward the club room door. Just to make sure he hadn't entered.

"But some, eh?" Simon's grin transformed his face to devastating. "Your receptionist time is over in a few minutes. Will Nathan show you around?"

"No. He's teaching in Maine for the summer." *Thank heavens.*

"Ah. Then join us when you're off, and I'll help you find someone nice to play with."

Play with? Her breath caught as if snagged on one of her ribs. By the time she finished coughing, the couple had already entered the main room.

Abby managed to smile at the next three men waiting at the desk. Hunky, but from the spiked collars around two necks with leashes to the third guy, she knew none of them played on her side of the street. Sometimes sexual orientation wasn't obvious—although it certainly had been with Xavier. Simply from the way he'd touched her, she knew he really, really liked playing with breasts. The thought sent a flash of heat to her lower half.

The guys ran their membership cards through the reader and held them up for her to check the photos. "Thank you. Have a wonderful night." As they disappeared into the club, she jotted down some notes.

"Hi." The leather-clad Dom wasn't far past twenty-one—at least five years younger than she was. After swiping his ID card, he leaned an arm on her desk.

"Can I help you?" Abby asked.

The young man grinned. "Give me an hour and I'll show you." Then he noted her collar, and his smile turned rueful. "If the Master of the house permits."

She laughed as he sauntered into the club. Not that she wanted him, but he was cute, and the well holding her ego had needed filling. After all, she sure wasn't a beauty like some of the women here. Not even close.

The angel who assigned bodies had obviously been in a bad mood when Abby was born. Her stepsister had received long, thick brown hair to match her dark eyes and golden skin. Abby got blonde hair that she wore short because the strands were so fine that her ponytail was no thicker than a cotton swab. Dark eyes? Nope. She had weird gray ones, not even bright enough to be called blue.

Tall and slender like Janae? Nope. Abby was a pear—a nice, healthy shape as long as you liked a fat butt. She had nightmares of someone tagging her ass with a WIDE LOAD sign. *Shudder.*

The angel hadn't been completely evil, though. *I got breasts.* And tonight they were showcased in a black corset. Her black leather skirt showed off her shapely legs but was long enough to cover her bumpy upper thighs.

Last month she'd read that a man's connective tissue aligned horizontally with the skin, whereas a female's went perpendicular—which was why women got lumpy cellulite and men didn't. *And doesn't that totally prove that God is male?*

She frowned upward to where God dwelled with his parsimonious angel. "You should be ashamed. Both of you."

"Excuse me?"

At the sound of the deep, deep voice, she started, and her pen made a suicide dive to the floor. She bent, wrapped her fingers around it, and gulped as two oversize black boots moved into her view. After straightening up, she plastered on a smile. "Good evening, my liege."

"Abby." He studied her for a minute. "You're wearing glasses."

She'd forgotten how he affected her. Her heart was pounding like a five-year-old with a new drum set. "I'm not used to being up late, and my eyes had a tantrum when I tried to put in my contacts."

"I see. The glasses are quite beguiling."

"Oh *please.* I look like a nerd." Or so Nathan had always said.

"I like the combination of fetish and studious." His gaze lingered on her cleavage. "You look like a librarian who wants to go back in the stacks and fuck."

As her mouth dropped open, he picked up her limits list from the desk and glanced over it.

Warmth flowed into her face as she remembered the disconcerting list of erotic choices. Maybe she should have checked *no* to them all.

He set it down without speaking. When he grasped her wrist, the zing was so loud that her ears rang, like hearing door chimes on amphetamines.

Apparently he didn't hear them. He turned her forearm over to check the line of black dots. "Good. No reaction to anything."

"Nope." As his thumb made circles on her wrist, shivers climbed her arm. Heavens, how could being touched do this to her?

His dark eyes crinkled before he released her and gestured with his fingers. *Stand up.*

"Uh. Yes, sir." She stood.

As he looked at her, his black brows pulled together into a frown that chilled her. Compared to him, the most intimidating professor at the university seemed like a lamb.

"Sir?"

"Did I mention less clothes?"

Her chin rose. "This skirt is shorter."

His hand closed on her shoulder. "I obviously confused you. So. Let me clarify. If you wear something that covers your breasts and stomach, then I expect nothing more concealing than a thong on your lower half. If you wear a skirt or pants, your breast may be covered with only chains or a set of nipple clamps."

Only a thong? With her butt? Did he have no clue about women's insecurities at all? She gave him the stare she reserved for students playing games on their cell phones.

When his eyes filled with obvious amusement, she wanted to hit him, right on that oversize, muscled chest. Even as her lips pressed together, a shiver of excitement ran down her spine and set her lower half to tingling. What would he do to her if she defied him?

He bent, his mouth less than an inch from her ear, his breath ruffling her hair. "Don't push me, little fluff."

Even as she stepped away, she caught his exotic masculine scent, and her toes curled under.

The inner door opened, making Abby drop back down in the chair.

The late-night receptionist stepped into the room and halted at the sight of Xavier. Lindsey's streaky, shoulder-length hair was tangled, and marks from a gag remained on her cheeks. Her gaze dropped. "My liege."

"Are you prepared to take the desk?" he asked.

"Sure." She smiled at Abby. "You got anything I need to know?"

Abby kicked her brain into gear. "I put filled-out applications in the red folder. Questions and messages for Xa—uh, my liege—are in the MY LIEGE tray."

"You're purely amazing." Lindsey turned to Xavier. Although she had to be around thirty, her grin made her appear like a mischievous teenager. "Sir, it's not my place to butt in, but please keep her? Pretty please?"

Xavier chuckled. "I'll consider your request, pet." He crooked his fingers at Abby.

One part of her mind wailed, *He's going to mess up my fieldwork time.* The other part was dancing with anticipation. *What is he going to do with me?* Shoulders back, she walked around the desk to him.

He curled his hand over the back of her neck, covering her collar, and steered her into the club.

"Do you need me for a demonstration?" The thought started her heart tapping like a woodpecker in a termite colony. He mustn't use her; she had research to do. Yet her breasts kept replaying the way his fingers had felt. Her nipples jutted hard against the thankfully stiff corset top.

"There's a Dom I want you to meet." He didn't wait for an answer but guided her downstairs to where a sandy-haired man about her age stood in front of a Saint Andrew's cross.

"Seth, this is Abby. She's the new receptionist and also new to the lifestyle. Since she doesn't have a Dom to play with, I thought she might be a good choice for you to start with."

Wait. She stared at Xavier. "I'm not here for—"

"Your time as receptionist is up." Xavier's eyes narrowed. "You joined the club to learn about BDSM, correct? I mentioned last night that this isn't a place for voyeurs. If you merely want to watch someone having sex, there are better places for you."

Oh no. She needed Dark Haven. "No, I'm here to...learn." *Good word.* "I'm just nervous." And that was the full truth.

"That's normal," Seth said. "Come on. Let's talk awhile and work on what kind of a scene you'd like. I'll ease you in gently."

"Very good." Xavier gave her a nod and walked away.

He's leaving me here? She managed to refrain from running. Instead she squared her shoulders and smiled at Seth. He had nice eyes. Gentle. "Well, what happens now?"

FEELING AS IF he'd abandoned an orphan, Xavier asked Angela, the late-night dungeon monitor, to keep an eye on Seth and Abby.

If he'd stayed, she would look to him rather than Seth. Even worse, with those big gray eyes on him, he'd have had a hard time staying out of the scene. She was very appealing. Intelligent and submissive, with a hint of vulnerability.

But aside from demonstrations, he refrained from playing with his staff members. He'd discovered too many submissives expected that club play would lead to a D/s relationship. In his case, it wouldn't.

To avoid temptation, he crossed to the other side of the room and took a seat to watch Simon lightly flogging his submissive. Rona wore only a golden necklace—her collar. She was a charming, self-possessed woman, and intelligent enough to keep Simon on his toes. His friend had needed someone like her for a long time.

At one point Simon stopped the flogging. He slid a rabbit vibrator into Rona's cunt and strapped it in place. "There you go, lass. That should keep you awake."

Her arms were chained to the low ceiling beam, or she'd have punched him. Instead she muttered something, her eyes sparking.

Simon flipped the switch, and her back arched. "I don't mind if you come, Rona, but if you make any noise whatsoever, I'm going to be unhappy."

Xavier grinned. Simon knew his sub well.

Her mouth pressed closed as she tried to muffle her moans. Simon resumed the flogging, stopping frequently to change the vibrator settings. Soon Rona was almost purple as she teetered on the edge of an orgasm.

With a low laugh, Simon flicked the ends of the flogger over her breasts. She lost the battle and climaxed with a satisfying wail.

Nice session. Smiling, Xavier rose. Time to check on Abby.

"My liege." An uncollared submissive knelt in his path. "May I serve you in any way?"

He didn't know the pretty brunette. Although Dark Haven was private, new members constantly cycled in from the classes and recommendations. New or not, she needed to learn manners. "Look at me."

When she lifted her face, triumph accompanied the hope in her eyes.

"In this club a Dom approaches a submissive, not the other way around. The choice is up to the Dom. The offer comes from the Dom. Kneeling and offering might work for you elsewhere. Here, it will not. Do I make myself clear?"

She dropped her gaze and cringed. “Yes, my liege.”

“Excellent.” He softened his voice. “If you’d like to meet someone or if you have problems, you may request to speak with me.”

“Yes, sir.”

“Do you know anyone here?”

She nodded, and her flush increased.

His irritation grew. “You’re here with a Dom? Your Dom?”

“Yes, sir,” she whispered.

He was tempted to toss her right out of his club. The disloyal beauty was apparently used to manipulating the men around her. “Take me to him.” When she started to stand, he shook his head. “You weren’t given permission to rise.”

Her eyes widened.

“Move.”

Unlike many Doms, he didn’t often make a submissive crawl, but in her case... She made her way across the room to kneel beside a man watching a scene.

Xavier recognized him. A longtime Dom, not strict, more into sex than dominance, and rich, which explained his lovely, young submissive.

Johnston glanced at her. “Tisha, what are—” He saw Xavier and rose. “Xavier. Is there a problem?”

“I’m afraid so. Your submissive offered to serve me.”

Face darkening, Johnston stared down at her. “You said you needed the restroom.”

“I...I just thought...”

No, she hadn’t thought. Xavier took a step back.

“Do you want anything done?” Johnston asked him.

"I'm sure you'll deal with her appropriately." As Xavier walked away, he heard a squeak behind him. Johnston might not normally be hardhanded, but that wouldn't help the girl this evening.

Dismissing the annoyance from his thoughts, Xavier strolled through his domain. The energy in the dungeon was almost palpable. Some evenings were better than others. Sometimes, whether due to a bad scene or a bad mixture of play, the ambience could feel disjointed. But tonight the cries and moans and rhythms flowed from one side of the room to the other until scenes took on an added resonance.

But not all scenes. Apparently he'd done a poor job matching the receptionist and Seth.

Off to one side, the dungeon monitor watched with a frown. When Xavier nodded a greeting, Angela jerked her chin at the scene. "The bottom isn't engaged at all."

"I see that."

Although fairly new, Seth also realized he wasn't reaching Abby, and his frustration showed. He hadn't bound her but had her gripping the cross as he lightly flogged her ass.

Xavier put his hands behind his back and considered. True, he'd pushed her into doing a scene with Seth, but she'd joined the club to learn. Had volunteered to be a receptionist so she wouldn't have to wait. But she wasn't even trying to be part of this session.

He'd topped submissives who'd needed to be pulled into engagement, but Abby was not only distant; her head wasn't anywhere in the area. He followed her gaze to where a switch was topping a younger couple under the supervision of her Dom.

Xavier's eyes narrowed. Although focused on the four people, Abby showed no signs of arousal. She had the expression of someone watching an interesting TV show.

Seth tossed his flogger into his bag, stepped in front of her, and said something.

Abby nodded. As she moved away from the cross, stretching her arms, Seth walked over to Xavier and Angela.

"That didn't go well," Xavier said.

Seth shook his head. "That was the flattest scene I've ever done. She wasn't with me at all. She's not mine and I don't know her, so I wasn't comfortable increasing the pain to draw her back."

"She didn't even try, Seth. Not your fault." Xavier watched as Abby rubbed her shoulders. "Since she's my responsibility, I think I'll show her where I expect her head to be when she participates."

Seth grinned. "Poor subbie."

Xavier summoned a barmaid to fetch his toy bag and joined Abby.

"Hey." Her smile faded at his silence. "My liege. Sorry. I'm not used to—"

"That's obvious." He kept his voice low but hard, akin to a swat on the ass. Her eyes widened. Yes, he had all her attention now. "When a submissive is in a scene, where should her gaze be? Her awareness?"

The tiny muscles in her throat worked. "On the scene."

She *was* very new. "No, Abby. On her Dom. Unless you're instructed to look at the floor, your gaze stays on the Dom. Even if you're looking down, the rest of your senses stay focused on the Dom. Where was your attention?"

Her flinch was obvious. "On another scene."

"Exactly." He set his hand on her shoulder, pleased at the tiny quiver that displayed her physical awareness of him. "As staff in Dark Haven, you're in essence my submissive, which means I choose your play partners. For that scene, Seth was your Dominant, and your behavior was disrespectful to both him and me."

"Oh." She caught her lower lip between her teeth and gave him a penitent look. "I'm sorry, my liege."

"I forgive you. And I'm going to work with you to ensure it doesn't happen again." He guided her to a bondage table and covered the surface with a cloth from a service stand. "Climb up."

Chapter Five

"*Malum!*" she muttered in Latin under her breath. A *bad thing* indeed. Xavier seemed more irritated than angry, but he certainly didn't pull his punches. His bluntness, unleavened by any courtesy, was unsettling. Was this kind of honesty a Dom trait?

Wouldn't that be an interesting research topic?

When he made a threatening noise, she dragged her attention back and quickly climbed onto the table. The padding under the rubber-backed sheet was black leather, like an ominous version of her doctor's exam table. Wider, though. The dangling straps and inset D rings didn't alleviate her insecurities at all.

"Lie back," he directed. A barmaid handed him his overnight-sized leather bag.

Too insecure to comply, Abby stared at the bag. He'd have *stuff* in it. As a cry came from across the room, she glanced toward the scene she'd been watching and—

Disconcertingly powerful hands closed on her shoulders, and Xavier pushed her flat on her back. "I don't think you're deliberately disobedient, Abby, but you're quite distractible." His lips twitched. "You'll dent a Dom's fragile ego if you don't pay attention to him."

He really did have a sense of humor. It wasn't slapstick blatant but almost hidden. And attractive. "You don't have a fragile ego." Not even close.

Pillowing her skull in his palm, he leaned on his arm. He stood close enough she could smell his aftershave of rich spices with a hint of exotic resins. Tiny flecks of gold warmed his dark eyes. His lips looked hard, but she remembered their velvety texture.

He kissed her. His firm lips moved over hers, then teased her mouth open. His tongue swept in, stroking hers in a leisurely plundering. Gripping her hair, he pulled her head back, giving him a better angle to take her mouth. His growl of approval whispered down her spine even as his hand curved around her jaw, securing her more fully. Aggressive—too aggressive—yet heat smoldered under her skin as if she stood in front of a wall heater.

Heavens, the man could kiss. *Don't get swept away.* Regaining her self-possession, she tried to experiment, teasing with her tongue.

He lifted his head. "You have a very active mind, little fluff. Tonight I'm going to find out what it takes to turn your brain off."

"You…what?" Her brain was who she *was*. She tried to sit up.

He chuckled and flattened her, reinforcing the movement with a look that promised bad things if she didn't stay put. When she stopped struggling, he buckled a cuff on her left wrist and clipped the D ring to the side of the table beside her thigh. Then he did the same for the other wrist.

Well, this kind of bondage wasn't too bad. She had a lot of freedom still, and her legs were free.

He started unhooking her corset.

"What are you doing?"

His face held amused exasperation. "Abby, how many submissives have you noticed wearing clothing during a scene?"

"Um. One."

A smile flickered over his lips. "And that was because…?"

"The Domme wanted to cut his shirt off with her whip."

When her corset fell open, he pulled it from under her and tossed it on a chair. The air cooled her damp skin and tightened her nipples.

He removed her skirt, and thank goodness she'd indulged in buying sexy underwear. The corner of his mouth lifted as he ran a finger across the lace of her dark-red, cheeky panties. "Nice. Lace and red both look good on you." The compliment delighted her, but when he started to pull the pantie off, she instinctively closed her legs.

He administered a sharp slap to the front of her thigh.

"Ow!" The spot burned. The realization that he wouldn't let her get away with anything sent a quiver of vulnerability through her…and woke excitement in her belly.

He continued stripping her as if he hadn't done anything unusual. *Does he smack women every day?* The pantie landed on top of her corset. When he rested his wide palm on her bare stomach in the same way another man might take her hand, the casualness of his touch shook her.

"Abby, I've indulged you up to now because you're new. You said you'd done some reading about BDSM?"

"Yes, sir."

"Then you know, intellectually, at least, how to behave."

His sharp gaze sliced a pathway through her thoughts. "Yes, sir."

"Do so. I warn you, if you start watching other scenes, I'll increase the intensity here." He picked up a strap, letting the end trail over her stomach. "We Doms are rather competitive, you know."

Intensity? That didn't sound good at all. Yet she was aroused. Her skin felt so sandblasted that each brush of the leather set her nerves to firing.

Xavier secured the strap below her breasts, pinning her to the table. "Can you breathe?"

She couldn't sit up. Couldn't escape. "I…I don't…" Like a flooding river, anxiety roared in her head.

"Take a slow breath." His smooth voice broke through the noise and panic. "Another." As he stroked a warm hand up and down her arm, her heart slowed. Her mind turned back on.

Why in the world had she gone off like that? She'd watched bondage scenes with no uneasiness. But this was more frightening than being restrained. Xavier had neatly plucked control from her without her seeing it coming.

With Nathan she'd always backed off before he'd got to this point. Because…because a small part of her worried that if she angered him, he'd leave her restrained—or worse, would do something she didn't want.

Xavier had sneaked up on her. He was the most self-confident man she'd ever met, like how he simply waited for her to get comfortable. Somehow she knew he wouldn't risk her safety even if he lost his temper—which she doubted happened during a scene. This Dom was all about control and responsibility.

"Ready?"

Sucking in a breath, as if she were preparing for an injection, she nodded.

He picked up another strap. "Remember your safe word is *red*. You tell me if the restraints are uncomfortable or if you get too anxious with them. Do you understand, Abby?"

His voice reverberated down to the inner person deep inside her. "Yes, my liege."

"Very pretty." His light kiss was a reward.

But her nervousness rose again. Maybe she trusted him—mostly. But to give him all the control? She never let that happen—especially with sex. Yet her defenses were slipping out of her grasp, as if he'd rolled over in bed, taking her sheets with him and leaving her exposed. "I don't know if I can do this."

Never looking away from her face, he fastened another strap, this one above her breasts. The pressure tightened the skin and made her breasts mountain up between the straps. "I see this is frightening to you, Abby. Can you trust me to give you what you need?"

"Need? I'm not sure we have the same definition of the word."

Appreciation of her response lit his eyes. "Submissives and Dominants often disagree over what a sub needs, even when viewing the same problem." Leaning on his forearm, he fondled her breasts almost absentmindedly. His gentle plucking of her nipples fired sizzles of heat downward until her labia and clitoris tingled.

Another strap went across her pelvis. “For example.” His big hand flattened over where her ugly stomach pooched out. “You look at yourself and think you need to lose weight.”

Exactly. This was why she *needed* to stay in clothing. Her lips tightened.

“I see you and think you should accept the beauty of your body and stop searching for flaws.” His voice held an inescapable firmness. He leaned down, hands curving on each side of her waist as he nuzzled her belly. “Mmm. All this softness is incredibly seductive, Abigail.”

His words might not have convinced her, but his heavy-lidded look of pleasure and the way his hands lingered and stroked provided confirmation. Besides, he was *my liege*. He didn’t need to hand out pretty compliments to seduce. Any unattached submissive in the club would—and did—beg to be with him.

Had he called her Abigail? She frowned. “My name is Abby.”

“But Abigail is correct, is it not? It’s on the forms.” He put a cuff around her left ankle and clipped it to the lower corner of the table. After pulling her legs wide apart, he restrained the right leg.

“What are you doing?”

“Whatever I want.” He held her gaze with his.

The table seemed to drop a foot, leaving her stomach behind.

Smiling slightly, he set his palm over her pussy, and the heat and pressure against her clitoris shivered through her. “Although I won’t use my mouth or cock down here, I intend to use my fingers—and other things—on you, Abigail. Is that a problem?"

"Other things?" She stared. "No matter what people in high office might believe, that's still a type of sex."

His chuckle was like dark chocolate for the ears. "Yes, it is." He brushed over her outer labia and held up his fingers to display the glistening wetness. "Again, is this a problem for you? Or are you a virgin?"

When she glared at him, he swatted her thigh. Harder.

Her skin stung, and she couldn't move to rub the burning. *Don't glare at the Dom, moron.*

After shaking his head in a reprimand, he waited.

"I'm sorry," she muttered. The light pain seemed to drain from her leg to her core, which had started to throb with need.

"I daresay you'll learn manners eventually." His hand returned to lie against her pussy, right where she was the wettest. "Now answer my questions. Politely."

"I'm not a virgin." *Which I'm sure you knew.* "I hadn't thought about touching. Sexually." She hadn't planned to do anything, and now here she was, naked, strapped down, and being openly stimulated. Wasn't this wrong? Didn't she love Nathan?

How could someone else excite her?

But Nathan hadn't wanted her. She was free to act as she pleased. In fact, he'd probably found someone else already. The realization made her feel lonely even as her anger rose.

Xavier's gaze grew more intent. "That's an excessive amount of thinking for a simple question."

Sex is never simple. "Touching and…things…aren't a problem."

"Very good." Now that she'd told him he could touch her, the jerk moved his hand away. How perverse was that?

Her attempt to rein in her glare probably exploded brain cells throughout her skull.

His lips pressed together, and he was obviously trying not to laugh. "Abby, you're truly a delight." With one finger, he guided a lock of hair behind her ear. "Now, I could blindfold you to keep you in the present, but you'll be more comfortable if you can see me."

She nodded even though he wasn't asking permission—merely telling her what would happen. Undoubtedly this was his version of negotiation. After all, he'd seen her limits list. She began to think she should have marked *no* to a whole lot more items.

Which way did most submissives choose—to try or to refuse the majority of the options? Wouldn't that be a great subject to research? She'd theorize that submissive traits would lead people to—

Xavier made a warning sound.

She blinked and realized he was staring at her. *Uh-oh.*

"You are something, pet," he murmured. He stroked a finger across her lower lip, down her chin, the slow progress of his warm fingertip excruciatingly sensual. After circling the hollow of her neck, he kissed her there, his lips velvety, before his finger trailed along the highest strap. Her breasts, already compressed, tightened further, and her nipples throbbed as if demanding he detour to attend to them.

His touch slid between her breasts, circled the left, then spiraled inward to the nipple.

Oh please, touch me.

He plucked the peak gently, and the sensation felt like light bursting through stained glass, brightening everything in her body. The next pull was harder, making her labia throb as well. When he pinched and held without releasing, the pain lit something deep inside her, sparking a disconcerting sensation of pleasure.

Her thoughts wavered as her need to escape conflicted with the desire to arch into his grasp.

Smiling, he released her nipple, and blood flowed back in with a rush. "These will be a beautiful, deep red when I finish," he said, not looking up. His finger circled the areola.

Her clitoris tingled and burned, but she didn't want him to...to touch her. Not there. Except she really, really *did* want him to. *No. Yes.* Gritting her teeth, she looked away from him, trying to distract herself. She was supposed to be doing research, after all, not letting some...person...play with her. What kind of a slut was she anyway?

Across the room, the Dom scrubbed the equipment while the Domme dispensed water and hugs to the blanket-wrapped submissives. How did two Dominants decide who was in—

"You're deliberately diverting yourself," Xavier stated. It wasn't a question.

Her gaze shot up.

"I thought you became sidetracked by the activities around you—that you needed to discipline yourself—but that's not it. You mentally escaped from here, much as someone would run away on foot. Why?"

"I... The scene over there was interesting."

His black brows drew together, and his eyes hardened. "No. You looked over there to distract yourself. You performed the same maneuver with Seth." He leaned a hip on the table, completely at ease, conversing with her while she was naked, legs open for everyone to see her genital area. "I don't think there's any question you're submissive, Abigail, and that you're aroused. Does arousal make you so uncomfortable you need to escape?"

As a flush flooded her face, she pulled and twisted, wanting free of the straps. Who was he to question her about her feelings?

He cupped her breast, using his thumb to idly toy with the nipple. Her back started to arch, and she stiffened. *No.* The feeling of need was...wrong. Her responses weren't under her control—her body was short-circuiting her thoughts.

"Are you afraid of being aroused?"

"Of course not." *Fear* wouldn't be the right word. Uncomfortable...definitely.

His eyes narrowed, his gaze intent. He rolled her nipple between his fingers, and her eyes closed at the rush of sensation. When he stopped, she struggled to pull herself together, to—

"It's the loss of control that bothers you," he murmured. "Not the arousal, especially, but it destroys your ability to stay in your head. To think." He leaned down to stroke her face. "Little fluff, don't you realize that's what being submissive is all about? Giving up control so you don't have to think or worry? For the time we are together in this scene, thinking is my job."

His words sent a stab of fear and—and something hopeful—through her. Low in her belly, a disconcerting flutter of anticipation started, like the flapping of a curtain in a freshening storm. “Xavier.”

“Try again.”

“My liege, I don’t want... This isn’t...” She couldn’t *think*.

“You don’t have to analyze it here. Do you trust me, right now, to control this scene—and you—for the next half hour to an hour?”

If she said no, she’d hurt his feelings. And she did trust him. Mostly. Could she let him have his way? “You won’t gag me?”

“No, Abby.” His smile was tender. “You’re not ready for that.”

But what would he do? She wanted to find out...kind of. “All right.”

“Good girl.” To her consternation, he pulled her glasses off.

“No!”

He squinted through the lenses. “They’re for distance, hmm? Can you see my face?”

“Somewhat, but not as well as when they’re on.”

“And the other scene?”

She turned her head. Anything farther away than about three feet turned blurry. “No.” Being half-blind was too, too scary. “I want my glasses.”

“No.” The absent way he said it, as if she didn’t have a choice, set off an odd shimmer in her bones. He regarded her soberly. “You’re scared without them? More than being bound to a table?”

“I’m trying not to think about bondage,” she said grumpily.

He grinned, swift and wonderful.

"And yes, I'm scared. What if something happened, like a fire?" She wouldn't be able to find her way out. "Or a terrorist attack. Or zombies."

He chuckled. "I do like submissives with imagination."

That wasn't imagination—just being prepared.

"First, I would never, ever leave someone who is restrained." He laid his hand on her face as if to promise. "However, we can compromise. You may keep them close." He tucked her glasses beside her thigh, where her fingers could trace the metal. "Not in your hand, though—you might crush them without realizing it."

How would that happen? As her anxiety increased to the level of a thesis defense, his lips quirked.

From his bag he pulled an eight-inch box, a water bottle, tiny hand wipes, a... Was that yogurt? Finally he took out a vibrator, still in its packaging. "This is your first toy from me."

I didn't ask for a toy.

He ran his hand between her legs, tracing her folds, sending her body into joyful anticipation. Her clit throbbed with demand. His finger circled as if measuring for size, then thrust inside, almost like a medical exam...only no doctor had ever made her feel like this.

Knowing she couldn't avoid his intimate touch—or anything he chose to do—sent waves of heat through her. And worse, she couldn't direct where she wanted his hands. She tried to tilt her hips up, to get him to pay attention to her clit, but the strap over her lower belly prevented any movement. Her skin felt as if it were on fire.

He added another finger, stretching her. The fluttering in her belly grew as he explored her and watched her, as if getting her accustomed to his touch. When he stroked a spot inside her that made her feel as if her clit had turned upside down, she made a gurgling noise.

"Oh?" He lingered, rubbing that place over and over, relentlessly increasing her needy hunger until even her toes strained upward.

"Good girl," he said and slid the toy into her vagina. The shaft was cool and soft and slick and so much bigger than two fingers. She shuddered as it stretched her.

He flipped a switch, and the mild vibrations didn't hit anything important—like her clit—yet her body felt as if he'd ratcheted up the pressure.

When he pulled on a pair of gloves, she stiffened. "What… I marked *no* to blood play."

"Abigail."

He knows that. She swallowed hard before craning her neck to check the items he'd put on the table. No knives. No needles. Okay. Maybe.

The vibrations were making her clit burn with need. Her body felt…strange. Unfamiliar. When her gaze tracked over toward the other scene, she caught herself. She really did try to escape, didn't she?

And now she wasn't paying attention to the Dom. She forced her gaze back to him.

"Don't worry, pet." His dark eyes were too perceptive. "You're not going to have a choice about thinking in a minute. I won't permit it." He inserted a cotton swab into one vial and painted her left nipple with the liquid. It smelled like what he'd smeared on her arm yesterday. Like Christmas candles. Or cinnamon. He wanted her breasts to smell like pie? Was there such a thing as a smell fetish?

He shook his head. "That mind of yours is a busy one." He did the other areola.

As the cool air touched her wet nipples, they bunched into hard peaks.

Without saying anything, he tossed the cotton swab into the basket, followed by the gloves. He moved slowly, deliberately, as if in a ritualized dance, as he tightened her ankle restraints and ran his hands over her trim calves. When he continued upward past her pretty knees, she wanted to hide. "You have beautiful legs, Abby."

And fat, white thighs. You bet.

"Pale skin has a fascinating texture." His smile glimmered for a second. "Like Egyptian cotton sheets with a thread count of six hundred or so."

Delight at the compliment ran through her, increased by the way he stroked her thighs, showing he was enjoying himself. She held her breath when his calloused fingers curled around her hips, and his thumbs caressed the crease outside her labia. So close.

He leaned over and kissed her stomach, and she really, really wanted those lips farther down. Why had she set limits like no sex? *I want sex.*

His kisses descended until his breath ruffled the fine curly hair covering her mound.

"I…I don't shave there," she offered. "I—"

"Sometimes I insist on it. Sometimes I don't," he said. He fluffed her curls, sending a jolt of heat through her. "At the moment I don't want you to shave. I like the white-tipped look against all that pink."

His finger circled her belly button idly, as if he was killing time, waiting for…

Oooh, my breasts! Each nipple felt as if a wet mouth had closed over it, and the warmth increased steadily into heat. Her breath caught. He'd swabbed that ointment on her. No wonder he'd worn gloves. "You…"

"Me." His voice took on a hint of steel. "You don't speak again, unless to use your safe word or *yellow* to indicate you're frightened."

"I was at *yellow* the minute I walked in the door."

His laugh was as deeply masculine as his voice. "Then tell me when you reach orange."

After donning new gloves, he chose a different vial and swabbed the outside of her inner labia. A minute later, the tissues turned cool, like an icy breath mint with a decided bite. Her nipples continued to grow hotter.

Uncanny sensations coursed through her: cold here, heat there, vibrations inside. She needed more. Something. When he picked up another vial, she tensed. *I don't want that. I want sex.*

He held up the dampened cotton swab where she could see it, and the longer he waited, the more she felt everything he'd already done. A terrifying anticipation bubbled in her veins.

With a faint smile, he slowly and thoroughly rubbed the swab on her clitoris.

Oh, oh, oh. The roughness of the cotton was an exquisite torment. She inhaled hard, breathed out. In. Out. Nothing happened. She took an easier breath. That one wasn't so bad.

Setting the swab and gloves aside, he stroked the outsides of her breasts, then trailed a finger down the center of her torso to above her pubic mound. Playing with her, fondling her, letting the vibrator, the ointments keep her arousal at an uncomfortable pitch. But why—

The stuff on her clit turned *hot*. Unlike the heat on her nipples, this was a thousand fiery needles attacking the nub of nerves. *No*. Sweat broke out on her upper lip, then over the rest of her body. It was too much. Vibrating inside. Her nipples burned, her folds felt icy, yet the most sensitive spot was on fire.

He bent and blew a stream of air right at her pussy. Her back arched as everything increased. *Cold. Hot*. She moaned.

"There's a good girl." With a low laugh, he upped the vibrator one notch.

Her insides clenched around the shaft as sensations rioted over her. Hot and cold and biting hot, and her core trembled around the buzzing vibrator.

In the stew of overload, she heard someone laugh nearby, and the smack of a paddle, and a scream. She inhaled the fragrance of cinnamon. Peppermint. The air seemed to billow around her, and she couldn't focus. Too hot, and yet not, and as each second passed, the need to come clawed at her until her body shook with it. "I... Please..."

No, wasn't supposed to talk. She bit the words back, feeling as if the ground were quaking.

A sound made her look up. Xavier had pulled on new gloves and squirted on lubricant. Standing beside her hip, he watched her as he ran slick fingers around her burning nipples. Slow, hot circles. Down below, her folds were cold, but her clit felt as if tiny teeth gently gnawed at it, and now... The lube cooled her areolas and then heated them more.

When he rolled her nipples between his hard fingers, edgy pain joined the sensual collage, and her body shuddered. Her whole core had become one giant nerve.

"Pretty little Abby. I like seeing your eyes go unfocused." His voice was a low murmur, a soothing background to the upheaval inside her.

She wanted to say something, only couldn't escape the hold her body had. Too many things were divorcing her brain from any ability to process. Her insides coiled as the pressure grew higher and higher, but never, ever enough.

Her legs tried to draw together to rub her burning, aching clit. Nothing would move. Her hands fisted as another wave of heat rolled over her. She stared up at him helplessly.

He leaned forward, his gaze trapping her, so dark and direct and pleased that a whimper escaped her.

"That's a good sound. You're ready, aren't you?" He moved his left hand between her legs, and his lubed fingers rubbed her clit with featherlight strokes. Even the lightest friction... She moaned as her core contracted around the vibe tightly that vibrations shook her body. The pressure grew with each slow stroke of his slick fingers, coiling tighter and tighter. Her back arched, holding, holding...

Then his finger firmly pressed on her clit even as he wiggled the vibrator in a circle. Outside sensations and inside ones merged in a glorious rush, knotting and blowing apart. A tidal wave of pleasure broke over her. Her insides convulsed, tightening around the vibrator, and the feeling of being penetrated sent her higher.

Xavier's fingers slid over her clit, and another breaker hit, shoving her further into the ocean of sensation. Drowning her in it. She gasped for breath and quaked as lingering waves rolled over her.

Her body eased down in shuddery jerks until she could feel her heart and hear herself breathing.

"Very nice," Xavier said, his low, smoky voice filled with approval. "Go again." He leaned down and blew.

The gust of air slid first over her pussy, chilling the ointment, and then over her clit, where heat erupted like a volcano. Her body arched up in a terrifying convulsion of pleasure before dropping her back limp to the table.

THE LITTLE FLUFF certainly wasn't thinking of anything else at the moment.

Pleased, Xavier watched her pant for breath. Sweat-dampened hair clung to her temples, and her face had turned a gorgeous pink. She stared up at him with unfocused gray eyes. He changed gloves again and tugged on the vibrator. She gave a delightful gasp, and her cunt clenched, trying to keep it in.

A shame he couldn't replace the toy with his cock.

He kept an eye on her expressions as he removed the peppermint, cinnamon, and hot pepper ointments with the various cleaning agents he thought best. Nothing worked perfectly, and she'd still have a residue of heat. Then again, he rather enjoyed knowing a scene would linger, not only in a submissive's mind but also on her body.

He released the restraints and put her glasses back on. Not that she was seeing much. He gently sat her on the floor at his feet and tucked a blanket around her. She sagged against the table leg as he cleaned the scene area and handed off his bag to a staff member.

After taking a bottled water from the nearest service stand, he lifted her into his arms.

She squeaked and froze.

He grinned. Submissives had the sweetest startle reflexes. "Shhh." He rubbed his chin on her silky hair. "I've got you, Abby. Take a breath."

Not moving, he waited, willing to stand all night until she relaxed. Until she physically showed him the trust he wanted. The submission he demanded.

Her little body stayed stiff, and he knew her instincts would be screaming that he might let her fall. After an orgasm, she was very vulnerable, very open to emotions. Holding her like this, keeping her both dependent on him and safe, would start building the trust she needed to have in him.

A minute. Two. Her exhausted body melted.

"There we go." He kissed her hair, pulling her closer. She was so soft. Not light, but she had a nice heft that let him know he held a woman. Someone who wouldn't break under his weight and his size.

No, don't go down that path. She was his receptionist, not his submissive. But even as he'd pulled her into the play, she'd involved him just as deeply.

Of course he could tell himself the scene tonight was just a lesson given to a staff member.

He tried not to lie to himself. He'd enjoyed this scene far more than mere instruction would warrant. He wanted to play with her again, to see how much further he could take her. To hear and feel her response when he entered her. When he took her gently. Or roughly.

He settled into one of the oversize leather chairs in the center of the room. The unwritten, occasionally idiotic Dom rules said he should set her on the floor between his feet to reinforce her submission. With a shrug he pleased himself and adjusted her on his lap as comfortably as possible, considering her soft ass rested on his rigid cock.

Her damp skin held the light scents of an almond lotion and lingering cinnamon. Combined with the fragrance of her arousal, it made her smell like a sexual pastry.

No fucking the dessert, Leduc.

Instead he took her lips again, hard and rough, and felt her body sink further into submission.

She was quite a puzzle—wanting to submit yet fighting it.

An experienced Dom often played with submissives whose styles clashed with his. Xavier preferred being on the same wavelength, riding the high of anticipating a submissive's responses, knowing exactly what to give her to elicit the reactions he wanted.

But this little fluff was a contradiction. Working with her was like searching for a favorite radio station in the mountains. The music between them was perfect...when he managed to get her tuned in.

He hadn't had this much fun in a very long time. Wasn't it a shame he couldn't take her home and keep her?

Chapter Six

On Tuesday Abby nuzzled a furry body, grinning at the scent of puppy breath. "You are so cute," she told the tiny fuzz ball. Sure, she'd said the same to the others, but she meant it each time. "You're going to make someone a wonderful pet, and they'll love you more than you can understand."

Tippy stared into her eyes, licked her chin, and accepted every word she said.

"So why do you guys get someone to adore you, and I don't?" If reincarnation existed, next life she'd demand to be a pampered pet. Snuggled and fed. And carried.

Who knew that being carried could be both scary and seductive? She shivered. Xavier had scooped her up like a puppy.

He'd held her in his lap as if he had nothing better to do. And when he'd kissed her, he'd made that approving sound low in his throat, the tone that turned her bones to melted butter.

Okay, getting a little warm here.

She returned the puppy to the wading pool. Tippy squirmed his way between blankets and siblings, earning small complaints, then, legs trailing, dropped into sleep. Wakened from his slumbers, Blackie rose and stumbled through the pile of bodies, trying to find a new place to settle.

That's me, Abby thought, not able to fit in and blundering around. Bad enough in an academic setting where she mostly belonged, but in Dark Haven? Whew. She kept expecting someone to yell *imposter* and toss her out the door.

"Sleep tight, my dears." Abby made herself a pot of tea, got her notebook, and stepped outside to her tiny half of a backyard. Her stepfather had given her the down payment for the duplex as a graduation gift—*thank you, Harold*—and the money from her renters paid the mortgage.

She set the tray on the small wrought iron table and took a chair. As the breeze whipped her baggy silk pants, she smoothed down her embroidered tunic top. She'd bought the *salwar kameez* in India and discovered that the soft materials made perfect lounging wear.

After pouring a cup of tea, she leaned back to enjoy the beauty of her yard. When in England, she'd fallen for the cottage gardens and duplicated them as closely as possible here.

Honeysuckle climbed the dark wooden fence that separated her yard from the other half. Morning glories were trellised along the back of the house. Behind the fragrant heritage roses, her hollyhocks had reached waist high. Patches of lavender, rosemary, and sage added the clean scent of herbs to the air. In the beds, zinnias, marigolds, and impatiens made bright splotches of color, and white-flowering geraniums in containers lightened her tiny patio.

At the sight of a few weeds, she stood, then sat again. No, she needed to work on her paper. Nibbling on the eraser, she considered and then wrote out her thoughts about her last weekend. When a physical description of a Domme slipped in, she erased it. She absolutely wouldn't risk revealing anyone's identity.

She was already in an ethical gray area. *When does observation become invasive?* Was it wrong to research dynamics at a football game without getting consent from the thousands of fans? How about a classroom? And what if the subjects were breaking the law or in an urban gang or alternative lifestyle? What if knowing they were being watched would change their interactions?

Not having their consent made her uneasy, but they seemed quite happy playing in front of other people, so would they really care?

She shook her head and concentrated. Would the tiny Dark Haven community be considered a family or a tribe or maybe a feudal society? The club members treated Xavier more like royalty than a father figure. Even the other Dominants deferred to him. He had "councilors" like Simon, and a Dom everyone called the Enforcer.

The submissives... She tapped her pencil on the paper. They had their own hierarchy, but she didn't quite grasp how it worked. Of course, some subs weren't even allowed to speak, and silent greetings and smiles were hard to categorize. To add to the complexity, both Dominants and submissives could be male or female. She hadn't realized the social network would be as complicated or her analysis of it so time-consuming.

Last Saturday she'd lost quite a bit of observation time during that scene with Xavier. She shifted in her chair. Just the memory made all her female parts tingle. The mixtures of burning and coldness had been overwhelming.

Add in the way Xavier had taken control, doing exactly what he wanted with her. She pursed her lips. She hadn't had one coherent thought from the application of the first chemical to when he'd stopped kissing her. Talk about sensory overload.

Her research had suffered, but she'd certainly experienced very erotic dreams since. And played with that new toy Xavier had given her. She'd thought of him each time.

She took a big gulp of her tea, burning her mouth. He was the reason she had trouble concentrating on her essay. How was she ever going to face him again? She felt her color rise. Using that stuff and his fingers, he'd made her climax so easily it was humiliating.

Even worse, Nathan was a member of Dark Haven, so he and Xavier must know each other. What if he told Nathan about her?

She raised her chin. Did she care? Nathan had broken everything off. Still…how would Nathan feel if he knew Xavier had put her in the bondage that she'd never let Nathan use?

With a sigh, she watched a hummingbird sample the flowering sage. Even if he'd dumped her, she didn't want to hurt him. She still missed his company and how they would sit out here and discuss research and statistics. She'd liked having someone to date and someone in her bed. She'd been a girlfriend. Had felt like a normal girl.

You are normal, you moron.

Sometimes. Intellectually brilliant, socially retarded. Graduating high school at sixteen hadn't been too bad. But the guys in college had called her jailbait.

Then she'd received her doctorate a year after she'd been able to legally drink.

Really, she should have scheduled social interactions the same way she had her classes. Maybe then she'd have known how to date. Of course, each time she had actually found a boyfriend, her stepsister had stolen him away.

Nathan had lasted the longest. She'd had hopes... Blinking hard, she took a sip of tea.

Get over it. Everyone suffers disappointments. She had a job—at least until spring. A nice house. A good family. And hey, she had her health too.

A squeak from inside made her smile. Even puppies had problems. Who was she to complain? Nathan was gone, but in his place, she had kinky evenings and an interesting research project.

The phone rang, and she ran into the house to answer, puffing slightly. *Must add exercise to the list of things to do this summer*. In fact, sex with Xavier would undoubtedly be hot, sweaty, and burn lots of calories. *I didn't need that picture, thank you very much.*

"Hello?"

"Abby, sweetheart. How are you? Did you have a nice weekend?"

"I'm good, Mom, and my weekend was okay." *I was tied to a table in a kink club*. Someday she'd decide if she was proud of herself or appalled.

"Friday is Grace's birthday, and I'm making all her favorite foods," her mother said in her warm voice. "Can you come to an early supper? Around five?"

Birthday. Abby winced. She'd marked the date on her calendar and planned to gift-shop on Sunday. Instead she'd spent the day researching other papers about BDSM. *I'm scum*. "Of course I'll come."

"Wonderful. It's been a while, and I miss you."

"Me too." Smiling, Abby ended the call. Her mom was the best, and her stepfather, Harold, was a pretty good deal as well. And they'd given her a little half sister.

Her smile soured. A shame she'd also gotten a stepsister as well. Harold's daughter, Janae, two years older than Abby, never missed a chance to insult the *interlopers*, Abby and her mom. They'd upset Janae's perfect world where she was the one and only child, and she'd never forgiven them.

Abby frowned. Really, if Janae had possessed a different character, Harold's doting behavior wouldn't have spoiled her. But Janae was a walking, talking example of nature over nurture—she simply had a rotten personality.

* * * *

On Friday, after tapping lightly on the front door, Abby let herself in to her parents' home. "Helloooo."

The large living room in sedate blues and greens was empty, but the arched windows to the backyard showed smoke rising from the grill.

"Abby, you're here. I'd begun to worry." Her mother bustled out of the kitchen to enfold Abby in a patented mommy hug. Maybe someday Abby would be able to dispense love with the mere tone of her voice.

"I needed to feed the pups one last time before I left." And clean up the mess. How did a fixed amount of intake create twice as much output? *Don't want to research that one, thank you*. "Are the presents outside?"

"Yes. And thoroughly shaken and checked out. She's already figured out at least three."

Won't figure out mine, Abby thought smugly. She'd put the small box with the bracelet and earrings set into a file-sized box.

As she walked onto the patio, Grace jumped up. "Abbeegale!"

Wrapped in a spinning, bouncing hug, Abby squeezed back, laughing. How had her quiet mother and dignified Harold created a child with all this energy?

Grace let go and checked Abby over. "You look good," she said in delight. "More happy or something."

"Why, thank you." Abby tilted her head. "You look older." In the past year her adorable little sister had transformed into a stunning young woman. Long reddish-blonde hair, big green eyes accentuated by a fair amount of makeup, tight clothes on her slender body. She could be one of Abby's university students.

"Yes, you look very...healthy, Abby." Janae leaned a hip on a patio chair. Her lips curled in a smile as fake as her sweet tone. "You might want to avoid the cake. Lots of calories."

After the sweetness of her mother and Grace's welcomes, Abby hadn't braced herself for her stepsister's animosity. As the insult dug deep, she grew aware of how wide her hips were, how her breasts made their own platform, how slender everyone else was, including her mother. "Thanks for the suggestion," she said lightly.

Forcing a smile, Abby visualized herself enclosed in a shroud of ice and then thickened the insult shield until the temperature seemed to drop. She'd learned the skill under the barrage of her father's screams. After Janae had come into her life, she'd perfected the technique.

Harold came from the kitchen, carrying a plate of steak. "There's the professor!" He set the food on the wide table and gave her a hard hug. Hands on her shoulders, he held her out. "You look far too pretty to be a Doctor Bern."

She smiled at him. Janae had inherited her father's slimness, but the gene for compassion had skipped her entirely. "It's good to see you too."

An hour or so later, after present-opening and Grace's favorite meal of high-cholesterol, high-calorie steak and baked potatoes, the conversation started to lag.

Janae rose. "I'm going upstairs to pull out some summer clothes."

As Harold left to check the stock reports and Grace ran upstairs to flaunt her presents on Facebook, Abby and her mother retired to the kitchen nook.

Ignoring the fresh coffee, Abby boiled water for tea. She definitely needed something to rev her up. She'd stayed up late all week to work on her essay. Then last night her young teaching assistant had quarreled with a boyfriend and spent the night in Abby's living room, crying and talking. It wouldn't have been that bad…except the puppies had missed the *let's sleep in* memo. Two hours' sleep wasn't adequate, not on top of all the other short nights. Tonight at Dark Haven was going to be rough.

"How are you holding up with Nathan gone?" her mom asked, settling down at the tiny table.

Stalling for a good answer, Abby poured water into the teapot, and the bergamot scent of Earl Grey filled the air. "He hasn't been gone that long. And I've been busy."

"Will you have time for a vacation this summer?"

"I'm teaching the short summer session, which gives me most of August off. Only…I might be job hunting for a new position for spring semester." Her mouth twisted. "The university is talking cutbacks, so I'm writing a quick research paper to enhance my résumé."

"Oh." Her mother's brows drew together. "Not something you enjoy. What are you working on?"

"Well, I had to find a project interesting enough to be memorable."

"And?"

Abby gave her a half smile. Thank goodness her mother was a liberal individual. "I'm studying a BDSM club."

The coffee cup hit the end table with a thud. "You what?"

"It's *research*, Mom." Abby picked up her cup, hoping her mother wouldn't notice the flush heating her cheeks. Did research involve Xavier touching her…intimately? Sliding a vibrator into her vagina?

"Heavens." Her mother leaned back in the chair. "What did Nathan say? He agreed to let you wander around a club like that?"

"Perhaps it's better that he's not in town." Abby grinned. "I must say, it's an interesting place. People are—"

"Why, Abby, I think you'd make an excellent slave," Janae said from the doorway. "But if you're going to run around naked with only a collar on, you should start on a serious diet."

"Thanks for the suggestion." The insult went nowhere this time. Not with the ice shield in place.

As Janae smirked and left to bid her father good-bye, Abby glanced at her mother. "Bet you're glad she doesn't visit often."

"I always hoped she'd stop resenting us, but it's not going to happen. Poor Harold has no idea how nasty she is, and I never had the heart to tell him." Her mother gave her a repentant look. "I'm sorry she made your high school years so miserable. I should have taken her to task or something..."

Abby shrugged. The insults—and losing any boy who showed a hint of interest—had been painful, but she'd survived, and after Janae, sarcastic professors were a piece of cake. "It's not your fault. We both avoid confrontations." Even now the thought of someone yelling—of Dad yelling—made Abby cringe. But Mom had suffered the worst. Abby had been a child and able to escape to school; her mother had never been able to get away.

"I feel as if I should—"

"No, you shouldn't." Abby patted her mother's hand. "Having you happy, and having Harold and Grace in our lives, is worth putting up with a bit of bitchiness. Someday someone will give Janae a wake-up call. It won't be us, but that's okay."

Chapter Seven

Friday night, at a table in the upstairs club room, Xavier watched Michael conduct a violet wand scene. The older Dom wore a contact pad, and the electricity passed through him. As sparks leaped from his finger to the submissive's bare ass, the well-rounded woman squirmed violently on the bench, trying to evade the bite of the current. Good entertainment for the crowd.

Xavier glanced around the room, pleased with the number of members present. Even at midnight the dance floor was packed, the bar and tables busy.

There was Abby, over by the door. As his spirits lifted, he shook his head ruefully. Although a Dom needed to be able to read his own emotions like a book, the knowledge gleaned wasn't always comfortable.

She's a member of the Dark Haven staff, not my submissive. He should remember that. When her gaze met his, he motioned to her.

Looking all around, she crossed the twilit room, so fair-skinned and blonde she almost glowed. The show on the stage halted her completely. Although the music of Terminal Choice from the dance floor drowned out the faint sizzle of the wand, the submissive's yelps came through clearly. Abby's rapid retreat indicated her opinion of electrical play.

As she drew closer, Xavier frowned. Her gray eyes were reddened, and the translucent skin beneath showed dark circles. "Welcome back."

"Thanks." She caught his raised eyebrow and added a hasty, "My liege."

He understood her difficulty with the automatic respect. Although he'd topped her in one scene, he wasn't her Dom, and she didn't have the habit of calling every Dominant "sir" that many submissives acquired. However, he did insist his staff be respectful.

"I'll give you one more night to improve your courtesy," he said gently and saw her brows draw together as she mentally added, *Or what?* He didn't answer her unspoken question. Explaining consequences served well at times, but silence could be far more effective…if the submissive possessed an active imagination.

He could see hers was hard at work. She really was delightful. "Clear?"

"Yes, sir."

After nodding acceptance, he shifted his attention to her attire. She'd ignored his directions about her clothing. Again. "Abigail, return to the desk and remove either the bustier or the skirt. Put your collar on. Return here."

Her mouth opened, closed, and a flush lit her cheeks.

He turned his gaze back to the stage in an open dismissal and punishment. Her footsteps trailed away.

A few minutes later he heard her stop beside him, and he glanced up.

Collared. Naked from the waist up. He'd have let her wear something slightly less revealing if she hadn't defied him. Her arm muscles were rigid, as if she had to quell the need to cover herself, and her face turned an enchanting red.

He'd forgotten how enjoyable the modest ones were. This one blushed more beautifully than anyone he'd ever seen. "You have gorgeous breasts, little fluff. I'm pleased to share your beauty with my friends."

Her mouth tightened—not a normal reaction to a compliment, and neither was her clipped, "Thank you, sir." Expressionless, she kept her gaze on the stage.

She was quite the piece of work. "When talking to a Dom, it's good manners for the submissive to be on an equal or lower level. That means if he's sitting, you kneel."

After a moment of obvious reluctance, she knelt in front of him with an awkward charm. He studied her, trying to read how she felt. He could see a hint of shock—that of a career woman ordered to kneel. Yet her nipples had tightened, and her back arched. Did the little feminist find it exciting to be at his feet? Quite likely. Perhaps someday he'd tell her how it pleased him to have her there.

For now he had other subjects to pursue. He leaned forward, resting his forearms on his knees, invading her space. Taking a slow breath, he inhaled her delightful fragrance, like a brisk spring with a hint of flowers. "Tell me why you chose to remove your top rather than the skirt." After all, she'd probably worn panties and would have been more covered.

She shrugged. "It was easier."

His mental deceit detector clanged. "I'd prefer an honest answer."

Her gaze never met his. "It seemed less naked."

WHY WON'T HE stop prying? As Abby shifted her weight, trying to find a comfortable position on the hardwood floor, her breasts wobbled. Without the bustier, her stomach's roundness was in full view. Janae's *you're fat* comments from earlier still lingered, and now Abby's mental armor chilled with every glance that probably held disgust.

The weight of Xavier's attention bowed her shoulders, but at least it couldn't penetrate the ice around her. Why wouldn't he just leave her alone?

"Let's try it this way," Xavier said, his tone even. "Tell me your thoughts as you decided which garment to keep on and which to remove. All."

Lay out her reasons like an exam paper to be graded? She felt the ice around her thicken to keep his influence minimized. "That was it. Really."

"Abby. Look at me."

The firm command sliced through her, and she tipped her head back. His eyes were black. Intent. The demand in them chipped at her armor.

"Keep looking at me," he said softly. His knuckles brushed down her neck, down her chest. His hand was warm, melting the ice around her as he cupped her left breast and weighed it in his big palm. Her nipples tightened painfully, making her toes curl. As he circled the areola with his thumb, his gaze kept hers trapped. She swallowed as the rush of heat inside her blasted away her defenses.

"That's right." His voice was soothing; only she didn't understand what he meant.

He leaned forward and kissed her firmly. "Your inability to share your thoughts and emotions is something we'll work on. But this time I'll help. When you tried to decide what to remove, your first thought was that you wanted to show off your breasts."

A startled laugh broke from her and made the fine lines at the corners of his eyes crinkle.

His hand shifted, sliding under her neglected breast to caress...to heat. "That would be no. Actually, since you're female, your first thought was probably that one part of your body is less attractive than another."

He'd plucked the worry right from her brain, and she jerked slightly.

"Yes. Tell me how you feel about your breasts, little teacher. Three adjectives, please."

She tried to look away, to get some mental distance to think. His free hand curved under her jaw, an iron trap holding her face up. He'd not let her escape. A shiver shook her as the feeling of exposure went from external to internal.

"Abby?"

Breasts. Her breasts. "Heavy. Nice." She did like her breasts. Although there were times... "Awkward."

"Awkward?" One eyebrow rose, and humor glinted in his eyes. "I'm looking forward to discussing that one."

Hell will freeze over first, thank you very much.

Despite her silence, he smiled. "Oh yes, we will. We also need to work on letting you view yourself in a better light." He stroked one breast, then the other. "They're more than *nice*. My adjectives: lush, lovely, responsive." He tugged on a nipple, and heat sizzled a path to her groin. "Your nipples are... Hmm. Like fragile, pale-pink roses on a canvas of snow."

Even through the flush of delight from the compliments, she stared. Men didn't use poetical phrases, especially a man who looked like a leaner, deadlier, darker Rhett Butler—an aristocratic pirate.

His smile flickered, undoubtedly at her expression. “I had an excellent private school education.”

What would she bet that his elusive and faint accent originated in a *European* private school?

He gave a very Gallic shrug, and his expression lightened. “I want three adjectives for what your skirt covers. Ah, no, I’ll make it more difficult. Three descriptive words for your hips and ass. Three for your pussy.”

“What?” Her attempt to lean back was defeated when his fingers tightened on her jaw.

“Now, Abigail.” A note of steel entered his tone.

The pit of her stomach dropped. Under his hands, his indomitable gaze, she couldn’t *think*. The words spilled out. “Fat. Ugly. Jiggly.”

His expression didn’t change. “All right. Your pussy?”

She wet her lips. Her ice shield had disappeared. His control of her face was intimate, his gentle stroking of her breast even more so.

What did her pussy look like? She thought of the times she’d used a mirror down there. *Ew*. “Wrinkly. Uneven. Ugly.” As she heard the words come out of her mouth, she wished she could take them back.

“I see. So you hide everything under a skirt and wish you could be tall and slender and tan.”

As her college students would say, *Well, duh*.

“Have you ever seen a Christmas tree farm?”

Interesting divergence from the topic, but it worked for her. Trees were a safer subject than intimate body parts. “Sure.”

“Did you find it awe-inspiring? Did you have to stop and catch your breath?”

The sight of acres of straight rows of green triangular trees? “Of course not.”

“What about a regular forest filled with tall and short, old and young trees, snags and all? The first time you saw one, did it feel like a miracle?”

On her first trip to Yosemite, she’d been ten. Her father had died of brain cancer the month before. A few trees had appeared, then more and more. She’d felt tiny, dwarfed by the immensity around them. When Mom had pulled over, Abby had gotten out and simply stared. “Yes.”

“Then understand this, little fluff: diversity is God’s gift to the world.” His lips quirked. “The thought of a planet filled with blonde Barbie dolls could give a man nightmares.”

When a laugh escaped her, he smiled and leaned forward to whisper in her ear. “As for wrinkly, uneven, and ugly, you’ve never seen your cunt when you’re aroused. Then it’s swollen and pink and wet. Puffy and soft and incredibly tempting.”

As her face flamed red, he released her.

“My liege.” Dixon waited off to one side.

“Yes, Dixon.”

“I have a member with some questions. Do you have time to speak to him?”

"Certainly." Xavier kissed Abby, and even without any tongue or open mouth, the sensation left her shaken. "Check in with me before you leave."

"Yes, sir."

"Enjoy your free time, pet." He walked away. His white shirt fit his broad shoulders perfectly. The fabric tucked into his black slacks, revealing the long muscles on each side of his spine. As usual, he'd worn his thick black hair in a braid down the center of his back, and it directed attention to a truly noteworthy butt.

What would he look like with his clothes off? She shook her head. She wasn't doing that kind of research—no matter how much fun it might be. *Get back to work, Abby.* Realizing her chest ached, she laughed, releasing the breath she'd held.

"Hard not to stare at Master Xavier, isn't it?" Simon's wife stood beside the table, waiting patiently.

Abby rubbed her chin—*good, no drool*—realized her position, and clambered to her feet. "Rona, right?"

"That's it." The blonde nodded toward a dozen or so people clustered at various tables in one corner. "Would you like to meet some members?"

Abby glanced over and caught Simon's disconcertingly keen appraisal. Pulling her gaze away, she looked at the others. The mixture of men and women were in a variety of postures. Some submissives knelt, some sat on their Doms' laps, and a few had chairs. One kneeling man had a tiny tray-like device attached to his head so his Dom could put his drink on it. Another sub was being hand-fed.

How fun...and exactly what she needed for her paper. "I'd love to meet everyone."

"Perfect." Rona led the way. "People, this is Abby, the new receptionist."

The chorus of welcomes heartened her.

"Thank you. It's nice to be here." A little nervous under the assessing gazes from the male and female Doms, she fingered Xavier's collar—no, the Dark Haven staff collar.

Rona patted an empty seat beside Simon. "Unless you're more comfortable on your knees, it's all right to sit in a chair. You don't have a Dom to tell you no, and the club doesn't require high protocol unless Xavier dictates otherwise." She sat down on the other side of her Dom.

"What's—"

"High protocol?" interrupted the buzz-cut, blond Dom lounging at the adjacent table. Dressed in ripped-up leathers, he gave her a slow once-over. His jaw was big with a cleft chin, and he looked like a movie drill sergeant—the one who always bellowed at some timid private. "High protocol is a certain set of behaviors and rituals—it's the D/s version of bringing out the fancy silverware. Submissives kneel, eyes down, never speak unless permitted. That sort of thing."

His gaze said that he enjoyed that sort of thing, and Abby wanted to scoot her chair back from the table.

"Relax, pet." Simon squeezed her shoulder in such a comforting way that she didn't even worry about being half-naked. "Wearing Xavier's collar means you can't do a scene without his permission. And he wouldn't let deVries play with you." He gave the hard-faced man an easy smile that was both a compliment to the Dom and reassuring to Abby.

A female submissive farther away sighed noisily. "I saw Master Xavier play with you last week."

Great. Had everyone seen her spread-eagled on a table? "Uh. Yeah."

"He doesn't do full scenes often. I wish he would pick me for one." The freckle-faced redhead sighed again.

A stunning brunette tossed her hair back over her chain-mail dress that left nothing to the imagination. "I wish he'd take me as his slave and do the twenty-four/seven deal."

"But he never brings any slave from home to the club," the redhead said. "What good is that?"

Lindsey stepped behind the redhead and patted her head. "Mandy, my child, if he's fucking you at home, who cares about coming here?"

"Oh. Right."

Lindsey dropped into the chair next to Abby.

"Who's minding the reception area?" Abby asked.

"Another sub can't afford the dues, so she volunteered. Which is good—they can't count on you and me every single weekend, right?" Lindsey's PVC bustier was short enough to expose a slender abdomen. She tugged at the top, then rose and openly adjusted her vinyl hot pants. "You'd think they could make these clothes more comfortable."

"Undoubtedly men design them," Abby said, hearing a huff of laughter from Rona. "So are you going home or—"

"Not a chance." Lindsey rubbed her hands together. "I'm fixin' to find myself a big ol' Dom to play with."

Abby snorted. She'd always heard Texans were bigger than life. Well, Lindsey stood only an inch taller than Abby, maybe five feet seven, but her attitude definitely qualified. She wasn't scared of BDSM—she was revved. Like Grace, she'd dive right into the ocean while Abby would stand on the beach calculating temperature, depth, and salinity. "Do you have someone in mind?"

"No." But Lindsey's glance at the very big blond Dom gave her away.

DeVries's return gaze held more assessment than appreciation. "You're not up to my speed, little girl. Find yourself a baby Dom."

The red in Lindsey's face drowned out her few freckles. She sat up taller. "Ah don't recall asking you. Sir." She turned to Abby. "I need some water."

As Lindsey walked away, Abby gave deVries a glare that made him grin.

"Abby." Simon patted her arm.

"Yes, sir?"

"Xavier asked me to answer any questions you had. Now that you've had a couple of nights to get acclimated, does anything come to mind?"

She bit her lip. "Actually. Kind of. Can you show me what that cane with leather on the end feels like?"

* * * *

Abby curled into an oversize leather chair in the dungeon and tried to force her brain into alertness. If she didn't get a good night's sleep, she might turn into a zombie. She glanced at the clock near the stairs. Already two hours past her normal bedtime.

Even the sore spots on her back weren't keeping her awake, although—at the time—they'd been quite the wake-up call. Especially the crop. When Simon had given her the sampling she'd requested, the innocent-looking cane with leather on the end had hurt worse than his giant-sized flogger.

Concentrate. Blinking gritty eyes, she took mental notes as she watched a middle-aged Dom use various toys on a pretty brunette. A paddle, a leather strap, a cane. She now understood the variations in how one person might dominate another. The genders displayed different styles as well. The Dommes often did more sensual play but also seemed to like the psychological. Although some were even rougher than the men. And the—

Long legs in black slacks blotted out her view and didn't move.

"Excuse me, please." Annoyed, Abby tilted her head back, her gaze moving up. A black belt around a flat waist. A muscular chest under a placket-style white shirt. The sleeves were full, the cuffs set with ornate silver cuff links. Xavier's attire didn't belong in this century. No wonder he reminded her of a pirate.

His neck was corded, his jaw razor sharp, his mouth firm and beginning to smile.

Am I supposed to stand up? "Good evening, my liege."

He set his leather bag down beside her chair. "You have an interesting way of viewing a scene. No...not viewing. Studying. You focus completely. Do you feel anything when you're watching?"

A touch of anxiety ran through her. Surely he couldn't hear the mental notes she took. "What do you mean?"

"I don't think you and your body talk. Communication is important."

"I—"*Communicate with my body?* "We talk. When it says it's hungry, I feed it."

He tugged on a lock of her hair. "When your body says it's aroused by watching a scene, do you listen?"

Aroused? To her shock she realized she was damp between the legs. Her gaze shifted. "Have you noticed the way that Dom over there is—"

"Now you're verbally evading." He didn't smile, but creases appeared in his cheeks. With his boot he nudged a high footstool closer to her chair and sat down on it in front of her. He leaned forward, forearms on his thighs, deliberately invading her personal space. *Again*. "Abigail, your 'pay,' like most of the staff in Dark Haven, comes in two parts: First, membership in the club. Second, learning about the lifestyle. The questions I ask help me understand what you need to learn."

Did his teaching methods have to be so personal? Still, he was being logical. "You're right." She frowned. "You have a lot of staff, though. Don't you get tired of"—*terrifying? intimidating?*—"instructing each person?"

"I don't teach everyone, but I enjoy helping out now and then." He ran his fingers through her hair, fingering the strands. "Especially with pretty blonde fluffs."

Fluff. Didn't that make her sound as if she hadn't had an original thought in her whole lifetime? She gave him her professorial hell-will-freeze-over-before-you-get-an-A frown.

And received back a tap on her lips. "Have you heard the term *impact play*?"

That was what the Dom in the nearby scene was doing—using lots of painful toys that made nasty red marks on the skin. "Yes. Sir."

"Frown at me again, and you'll get a personal acquaintance with the definition."

Her mouth dropped open, and he slid his finger inside. "Suck on me, Abigail. I want to feel your tongue."

Why the dark command sent a wave of heat straight to her genitalia made no sense. She closed her lips and sucked, running her tongue over his fingertip. Then his heavy knuckles. Calluses added rough spots. He pulled his finger back, pushed in again, and the movement was so similar to…something else…that she could almost feel him inside her.

He straightened, then set his hands on the chair arms to cage her. His kiss was long, wet, and deep, and even his tongue dominated hers. When he withdrew a few inches, his black eyes were level and controlled despite the heat radiating from his body. "Can you think of a reason I shouldn't fuck you when I play with you tonight?"

Lots! Only her brain couldn't provide even one. He wasn't a guy-slut. Women threw themselves at his feet, but he hadn't accepted any that she'd seen. He wanted *her*. And she and her body apparently communicated just fine, because she knew she really wanted him.

What would being with Xavier be like?

His eyes never wavered.

She swallowed. "I can't think of a reason." Except anxiety. Fear. Worry. Embarrassment.

"Honesty becomes you, pet." His gaze showed his approval. "I have a couple of scenes to oversee before I can get free. Are you doing all right on your own? Is anyone bothering you?"

"No, sir." The formality slid out without her thinking about it. "A few have asked me to play, but—" She touched her collar.

His hand cupped her cheek. "The collar is for protection, not ownership. Unless I think the Dom would go too far past your comfort level, I'll give you permission to play."

"I understand." His words sent a trickle of hurt through her. Didn't any man ever want to keep her for his own? Pretending to look for her drink, she shifted in the chair and turned away from him.

"Stop." Xavier stood and gripped her shoulder, forcing her to lean forward. His fingers ran down her back, and she flinched when he touched a sore spot. "Explain these marks." The steel in his voice was icy cold.

"I... It wasn't play. Sir. It—"*Don't yell. Please don't yell at me.*

"Xavier, I gave her the marks, but not during a scene." Simon strolled over and sent her a reassuring smile. "She wanted to know how some impact toys felt, so before Rona and I started to play, I gave Abby a light, medium, and hard strike from a flogger, a signal whip, and a crop. Nothing else." His eyes narrowed. "You asked me to answer her questions. I apologize if I overstepped."

Xavier didn't release her. His hand closed over her nape, just above her collar, as he traced one tender spot with his other hand. A tremor shook her. "She marks nicely, doesn't she?"

"Almost too easily."

His anger had dissipated, and she relaxed. As his finger skimmed slowly over each stripe, the sensation was...more erotic than anything she'd ever felt.

He released her. "No apologies needed, Simon. Answering questions is what a Dom does. Although I daresay you knew I meant verbal answers, not physical ones." The look he gave the other man could have frozen fire.

"Would you prefer I not answer her questions—physically—again?"

Abby tensed. Why didn't Simon stop? He'd explained to Xavier. This felt as if he was...almost pushing him.

Xavier gave him an unreadable look. "Exactly so. Verbal only." He nodded at the stairs. "Rona is waiting for you."

"And my lass has a temper." Simon smiled at Abby. "Find me anytime you have more questions you need answered."

Oh, like that would happen. Was Simon *trying* to start a fight? She glanced at Xavier's face, and her insides clenched. Dixon had been right. Upsetting him wasn't something she ever wanted to do.

How could she fix this? And why did his anger make her IQ drop lower than her age? "I'm sorry I upset you, my liege." She stared at her fingers.

He gave an exasperated sigh and used a finger under her chin to tilt her face up. "Like many Doms, Simon manipulates events to get the outcome he wants. You did nothing wrong, pet."

His smile rearranged her emotions, putting them in order. Her muscles eased. "Thank you, sir."

"Have you got a thong or underwear on under that skirt?"

She stared. "Excuse me?" His lack of response was weighted with annoyance. "Yes, sir."

"No underwear beneath other clothing. Understood?"

Well, wasn't he just the autocrat? "Yes, sir."

He pulled her to her feet. "Remove it."

She got three steps toward the restroom.

"Here, Abby. Off. Now."

Her attempt at a frown died under his black gaze. With a silent sigh, she reached under her skirt and slipped her panties off.

He removed an item from his leather bag. "Wear this instead."

Pantie briefs made of tight rubber. She tugged them on. Not comfortable, especially with the hard lump over her crotch. She gave him a suspicious look.

"Yes, that's a vibrator. Your task is to keep count of the times the vibe turns on." A smile played at the corners of his mouth. "But no matter how much it *turns you on*, you may not come."

Have an orgasm here? In front of everyone? "No problem, sir."

"I'm pleased you have such excellent control." The dryness of his voice made her recall how she'd climaxed last week. In front of everyone.

Her cheeks heated.

He leaned down and gave her a slow, drugging kiss that turned her on far more than any vibrator ever could. "I'll find you in a bit."

Chapter Eight

In the next hour Xavier dealt with a hysterical slave and then a quarrel about music selections on the dance floor.

After that he broke up an altercation between two Doms over a submissive. Even worse, the sub had incited the fight. The young men were still learning about D/s, so instead of coming down on them, he told them to discuss how a submissive had jerked their chains rather than the opposite.

He removed the sub from the equation. Harmonie certainly didn't live up to her name. She'd caused problems before, and his tolerance had ended. He had a staff member escort her to the main floor, where he kept an area roped off for public punishment.

Mitchell, a stocky Dom from Australia, stripped her, and then Xavier used the controls to lower the wooden pony to knee level. As the narrow board swung from heavy chains attached to a low rafter, the short woman moved to straddle it.

Xavier raised the pony up. When the board reached Harmonie's groin, Mitchell clipped her wrist cuffs to a horizontal chain running between the heavier front and back ones, giving her a way to balance herself.

Xavier winched the pony up slowly, until the brunette went up on tiptoes to get her pubes off the board.

The board wasn't sharp but was damn narrow, reminding him of his youth when he'd slipped while climbing over a fence. His crotch had slammed onto the one-inch board. His balls had felt as if they'd jammed in his throat, which probably explained his strangled wheezing.

As long as Harmonie stayed on her tiptoes, the pressure would be off her pussy. Xavier studied her weight and muscle tone. After about fifteen minutes, her calf muscles would give out, and her weight would come down on her crotch...on a narrow board. Riding the wooden pony served as a painful punishment, and one that rarely translated to erotic, especially with no other stimuli.

"Harmonie, you will remain here for half an hour, thinking about your behavior. If you're silent, Mitchell will release you, and you can resume play." Although her cunt would hurt enough that she'd probably go home. "If you make noise or use a safe word, you'll be barred from the club for a month. Are your choices clear to you?"

"Yes, my liege," she whispered.

He glanced at Mitchell. "Put the sign on her, please."

"Be a pleasure." Mitchell hung the wooden sign on her, BAD SUBMISSIVE, and took a seat at a nearby table. He'd monitor her condition and release her if needed.

Xavier shook his head. He doubted Harmonie would change her behavior. She was more concerned with getting attention and sex than about serving another.

In contrast, Abby had an instinctive desire to please. She'd been distressed at his anger. Attention made her uncomfortable.

After double-checking the punishment scene to ensure everything was safe, he headed down to the dungeon.

Hair tangled around her face, Abby sat near the center of the room. Elbows on one chair arm, she'd curled sideways so her bare breasts were covered by her arms. Nicely modest. Her big eyes were intent on a Mistress performing cock-ball torture.

Xavier's own balls drew up in sympathy. Testicles weren't meant to be flattened.

Taking a position in a corner of the room, he noticed Abby's attention had shifted to a group of older leather men with their subs kneeling properly on the floor. Why would she watch them instead of the scene?

Well, she wouldn't be observing anything soon. Xavier reached in his pocket and flicked the remote to a low setting.

As the pantie vibrator came on, she jumped. Within seconds her spine turned rigid, and her hips squirmed nicely. She looked around but didn't spot him in the shadows.

Although she tried to resume watching the nearby scene, her weight shifted over and over. He'd broken her concentration. Excellent. He flipped the remote off.

She relaxed into the chair with a sigh.

Then he kicked the controls back on and upped the intensity a notch.

Face flushing, she surged to her feet. With a stiff-legged gait, she moved to the next scene and pretended to watch it. After a couple of minutes, sweat sheened her skin. Good enough. With a smile he turned the remote off and headed away to make his rounds.

Upstairs the bartender pointed him toward a member who'd been drinking and tried to take his sub into a theme room. Per club rules, alcohol was for after a scene, not before. The man hadn't known the locked *I had a drink* bracelet contained a device similar to those used to prevent shoplifting. After speaking with Xavier, he and his submissive decided to dance instead.

Xavier checked on Harmonie. She was still able to rise onto tiptoes for a break. Sweating and squirming but silent, she displayed more determination than he'd expected.

Back downstairs Abigail had settled down to watch Angela's scene with her submissive, Meggie. Nice choice, since the Mistress was an expert with wax play. Deep into subspace, Meggie sighed and moaned.

A shame to distract the little fluff, but... Xavier pulled out the remote. As the lights on the remote flickered according to the setting, he selected an alternating rhythm that went well with the music.

Abby jumped to her feet, walking fast as though she could escape. She stopped a minute later, and he saw her muscles tightening as she neared an orgasm.

He turned the vibrator off and watched to see what she'd do.

She lowered her head and hugged her waist in a self-comforting movement. Huddled in on herself, she appeared more shaken than aroused, and that certainly wasn't the point of this exercise. He walked up behind her and wrapped his arms over hers.

She stiffened, trying to pull away from him. Angry and upset. Rather than releasing her, he backed to a couch and pulled her down onto his lap.

"Abby, take a breath." He added enough edge of command to see it done. "Now lift your middle toes on your left foot up. Down."

As she concentrated on the movement, her ability to remain rigid failed, and she sagged against him.

"That's a good girl."

Holding and warming her with his body heat, he waited until her color had returned. "You didn't like the vibrator." He made it a statement. "Why?"

"It was okay."

"No. Think about your answer for a minute. Then make it an honest one—not one intended to pacify me."

Startled, she looked up at him. After a pause, a dimple appeared in her cheek, reassuring him that her sense of humor had returned. She said, "In the BDSM books, I read about honesty and thought, of course you need to be truthful. I didn't realize it was so difficult."

For many submissives, emotional transparency was more painful than getting flogged. "Difficult for both Dom and sub." Pleased with her, he ran his knuckles over her cheek. "I'll go first and show you how." He thought for a second. "I liked how you jumped, and how arousal lights up your skin and eyes. I enjoy having the power to do that right in my hand. Seeing you wiggle made me hard."

"Oh my," she said under her breath, and he chuckled at her appalled tone. How long had it been since a submissive made him laugh?

"Your turn, Abigail." He gave her a question to hang her answer on. "Did the vibrator hurt you?"

Her tiny sigh at his persistence made him smile again. "Um. No. But I didn't like the jump or surprise. Or being aroused."

What? "You didn't mind last week. What's different tonight?" He thought he knew. Did she?

Silence. "Maybe because you were with me then. It felt...safer?"

And perhaps more intimate with my hands on you. "Fair enough. You should know, though, I was always close and watching you whenever the vibrator was on."

"Oh." The last bit of tension drained out of her body.

Yes, he'd erred, damaging some of her trust in him. Regret weighted his shoulders. Not all scenes went as desired, but since the control belonged to him, the blame for failure was his as well.

He laid his cheek on her silky hair, inhaling the light fragrance. "I'm sorry, Abby. The remote wasn't a good choice for you. I thought it would teach you to listen to your body without putting you on display. I never intended that you should feel abandoned."

ABANDONED. DIDN'T THAT make her sound like a five-year-old on her first day of kindergarten? Yet Abby knew he wasn't wrong. She'd felt alone. But the way he held her close and rubbed his face in her hair was shrinking the hollow place inside her.

Discussing what had happened was oddly intimate. Unfamiliar. Sure, she'd had boyfriends, but even in bed, they preferred the *wasn't that great sex* sort of discussion.

Unfortunately, with Xavier, the pendulum had swung too far in the other direction. His probing questions and intent study were intimidating.

"Well, pet, since remote play is out, I'll have to do this up close and personal." His chuckle had a wicked edge to it.

Arousal shot through her at the thought of receiving more personal attention, but she wasn't here for that. *Yeah, explain to him that you're just here for the research.* "Uh. There's no need to worry about it. I mean—"

"It's a Dominant's prerogative to worry." He ran a finger over her lips, and the simple touch started her on the upward path to arousal. "Since you're right here in my lap—not far away—we might as well use this toy. I'd like to know if there's anything else you dislike about it. No need to count, and you can come if you want."

Before she could stop him, he'd flicked it on again. Her protest came out in a low "Nooo" as the vibrations hammered lightly against her clit. The sensitive ball of nerves, already teased, flared to life and tightened.

When a tiny moan escaped her, the laugh lines bracketing his mouth deepened. "What do you think of this vibrator? Sales reps for sex-toy companies are always asking me for feedback."

Her clit hardened, thickened. A coil of pressure built inside her, and she tried to ignore it, even as her thoughts went foggy.

"You're still fighting what you feel, pet. Perhaps my hands need to be on you." His deep voice said words, and she heard them, but they didn't make sense.

He slid his right hand under her skirt and skimmed it up her bare thigh.

"No. Don't." She struggled, pushing at his arm. He'd touch her in front of everyone?

"Abby, you did a scene with me last week."

"I wasn't thinking then."

"Ah. Of course. But you know, I don't want you to think." To her relief he removed his hand—and captured her wrist. Then the other.

His left arm remained curved under her shoulders, and he pushed both her wrists into that hand, trapping her arms off to one side. "Lucky for you, I like holding down unwilling submissives." To her horror, he picked up the remote, upped the setting on the vibe, then put his right hand back under her skirt.

As harder vibrations hammered against her clit, need washed over her. "*Di te perdant*!"

He laughed. "The gods won't destroy me for playing with a pretty little fluff."

Great. His fancy education had included Latin. The vibrator hummed, increased, then stopped. Hummed, increased, stopped. Cycling up and slowing before she could come. She inched closer to a climax, shuddering with the feeling of inevitability.

But she couldn't get there. She was stuck. Teetering between *No, I won't come* and *More*.

He pulled her closer to him, and she pushed her forehead against his chest, panting for air. Just come, she told herself. Only, her brain wouldn't stop, and her body wouldn't obey.

She felt him kiss the top of her head. "Thinking again, Abby? Look at me now." His grip on her wrists tightened.

She looked up.

"Do you realize I can do anything with you, touch you anywhere...and you can't get away?" The ominous glint in his eyes demanded that she try.

She futilely struggled and couldn't escape. Couldn't even make him exert himself. The knowledge shook her, cracked the container holding her thoughts, and they drained away.

Under her skirt his hand moved up. His thumb pressed on top of the vibrator, adding more pressure, even as he slid his fingers through the right panties' leg hole. He circled her entrance with a slick finger, then firmly pushed inside.

Like a kite ripping free in a high wind, the ruthless penetration spiraled everything out of her control.

He thrust into her harder, pulled back, thrust again, and she shuddered, clenching around him. As unyielding as his grip, his black gaze trapped hers.

Another finger joined the first, and the slight stretch, the determined invasion, was too much. Her body went rigid as everything coalesced and dragged each nerve into one bright, bright moment of sheer sensation. And then it all fireballed, rolling outward, searing her veins, her nerves, and her skin with wrenching pleasure.

His fingers twisted inside her, stretching her, while his thumb pulsed the vibrator on her clit, and another wave of pleasure hit, and another, until she was shaking and gasping for air.

After easing out, he licked his fingers with a pleased sound. "You're as sweet as I thought."

Although he turned the remote off, the hum lingered in her bones. A tremor shook her.

"Shhh." He released her wrists, cuddling her like an unhappy kitten.

She stared at him, knowing if he let her go, she'd fall. Only she was already falling, pulled off balance by his eyes.

A scream from nearby broke her paralysis. As she wrenched her attention away, the room came into focus.

Music and moans and sounds of blows. People talking quietly. Some walking past, glancing at her and Xavier.

Her spine straightened. He'd made her come, right out in front of everyone. *Again.* Feeling furious, she tried to wiggle upright.

"I want to hold you now, Abigail." His voice was low, his faint accent adding an exotic element. "However, if you're that energetic, I'd be happy to test every variation the remote has. I believe there are ten."

Oh, absolutely not! She gave him an appalled look.

And he burst out laughing, full and open and surprising.

In the periphery of her vision, she saw people turn to stare at him.

His focus on her didn't waver. He petted her, stroked her hair, traced his finger over her collarbone and down between her bare breasts. When he curved his hand around her left breast, his gaze was intent on her face, making her feel more naked than if she'd stripped completely. He watched her as his thumb brushed over her nipple.

Deep inside, her body responded to his touch as if he'd picked up the string and was reeling her kite in.

He smiled; then his thumbnail scraped the peak lightly. Her back arched as heat blossomed low in her belly.

She heard a tiny sound and realized the watch on his wrist was vibrating. He frowned, then kissed her forehead. "I need to check on something upstairs."

"That's fine." Coldness swept through her. Emptiness. "I'm ready to head home."

He studied her before shaking his head. "I don't think so."

"What?" With him steadying her, she managed to stand. Her breasts wobbled as she staggered a step. She was slick between the legs, and the sadistically designed panties kept the hard vibrator pressed against her very sensitive clit. "I'm leaving."

"You're not functioning on all burners yet, Abby." He enfolded her in a soft, laundry-scented blanket from the service pedestal. When he pulled her closer and kissed her gently, her willpower flowed away like ashes in a strong wind. "You'll remain with me until I know you've recovered."

As they walked toward the stairs, she realized he might be right. The floor seemed to be moving up and down, and only his arm around her kept her going in a straight line. The books said submissives might have an altered mental state after painful scenes like spanking or whipping. "We didn't do anything intense. You didn't hurt me, so I should be fine."

"You had no pain, but you went through some nasty emotional shifts, little fluff. And then—did you know you're beautiful when you come?" He smiled down at her and traced a line over the heat in her cheeks. "Look at you blush."

Upstairs he guided her around the tables to the center of the room, where a woman straddled a wooden board. The width of the board was so narrow that the top edges disappeared between her outer labia. She wore a big sign proclaiming BAD SUBMISSIVE.

Tears streamed down the brunette's face, and she choked on sobs, obviously trying to stay quiet. People detoured around the area, some commenting loudly about "brats" and disrespectful submissives, their voices filled with disapproval.

Anger flared in Abby. "What are you doing? You let—"

"Sit here, Abby." Xavier pulled a chair out at an empty table and set down a bottled water. When he withdrew his arm, her knees buckled, dropping her onto the chair.

After speaking to a man sitting at a nearby table, Xavier strode over to the tortured woman.

Abby managed to get halfway to her feet before dizziness knocked her back down. Head spinning, she gripped the table. But Xavier was standing in front of the brunette, so maybe he would do something.

If he didn't help the poor woman, he'd find out what a scene really was. Everything in Abby cringed at the thought, but her mouth pressed together. She'd do what she had to do.

"Harmonie." Xavier had crossed his arms over his chest. "Tell me what you did wrong. And why."

"I tried to get the Doms to fight over me." The submissive shook with her sobs. "Because I wanted more attention. I'm sorry." She bowed her head; the tears never stopped.

Xavier stayed silent as seconds ticked by, and Abby's anger grew. "Accepted. If you see the Doms and if they permit you to speak, you may apologize and tell them I handled your punishment."

Relief spread across her face. "Thank you, my liege."

Xavier nodded to the man who at the table. "Mitchell, if you would..."

Mitchell walked over to a control box. The board lowered. With an arm around the woman's waist, Xavier released her arms and lifted her off the device. She turned her head into his chest, sobbing frantically, and he held her, letting her cry.

Abby sighed at the sight. A man who wasn't afraid of a woman's tears. Then her fury rekindled. *That poor, poor woman.* What kind of a horrible torture was that? And Xavier had obviously ordered it.

Carrying a blanket and bottle of water, Mitchell spoke to Xavier. "I'll take her to the quiet room and get her stabilized."

"Thank you." Xavier passed her over, saying, "You may return anytime after tonight, pet."

As he headed back to Abby, she heard the woman ask Mitchell, "Was I quiet?"

"Hardly." The Dom snorted as he guided her away. "But you tried. He let you off easy, love."

Easy? Abby couldn't believe he'd said that. Tears still ran down the woman's cheeks, and she staggered as Mitchell assisted her across the room.

Abby glared at Xavier when he sat down beside her. "Why would you do that to someone?"

Not answering, he glanced around, assessing what was going on. His gaze returned to her. "That was punishment, Abby."

"But I thought..." She would far rather be hurt and get it over with than be put on a board and left to suffer. With a sign. Humiliated. "I thought submissives were whipped or spanked. Not something like that. It was horrible."

"That's called riding the wooden pony. For some subs, their Doms' disapproval is punishment enough.

Some need pain. However, Harmonie enjoys being whipped. And she's also rewarded by receiving the complete attention of a Dom." He motioned to the hanging board. "This left her isolated and embarrassed, essentially a painful time-out."

His logic didn't alleviate the shaking inside Abby, the feeling she'd been wrong about him on some basic level. She felt as if she'd opened the door to a friend and found Freddy Krueger instead.

"What you occasionally see in a public place is known as *funishment*, and it's a type of play. A sub acts out and gets punished, but in a way they both enjoy. It's harmless as long as they acknowledge it's for fun—and the Dominant likes that behavior. Most don't. Subs usually know how far they can go and won't cross the line from cute sassiness into true disobedience or disrespect, since the last thing a true submissive wants is to embarrass her Dom." He drank some of her water and set the bottle back on the table. "Harmonie's behavior wasn't sassy or cute."

"So you hurt her."

"I did, and hopefully enough that she won't repeat the offense." His eyes were level…and shadowed. She'd started to learn to read his face. He hadn't enjoyed inflicting pain on Harmonie.

Relief swept over Abby. A wave of fatigue followed, and she sagged in the chair.

Xavier's eyes narrowed. "You're exhausted. Did you drive here?"

"Taxi." She yawned. "I need to go home."

"Yes. You do."

As she scrubbed her palms over her face and tried to remember where she'd left her clothes, Xavier talked with someone, then rose and scooped her out of her chair.

"Hey!"

"If you wiggle, I'll drop you."

She froze. The floor was a long, long way down, and despite her ample padding, a fall would really hurt.

He took a couple of steps before his lips quirked. "I don't mind if you breathe, pet. In fact, I recommend it."

Oh. No wonder her ears were ringing. She hauled in a breath and heard him laugh.

* * * *

Xavier glanced at Abby. After tucking her into his sports car, he'd tilted back the seat, and she'd dropped off two seconds after giving him her home address. The sight of her sleeping, as trusting as a child, squeezed something deep inside him.

Following the GPS directions, he reached a quiet residential area of Mill Valley. The neighborhood was mostly two-story clapboard houses built in the nineteen hundreds. Hers had been converted to a duplex, he realized when he helped her up the walk. Taking the key from her clumsy fingers, he unlocked the door and stepped inside. The scents of flowers, cleaning solution, and a rather pungent odor greeted him.

The light revealed a room with delicate floral wallpaper and the graceful curves of French furniture. A gilded mirror hung over a whitewashed fireplace with an eccentric array of antique candlesticks on the mantel. A worn needlepoint carpet covered part of the hardwood floor. The ambience felt oddly like a school friend's home in the south of France.

Mouse-like squeaks came from the far corner. “What have you got in here?”

“Puppies. I foster puppies for the animal shelter. They have a better chance of survival if not exposed to the germs there, especially since they don’t get their mother’s milk.” She yawned. “I have to feed them now.”

Of all the endings to the night, this wasn’t one he could have foreseen. Huffing a laugh, he crossed the room. In a children’s plastic pool, five round balls of fur stared up at him with hopeful black eyes. They were barely the size of his fist. “Where’s their food?”

“The legendary Master Xavier is going to feed puppies?”

She really was adorable. “I have a feeling you’ll fall asleep halfway through.”

“I’m fine.” Her defiant shake of the head didn’t succeed in making her look more awake.

“Of course you are.” With a snort of amusement, Xavier pushed her toward the high-arched opening to a dining area, then into the kitchen. Creamy yellow cupboards, stuccoed walls on three sides with a faux stone wall behind the oven. Dark granite counters and shuttered windows. Painted tile backdrops. Woven baskets and bright ceramics. “That was France. This is Italy.”

Her eyes narrowed. “And I’m betting your private school was in Europe.”

“Clever girl.” She kept surprising him. One moment she was filled with confidence, sharp as a new-forged blade, and then she’d change...like now.

“Um.” She looked at him uncertainly. “Would you like some wine?”

"Thank you, pet, but no. I don't drink." His mother's people were Native American, but it was his pompous French father— "My father was an alcoholic."

"Oh." Her look of sympathy wasn't unexpected, but the compassionate pat on his hand was. "It's hard when parents aren't up to the job." Moving sluggishly, she mixed a tiny amount of thin gruel. "Can you give them this while I get the bottles ready?"

"Certainly." In the living room, he set the dish in the wading pool, then moved it when a puppy tried to walk into it. "Drink it," he advised.

The pup planted its butt, stared up, and whined in an obvious *give me a bottle* demand. Scooping up the ball of fur, Xavier studied the serious expression. Dark eyes, silky, curling hair, folded-over ears. "What breed?"

"We think they're mostly spaniel and poodle. Someone left them in a box outside the shelter a week or so ago." Abby knelt down, surrounding herself with small bottles of milk.

When he took one, she gave him a startled look as if she still didn't believe he'd help.

She couldn't have stopped him. After settling the pup on his knee, he offered it the nipple, then grinned. The little beast definitely knew how to suck.

Abby picked up a black fuzz ball and gave it a quick kiss before starting the feeding.

Xavier smiled as one puppy stuck its nose in the bowl, realized the mush was edible, but couldn't figure out how to proceed. Its first endeavor resulted in a sneezing fit. "Still on the bottle, I see."

"I offer a little to get their stomachs ready, but it'll be another week or more before they're really weaned." She smiled. "My life will quiet down."

Xavier's puppy was sucking strongly, the tiny stomach rounding out. The waiting three bounced around, filled with energy. In contrast Abby was fading fast. She'd slump, then jerk upright as she fought off sleep, obviously determined to see her charges fed.

Someone had a big heart.

His puppy finished at the same time as hers. Xavier set them both in the pen and took Abby's bottle from unresisting fingers. "To bed with you. I'll finish the rest."

He pulled her to her feet, led her up the stairs and into her bedroom. Not a European decorating scheme this time. The lighting came from sconces on the wall. Richly textured fabric in a dark red draped the high, arched windows. The decor was both exotic and intriguing. Oriental carpets covered the hardwood floors. Her bed was a masterpiece of Moroccan carving, giving him tantalizing ideas of silk bondage.

Xavier glanced at the woman beside him, delightfully fair in the dark sultriness of the room. "You have harem-girl fantasies?"

"Mmm. Kidnapped. Carried off. Desert tent."

How nice. He did enjoy abduction games—and she probably wouldn't even remember she'd spoken.

She hardly noticed when he stripped her down, set her glasses on the bedside table, and tucked her into the bed. He ruffled her silky hair and went downstairs to finish feeding the fur balls.

Chapter Nine

Abby woke and yawned. Dawn lit her curtains, shadowing her bedroom. The sheets had created a cozy nest around her naked body. Naked? How had that happened?

Xavier had driven her home. Then… *I fed the puppies*. No, she'd only fed one. She frowned as she inhaled the fragrance of sandalwood from the trunk at the foot of the bed, a hint of shampoo from the bathroom, and…Xavier's exotic, musky aftershave. He must have undressed her and tucked her in.

She bit her lip, remembering the previous night at the club. *Take your underwear off. Tell me this. Lie back.* She'd let him tell her what to do as if she couldn't think for herself. He'd touched her how he wanted, made her climax. What kind of a weak person was he turning her into?

This isn't me… Or maybe it was. Each night it had been easier to trust him and let him take the reins. And when he did, it gave her the feeling of being lodged solidly in her own body—a body she liked.

On the other hand, when she'd worn that vibrator, her whole world had seemed to shatter, leaving her alone and lost. She shivered.

"You're awake." Slow, deep voice.

With a gasp she sat straight up. Xavier was stretched out on top of the covers. “Malum! What are you doing here?”

“It’s not a *bad thing*, pet.” Making a grumbling sound, he propped his head on his hand. “You were barely conscious, and I was worried.” Although his hair was loose, he still wore his clothing. A night’s growth of beard shadowed his jaw, and the dim light turned his face dark and forbidding. Yet when he curled his fingers around her wrist, the warmth of his palm and the careful power were disconcertingly reassuring. “What we did at the club shouldn’t have affected you so much.”

He had stayed. “My problem was just a lack of sleep. I had a younger friend who needed a shoulder to cry on the night before, and the puppies wake up early.” Speaking of waking, she vaguely remembered him shaking her and asking her questions during the night, making sure she was all right. Was that part of his appeal? That his sense of responsibility and caring equaled the darker aspects of control and command? “Anyway, thank you.” *I think.* She’d never dreamed she would end up with Master Xavier in her bed.

As if he’d heard her worries, his grin flashed in his shadowy face. “Relax, fluff. I won’t jump you.”

Or tie me up and do horrible—interesting—things to me? She swallowed against a dry mouth. “Well, that’s reassuring.”

His eyes narrowed, and he pulled her down beside him. Propped up on one elbow, he studied her as he traced his fingers along her jaw. His touch was assessing. “Then again, I could stay.”

Let him decide.

“Do you want me to stay, Abby?”

"Why do you always ask me these questions? I thought you were supposed to be in charge and everything."

A smile lifted his lips. "In the beginning, until a Dom learns to interpret a submissive's body language, it's safer to ask. In addition, you need to learn to read your own desires, so you can express them openly to both of us."

I hate reasonable answers. Especially when she felt as if he wanted her to open a vein and bleed emotions. His gaze stayed on her, level and patient, and she…really wanted what he could give her. *The body has spoken.* "Please, stay."

"Good girl." His approval washed over her, patching up the holes in her defenses. "In that case, I'll be happy to take complete control." The molten heat in his eyes sent a shiver along her nerve endings. "You may say, 'yes, sir,' now," he prompted.

Complete control. The words came out shaky. "Yes, sir."

"Little fluff, I'm not going to hurt you"—he leaned forward and kissed her, possessing her lips, her mouth, then drew back an inch to finish—"much."

Anxiety and anticipation sizzled through her.

Rising over her, he stripped her covers away and straddled her. As his groin pressed against her, she realized with a twinge of concern that she was naked and he wasn't.

"I—" She tried to cover herself, but he caught her wrists.

"You were without a top at the club, pet."

"That was different." He hadn't looked at her this way, with a man's desire in his eyes. Warmth flowed over her body as if she were wrapped in a heating pad.

After a moment he released her. Unable to help herself, she flattened her hands over her breasts.

When he laid his hands over hers, she had a second of confusion. Then he used his fingers to bend hers, guiding her to pinch her nipples.

No. No way. She tried to yank her hands away.

He was obviously trying to keep a straight face. "If you cover up what is mine to play with, you'll do the playing for me." He paused. "Would you rather I do the work?"

She nodded frantically.

After allowing her to snatch her hands away, he ran his wide palms over her, easily cupping her large breasts. His low hum of appreciation stroked her ego as wonderfully as his fingers did her nipples.

He closed his lips over hers again. His hands didn't stop, and her breasts swelled until the skin felt tight. He released her lips and nipped her jaw.

His black hair spilled over the rippling muscles of his shoulders, tempting her unbearably. She reached for him. Hesitated. "Um. Can I touch you?"

"Good girl. I'm pleased you thought to ask." He wrapped her fingers around the headboard carvings. "Keep them here. If you obey, I'll permit your touch in a bit." His tone dropped to a menacing warning, his slight accent stronger. "Don't let go, Abigail. No matter what I do."

Her insides were turning into a lake of lava. "Yes, sir." But what was he going to do?

He teased his tongue along the rim of her ear and kissed the hollow below it. Goose bumps ran down her arms.

Sitting back, he studied her, his gaze sensuous as it lingered on her face, her breasts, her groin. “You’re a beautiful woman, Abby.”

Sure she was.

He chuckled. “Such a cynical look.” When he lightly pinched one nipple, heat arrowed straight to her clit. “It’s not wise to disagree with the person topping you.”

“No, sir.”

He was laughing at her, as if he knew how badly she was starting to ache. And that pinch… Her nipples were peaked, begging for his touch.

He bent and licked over one before puffing a breath over it. *Hot. Cold.* He did the same to the other, alternating back and forth, until they throbbed.

“Hmm.” To her dismay, he moved up to kiss her again, and her arms shook with the need to push him back. Move him down. Her hips squirmed under his.

“No, pet. Stay still.” His hand gripped her hair, holding her and restraining her as his kiss turned rougher, and he took what he wanted, deep and wet. The feeling of being held that way was…so erotic. His teeth closed on her chin, trapping her with the not quite painful pressure as he pinched her nipples.

A bite to her neck, a harder one on the long muscle of her shoulder. The pain of it flared, then simmered like spice added to a soup. His hair brushed over her skin, a cool touch in contrast to the burning inside her. He slid his tongue along her left collarbone as he moved down. Each nip created a tiny pain, and he was driving her mad with an urgent hunger. Her breasts ached as he inched lower.

"I like your almond lotion," he murmured. "You smell edible." His teeth pinched the outside of her left breast before the pull of his mouth on the nipple made her moan. He released her to lightly bite the outside again, slightly farther down, then returned to the distended tip.

Back and forth, he circled her breast, alternating a stinging nip with sucking on the peak, creating a circumference of tiny pains with a center that ached more with each second.

When he'd finished the circle, he lifted his head. She tensed, anticipating the next bite on the outside, but his lips paused over her areola...paused... Then his teeth lightly closed right on the peak.

She felt a quick pain before searing pleasure blasted through her, and she half screamed, half moaned.

He moved to her other breast.

Not again. She couldn't bear it. She grabbed his shoulders.

He closed powerful fingers over her wrists, pinning her arms to the bed over her head. "Where did I tell you to put your hands?"

"Xavier." She whimpered, half floating in a fog of sexual need.

"Abigail." The sharpness of his icy voice cut like a whip.

"My liege. Please, I..." Begging wouldn't work. He was in charge. "I'm sorry."

When he opened his grip, she closed her fingers around the carvings on the headboard. The wood felt cool and satiny under her fingertips.

He waited for a moment before nodding approval. "You'd have an easier time if I tied you, pet, but we haven't reached that level of trust yet. Not when you're at home with no one else around. You'll have to restrain yourself." He stroked her lips with a calloused fingertip. "Remember our discussion of funishment?"

She nodded.

"If you let go, you'll discover how it works. And at least one of us will think it's fun."

Oh no, not going to happen. When her fingers tightened on the spools, amusement lit his eyes.

He nipped the outside of her right breast. Her left nipple still stung from his teeth, and he pinched it lightly with his fingers, prolonging the throbbing. His lips closed and pulled over the right peak. And he slowly circled her right breast as he had the left, alternating light bites with sucking.

With each repetition, her body grew stiffer in anticipation.

He completed the circle and lifted his head. Paused.

Oh sweet heavens. Her breathing stopped.

His teeth closed on her right nipple and tightened slowly, like breast clamps. Pain streaked through her, but the aching tip blossomed with pleasure as well. His tongue swirled, adding a wet heat, and he bit again. Harder.

"Ow— Ooooh, God, wait." The pain erupted into a shocking pleasure that filled her body. Her hands opened, releasing the spools. She arched toward him, needing more. Less.

Still holding her between his teeth, he gripped her elbows, keeping her arms over her head.

She struggled against his restraint, yet the sinking feeling in her belly increased at the power in his hands, at the unyielding control.

When he lifted his head, blood rushed back into her nipple, and she moaned as it pulsed with every heartbeat. He closed her hands over the headboard again and moved down. His long hair trailed after him, feathering over her breasts.

When he licked her soft, round belly, the skin quivered. He slid lower. His breath swept over her mound, and her breathing hitched. He was... Doms didn't do oral sex. Nathan never did—he'd said it was her place to serve him.

"I..." She swallowed. "My liege, you don't have to do...that."

To her consternation he stopped and sat back on his calves. Still fully clothed. "Abigail. Do you have permission to speak?"

She whispered, "No, sir."

"Correct." A crease appeared in his cheek. "I'm glad to know I don't have to do"—his lips quirked—"*that.*" In an arrogant, possessive move, he flattened his hand between her legs.

The pressure right where she ached the most made her hips squirm.

"Do you, by any stretch of the imagination, think I need your permission to do or not do something? Outside of stopping if you use your safe word?"

The look in his eyes was merciless. A Master's look. He'd do what he wanted, and if he wanted to put his mouth on...her...he would.

He tapped her clit, and she clenched at the frisson of pleasure. "Right now this cunt is my toy to play with as I want." He pinched her aching nipples, pulled, pinched harder. The pain streaming through her blossomed into pleasure. "These breasts are mine." His finger ran around her lips. "Your mouth is mine, and I may yet want to use it."

Each uncompromising statement made her body grow tenser. Hotter.

"Since you saw fit to interrupt me, you obviously need a lesson in how annoying interruptions can be." His mouth curved in a lethal smile. "You have my permission to speak as long as you're begging."

Begging. Oh, get real. He pinched her nipples again, rolling them between his fingers until a relentless thrumming filled her world, settling low in her belly.

After tossing his hair behind his shoulders, he slid down and licked over her pussy, teasing her with the flicker of his tongue. She gasped at the dazzling pleasure. Under his hot, wet attentions, her clit hardened as the tissues engorged with blood.

He nipped her inner thigh, making her yelp. Even as the sting sizzled and faded, he laved her clit with his tongue. Bit her other thigh. Back to her clit. Again he was alternating each tiny pain with exquisite pleasure, and her whole body stiffened as she recognized the terrifying pattern—one with her clit as the center.

His tongue lingered over the nerve-filled nub, increasing the needy tension. Her muscles tightened; her hips lifted.

He moved. A nip stung her outer labia—*pain*—before he returned. *Pleasure.* The air grew so thick she could hardly breathe.

She wiggled her hips, trying to escape the sting, trying to make him lick more. He circled her clit, once and again, and as she strained upward he slid two hard fingers into her, stretching her abruptly. Nerves ignited until need tormented her whole lower half.

His tongue continued, around and around, and she was going to come, actually come and—

He stopped, and his black gaze met hers. “Interruptions are annoying, aren’t they?”

Her mouth opened in a soundless protest. She would have come. Could have. Her eyes closed. He knew exactly how close she’d been. He could have pushed her over…if he’d wanted to.

Deep inside she started to shake. He didn’t have her in bondage, but she had no control here at all. Whatever he wanted to do, he would.

“That’s it,” he murmured. “The decisions are mine. Your body is mine. Let go, Abby.” As he lowered his head, she realized his fingers were still inside her. Pressing deep.

Her clit had started to soften, but with the first touch of his breath, it swelled to bursting.

“Very pretty.” He circled his finger around the nub, the rough skin a shock after his soft tongue. “You’re pink and shiny, not hiding from me any longer. The hood”—he teased something on the top, and she gasped at the intense feeling—“is pulled back, giving me full access.” His merciless gaze met hers. “I expect full access to everything.”

The shaking in her core moved outward until her whole body trembled. She needed…needed. She felt like crying. Felt like crawling into his arms.

He pushed her outer labia apart so his teeth could close on one inner fold. His tongue lashed the flesh, bathing her in heat as he bit down to just over the edge of pain. He released her, and his tongue whipped over her clit. And then he started to thrust his fingers in and out.

Her senses couldn't keep up.

He lightly bit the other fold while the first still ached. He licked her clit, teasing it upward, upward…

He stopped.

Oh God, she didn't climax that easily. *Don't do this to me.*

His eyes met hers again. She burned, throbbed; she needed him *there*. Right there.

But his head stayed up. He watched her as his fingers slowly pumped in and out, pushing her, making her ache more, but never enough.

Her lips closed on the word *please*, and only a moan escaped. Would he be angry if she didn't come? Would he—

His teeth scraped on each side of her clit. Tightened.

She froze. The stimulation was so intense, so painful, so much. The nerves were pulsing in his grip. He held her there, trapped, and helplessness drowned out everything, winding her higher and higher.

He thrust harder, adding to the tormenting pleasure, and the jolt broke her words loose.

"*Pleeeze. Oh please.*"

When her hips tried to rise, his teeth tightened in warning. Her muscles went rigid, turning her into an unmoving concrete statue. Each relentless thrust pushed her closer, and she hung there on an excruciating edge.

He released her. Blood surged back into her clit in a flood of pleasure and pain, and then he sucked on the nub, pulling forcefully, tonguing the very top.

Her concrete body shattered. "*Ahhhh!*" Sensation ripped through her, filling her world with wrenching pleasure.

Hard hands held her down as he sucked again, and her body arched again, completely out of her control. The room turned white. Her pulse roared in her ears as each convulsion shook her, yet she wanted more.

His laugh vibrated her oversensitive nerves, and she spasmed again.

She was still panting and shuddering with aftershocks when he pried her fingers from the headboard and flipped her over. With a yank he pulled her up onto her shaky arms and knees. "Don't move."

Her head hung as she struggled for air.

She heard him unbuckle his belt, unzip his slacks, and tear open a condom wrapper. The cool strands of his hair washed over her back as he pressed against her entrance, as he started to push into her. And oh, she wanted him inside, filling her…

Hard and thick and hot, he slid partway in. She was so, so wet, but he was bigger than she was used to. Her body stiffened, protesting the intrusion, and she leaned forward. Away.

His hands tightened on her as he gave a laughing snort. "Sorry, little fluff. I'll go slower." He rocked his hips, edging into her slowly, stretching her to his size. Inch by inch, until his thighs were hot on the backs of her legs and his balls bumped her pussy.

As she throbbed around him, she bit her lip, unsure if she was comfortable or not. Mostly not. He was impossibly large.

And his ruthless control unsettled her. Heated her. She glanced over her shoulder. The faint dawn light showed his face was hard, almost…cold.

He met her gaze, then firmly pushed her forehead down on her arms. "Don't move." His powerful hands gripped her hips as he slid out and eased in, experimentally. Another slow stroke and pleasure blossomed inside her again.

"All right, then." He pulled out…and then slammed into her. At the burst of sensation, her back arched; her head jerked up.

He set his hand on her nape, pushing her down onto her forearms again.

He paused a second as if to be sure she'd stay. His fingers curled around her hips and tightened into an unbreakable grip as he pulled her bottom higher. And then he truly started. Hard stroke after hard stroke, movements changing—pace never relenting.

The primal rhythm wakened nerves, and a spot inside her grew more and more sensitive. With a shiver she clenched around him, needing more.

"You are a never-ending surprise," he said lightly, and he changed the angle of his cock, driving into that responsive area with short, demanding stokes.

Her insides drew together, like a sun gathering into itself, and…and…the area went nova. Blinding light and heat shot outward, searing and sizzling all the way to her hands and feet, wave after wave with each undulating spasm of her core.

With a rumble of enjoyment, he plunged deep. Over and over he yanked her onto his cock, before he pressed fully in and came in urgent pulses. Even after he finished, he held her immobile, and she could hear his deep, even breathing, as disciplined as everything about him.

She lifted her head.

He pushed her down again. "Stay put for a minute, Abigail." His voice was husky, lower than normal, a little rough, and he'd said her name…oddly. Slower. As if uncertain he liked the taste of it. Then he sighed and withdrew.

She waited, unsure if she should move. Unsure if she could. Her insides rippled as if still being pounded.

He rose to stand beside the bed. His fingers closed over her nape, his grip unyielding, and a hard slap on her bottom made her yelp at the unexpected pain. "This is for your inability to stay where you were told. Next time you won't forget."

A stinging slap landed on her right buttock, then two more. Her skin stung. Burned.

"What do you say?" he asked.

"I'm sorry, sir." *Ow, ow, ow.*

"Very good." The distance was gone from his voice, and a knot in her chest released. His hands caressed her bottom, spreading the pain, easing it. "You have a gorgeous ass, and it holds handprints beautifully."

Oh, well, how nice for me. Only she couldn't summon any anger, not under the gentle touch of his hands. "Thank you, sir."

He lifted her off the bed in a head-spinning move and set her on her feet. "Go shower. The pups are waking up."

She took a step away, feeling...lost. After being so close to him when she'd come, he'd shoved her facedown as if he didn't want to look at her, and now he was pushing her away. She rubbed her arms. How could she stand next to someone she'd just made love with and feel lonely?

He said something in French under his breath and pulled her into his arms, surrounding her with warmth and strength and comfort. His long black hair fell forward, curtaining her from the world as he pressed her cheek against his shoulder. "Thank you, Abby. I enjoyed being with you. Perhaps more than I expected to."

The unhappiness eased slightly.

But he didn't stay.

Chapter Ten

With an exasperated grunt, Xavier laid the pen down on his office desk and walked over to his wall of windows. Fog had rolled in off the ocean, and the normally spectacular view of San Francisco Bay from the Financial District was gray and grim.

He couldn't see Dark Haven in the South of Market from here. Instead he looked toward the north, where Abby fostered puppies that needed her help. And she'd given it, just as she'd given him anything he asked for.

Shame weighed him down as he thought of how he'd left her so abruptly. Spending the night had been foolish, although he hadn't had much choice. No Dom abandoned a submissive unable to care for herself.

But to have taken her in her own bed? *Idiot.* He always insisted a woman come to his house, so when he was gone her home would contain no painful memories to expunge.

Catherine had left her ghost behind in their home. Every room reminded him of the places they'd made love, her laughter at the dining table, her on her knees in the foyer waiting for him to return.

Over the years the phantom images had faded. Now she haunted him only occasionally...during sex. A woman's features would blur into Catherine's freckled face, her vibrant red hair, and her blue-green eyes. The occurrences left him guilt-ridden, as if he'd deceived both his wife and the woman in his bed.

Saturday night with Abby had been...different. She had a comfortable personality, giving and intelligent, sweet with a wry sense of humor. Her subconscious response to him was compelling, and in the club, she'd given him one of the prettiest orgasms he'd ever seen. He enjoyed the musky spice of her scent, her husky moans, and her surprise when her body overrode her mind.

He rubbed his chin, remembering her sweetness with the puppies and how she'd put their needs before her own. He not only liked her, but his urgency to bury himself inside her quivering, soft body had been unsettling. Only his wife had tested his control like that—and in taking Abby, needing her, glorying in her, he'd felt as if he betrayed Catherine.

That was foolish, of course. Catherine was dead. Like a blazing meteor, she'd lived her life to the fullest and departed as quickly. She would yell at him for the way he'd dealt with her death.

He shook his head. *But I don't want a replacement.* He had no intention of replacing his sun goddess with a moon maiden—he just needed a new slave.

Not someone like Abby. The teacher was a Dark Haven staff member. He owed her his protection and some instruction. Nothing more. And he needed to stay within those boundaries despite the temptation to take her home. If he didn't, she'd end up hurt in the end. Avoiding her would be better; she'd understand without an explanation.

He should ask Simon to find her some experienced, reputable Doms to play with. Yet the idea of her with someone else was unpalatable. As he watched the fog start to dissolve under the weight of the sun, he knew Abby wasn't the only one who might be hurt.

Mouth tight, he yanked the curtains shut.

At his desk he frowned at the pile in his in-box and the long list of e-mails displayed on the screen. This hadn't been a productive Monday morning.

Two e-mails and one letter later, his middle-aged administrative assistant tapped on the door before opening it. "Marilee Thompson is here. Rona Demakis sent her."

"Yes, Rona warned me." The hospital administrator said Marilee had escaped from an abusive husband and ended up in Rona's hospital with internal bleeding. Two children. No skills. No job history. Rona suspected the woman couldn't read.

"Bring her in, please."

Short and round, Ms. Thompson might have been pretty if her face hadn't been puffy and purple-green from bruising. Xavier tamped down his anger and motioned toward the sitting area on the far side of the office. "Ms. Thompson, please have a seat."

"Mr. Leduc." Clad in an ugly brown skirt and white shirt, she stood straight, hands trembling. "I...I didn't realize. I'm sorry to have taken your time." She turned to leave.

He shook his head. Although comfortable, his office was designed for intimidation. Just another tool for a canny businessman to employ. But meeting her downstairs might have been wise. Too late now. "Marilee, if you leave, Rona will yell at me." He smiled and saw her relax a fraction. "Please, sit."

She perched on the edge of a leather chair. Abby's smallest puppy had shown the same timidity when venturing too far from the pack.

Xavier sat on the couch, stretching his legs out. *See, I won't attack.* "I admire your courage in leaving your husband and coming all the way here from the Midwest."

She stared at her hands.

"My mother was in a similar situation. She ran to San Francisco from New Orleans."

That brought her head up. Her eyes were dark brown, the color of his mother's. "And she took you along?"

"Not exactly."

"She left you with him?" Marilee frowned.

"No, she wouldn't have done that. I was at a European school and didn't even know she'd left." When she'd missed her weekly calls, Xavier had called home. His father had been incoherent with rage—and alcohol. Xavier's lips tightened. He hadn't known his father had turned abusive, but the neighbor had described his mother's condition when she ran. "I stowed away on a boat, worked my way across the ocean, then hitchhiked to San Francisco."

"My goodness. How old were you?"

"I turned seventeen two days after I arrived. I was certain I could help her." Xavier gave her a rueful look. "Instead I was one more burden."

"You poor baby." Her compassionate expression showed she no longer saw him as intimidating but as a child like one of her own.

Softhearted women pulled at him every time.

"My mother deserves the sympathy. She had no marketable skills and ended up holding down three jobs." She'd insisted he finish school, which meant he could only work part-time. Food wasn't plentiful; clothes were secondhand, treats nonexistent. Then his father had died, leaving everything to Xavier. At least he'd had a few years to pamper his mother before she died. "But she never gave up."

Marilee's spine stiffened in an obvious sign that she wouldn't quit either.

"Rona said she found you somewhere to stay while you heal. Meantime, we'll concentrate on finding you a job."

"Once the doctor gives the okay, I can clean. Bus tables. Do yard work."

No heavy physical work for a while, Rona had said. But light labor usually required reading. "Marilee, I need you to be honest with me. How much can you read? Do you know your letters? Can you sound out words at all—or do you memorize them?"

Her head went back down, her hands clenched.

He waited patiently. As a Dom he'd learned that silence often extracted more answers than persuasion.

She drew in a slow breath. "I've learned the letters—I just can't do anything with them. I memorize what words look like."

"Thank you. I know that wasn't easy to share."

With his smile, she relaxed. "Job hunting isn't easy. Not when…"

"Stella's will find you a job, and unless you object, we'll get you reading classes as well."

The spark of hope in her dark brown eyes was his reward.

After she'd left, Mrs. Benton came into his office. "I helped Ms. Thompson set up an appointment tomorrow at Stella's."

"Excellent. Have one of the secretaries—a kind one—assist her in filling out an application."

"Of course." Mrs. Benton waited, not bothering to take notes. The woman had a trapdoor memory.

He rubbed his chin, considering. Pam Harkness wasn't the most experienced placement counselor but had a way with frightened women. "Assign her to Ms. Harkness. Let her know we need to find Marilee a job, or Simon will kill me."

His admin laughed. "We'll do our best." And they would, simply because they cared.

Most of the Leduc Industries and Stella's personnel had experienced the same nightmare—lacking skills and unable to find a job.

"I will entrust her to your care, then. Thank you, Mrs. Benton, and please keep me informed as to her progress." As the door closed, Xavier smiled. When he'd hired the insecure, almost-in-tears Mrs. Benton, he'd never imagined how a degree in business would transform her into someone so formidable.

Xavier turned back to his work, firmly putting aside his new ghost—one with wispy blonde hair, pale skin, and unhappy eyes the color of the fog outside.

* * * *

So. What now? After her Saturday receptionist duty, Abby walked through the crowd on Dark Haven's main floor, trying not to look for Xavier.

He hadn't shown up on Friday. DeVries—Xavier's Enforcer—had uncollared her and Lindsey. Abby'd been nervous, but he'd grinned and reminded her that he couldn't whip her without Xavier's permission. After he'd strolled away, Lindsey admitted the Dom scared her—almost as much as he turned her on.

Talk about insanity. Being attracted to deVries was like a moth saying, *Hey, let's go check out that awesome bonfire.*

Unfortunately Abby had also flown too close to a fire—the dangerous one called *my liege.*

This evening Xavier had arrived late, and when he'd come into the reception area, he'd been distant, both emotionally and physically. She hadn't realized how often he'd invaded her personal space until he stopped. Her wings were definitely scorched, and she'd hit the ground hard.

Pulling in a pain-filled breath, Abby looked at the people around her. Mistress Angela was in a latex bra, mesh tank top, and latex pants tucked into lace-up, knee-high boots. Her submissive wore only a loosely woven mesh dress.

Last week Xavier had decided the current fetwear was boring and arbitrarily declared Saturday a "see-through" or mesh night. Apparently his quirks were well-known, and the members always checked the club calendar for surprises. She had to admit, some people had a real talent for dressing up.

Wanting to look good, Abby had bought a prom dress from a secondhand store. She'd worn only the overlay, and her white skin showed clearly from under the soft pink lace. The Doms had been giving her lingering looks of appreciation.

Xavier hadn't even noticed.

It hurt. *Moron, you let yourself get attached.* She'd blindly followed a trail that had petered out, leaving her lost and unsure what to do. She bit her lip. Whatever stupid thing she'd done during sex must have been bad, since he'd already been retreating when she rose from the bed.

The sound of bickering caught her attention. She looked to see a Dom and his partner arguing over the submissive's flirtatious ways.

I'm here to observe. Nothing else. Taking mental notes, Abby chose a nearby table. If she didn't get her research done, she was doomed.

Around her, people talked, laughed, and danced to the industrial rock music. She leaned her arms on the table and stared at the grain of the wood. If only the project were over, she could go home and not return. But she had a job to do.

"How're you doing, girlfriend?" Dixon sat down beside her and pushed over a can of diet soda. "You look like you need this."

Totally out of the blue, her eyes pooled with tears.

"Oh, shit, don't do that." He scooted his chair closer and patted her hand frantically. "If the big boss thinks I made you cry, he'll give me over to the Enforcer, and I'll get caned, and not in a good way.

She sniffled and managed to laugh. "Sorry." What was the matter with her? She rarely cried—and never, ever in public. But her emotions felt abraded to the point of bleeding. "Xavier won't care. No worries."

Dixon's eyes rounded. "Christ on a crutch, *you're* why he's in such a pissy mood?"

Her hopes lifted...and crashed back down. "Don't think so."

"Be gnarly if my liege was crushing on you, but damn, girl, you'd be insane to hook up with him. I mean, sure, everybody knows he's awesome at scenes and sex." He fanned himself. "But he's not into relationships, so don't you waltz down that path. You hear what I'm sayin'?"

"Oh, I hear."

"If you even look like you're getting a hard-on for him, he'll kick your ass to the curb."

"Yeah, well...too late." Her eyes filled again. *I don't even know what I did wrong.*

"What's the problem here?" A hard hand closed on her shoulder in an unyielding grip, and the unspoken *don't move* paralyzed every muscle in her body. Xavier's voice was cold, turning her bones to ice. "Dixon, what have you done?"

The slender submissive landed on his knees in the smoothest shift she'd ever seen. "My liege, I didn't..." Dixon glanced at her, and then his chin jutted out in uncharacteristic belligerence. "*I* didn't cause her tears."

Oh, nice. Humiliate me, why don't you? As the grip on her shoulder tightened painfully, she glared at Dixon, but he didn't notice. His gaze stayed on Xavier for a long, long moment before dropping to the floor.

The silence from Xavier grew until it filled every molecule of space around the table. "I see."

I've had enough of this. Bursting into tears had reached so high a possibility that it shook her. *I want to go home.* She tried to push away from the table.

Xavier shifted, his hip keeping the chair from moving. He didn't release her. "I'll deal with you in a minute, pet."

He turned slightly and raised his voice. "Master deVries."

Dixon gave a horrified squeak like a puppy that had fallen off a step, and dropped his forehead to the floor in abject surrender.

Abby watched the heavy-jawed Dominant approach. He scanned the group with sharp, gray-green eyes and lifted one eyebrow when Dixon didn't move. "Can I be of assistance here?"

Oh no, what did Xavier want with him? His reputation was…scary. Past scary. A bisexual sadist. She shivered, and his lips curved in a sensual smile as he drank it in.

Xavier set his boot on the back of Dixon's head, pressing his forehead into the floor. "If you have time to spare, I have an interesting dilemma."

DeVries's eyes lit. "I have a bit of time."

"Dixon was brave enough to be honest with me, but disrespectful in doing so. I'd like him rewarded for his courage and punished for his attitude."

"Ah."

The gleam in the man's eyes made Abby stiffen. "No! He shouldn't be punished. I won't—"

Xavier's wide palm covered her mouth even as he caught her hair in his fist. "Loyalty is a fine thing. Stop while I'm still admiring it."

She tried to wrench away, and the pull on the strands turned painful.

DeVries chuckled. “Be fun to haul these two up, side by side, and find out who would scream—or come—first.”

No. Oh no.

“Thank you, but I intend to work with this one alone.”

“Pity.”

Xavier lifted his boot. “Dixon, go with Master deVries. Remember to thank him when he’s finished with you.”

“Yes, my liege.” Dixon knelt up. He gave her a glance that showed both fear and excitement before looking at the Enforcer.

“Lose the clothes, boy.”

Dixon stood and pulled off his mesh top and biker shorts.

“Nice fat balls. I have some clamps and spiked chains that should be just right.” He removed the crop hanging from his belt and put the wood between Dixon’s teeth. “Hands and knees. Bad boys don’t walk.” After snapping his fingers, he strolled away.

Dixon shivered once, then dropped and crawled after him.

As the two headed toward the dungeon stairs, Xavier released Abby. He settled into Dixon’s chair, leaned back, and stretched out his legs. The silence grew. His gaze stayed on her. What was he waiting for?

Oh. She dropped to her knees before him, not nearly as gracefully as Dixon had managed. It took an act of will to lower her eyes.

Who knew silence could turn the air thick and sultry? Like a tropical paradise. *Like hell.*

“I caused the tears?” he asked finally.

"Of course not." Perhaps it was good that she was staring at the floor. "I simply had a bad day at work."

A minute passed. What was this, death by silence? Her teeth gritted together.

"Try again."

Di te perdant. "Excuse me, *sir,* but we're not in a relationship, so my feelings belong to me." A tremor ran through her at the memory of his hand between her legs and his deep voice saying, "*Right now, this cunt is my toy to play with as I want.*"

When he leaned forward, so powerful and confident, goose bumps rose on her arms. He traced the top of her collar, and the brush of his calloused fingertip flared heat inside her. "What are you wearing, pet?"

She should slap his hand away. "A collar. Sir."

"Whose?"

She started to say *the club's* and thought better of it. "Yours."

"I'd say that's a type of relationship, wouldn't you?" Despite his mild tone, anger underlaid the words.

Every cell in her body cringed. She'd made him mad. Any second now he'd yell and scream names at her and... Her breathing turned jerky. What could she say to keep him from getting more upset? "I'm sorry. Whatever I did last week, I didn't mean to. I'm—"

"Look at me," he said, his tone without any emotion at all, as if he'd buried his fury in ice.

Her gaze rose to meet his black, unreadable eyes.

Forearms resting on his knees, he studied her intently. "When I left so quickly last week, it hurt you."

She couldn't conceal her flinch. *Don't make him mad. Madder.* "It was silly of me. There's nothing between us, after all. We just had sex."

"Yes, we certainly did."

She so, so wanted to ask him what had happened, what she'd done, but the words wouldn't come. More questions would anger him further. Make him yell at her.

His gaze didn't falter, as if he were trying to read her soul.

"My liege!" A submissive Abby didn't recognize ran up to the table. Her eyes were wide. "There's a policeman at the door. He insists on coming in."

When Xavier released Abby's gaze, she felt as if she were falling backward. Straightening her shoulders, she hauled in a breath.

Xavier stood, looming over her. "We'll talk when I get back, Abby."

Sure, and I'll hear how you didn't mean to hurt me, but—blah, blah, blah. She turned her gaze to the floor, waiting until his boots moved out of her sight. Time to cut and run. But what about the research? Torn, she pushed to her feet.

"Abby, I was looking for you." Simon walked over, his wife beside him. Indifferent to Xavier's dictates, he wore a suit.

Rona had dressed for the evening, though, in a transparent halter top. Her calf-length black skirt had long rectangles cut from it and exposed her flesh each time she moved. As always, her thick gold choker ringed her neck. When she looked at Abby, her smile died. "Are you all right?"

"Fine. It's been a long night."

When Simon's eyes narrowed, she held her hand up. "Please. Don't make it a longer one."

"Clever defense," he said. "All right."

Abby managed to curve her lips up. "You were looking for me?"

"Rona and I thought you might enjoy a Fourth of July party at a mountain lodge near Yosemite. You'd meet lifestylers outside the club. This year the Mastersons are having a barbecue with vanilla activities at their place. In the evening, we'll head up the mountain for the Serenity Lodge's dungeon party."

"We'd spend the night in delightful little cabins at the lodge," Rona said.

Abby glanced toward the door through which Xavier was disappearing. If she saw him all day long, she'd end up hiding under a bush in tears.

Simon followed her gaze and gave her a speculative look. "Although Xavier has a standing invitation, he hasn't visited Serenity in the last five years or so."

He wouldn't be there. The knowledge was almost as dismal. She opened her mouth to refuse and stopped. If she went, she'd have hours to conduct her studies. At an informal party, she could chat and ask questions. Maybe obtain all she needed—in which case, she wouldn't have to return here.

The thought of never seeing Xavier again stabbed her so hard she couldn't breathe for a moment, but it passed. Everything always passed. "The hosts wouldn't mind?"

"Jake and Logan Hunt are used to me inviting a batch of city kinksters to their play parties. For the Mastersons' barbecue, the invitation is for anyone in the area. The entire town attends."

"Well, then, thank you. I'd love to go. Is there a map or something?"

"It's mountain driving, and some of the roads are rough. Is your car up to it?"

Ouch. Her little car bottomed out even on driveways. "Well—"

"I'd like to have her drive up with us, Master," Rona said softly.

Simon nodded agreement. "We'd enjoy your company, Abby. How about we pick you up in the morning?"

It would keep her from chickening out. "That would be wonderful. Thank you."

WHEN XAVIER RETURNED, he was shaking his head in annoyance. The beat cop sent to deal with a street fight had simply assumed the problem was at Dark Haven.

Wrong. As usual the problem was at the redneck bar farther down the street. The bouncers would break up an altercation, throw the drunks out, and they'd continue their battle outside.

Xavier had escorted the officer to the bar. The patrolman was new with a few unfortunate prejudices. Although alcohol was available if people didn't play, Dark Haven discouraged drinking. If a member wanted to fight, there were usually some others who would happily pull out the mats and get down with rough body play. In BDSM even fighting was consensual.

Xavier went past Lindsey and entered the main room. No Abby. Frowning, he returned to the reception area. "Did Abby leave?"

Lindsey nodded. “Master Simon uncollared her before he and Rona walked her out.”

Xavier glanced at the wall clock. “It’s not very late.”

“Oh, they’re planning to get an early start.” Lindsey gave him a quick glance. “For that party in the mountains. Around Bear Flat.”

She hadn’t waited for him. Hadn’t wanted to see him. “I see.”

Chapter Eleven

In the backseat of Simon's big SUV the next morning, Abby watched the trees whizzing by. They'd started early, crossed the dry Central Valley, and entered the foothills. Already the mountains loomed larger, and pine scented the air.

Hopefully the trip would be valuable. Urgency bit at her since she had only three more weeks to collect data and get her article in before the end of July. Time was speeding away. And she'd had to cut another section where the information contained too much identifying detail.

But her paper was interesting. Wonderful, really. Her fieldwork had shown how tightly knit the community was, and how diverse and open-minded, not just about genders and relationships, but everything. *Your kink is not my kink, but it's okay.* The rest of the world could learn something from Dark Haven. She dearly wanted to share the insights she'd gained.

In the passenger seat Rona turned and motioned to the large cooler beside Abby. "Can you get me a diet cola?" She patted her husband's thigh. "Simon, do you want something?"

"I'm fine, pet." He tapped the coffee Thermos in the holder. "Polluting caffeine with bubbles is like dumping toxic waste in a river."

"Oh, Crom, thanks for that disgusting visual." Rona accepted a can from Abby. "Grab yourself something. We brought a variety."

"Thank you." Abby picked out a root beer and sipped the icy-cold liquid. Meeting Simon's gaze in the rearview mirror, she wrinkled her nose at him. "It so happens that I think carbonation and caffeine go together like cake and chocolate."

His grin was lethal. With his black hair, black eyes, and darkly tanned skin, he sometimes seemed far too much like Xavier. Although Simon was probably Greek, and Xavier had mentioned being Native American and French, they both were tall, dark, and dominant.

"And what's a *crom*, by the way?" Abby asked.

"Oh, sorry. It's the god of Conan the Barbarian." Rona grinned. "I raised two boys and convinced them to use it instead of the F-bomb."

"Clever." Very clever. Grace would enjoy that one.

Rona wiggled in her seat to face Abby more comfortably. "I've been wondering something—and you can tell me that I'm being snoopy but—"

Simon snorted. "You're being snoopy."

"It wasn't you I was speaking to. *Sir*."

His gaze flicked to Abby's in the mirror. "Nosiness is an unfortunate trait of nurses. They assume they need to care for everyone, and they're accustomed to prying into a patient's personal business. After decades of asking people if their bowels have moved and what color their urine is, a nurse's boundaries become skewed."

Abby sputtered with laughter.

Rona frowned at her husband. "If you weren't driving, I'd hit you."

His smile was slow and ominous. "If I weren't driving, I'd paddle your ass for threatening me."

They were so well matched. Abby sighed a little. She and Nathan had been fairly in tune intellectually, but Rona and Simon had a constant sexual hum going.

She frowned. With Xavier, the electricity was there, but they sure didn't know each other. *And never would.*

Rona turned again, her thick, wavy hair falling over her shoulder. "Back to snoopyitis. Simon said Nathan introduced you to him. Why didn't he ever bring you to the club?"

Abby's drink stopped partway to her mouth. That was a good question. He'd never invited her, just tried to do bondage at home. "Maybe he thought I'd get scared off." She huffed a laugh. "Which might have happened if I'd seen the piercing stuff first."

Rona winced. "True. I almost ran out of the place the first time I saw someone inserting needles into a breast." She rubbed her head on Simon's arm like a kitten. "Are you seeing Xavier now, then?"

"No!" Glancing at the mirror, Abby noticed Simon's quizzical look. "Xavier isn't... No." She gave a helpless shrug. *He went to bed with me and decided I'm not his type. Or something.* When her eyes prickled with tears, she turned to look out the window. The trees were getting taller. A long way down, a tiny stream sparkled in the sunlight. A hike would be nice right about now. The car felt far too closed in.

"Did you know that Xavier's wife died a few years ago?" Rona asked.

"Rona," Simon said in a warning tone.

"From what people say, they were good together, and I doubt he's ever let her go. Nowadays he sees several women at any given time, and each one is in a separate 'box.'" Her fingers put quotes around the word. "The club play partner, the slave at home, the social date. It's really—"

"It's not appropriate to discuss him behind his back, lass. Would you like to be gagged for the rest of the trip?" Without looking away from the road, Simon reached out and tugged Rona's hair.

"No, Sir. Absolutely not, Sir. I'm sorry, Sir." Rona winked at Abby, then faced the front.

Darn Simon. Just when she was getting some information. She considered smacking the back of his head, met his gaze in the mirror—eyes as black as Xavier's and with as much power—and hastily abandoned the idea.

So Xavier hadn't ever been serious about her in the least. He didn't want anyone that way. Still, she obviously wasn't even someone he'd play with at the club anymore. And that hurt.

* * * *

In a tiny mountain valley, the Mastersons' home was sided by forest on the left, fields and fences on the right. Parked vehicles formed rows from the house to the massive barn and edged the sides of the dirt road. As Xavier shut off his car, he saw a young couple—burdened with bags, towels, and a pie—cross toward the house. An adolescent dashed past, followed by an older woman at a slower pace.

The late afternoon sun glared down on the massive two-story log cabin. A porch wrapped around the building, tying the various extensions together. From the look of the construction techniques, the cabin had apparently expanded both vertically and horizontally, which was good since Virgil Masterson had mentioned he and his two brothers lived here. With the livestock and offices for their wilderness guide business, staying on-site made sense.

It had been years since he'd been to this area, although he'd met many of the local Doms who visited San Francisco to play. The Hunts and, recently, Virgil Masterson had often been to the club. What kind of Dom had Virgil become?

Simon had said that Summer was still Masterson's submissive. Xavier looked forward to seeing the little nurse who'd once been a Dark Haven member.

Still stalling—and knowing he was—Xavier leaned against his car. His brain felt exhausted, since he'd second-guessed his decision all the way here. What was the little fluff doing to him?

Abby had fit quite nicely into the *club play partner* slot—until she'd tempted him into wanting more. Never before had he run into difficulty keeping a woman within the bounds he set for her. Like Destiny. He'd enjoyed the previous long-term receptionist, been pleased with her capabilities and quirkiness, occasionally played with her in Dark Haven, but never had the urge to take it further.

With the slaves who entered his house, the minute one walked in the door, he'd begin evaluating her for her next Master. It was always a mutually agreed-upon, commitmentless arrangement.

He had boundaries for his women. But with Abby, the desire to know her more fully was like smelling coffee and bacon with a locked door barring the way to the kitchen. He'd secured the deadbolt himself.

As he thought, he watched an eagle circle overhead, probably confused by the event. He sympathized.

Ever since he'd met Abby, his memories of Catherine had grown distant—as if the bond tying him to her was eroding. Conversely sometimes it seemed as if she'd leaned over his shoulder to give him advice. He smiled ruefully. She'd been a full-time slave, wanting nothing more than to serve him. For her, he'd assumed the Master role, although it didn't suit him—but she'd been happiest under a strict regime.

Not that it had kept her from voicing an opinion. After obtaining permission to speak freely, she'd kneel at his feet and scold him if she thought he needed it. She'd have scolded him about the coldness he'd shown to Abby.

He'd hurt the little fluff. As openhearted as Catherine had been, Abby was more vulnerable and definitely less experienced in the lifestyle and in sex.

Pulling away had seemed like a good decision, a chance to reset the boundaries, but he'd made her cry, and seeing her in tears had been like a fist to the belly. He'd wanted to hold her. To take her home and play with her there. To wake up with her in his bed and enjoy her soft mouth. To hear her husky laughter and verbally fence with her in a way he'd never experienced with a submissive.

She was supposed to stay his Dark Haven play partner, but he wanted more. Just this once he'd relax the dividing line between the club and his home. Maybe she'd be interested in exploring the lifestyle outside of the club.

"Xavier."

He turned.

Smiling widely, Virgil Masterson crossed the gravel from the barn. The sandy-haired cop wore jeans and a T-shirt that barely stretched over his broad shoulders. "It's damn good to see you."

"And you." They shook hands. "You have quite a place here."

"We like it." Virgil led the way toward the house. "Simon plans to arrange a wilderness trip later this summer. You should come."

No need to tell him the lure today was a particular gray-eyed submissive. "It would be good to get away from the city more often." It was true. He'd never allowed himself to become so city-bound before.

"I'm glad you came early enough to join the Masterson portion of the day, before everyone heads up to Serenity Lodge." Virgil grinned. "This is the first year we've added *adult* games to the fun."

"I thought the entire town of Bear Flat came to your barbecue. Won't you have children here?"

"My brother keeps a fenced-off area back in the forest for black-powder rifle tournaments. The children and vanilla adults will stay here and have a war on the lawn, and the kinksters will move to the more private field of battle. Doms versus submissives."

Xavier had a vision of winning a war with the prize a soft, sweet submissive. One with foggy gray eyes. "That sounds interesting."

* * * *

The Mastersons were amazing. At a picnic table on the enormous deck, Abby ignored the women chatting around her and stared at the kaleidoscope of activity in the wide backyard. She'd been impressed by her parents' annual anniversary gathering with a hundred or so guests.

The Mastersons' Fourth of July party included the entire *town* of Bear Flat.

The red, white, and blue theme ranged from the cups, plates, and table decorations, to cakes and cookies brought by guests, to bunting and streamers on the railings. Down the slope from the house, a tree-lined creek kept children occupied; other youngsters screamed down a waterslide or played soccer. A wading pool and fenced "corral" were surrounded by comfortable chairs for mothers to watch their toddlers. At the tables scattered over the lawn, older guests played poker, board games, or dominoes while hashing over gossip and politics.

"Abby, are you coming to our party tonight?" Rebecca asked. The very pregnant redhead was married to Logan Hunt, one of the brothers who owned the Serenity wilderness lodge up the mountain. Simon said the dungeon play there was the highlight of the trip.

"That's the plan, I guess." But who would she know? She glanced at the women. Just Rona and Lindsey? Pregnant Rebecca sure wouldn't be doing any scenes.

Across the table sat tiny, dark-haired Kallie, wife of Jake, the other Hunt brother. Summer was married to Virgil Masterson, one of the barbecue hosts, and was as fair as Kallie was dark.

"You're both going?" Abby asked.

"Not me and Virgil." Summer turned sideways to rub her bare foot on a sprawled-out, half-grown dog. The spaniel closed its eyes in bliss.

Abby sighed. Her renters had been delighted to babysit the puppies, but she missed them already.

"We'll oversee the adult war games here and call it a night. Virgil doesn't like public scenes." Summer pointed at Kallie, who was Virgil's cousin. "And he never, ever wants to see Kallie playing with Jake. He said he'd have to wash his eyeballs with bleach."

Kallie choked on her hamburger. "Trust me, the sentiment is mutual." She grinned at Abby. "Last year Virgil had fits about me dating someone into BDSM." She dropped her voice to a low growl. "'*Don't fuck with her, Hunt, or I'll pitch the badge and beat the shit out of you.*' They even got into a fight on Main Street. Then Virgil goes off and gets his own submissive. Two-faced bastard," she said lovingly.

Oh, talk about complicated relationships. Taking a sip of her iced tea, Abby added another mental note: *Must consider how other "family" dynamics affect a BDSM network.* At this rate, she'd have more questions than she did answers.

Hopefully tonight she'd have a chance to scribble out her impressions. She had more late nights in front of her, but she might, *might* get done in time.

She smiled as the guys around the barbecue burst into laughter. At a table on the grass, two old men were amiably insulting each other over a checkerboard. A child skidded down the waterslide on his chest, screaming in excitement. So many sounds of happiness.

"Don't worry about tonight." Rona patted her hand. "Simon and I will watch out for you. Usually about a third of the people are from Dark Haven, and you know them."

"It's my first time too," Lindsey said in her soft Texas drawl.

Kallie smiled. "A couple of people are flying in, and we'll have the local lifestylers. There's some good-looking Doms around here if you like the rugged type."

Abby thought of Xavier. He went past rugged into a deadly sophistication. *No, don't think about him.* How would an outside party affect the dynamics of the Dark Haven group? Would a stranger enhance the "family" solidarity or detract from it? "Do the groups interact well together?"

"Pretty much," Rebecca said. "The locals are less into edgy costumes, but there's no difference in how people play."

"Costumes?" Abby's stomach took a nosedive. "Uh. I'm not sure how to dress. Is this, like, formal fetwear, or a jeans and T-shirt party?"

Rebecca frowned. "Why would any woman wear a T-shirt? Talk about unattractive."

"It's Becca's mission," Kallie said, "to put women into sexy clothing. She did the same for me last year."

Becca sniffed. "Before meeting Logan, I dressed like a businesswoman, but he showed me that men enjoy a woman's curves and how to show them off."

"Apparently he enjoyed more than just your curves, girl." Summer lifted an eyebrow at Becca's eight-months-and-counting stomach.

"Brat."

"You win." Abby grinned at Becca. "I'll donate my T-shirts to charity when I get home."

"That's the spirit." Rubbing her stomach, Becca gave Summer a victorious smirk. "But really, anything you want to wear tonight is fine. If you're submissive, you probably won't have much on by the end of the night."

"Well, see who came for the barbecue," Rona said, motioning to the right. "I thought he didn't come to Bear Flat."

When Abby turned, her heart stuttered to a halt.

With Virgil beside him, Xavier strode across the lawn toward the deck, his gaze on her. He looked…amazing. Dark tan, carved facial features, black jeans worn smooth with use, a western shirt in a subtle dark plaid, and well-worn boots. A black cowboy hat shaded his face and made his eyes unreadable.

He shook hands with Jake Hunt before Simon walked over and said something. Xavier's smile appeared, and he gave her another long stare before turning back to the men.

"I've never seen Xavier look at a woman with that kind of heat. Whew," Summer said. "Now I understand why Victorian women carried fans."

"You know him?" Abby asked. "I thought you lived here. With Virgil."

"I used to live in San Francisco. In fact, I met Virgil at Dark Haven during a western night calf-roping game."

"Let me guess—you were the calf?"

"Yep." Summer laughed ruefully. "Xavier, ever so sweetly, handed me over to the one Dom in San Francisco who had ridden rodeo. Virg had me thrown and hog-tied in seconds."

When the laughter died, Rebecca leaned back, her hands resting on her stomach. "I've never seen Xavier except at his club." She smiled. "Daylight doesn't diminish him at all, does it?"

Just the opposite, if that was possible. Abby watched the sunshine glow over his dusky coloring, aquiline nose, and strong jaw. He had the most elegant mixture of Native American and European ancestry she'd ever seen. A boy ran up to him, apparently admiring the thick black braid down his back. With a quicksilver smile, Xavier knelt to talk.

How could he appear so approachable yet be so distant with her? "Why is he here?"

"No telling. He's a puzzle," Rona said. "But Simon loves him like a brother. And he's definitely focused on you, honey." Her lips twitched. "Rebecca, we'll have to make sure our Abby looks extremely seductive this evening."

"I...I don't think he's interested, but thanks." Oh heavens, he was headed straight for them. If he yelled at her, she'd burst into tears. She glanced at the door to the house behind her and wondered if she could escape.

XAVIER HAD STOOD for a moment, enjoying the festivities. The mingling of ages, from babies to old ones, reminded him of the parties his mother had taken him to when he'd been young. Then his father had decided his heir shouldn't be tainted by a Native American heritage and had shipped him off to a European boarding school. His gut clenched. *Far in the past, Leduc.*

He walked toward the deck, taking in the sight of his pretty summer toy. Her fluffy hair glinted in the sunlight, her cheeks were pink, and the dark red top fit over her full breasts so low and tight that he hardened.

Halfway up the steps, he held his hand out to her. Their conversation needed to be private.

She stared at him, reluctance and pain and something else—almost fear—in her gaze, yet she came to him with a sweet compliance that melted his heart. She stopped one step above him, as if making sure she could run. "I didn't think you attended these parties."

Would she rather he hadn't? Unable to resist, he slid his hands under her shirt and over her bare skin. In the bright light he saw her pupils dilate and her lips redden. She roused so easily to his touch. He intended to rouse her more. Later.

"I wanted to be with you." The honesty he tried to maintain demanded this acknowledgment.

"Really?" Her surprised expression saddened him. He'd shaken her confidence in herself. Even worse, she didn't believe him. He framed her face with his hands and held her long enough to give her a hard, claiming kiss in case any men nearby had thoughts. In consideration of the children, he broke off before he wanted.

She'd curled her small fingers around his wrists, and her gray eyes had gone smoky. Lovely.

As he ran a finger over her lips, he looked forward to seeing them swollen from his mouth, his cock. If she wasn't careful, even a gag. "Come with me. We're going to talk."

Taking her wrist firmly—he'd seen how she'd checked for escape routes—Xavier led her across the sloping lawn. He stopped beside a table with a chessboard set up.

"White or black?" he asked politely.

She flinched at the sound of his voice. Her gaze flickered up and away, and under his fingers her pulse was speeding, which seemed strange. He often took a submissive to the edge of fear, but this wasn't a scene, and he hadn't pushed Abby at all. "Why are you nervous?"

"I'm not."

A lie. His mouth tightened.

She swallowed before asking in a near whisper, "Are you mad at me?"

She was worried he was angry? He studied her more closely. Yes, she looked like a child called to the headmaster's office. Odd. The most painful reprimand he'd ever given her was a few swats of his hand. "Why would you think I'd be mad at you, little fluff?"

Her clear gray eyes were wide, and he didn't resist the urge to move closer. Her rounded chin fit into the palm of his hand. "Tell me, Abby."

"I…I don't know. You look… I don't know what you're thinking, and you're not smiling." Her hands clenched together, and a shiver ran down her frame.

"You're afraid of me?" He had trouble believing it. Her lack of fear had been one of the reasons she'd drawn him.

"I…" She swallowed and seemed to give herself a mental shake before really looking at him. "You're not mad, are you?"

There. Back with him again. She definitely had some odd headspaces. "Absolutely not. I'm angry with myself for hurting you, Abby. But you've done nothing wrong at all."

"Oh." Her eyes took on a sheen of tears, and then she nodded. "Okay."

"Okay," he said softly. "Now, let's play chess." Her startled blink made him chuckle, and he gave her the absolute truth. "If I get you alone, I'm going to ravage you, pet." He stroked her soft, soft cheek with his thumb and wanted to fill his palms with— He removed his hand and stepped back. "We need to talk first."

"Oh, wonderful," she said under her breath. "Um. Chess. I'll take white."

Somehow she managed to make him want to laugh and hug her at the same time. Instead he seated her at the table and chose the chair across from her. "White starts."

Her bishop's pawn moved out. He took his turn. They played silently for a few moves until he realized she'd let the silence hang forever—in the other game they were playing. *Your move, Leduc.* "You affect me in ways I'm not used to."

Her gaze darted up to his, and, brave sub, she took her verbal turn, even as her bishop slid into position. "What ways? And if so, why did you...you..."

"I avoided you, yes. And that was the reason," he said. "Since my wife died, I haven't been with anyone who affected me other than physically." He cleared a space for his queen to move out.

As she spoke, he heard the hurt in her voice. "You didn't want to look at me when we made love. You turned me over."

This observation was harder to answer. "Actually..." He sighed. "Sometimes I see her face when I'm with someone. That feels wrong, so I avoid the missionary position." He needed to finish the thought for her sake. For honesty. "With you, I pulled away because all I saw was you."

"Oh." Her gaze dropped to the board. "I'm sorry about your wife. How long ago did she die?"

"Four years. And I've been comfortable with the way I live my life." He tried to think of what he wanted to say next.

"Tell me about her? How you met. Who she was."

He hesitated. He never spoke of Catherine. But Abby was watching him, her big eyes sad on his behalf. "She wasn't traditionally beautiful. Just vibrant. Her husband and I attended grad school together and stayed friends. She was his slave, and when he died she became lost in a way that independent women can't imagine. She wasn't helpless, but..." How could he explain? "She was a person in a sailboat without an anchor. You might be an excellent sailor, but if your anchor is gone, then every time you relax, your boat blows off course."

"I understand," she said softly. "I've seen that happen with elderly widows. For a slave used to a more encompassing control, it must be terrifying."

Softhearted Abby. "I couldn't tolerate seeing that, so I took her home." He lifted a bishop and rolled it between his fingers. "I'd only planned to keep her safe, but as time passed, we fell in love. She became my slave, my partner, my wife. When the local BDSM club went out of business, I started Dark Haven so she'd have a place to be with other slaves." *She was my everything, in every corner of my life and heart.*

Abby's brows drew together. "Now you have slaves at home and still play with others at the club?"

She'd heard some gossip, then. "Close. I date some women, I'll scene with club members or staff, and I'll keep a slave until I find her a Master." She probably should know that wasn't his true nature. "I actually don't enjoy being a twenty-four/seven Master." He half smiled, remembering an argument with Catherine.

"You're a big girl. You can pick out your own clothes."

"No. I should wear only what pleases you."

"Oh." With a finger, she pushed a pawn forward one space.

"Avoiding you didn't work, Abby. I'd like more." He moved his bishop. "So the question is this: would you like to explore submission outside the club?"

Her gaze came up long enough for him to see the desire in her eyes. Without answering, she set her castle into action.

He waited. They played for a few minutes, and he had her bishop, but she'd taken his knight in turn. Pawns fell by the wayside. "Tell me what you're thinking," he said.

The corner of her mouth rose. "I'm thinking that you're awfully bossy."

He grasped her wrists—so delicate in his big hands—and flattened her arms on each side of the board. "I am that, pet, and you enjoy it. Now give me an answer and not an evasion."

The flush in her face was a telling response to his control and attracted him in the same way his dominance did her. When she tried to pull away, he tightened his grip.

"You want to...play...with me outside the club," she said slowly. "But you'd still date others? We'd have no commitment to each other?"

He regretted the hint of unhappiness in her voice, but he couldn't give her what he no longer had. "No commitments. Let's play it by ear for now."

"Perhaps that would be wise." She turned a pawn in her fingers, studying the piece as if it held answers. "I think... Yes. I'd like to try. Sir."

He sat back and studied the board. She'd said yes. Why did he feel uncomfortable with that? Perhaps because his territorial instincts were yelling, *This one is mine.*

But he couldn't ask for what he wasn't willing to give in return. His instincts would just have to suffer.

He returned his attention to the game. When had she taken his queen? In fact, far too many of his pieces had fallen victim to the sweet little fluff on the other side of the table. His eyes narrowed. Her next move would put his king in check, and he had nothing to prevent it. "You *sneaky* little sub."

When she gave him a worried look, he couldn't keep from grinning.

And she laughed, more open than he'd heard before, a throaty, happy sound that ran up his spine and tightened his chest.

This one is mine.

Chapter Twelve

In the early evening, guests interested in kinkier games had piled into a long trailer heaped with hay. As Virgil's pickup slowly pulled the wagon down a tiny road, Abby recalled her grandmother's sentimental stories about horse-drawn hayrides. Gran might not have been so nostalgic if her rides had terminated in a kinky battle zone.

Still a bit unsettled from the talk with Xavier, Abby was grateful for the long ride. Too many surprises weren't good for the nerves.

He wanted to play with her. *Her.*

And he wasn't cold at all—if anything, he cared too deeply. She leaned back against him, reassured by his strong arm around her as the wagon bumped along. After hearing the pain in his voice when he spoke of his wife, she understood him better. What would it do to such a protective—and controlling—man if he couldn't save someone he loved?

Her heart ached for him—and a little for herself, because he obviously didn't want to care for anyone else. But she wasn't ready to jump into anything either. In fact, it was rather appalling how quickly she'd had sex with Xavier.

What kind of a woman had a relationship fall apart and jumped into bed with another man? Hadn't she loved Nathan at all? *I don't know anymore.*

The trailer came to a halt, and everyone spilled out into a wide clearing surrounded by thick forest. Abby balanced on the wagon side and looked around. Trails led off into the shadowy woods. On one side, various items were piled on hay bales.

"Come, Abby." Already on the ground, Xavier grasped her around the waist and lifted her down so easily that it took her breath. "I think Lindsey could use some support," he said, leading her across the clearing.

He stopped beside Lindsey and put his hand on her shoulder. "You're pale, pet. Are you all right?"

Lindsey nodded, although the spattering of freckles stood out on her face, and her brown eyes were wide.

And no wonder. First kinky games in the woods, then later tonight came the dungeon party. How could anyone come to a weekend like this alone? Abby squeezed her hand. Receptionists needed to stick together.

Fingering the white glow-stick collar around her neck, Lindsey gave her a grateful look.

Virgil Masterson stepped onto a hay bale. "Ladies and gentlemen, Tops and bottoms, Masters and slaves, Doms and subs, listen up." The cop was not only big but had a voice designed for crowd control. "This is a war game. Spectators and noncombatants, please remain by the truck. You'll get a ride to the end of the trail.

"The Dominants—I'm going to call you 'Tops' for ease of speaking—are defending their country. The bottoms are the invaders."

"Invading submissives? That just sounds wrong," someone said. Abby recognized Xavier's Enforcer.

DeVries wore a tank top that showed arms and shoulders thick with muscle. No wonder he could wield a heavy flogger for what seemed like forever.

Virgil grinned at him and continued. "All the trails lead to the same place, and the perimeter is fenced, so you can't get lost. Sing out if you run into trouble. Gerald and Garth"—he gestured to two men wearing orange vests—"are the monitors, and their word is law.

"Attached Tops, shoot only at your bottom. Single Tops can shoot at anyone wearing a glowing white collar.

"Bottoms, there are balls in the clearing at the end. Grab one and throw it into the wading pool. If you manage that, you've won, and your Top will owe you foot rubs or whatever." He pointed to a container with laminated paper cards. "Each Top picks five cards for potential prizes so his bottom has a choice."

"And how does a Dom prevent such an atrocity as having his submissive win?" The question came from Logan, and Rebecca slapped his arm in admonishment. His hard face softened, and he pulled her against him, her back to his chest. His hands smoothed over her belly with a reverent motion.

"Because the Tops get weapons—four pistols." Virgil pointed to water pistols filled with colored water on the hay bales.

"Sounding better," deVries said in approval.

Abby scowled. Talk about uneven odds. "I want a gun too."

"Dream on, little teacher." Xavier caught her fist before she could punch him. He stepped behind her and wrapped his arms over hers, pinning her arms to her sides. When she squirmed, he changed his position so each hand cupped a breast. The slide of heat through her was startling.

Lindsey glanced over and snickered.

"What are the black-filled pistols for?" Xavier asked Virgil.

Virgil grinned. "The black is the kill shot, and the bottom is dead. Now, if you don't kill her before she tosses a ball into the pool, she wins, and you might get stuck giving foot rubs for a week.

Abby glanced over her shoulder at Xavier. "I like foot rubs."

His arms tightened, and he whispered in her ear, "I like blowjobs."

The tremor that ran through her made him laugh.

"That's black. Why the other colors?" a Domme asked.

"Ah, now that's where it gets fun. Each color is for a different…orifice. Can you demonstrate, Logan?"

Grinning, Logan released his wife. He picked up three pistols and fired the first at Rebecca. Crimson liquid splattered over her bare foot. "Red means I get to enjoy her pussy." Another pistol. Blue covered her ankle. "Blue is for the mouth. She gets to suck me off." Brown hit her other foot. "Can you guess what brown means, sugar?"

She scowled at him. "The big *asshole* gets to use my asshole."

Abby joined the submissives in cheering her answer.

Logan narrowed his eyes at his wife. "That big belly isn't going to protect you, little rebel." He turned back to the crowd. "If your bottom is male, you can choose how to use the red color."

Virgil laughed and resumed. "If you've only hit your bottom with red dye before the kill shot, then you've only won her pussy. Nothing else." Virgil pointed to Rebecca. "You see how Logan got Becca with three colors. He potentially wins the use of all three orifices, but only if he nails her with the black *after* the three colors. No black on the submissive? You win nothing."

Summer pushed Virgil off the hay bale and stepped on. "See, bottoms? There's hope. Your greedy Tops will try to shoot you with all three colors and probably won't use the kill shot until the last minute. So unless you get hit with black, keep going."

Virgil yanked her over his shoulder and swatted her ass, making her squeak. "Bottoms, don't hide to avoid losing. You'll be declared a prisoner of war, and we'll take turns beating on you before giving you over to your Top for whatever he or she wants to do to you."

Every bottom in the crowd went stiff, and Virgil nodded in satisfaction.

"You got it, I see. All losing bottoms get displayed on the stage before being released to their Tops."

PUTTING THE LOSERS on the stage to exhibit them? Lindsey shivered. What would that be like? She didn't hold much hope that she'd win. She was in good shape, but some of the Doms were scary fit, and there might be more than one—*hopefully*—interested in shooting at her.

Lindsey glanced at Abby. Although Xavier was fondling her breasts, he was also holding her almost tenderly. Lindsey sighed silently. She doubted they'd be together long—Xavier had a real sorry reputation for submissive turnover—but they looked right. At least

Abby would know the person who'd claim her for a prize tonight.

What if I don't like who wins me? But she'd known the risk when she'd jumped on the hayride. No need to get all worked up until the end of the game. She tugged on the white glow-stick collar around her neck, then raised her hand like a schoolgirl. "Sir?"

Virgil set his wife down. "Lindsey, right?"

She nodded. "What happens if more than one Top shoots a bottom? And how do you tell who did?"

When deVries turned to give her a speculative look, she felt her face turn red. She glared at him. *Not you.* He had the personality of a half-drowned weasel.

"Excellent question. Single Tops, listen up. Those pistols are for you." Virgil pointed to a separate pile of weapons. "The red, blue, and brown *ammunition*"—he grinned—"also has sparkles. You'll get assigned a sparkle color. At the end, you can claim the appropriate prize—um, orifices—from any bottoms that glitter with your color. Black doesn't count. As long as the bottom loses—to whomever—all the Tops may claim their prizes."

Lindsey caught her breath. *More than one Top can use me?* On the drive out, Summer had asked if she wanted to be taken by more than one man. Lindsey had figured she was joking, but...the idea really turned her on too.

Virgil apparently read her surprise as confusion. "Lindsey, if you lose, and your body shows a red with pink sparkles, blue with black sparkles, and brown with white sparkles, then three Tops will pay you a visit." He grinned at her.

She managed to inhale but could feel her heart hammering. *Shoot, girl, what have you done?*

"Bottoms, do remember, the club safe word at Serenity, Dark Haven, and here in the war zone is *red*. Safe words are always honored," Virgil said.

"Lindsey, look at the bright side," Summer said. "If you don't get killed, you get to demand a prize from any Top who shot you. Single Tops, if you shoot two bottoms and they both win, you have to pay them both off."

SEEING THE WORRY on Lindsey's face, Abby patted her arm. "You okay?"

Lindsey fingered her white collar. "Mostly. The idea of two at once is kind of a whole 'nother thing. But I've thought on it before. Might be fun."

A threesome? The Texan had some courage, all right.

Xavier released Abby to run his hand up Lindsey's arm. "Simon only invites certain Tops and bottoms from Dark Haven. For this game, Logan and Jake did the same for the locals. You shouldn't end up with a Top who's totally ill-suited to you."

As Lindsey relaxed, Abby rubbed her head against Xavier's chest. He had a wellspring of compassion.

He put his arm around Abby's waist and bent to whisper, "You, however, are stuck with me, whether it suits you or not."

His breath brushed her ear and sent pinpricks down her neck.

Virgil pointed to a row of bowls on two hay bales. "Those are fluorescent finger paints. Mark which bottom is yours. For clarity, use only one or two colors, and keep your design unique."

Logan checked his watch. “Bottoms, there are sacks for your clothing, and water shoes to wear if you’re tender-footed. Tops, grab a belt, pistols, and five reward cards. Do some finger painting. The war starts in exactly ten minutes.”

Xavier released Abby. “Strip, put your clothes in a sack, and wait for me here.”

A rush of adrenaline went through her. “Everything?”

“Definitely.”

“I’m not—”*I don’t know if I want to do this.* “Not athletic.”

He tugged on her hair. “Excellent. I won’t have to exert myself to get all three shots in first.”

Her eyes widened. All three. She’d never had anal sex. Ever.

He walked a few steps and said without looking back, “Be naked before I return, or you’ll enter the game with my handprint on your ass.”

Uh-uh. She hurriedly stripped, shivering as she stuffed her clothes in a sack. The sun had disappeared behind the trees, leaving the world in a shadowy, semitwilight state. The air held a snowy mountain bite. She pulled on the rubber-soled booties to cushion her feet.

To her right, people had started finger-painting. One Domme made circles around her submissive’s cock. Another Dom was putting cat whisker stripes on a woman’s face.

A hard hand gripped Abby’s arm, and Xavier drew her close to the bowls of paint. After a second of consideration, he chose a bright blue. “Don’t move, little fluff,” he said. “I’m going to give myself something to aim at." He painted a circle around the outside of her left breast.

Her mouth dropped open. "You're going to shoot at me there?"

"Only with the blue pistol." A yellow circle followed, then another blue. He finished by painting yellow on her areola. After he painted her other breast, he smiled. "Perfect bull's-eye targets, don't you think?"

Her nipples had tightened to aching points just from the mere touch of his wet finger. Even worse, she was damp already from thinking about…what might happen after the battle. "You're a sick man," she muttered.

His eyes lit with laughter. "Turn around." He painted a target on her bottom, yellow alternating with blue. As the sunlight dimmed further, the circles started to glow.

"One more." He ran his blue-coated finger across her lower stomach, down her upper left thigh to the right leg, and back to her stomach. A circle around her groin. "Spread your legs."

No way. *No painting on my…crotch.*

A stinging smack hit her thigh, and she jumped.

"That wasn't a request, pet."

A quiver built in her stomach as she opened her legs. She felt odd, like an object or animal. Smaller. But excited as her choices fell away. He wouldn't let her sit on the sidelines as she usually did. He'd force her to participate fully.

He drew a circle from the top of her mound to the creases between her thighs and pussy. "Good. Stay in that position so it dries without smearing."

After washing his hands in the bucket provided, he returned and eyed her with satisfaction. "That gives me a few nice targets."

DeVries's laugh rolled out. "Much more fun than the range."

Abby's brows drew together. "You know how to shoot?"

Xavier's small smile was worrisome.

"We go to Simon's range every week," deVries said.

"Oh, lovely." There went her chance at a foot rub. She sighed and muttered, "*Nos morituri te salutanti.*"

DeVries scowled. "If you're cursing me, little girl, do it in English."

"It's what gladiators said before they got slaughtered in the Roman area," Xavier said. "*We who are about to die salute you.*"

"In that case, you have exactly the right mind-set," deVries said.

As deVries walked away, Xavier went down on one knee in front of Abby's open legs.

"What are you doing?"

"The air's getting cold. I'm going to make sure you stay warm." He grasped her thigh, holding her still. His other hand slid between the folds of her pussy.

"Xavier, no!"

He chuckled and pushed a finger up inside her, and she squeaked at the shock of his ruthless entry. He'd slid in so easily that he must have noticed… Her face heated.

"Yes, it's obvious you're excited, pet. I'm pleased." His hand tightened on her thigh in warning when she tried to move away, but with his finger inside her, she was well anchored. His thumb made slow circles around her clit, occasionally brushing right over the top, and her excitement rose.

"Stop," she hissed at him as her knees started to wobble.

"Don't worry. They'll fire the starting pistol before you come." His thumb pressed harder. "Probably."

The pressure in her center started to build and—

The gun fired, startling her. As Xavier released her and rose to his feet, Virgil announced, "Bottoms, you have a two-minute head start before the pistol sounds for the Tops. Run!"

Run? With my breasts bouncing and—

Xavier smacked her bottom, and she jolted forward, then kept going. Ahead of her the other bottoms ran, their bright, glowing patterns bounding like a herd of multicolored zebras. Abby veered onto the far right trail, and the scent of pine rose around her as the shadowy forest surrounded her.

The trail was wide and flat with narrower paths branching to small open areas. She slowed and entered one. A rope guarded one side, preventing access to a wooden deer silhouette several yards away. The clearings must be the firing ranges for the black-powder guys. Maybe she could hide? No, being punished by everyone sounded ghastly.

Under a tree, blankets had been piled in a heap. Her heart gave a hard thud as she realized they were for use after the battle. *Oh. My.* The Tops weren't planning to collect their prizes in the privacy of a bedroom. She swallowed hard.

Then her eyes narrowed as she stared at the quilts. Virgil hadn't mentioned anything about being sneaky.

Yes! Even as she ran forward and grabbed a blanket, the sound of the pistol split the air.

"We're at war. Tops, defend your territory or suffer defeat," Virgil yelled.

As shouts, whistles, and a rebel yell sounded, Abby wrapped herself in a light quilt and checked her body. Not one glowing paint strip showed. *Ha! I'm going to win, Xavier.* As she turned to leave the clearing, she noticed a smaller path leading to the next firing range. If there were more shortcuts, they'd be far safer than using the big trail.

Heavy footsteps pounded through the forest. A scream sounded and a shout of jubilation. "Your mouth is mine!"

More shouts, shrieks, scrambling sounds. A chill ran up Abby's spine. It sounded like a war zone. *Do not go on the trail.*

Sneaking toward the next shooting area, she spotted Logan in an orange dungeon monitor's vest. He grinned at her blanket-swathed form, touched his brow in a mock salute, and returned to the main trail.

She let out the breath she'd been holding. He wouldn't give her away.

Another clearing. She paused.

A submissive was trying to hide behind a tree, but her glowing white collar was like a beacon. With a start Abby recognized Lindsey. She started to step forward—

A stream of glittering liquid hit Lindsey between the breasts, and she let out a shocked scream.

Low and rough, deVries's voice came from the shadows near the firing point. "I'll be looking for you afterward, little girl. In case you can't tell, that was the brown."

Swearing under her breath, Lindsey scrambled back onto the trail, and her white collar disappeared.

DeVries strolled across the clearing, slowing long enough to glance at Abby and say, "If Xavier catches you with that blanket, you won't sit down for a week." The Enforcer's shadowy form moved away in total silence.

Abby realized she was shaking uncontrollably, her heart hammering. This wasn't a healthy sport at all. She really did feel hunted. Like prey.

Would Xavier be mad? Her chin came up. *Too bad.* She'd just make sure he didn't catch her. But to her dismay, the far side of the clearing lacked another shortcut.

Trying to be as silent as deVries, she moved onto the main trail. The paint designs of the bottoms stood out vividly; the Doms were dim shapes moving through the trees.

Well, if a Top didn't get close enough to see her wrapped up, he wouldn't know she was a bottom. *Be bold. Act as if you belong here.*

She stalked forward and barely dodged out of the way of a racing pair. The Domme swore as her shot missed.

Abby kept going. She turned one corner.

As she stepped around another, her blanket was ripped out of her hands. She yelped and spun.

"I'm not sure if that's cheating or incredibly smart, but it's over now." Xavier gripped her chin and kissed her firmly. "You know, you're so fair-skinned, you glow even without paint." He stepped back, and liquid splattered on her right breast.

Shot. He'd shot her.

"That was the blue pistol. Next is the brown."

"*Di te perdant*," she swore and heard him laugh. She dashed away, back muscles taut, tensed in anticipation of another spray of liquid.

She couldn't hear if he followed. As her pulse roared in her ears, she stepped behind a tree and tried to catch her breath. More screams. A man cursing. A smack of flesh and a yelp. Maybe someone else had found the blankets.

Behind Abby, lights appeared, one by one, swinging high above the trail. Someone must have hung glow sticks in the trees and now was bending them to make them light.

Virgil must be preparing to end the war. Time to go. She sure didn't want to get punished for being late. She stepped onto the trail, started to run, and got hit with a full stream of paint right on her bottom. Cold, cold liquid trickled down the backs of her thighs.

"That one was brown." Xavier's deep voice came out of the shadows. "Run, pet."

Growling under her breath, she darted away, trying to support her bouncing breasts. *Brown. Anal sex.* Her behind felt as if it were puckering in protest.

She passed two exhausted submissives and a Dom who almost shot her in reflex, before taking refuge completely off the trail. The debris on the forest floor dug into her feet despite the thin-soled shoes. An unseen branch scraped her leg painfully. Two shadowy forms went by, and from the height of one, she had a feeling it was Xavier. She was now behind him. Perfect.

Through the scant underbrush, she advanced toward the lighted clearing. Most of the nearby balls had been tossed into the wading pool or lay around it. She needed a way to get a ball without getting killed. Maybe if she approached from the other side?

Xavier had only shot her twice. Knowing him, he'd have to try for a third. *I can do it.*

She winced as branches tugged on her hair and scratched her arms, and perversely the small amount of pain made her even more aroused and wet. She might feel like prey, but her body wanted exactly what Xavier intended, and everything seemed to tantalize her senses. Even pain.

Slowly she worked her way around the tree line to the far side. Staying hidden and using a stick, she maneuvered a ball close enough to pick it up. A soccer ball. *Honestly, who thought up this idiotic game?*

As she held the cold plastic to her chest, the blue paint on her breasts smeared it. That color meant oral sex. She'd never been fond of giving blowjobs. Yet the thought of taking Xavier's cock in her mouth, knowing he'd not let her move away, how he'd make her take it deeper, was just plain hot. Feeling her pussy getting swollen and slick, she rolled her eyes. If this continued, she'd be running bowlegged.

A stage filled the far side of the huge clearing, and the calculating Doms had put the wading pool in the center of the area. She had to get closer. Very, very quickly.

Taking a firm grip on the ball, she charged across the open space, zigzagging in the proper soldierly manner. Nothing happened. Fixing her gaze on the goal, she increased her speed...and spotted Xavier off to one side, a pistol in each hand, like an old-fashioned gunslinger.

She zagged. Zigged.

Red hit her crotch. *No! Almost there.* She raised the ball to throw.

Black splashed onto her left breast.

THE SURGE OF triumph was fascinating, and Xavier grinned as Abby stopped dead, staring at the black dripping down her breast onto her stomach.

"Very colorful, Xavier," Logan called from the stage where a mixture of Tops and bottoms were standing. "Looks like you'll enjoy your win."

He planned to. Xavier crossed to his little submissive and curled his fingers around her soft upper arm. Although she glared at him, he felt a tremor run through her at his touch. Anxious and excited. Perfect.

Virgil greeted him as he led her up the stairs. "To keep the prisoners from escaping while the battle concludes, we have a variety of immobilization devices," he said. "Use how many you think best. Once she's restrained, clean the paint off her—otherwise you'll both glow in the dark."

Xavier glanced around. On one side were a couple of large dog cages, one already occupied. A three-rail fence ran along the back of the stage. The neck-high railing held chains and collars; the chest-high one had ropes with breast clamps. From the lowest railing, boards extended every few feet, and each had a condomed dildo bolted to it, sticking up and ready for use. "Interesting arrangements."

Virgil grinned and nodded at his own submissive, who'd been both collared and clamped. She scowled at him. "Some wouldn't agree," he said mildly.

"Narrow minds." Xavier closed his hand around Abby's nape, pushing her over to a board with a thin, short dildo.

She tried to pull away.

"Now, you decide, pet," he said gently. "You can politely put your cunt on the dildo. If you give me trouble or glare at me, I'll *put* you on it...and it will be in your ass."

Her eyes grew so big he almost relented. But the lights on the stage also showed the redness of arousal in her cheeks and lips. Her nipples were spiked and tight. She might think she didn't want to be displayed, but it excited her at the same time. And since she had no choice—except which orifice—she'd enjoy the experience without feeling guilty.

She swung a leg over the board.

"Wait." Before she could lower herself, he ran his fingers through her puffy folds. Very, very wet. His cock hardened to the point of pain. "Well, this shouldn't be a problem for you."

At her small sound of embarrassment, he nuzzled her hair. "Abby, the point of the games is to arouse little submissives—and their Doms. I'd worry if you weren't excited."

He kept his hand on her pussy, opening her labia and pushing down on her shoulder. Taking the control away from her. Her breath hitched as the dildo entered her, but he'd chosen one with a small shaft. If she'd been more experienced, he would have picked something she'd have to work at—something like what Lindsey would receive, if he'd read deVries's intentions correctly.

DAMNFINITO. STANDING ON the stage, Lindsey scowled. She should have been faster. Sneakier. The Enforcer had shot her twice, and Mitchell had gotten her once. Two men. Excitement shivered through her, accompanied by a big pinch of worry. DeVries didn't even like her, so why had he shot her?

As if summoned, the sorry-ass bastard strolled over. "Time to get you situated." He tilted her head up, studying her face for a bone-quivering moment. "You're a pretty one, all right."

A compliment?

Before she got over the surprise, he tangled his hand in her hair and pulled. "Come along." She tried to drag her feet, but deVries hauled her across the stage as he would a whipped hound dog.

When he stopped at a board with a dildo sticking up from it, she stiffened. "You're not fixin' to put me on that thing."

In answer, he pulled a packet from his pocket, ripped it open with his teeth, and squirted lube on the condom-covered shaft. "Not all of you. Just your asshole."

"My—" She stared at him, appalled.

"You've had anal sex before, little girl, and I intend to fuck you tonight. Might as well start getting you stretched out a bit." The reasonableness of his answer was belied by the hard, hot look in his eyes. He did intend to take her tonight, and he wasn't known for being gentle about it.

She shivered as electricity sizzled along her nerves like summer lightning. "I'm not up to your speed, remember?"

"I'm not going to whip you, Lindsey." His hand in her hair loosened, and he combed through the strands, stepping close enough that her almost nonexistent breasts brushed against his shirt. He bent and whispered in her ear, "But I am going to fuck you, long and hard."

Her insides melted like butter under a summer sun.

Mitchell walked up. "The dildo going in her pretty ass?" With a firm grip on Lindsey's ankle, he lifted her leg over the board so she straddled it.

"Seemed right." The Enforcer nodded to her. "Down."

Her knees locked. "No."

"Oh yes. Definitely yes." DeVries put an arm behind her and his hand in front. "Hang on to me, and we'll help you out. Mitchell, open her up."

Her hands closed on his thick forearm. He had light hair over the dark tan, and her fingernails dug into iron-hard muscles. She felt Mitchell spread her butt cheeks, and heat started to smother her reluctance. Two men were touching her.

As she bent her knees, the tip of the dildo entered her asshole, encountered resistance. Too big. She tried to surge up.

"Breathe, little girl. You can go as slow as you want…as long as you keep going." DeVries pinned her between his arms. In the floodlights, his eyes were the gray of steel and openly amused. "Don't even try to tell me you're not excited as hell."

She was, damn him anyway. As she relaxed her knees again, the shaft pushed in, burning and stretching despite the slickness. "Uuuhhhh…" It went deeper. Deeper.

By the time it was completely in, she was panting, and her abused hole throbbed in complaint.

DeVries lifted her chin. “Does it hurt, little girl?” he whispered.

She nodded.

“Good. Does the pain make you hotter?” His hand gently fondled her breast, and shivers ran up her spine at the unyielding look in his intent eyes. “Don’t lie to me, Lindsey. I’ll know.”

Sweet Jesus, he already knew the answer. She was so wet, she could feel the slickness on her thighs. The burning nerves in her bottom aroused her far more than she’d ever thought possible. “Yes.”

“Good to hear.” Still on one knee, Mitchell chuckled and squeezed her ass cheeks, adding to the sensations.

“I like that answer.” DeVries pinched her nipple, just enough so the light pain merged with that in her ass—and heat and need flared higher inside her. “You’re going to submit to us, Lindsey. Both of us at once,” he murmured. “My cock will stretch that tender little ass even more, and I’ll enjoy every minute of it.”

Chapter Thirteen

Abby stared as Xavier came over with a bucket of water, a spray bottle, and a sponge. "What are you doing?"

"Cleaning you up." He handed over a bottled water he'd stuck under his belt. "Drink this while I work." After spraying her with lavender-scented soap, he scrubbed her down, rubbing hard enough over her breasts to have her squirming on the dildo.

"I see you went way off the trail." Xavier said in a hard tone, turning her bloodied leg to the light.

Abby froze. He was angry. Was he going to yell at her? Now? "They didn't say we couldn't." Her voice shook.

His face gentled. "Relax, pet. I'm only unhappy at seeing you hurt. There were no rules about staying in the cleared areas."

Oh. He carefully cleaned her various scrapes and got a bandage from Rebecca for her leg. She felt...cared for. How could her fear turn to squishy softness so quickly? Sipping her water, she watched as Virgil announced the winners.

Two Doms won for their creative artwork and chose toys from a basket of prizes. The first Dom to "kill" his submissive got a prize. When the first submissive to throw a ball into the pool was announced, he did a graceful dance across the stage to select a vibrating cock ring.

Only five submissives had won, and they openly gloated as they picked their prizes from the cards their Tops held. The defeated Tops took their razzing from the other Doms with good grace.

Abby eyed them thoughtfully. This was almost like a family game, everyone involved but no pressure. The—

A pinch on her breast yanked her out of her thoughts.

"That head of yours rarely stops, does it?" Xavier turned when Virgil called his name. Apparently the judges had liked Xavier's targeted paint job, and even more that he'd hit each bull's-eye.

Becca walked over with the prize basket, using her belly to help support it.

After taking the basket from her, Xavier took his time examining the contents. Abby held her breath in terror at a huge dildo; mouthed, *no no no*, to the sharp-looking breast clamps; and cringed at the ball gag. Finally he slipped something in his pocket before she could see it. A packet of lubricant joined it.

Oh, that didn't look good at all.

AS VIRGIL DISTRIBUTED the final awards, Xavier smiled. Finally. His little war prize was squirming nicely on the dildo, and he looked forward to replacing it with his cock.

When people started leaving the stage, Xavier tossed a few essentials into a bag and returned to Abby. He helped her off the board and pleased himself by burying his face in the curve of her neck and shoulder.

Fragrant with lavender and her arousal, she smelled quite fuckable.

They cleaned the board up as Doms and subs moved off the stage. When a scream came from the forest, her eyes went delightfully wide. "What happens now?"

"You do what I tell you, of course. Stand right there." He bound her wrists in front of her, leaving one end of the rope loose to use as a leash. "Are you dizzy? Hurting anywhere?"

"I'm fine."

He smiled as she shifted her weight from leg to leg, rubbing her thighs together. The dildo would have left her pussy sensitive. The chill breeze—and her arousal—tightened her nipples to pretty pink spikes that called for his attention. In fact... He walked back to the supplies and grabbed a small tube of body lotion.

"What's that for?"

He could almost see her picking through various uses for lotion, and he chuckled. "Stop thinking, Abby. The only thing you have to do is what I tell you to do. Your job isn't to worry—it's simply to obey. Can you do that?"

Her breathing was rapid and shallow as she nodded.

"Very good." He held her arm as he guided her off the stage, but she was steady on her feet and still wearing the pool shoes. Excellent.

After releasing her, he used the leash to pull her toward a trail off to one side, setting a fast pace to take her out of her comfort zone. Reinforcing that she had no control.

He chose a clearing that had several dangling glow sticks. Whatever they did tonight, he wanted to see her face. Needed to. Shadows danced across the sparse grass as the lights swayed in the wind. The quarter moon was high in the sky, lending a silvery light, and Xavier shook out the blanket in the center of the clearing.

Frowning, Abby took a step toward the more secluded areas under the trees and cast him a look of appeal.

He ignored it. "Kneel."

As she dropped to her knees, he walked around her in a Dom's inspection, enjoying the sight. Her fairness made it seem as if the moonlight had come to life. A fairy-tale elf with a wonderfully lush body.

And her mouth…

"All right, my little war prize, time to pay." He stepped in front of her. She'd lowered her bound hands to cover her bare pussy, and when she looked up at him, he quietly set his foot on the leash.

Standing a few inches from her face, he took his time as he unbuckled his belt and unzipped his jeans. Her breathing quickened.

His cock had been painfully erect for most of the game and sprang free of his clothing with a heady rush of freedom. *Patience.* Age removed the ability to get off several times in a night, replacing it with the control to stay erect for hours. Since he planned to come in her cunt, he'd start with that pretty mouth.

After curving his hand behind her skull, he guided her forward, tilting his cock to a good angle for her. Her lips closed around him, and her hot, wet mouth slid down his shaft in a way that made his balls tighten. Gripping her hair with both hands, he set her to a fast rhythm.

The first time his cock went farther than her comfort zone, she tried to raise her hands, and the leash under his foot jerked. Another jerk. Her eyes lifted to his.

"Just your mouth, pet. Nothing else." He'd taken away her ability to control how she'd suck him off. He studied her face, her shoulder and neck muscles, then let her pull back until tiny puffs of air hit the head of his shaft. Anxiety was good, but he didn't want her terrified.

Her jagged breathing steadied, and after a few seconds, she pushed forward, loosening her jaw to take him deeper. Good little sub. She continued sweetly sucking and licking, even when he held her head still and started to thrust lightly in and out of her mouth. "You feel wonderful, little fluff."

She gave a tiny feminine grunt and worked harder. Her tongue licked a hot strip up the underside of his cock, circled the head, and ran down. Back up, teasing the thick veins on the way. He didn't force her to take all of him—they'd work on that later. Instead he made encouraging noises and kept a steady rhythm, pleased with how her eyes had closed and she leaned into her task.

Her thighs were pressed together—bad submissive—and he grinned as she squirmed, aroused by what she was doing to him. When she sucked harder, his hands tightened in her hair. Her enthusiasm and sweetness unraveled his control faster than any perfect technique could.

When his balls began to draw up, he stepped back, holding her hair to keep her from following. After the heat of her mouth, the cool night air was like a slap against his wet cock. "Hands and knees."

She gave him a hot, anxious look and wiggled herself into position, leaning on her elbows.

After zipping himself back up—which wasn't easy—he dug in his pocket for the prize he'd selected. A considerate person had taped a battery to the package, and he grinned. After lubing the anal plug, he pulled Abby's ass cheeks apart and drizzled lube over her small, puckered hole.

AS ABBY FELT cold liquid trickle between her buttocks, she panicked. Yes, he'd *won* her asshole, but he was huge. He'd kill her for sure—or she'd wish he had. "No. Please, Xavier!"

She tried to crawl away, but he gripped her hips and pulled her back.

"Relax, pet." His deep, calm voice steadied her. "I'm not going to take you anally. Not tonight."

Oh, thank you, God.

"However, I did win this hole, and I intend to play with it." He pressed something against the rim, and her anxiety skyrocketed. Sounding as if he was trying not to laugh, he said, "That seems fair."

No, no, it didn't. But he wasn't asking her.

The anal plug was cold and slick as it pushed in a little, retreated, pushed in farther. Burning spread as her muscles resisted, and she tightened them, trying to close against him.

"This is not behavior I like to see." The disapproval made her eyes burn.

"I'm sorry, my liege." Her fingers curled into the blanket as she forced herself to relax.

"Much better." The plug pressed lightly against her. "Abby, you'll find this easier if you push down, like you're expelling something."

Easier would be good. She tried. The plug felt smooth and huge. It burned as it stretched the ring of muscles, finally settling inside her with a soundless plop.

Uncomfortable and big—but not nearly as large as Xavier.

“Breathe, pet. Breathe.”

She hauled in a breath, trying to relax around the oddness of something…there. It felt foreign. Wrong. Exciting. As she shivered, the burn flowed outward to encompass her entire core, filling her with a monstrous need. *Please, take me.*

With a low laugh Xavier ran his hands over her bottom. “Look at you wiggle. I thought you’d enjoy that—as will I, since you’ll be extremely tight when my cock is in your pussy.

The promise—threat—made her vagina clench.

Without warning, he firmly rolled her onto her back. His hair had come unbraided during the hunt, and the black silk spilled over his shoulders and onto her stomach with teasing, feather-like touches. Despite his aristocratic bones, his moonlit face appeared almost savage.

And she wanted him with every beat of her heart. She opened her legs.

“Not yet, pet. I watched your breasts wobbling and bouncing all night,” he said. “I’m going to play with them before I continue collecting my prizes.” His grin flashed and disappeared. After pushing her legs together, he straddled her, settling enough of his weight on her pelvis to push the plug deeper, making her squeak. Making him laugh.

His crotch rested on her mound, and his jeans scraped just above her clit whenever he moved. Heat kept growing inside her.

He ran his finger under the ropes binding her. “Tingles or numbness or cold or pain?”

“No, sir.”

"Good." He lifted her arms over her head, setting her bound wrists to press on the top of her scalp. Holding her leash, he tipped her far enough to run the rope down her spine, between her buttocks and labia, then back up so the end rested below her breasts. His experimental tug proved that the rope rubbed the side of her clit and moved the butt plug.

Her breath caught when he tugged harder, setting nerves jangling in her pussy. Her ass. He smiled down at her. "If you don't move, I won't use the leash…much."

Leaving the rope lying like a threat against her stomach, he squirted his tube of lotion all over her heavy breasts. The scent of lemon and vanilla filled the air. His big hands fondled her, massaging the lotion in, then sliding up almost to her nipples and away. Acting as if he had all the time in the world, he simply…played. Pushing them together and gliding his palms in from the outside. Squeezing in a milking motion, first one, then the other.

Her breasts swelled. When his fingers slid over the tightly bunched peaks, she arched into his hands as the glorious sensation flowered outward.

"Mmmmh, I knew you'd react like this," he murmured as his sure hands never stopped in the most erotic massage she'd ever known. Her breasts felt tight, hot, and the heat grew, melting down through her body to settle in her pussy. Her hips wiggled.

He tsk-tsked at her and gave the rope a sharp tug.

The butt plug rammed against the sensitive nerves in her asshole at the same time the rope scraped beside her clit. Her too tight, needy clit. "Ahhh!" She couldn't keep from squirming even more.

He tugged on the rope in admonishment, but she could only groan. Everything down there throbbed, and she'd never wanted to be taken so badly.

"Getting a bit needy, pet?" A crease appeared in his cheek, and if she hadn't been dying, she'd have sworn at him. "Let's take care of your little problem, then."

He pushed her legs apart. As he pulled the rope away, she whimpered. Her clit felt raw and far too sensitive, pulsing over her entrance that begged to be filled. With hard fingers, he separated her labia and nudged the hood back. His smile flickered. "All puffy and pink. Very pretty."

He flipped her onto her hands and knees. With a hand under her chest, he mercilessly pulled her bound hands off to the right and lowered her onto her left shoulder. The side of her face pressed into the blanket, her bottom tilted up in the air, and she had no way to prevent anything that might happen.

She tried to move, and a hand between her shoulders held her in place. "Now you understand, Abby. The control is mine, and you'll take what I give you." As he leaned down, his eyes trapped her gaze, reinforcing the knowledge.

Left with no escape, her body relaxed into acceptance. As her mind bowed under the inevitable, a peaceful hum filled her head.

"That's my girl," he murmured and straightened. Calloused hands stroked over her back and downward. After kneading her bottom, he wiggled the plug, making her whimper at the unfamiliar zinging of nerves.

She heard his zipper, the rustle of a condom wrapper, and then the head of his cock pushed at her entrance. He slid in slightly, retreated, pressed farther with the same movements he'd used with the anal plug.

She groaned as he advanced. *Too tight.* With the plug in she was too full. When her thighs tried to push her forward and away, his grip on her hip tightened. "Easy, Abby."

His low voice called to her, wrapped around her. Pulling in a breath, she made her muscles relax again to offer what he demanded. To gift him with herself.

He stilled. Then he swept his hands down her spine in a rush of sensation, warming her with his heat and attention.

His cock pushed again. Farther. *Stretch, slide, stretch.* As she pulsed around the intrusion, the discomfort changed to pleasure but still was too much. Overwhelming, and she couldn't stop shaking. She moaned.

Startled at the sound, she tensed and realized she heard people in the forest—the slap of flesh on flesh, whimpers and groans and moaning. That meant they could hear her and Xavier.

He stopped, his thighs hot against hers. "All in," he said.

"Shhh!"

Even as she cringed at what she'd said, he laughed. *Laughed.* "Needless to say, trying to silence your Dom is a mistake." He tapped a finger on her bottom as he considered…as she throbbed around him, unable to move.

"Every time I thrust, you will give me a noise—a groan, a scream, or a moan—loud enough for everyone to hear. If not, they'll hear the sound of my hand on your ass."

No. No no no.

He pulled back and slammed into her. Oh, she couldn't. She swallowed her moan.

The splat of his hand—and her yelp at the stinging pain—was probably loud enough to be heard in Bear Flat.

He thrust again, and her lips instinctively pressed closed.

"Stubborn little submissive." He slapped her other buttock.

Pain burst; then the sting merged with the heat low in her pelvis.

His hand pushed between her butt cheeks, and the anal plug started to vibrate.

She jerked as every nerve back there jolted and tingled.

He chuckled. "I can feel the vibrations. Very nice." He pressed deeper inside her as if to enjoy and stroked his hands over her.

"Make noise, Abby." He slid out and plunged in hard. Her groan at the unexpected pleasure couldn't be stopped. When he was in, stretching her around him, the vibrations felt too, too intense. The slick slide of his hard cock out was…incredible.

"That's better. Keep the noise coming, pet." In. Out. In. Out. With each thrust, his hair washed over her skin, her cheek dug into the blanket, and her body shook with pleasure. She could hear her own moans as the pressure inside her built higher. It was so good and yet not enough.

He increased the pace, and the rushing in her head grew until she couldn't tell if she was making noise or not. He hammered her and then slowed.

She groaned. The air was thick. Hot. Sweat trickled down her back. Her core was too tight, throbbing and riding the edge of reaching the peak. But not.

He bent forward, his rock-hard chest on her back, and she squeaked as his cock bumped her cervix. His groin pushed the anal plug deeper. So full. Her moan came out long and deep, making him huff a laugh.

His hand settled beside her head, his arm a column on which his weight rested. He slid his other hand down her belly to her mound.

When one hard finger rubbed over her swollen clit, her entire body clenched. "Oooo. Oh God."

"Now that's a good sound, pet."

His finger went lower to slicken in her wetness. Then, with a hard thrust, his shaft stretched her, even as his finger slid along the tight nub. She gasped as the two sensations hit, and he laughed.

Laughed as he moved his finger over her, his hammering thrusts accompanying the movements like drums with a saxophone.

She tried to groan for him and realized she was moaning continuously. Vibrations beat at her from behind. His cock filled her. Emptied her. Filled her. And his finger never stopped teasing her clit, driving her higher and higher.

Pressure coiled in her core, in her whole lower half, pulling her senses after it, until her universe was made up of movement, the slick slide of his finger, of his cock.

Her thighs quivered, her fingernails dug into her palms, and slowly, inevitably, every muscle grew rigid.

"Let it go, pet," he murmured, and his finger went sideways, over the top of her clit. Everything inside her clamped down and then blasted open, sending pleasure singing within her veins, her nerves, down to her toes, until her body shuddered with it. Over and over.

Mercilessly gripping her hips, Xavier slammed into her, keeping the waves of sensation rolling through her. His fingers tightened painfully, and then he came inside her with a growl of satisfaction.

He leaned over her, his lips on her nape, his body hot above her, and she tried to rouse her mind, but it had gone dead. Erratic spasms made her jerk, her legs shook, and she was sure she'd had at least one heart attack.

"Hold on for a moment, pet." He pressed a kiss to her nape and squeezed her shoulder before pulling out and removing the anal plug as well.

Empty and shaking, she couldn't find the willpower to move.

"Let me get you unbound." With gentle hands he rolled her onto her back and removed the ropes. As he massaged the dented skin, she stared at him, feeling lost. A couple of minutes ago, she'd needed him physically; now it was all emotional. Tears prickled behind her eyes. *I don't like this.*

"Shhh. You're exhausted, little fluff." He slid down on the blanket beside her and propped his head up on a hand. His face was all shadows, while hers was in the moonlight, open to read as he stroked a big hand up and down her breasts, and her belly. Petting her, soothing her. His body warmed her on that side, and his hair tickled as the wind feathered it over her skin. “Just rest for a bit. I’m here.”

A breath shuddered through her as his presence filled the emptiness and went further yet, melting away her icy defenses. With trembling fingers, she laid her palm on the side of his face and felt his cheek curve with his smile.

Chapter Fourteen

Physically satisfied and emotionally unsettled, Abby sat on her bed, chin resting on her knees. Color filled the rustic, one-room cabin, from the blue and white quilt to the multicolored rag rugs. Outside, the wind sloughed through the surrounding pine and fir trees. The mountain was a very peaceful place.

Well, when the inhabitants weren't indulging in war games.

Although she'd hoped Xavier would stay with her, one of the Masterson brothers had dragged him away, wanting to "pick his brains" about a business problem. Odd, that. What would a BDSM club owner know about a wilderness guide business? Rather than waiting, she and Rona had taken Simon's car to Serenity Lodge to check in and get cleaned up.

She shifted on the bed, and the lingering tenderness between her legs reminded her of the feel of the anal plug and how Xavier's cock had filled her...and how he'd driven her to an orgasm that sent heat through her every time she thought about it.

He hadn't pulled away after sex this time. In fact, on the hayride back, he'd held her on his lap so firmly that she'd felt safe and happy and wonderfully within his power.

"Now why does that seem so...satisfying?" she asked. The bobcat in the painting on the log wall ignored her. Snooty cat. Her puppies had better manners; they'd listen.

Okay, think it through. Being held by a man was nice. She and Nathan had cuddled on the couch when they watched movies.

But Xavier's actions were more...dominant. He'd pull her into his arms without asking, arrange her, and touch her how he wanted, and with every further evidence of his control she'd melt into him a little more. He'd known. His faint half smile and the warmth in his eyes said that seeing her submit pleased him.

She wasn't sure it pleased her. More like scared her. A *lot*. Her emotions were dragging her toward him in a way she'd never felt before. Not even with Nathan.

Was the attraction to Xavier only because he was more powerful than Nathan? Maybe her feelings didn't have anything to do with affection. Maybe she was experiencing the basic reaction of a submissive to an over-the-top Dominant.

Come to think of it, she'd first been attracted to Nathan because he liked to take charge, and that side of his nature had given her a thrill. She stared down at her hands. So...as a submissive, she'd reacted to Nathan. But she'd also liked his company, his intelligence, the control he had over his emotions. But was that all? She winced. Had she thought she loved him when it was really friendship—and a few zings from being submissive?

Her desire for Nathan had decreased every time Xavier had held her. Touched her. Kissed her.

She frowned at the cabin, wishing futilely for a pot of tea to help her think.

Whatever she and Nathan had had between them didn't really matter, did it? In the fall, she'd see if they could still be friends.

After a glance at the bedside clock, she jumped off the bed and walked over to her bags. Time to get dressed for the evening.

Maybe there would be more sex. She grinned. She'd never figured she had much of a libido, but Xavier had sure changed her mind. She had to wonder, though—could anyone even walk when these weekends were over?

She'd loved watching him at the Mastersons' barbecue. She'd rather thought that the Dark Haven members put him at the top of the hierarchy because he owned the club. But at the Mastersons', even strangers had shown the same deference. *My liege* simply radiated confidence and power.

When a girlie sigh escaped her, she rolled her eyes in disgust, then laughed.

Abby picked up her new bustier, set it to one side, and looked at the choices for the lower half. Black skirt. Jeans. They'd seemed adequate before—but not for Xavier.

A tap on the heavy oak door sent her heart soaring for a moment until she realized the light knock sounded feminine. Not Xavier. Nonetheless, a diversion would be very welcome. She opened the door to her two friends.

"Hi." She smiled at Rona and then checked Lindsey's face. "Are you all right? I saw that deVries had shot you." The Enforcer wouldn't have gone easy on her.

"He sure did. Mitchell too. You know, the Aussie dude?"

"Two men?" Abby swallowed. "Seriously, did they—"

"I'm fine. DeVries got an emergency phone call and had to leave." She snickered. "He was sure aggravated."

Rona pursed her lips. "I haven't heard such cursing since an OR nurse knocked over a tray of sterile instruments."

"Oh." Abby let out her breath and eyed Lindsey. "So are we happy about this?"

"We are. Lord have mercy, can you imagine taking two guys when one is the *Enforcer?* No way. Besides, Mitchell was mighty creative without any help." Lindsey looked as contented as a puppy after a full bottle.

"Good." Abby paused. "So what about deVries?"

"Well…" Lindsey bit her lip.

Rona answered. "He gave her a kiss hot enough to melt glaciers, then said she owed him her mouth and her ass. And he damn well intended to collect."

"Maybe you should consider joining a different club," Abby said, half seriously.

Rona laughed. "We're dressing in Becca's place. Grab your makeup and tonight's clothes, and let's go."

"That would be wonderful." Abby turned back to her cabin. Was this another way in which the BDSM people created their tribe or family bonds? It made her think of *Little Women* and how the sisters always dressed together. A pang bit at her; she'd never gotten to enjoy that ritual. Janae had hated her, and Grace had been too young.

Becca and Logan's apartment took up half the second floor of the massive lodge. Kallie and Summer were already in the bedroom, vying for space at the sink and dressing table, using curling irons and straighteners.

In a comfortable armchair, Becca rested her hands on her round stomach and supervised. A massive Maine coon cat sprawled on the bed, occasionally turning a black-tufted ear to listen.

After greetings were exchanged, Abby laid her clothes on the bed and looked around. Comfortable and rustic. But there was only one bedroom in the apartment. "Are you going to be short on space when the baby comes?" she asked Becca.

"Jake and Kallie are building another cabin on the other side of the grounds. When it's done, Logan and I will take over the whole second floor."

"Oh, that'll be nice." Abby stripped off her T-shirt and bra.

In the bathroom, Kallie carefully stroked mascara on her lashes. "I get the best of both worlds—my own house and close enough to scarf down Becca's cooking."

"I can't believe you're not a trillion pounds, the way you eat." Becca scowled at Kallie, then down at her own stomach. "Me? I gain a pound from just sniffing a doughnut. And now I resemble the Goodyear blimp."

"You are not a blimp." The growling retort came from the door, and Abby squeaked, pulling a shirt in front of her bare chest.

Logan stalked into the bedroom and took Becca by the shoulders. "You're not only a stunningly beautiful woman, but when a man looks at you now, he sees a fertility goddess." His hard blue eyes lightened as he caressed her stomach. "For a millennium, men worshipped women who looked like you. As it happens, some of us still do."

When Becca's green eyes pooled with tears, Abby's did the same. How could a man who seemed so mean be so sweet?

Shaking his head, he wiped his wife's tears away and kissed the tip of her nose, then murmured, "If I hear that *blimp* word again, I'll spank your ass. Carefully, of course."

After retrieving a pair of black jeans and a leather vest from the dresser, he glanced at Abby and grinned. "No need to cover those pretty breasts, sugar. I not only saw them earlier, but I daresay Xavier will have them on display before the night is over."

She felt her cheeks turn scarlet.

As he strode out, Becca pointed at Abby. "Your face…"

The others were grinning, and Abby shook her head. "I can't get used to all this display stuff."

"Visual creatures, men." Tapping her chin absently, Rona studied her two choices of dresses on the bed. "In a way, the lifestyle is good for women. We're far too used to hiding behind our clothes and makeup. A BDSM scene strips more than emotions away. And when you're naked with mascara smeared over your face, it's a revelation to discover that the Dom still likes what he sees. That you can turn him on without the trappings."

Becca grinned and agreed. "Have you ever noticed how they all go brain-dead at the sight of breasts?"

That got a chorus of snickers.

"Even mine," Kallie said, patting her small chest as she left the bathroom. With her tiny size and short, waiflike hair, she reminded Abby of the big-eyed hobbit children in *Lord of the Rings*. Wearing a stiff leather corset that made the most of her bosom, a long skirt, and strappy stilettos that shouted *fuck me*, she turned in a circle for Becca.

Becca looked her over. “Perfect.”

Rona finally decided on a strapless vinyl dress in a golden color that matched her choker. Black ribbon bows held the sides of the dress a few inches apart. “Simon likes untying things.”

“That’s a great outfit.” Becca sighed and cast a rueful look at her stomach. “I miss sexy clothing.”

Lindsey popped out of the bathroom, her shoulder-length hair in bouncy pigtails, wearing a short plaid skirt and a white shirt with the tails tied. “One schoolgirl fixin’ to report to class.” She grinned at Rebecca. “When Rona told me you were preggers and didn’t know what to wear, I brought an outfit for you. We can go downstairs together.” She held up another plaid skirt altered to tie at the waist and a white maternity blouse. “Do you figure Headmaster Logan will punish my classmate for getting herself pregnant?”

Becca stared at the clothes for a second and burst into laughter. “Absolutely.”

Kallie shook her head. “Girl, you won’t be able to sit down for a week.”

Abby frowned at the delighted anticipation on Becca’s face. Some submissives in Dark Haven had craved getting smacked, and it never quite made sense.

“Oh, someone looks confused,” Rona commented. “No spankings or floggings before?”

“Um. I’ve collected a few swats from Xavier now and then.” Nathan had wanted to spank her once, and Abby had flat-out refused. Although the thought of Xavier doing more…

"Not the same." Kallie crawled onto the bed and grimaced when the corset defeated any slouching. The cat set a fist-sized paw on her knee to remind her of her duties. As Kallie rubbed its head, she mused, "Maybe I should give Xavier a hint that–"

"You will *not*," Abby snapped, using the autocratic tone and menacing frown that she'd perfected in her first year of teaching. *Still works.*

Kallie's mouth dropped open. "You're a Domme? I thought—"

"Teacher." Abby gave her a smug smile. "I got my doctorate so early, I was the same age as the undergrads I was teaching, so I needed the Stare of Death."

"Early, huh." Becca frowned. "I had a youngster in my dorm. When my friends and I were drinking and dating, she was still learning to deal with hormones and breasts."

"That's how it was." She'd sat alone, watching the "normal" college girls having fun. They hadn't invited Abby to join them any more than they'd have welcomed their kid sisters.

Kallie reached over her cat to squeeze Abby's hand. "It was bad being a tomboy, but being younger than everybody must have sucked."

This was what she'd missed out on in college. The fun and teasing and advice. And sympathy. Abby blinked and looked down at the shirt she still clasped to her chest.

"So is that what you're gonna wear, youngster?" Lindsey asked lightly. "I'm telling you, my liege won't approve of a T-shirt."

Abby gave her a grateful smile. "Really? I thought he'd love it."

"Better stick to your bustier." Becca nodded at Abby's clothing on the bed. "And I have a skirt you'll love. I'm sure not going to wear it this year."

* * * *

An hour later Abby followed the other women down the stairs and halted in awe.

The huge room had been transformed into a dungeon with freestanding Saint Andrew's crosses. Chains dangled from the heavy rafters; steel rings studded the log walls. A sex sling hung at the far end. The reception desk had inset D rings and was covered with a rubber-backed blanket. Coffee tables and couches had straps around the legs.

A small fire in the massive stone fireplace heated the room against the mountain chill. Amber-colored glass in wall lanterns spilled flickering light and left some areas in shadow.

A touch of anxiety ran up her spine. This was very different from the big Dark Haven dungeon. Smaller. Fewer people. More...personal or something.

"Amazing how a few chains can change the ambience, isn't it?" Rona came down the stairs and stopped beside her.

Near the door, Simon spotted his wife and strolled over. In an apparent concession to the rustic surrounding, he'd worn a white shirt and tailored slacks, without a suit coat. A gleam lit his eyes at the sight of the bows running down the sides of Rona's dress. "That's very nice, lass," he said, tugging one open.

She slapped at his hands. "I should have tied them in knots."

"Even better. I haven't played with knives in a while." He caught and kissed Rona's hand, holding her gaze in a way that made Abby sigh.

Would she ever have anyone who looked at her like that? Wistfully she turned away and fidgeted with her clothes. Her new dark-red bustier had black lacing she'd half undone to display a good amount of cleavage. But Rebecca's ankle-length skirt perfected the outfit completely. Somehow the black fabric had been sliced to shredded paper widths from hip to ankle. With such tantalizing glimpses of private areas, a man wouldn't even notice the width of the wearer's hips.

Simon turned to her. "You look enchanting. I know some Doms who would be delighted to meet you. Or are you waiting for Xavier?"

"I'm not sure." Xavier hadn't mentioned tonight. Obviously she should have asked. "I'll wander for a while and get the lay of the land."

Simon ran a hand down her arm. "All right. But Abby, I consider you under my protection. You're a big girl, so you may negotiate on your own behalf, but use my name if anyone gives you trouble. And I'm here if you want me to monitor a scene. Is that clear?"

"Yes, sir."

"The lodge's safe word is the usual, *red*."

"Yes, sir."

"Good enough."

She moved toward the center of the room, realizing she wasn't wearing Xavier's collar. Her legs felt shaky as if someone had taken away much-needed crutches.

As more people arrived, the music shifted to Whip Culture, and the Hunt brothers seemed to be everywhere. Jake was helping a Dom with a suspension setup.

Nearby, Logan was introducing a Dark Haven submissive to a local Domme. Slowly the equipment began to get used, and Abby wandered from one scene to another. A couple of Doms approached her, but she fended them off with "Later."

After an hour her spirits were sinking, and she dropped down on the leather couch to stare at the fire. Xavier hadn't arrived. For all she knew, he'd gone back to San Francisco.

Should I play without him? He'd been clear they weren't exclusive or anything. Maybe she should try a scene with someone else, just to see what it was like. The thought wasn't very palatable, though.

"Abby?" A man's voice. Familiar. Shocked.

Her head came up. "*Nathan*. What are you doing here?"

His gaze ran over her clothing, and his blue eyes widened. "I could ask you the same." Dressed in a leather jacket and black leather pants, he took a seat beside her.

Her brain felt as if it had started to spin. "Simon invited me. Did your summer term get cut short? Are you back for good?"

"No, I'm here for only a couple of days." He looked away. "You know how I like mountains. Since the Hunts plan to turn this into a family lodge, they'll have fewer parties, and I wanted to get this one in."

The pleasure—and discomfort—at seeing him seemed to be on a winding drive through her emotions.

Taking her hand, he smiled. "Our last conversation must have gotten through to you. I can't believe you went so far as to join a BDSM club to learn to meet my needs."

True, she'd planned that at one time, but… "Well—"

"Maybe our relationship wasn't as hopeless as I thought." He rose. "I want to do a scene with you."

He tugged her toward the back. Backing her up to a Saint Andrew's cross, he pulled his favorite metal handcuffs from his jacket pocket.

I hate handcuffs. With difficulty, she smothered the urge to refuse. She had experience now. Had been restrained before. And she'd just been wondering how she'd really felt about him—and about Xavier. Maybe she owed it to them both to try again. After all, she'd also been unconvinced about Xavier at first.

But wasn't Nathan supposed to ask her what she'd permit in a scene?

A handcuff snicked on her left wrist, and he clipped it to the upper arm of the X-shaped frame. He pulled out another set of handcuffs and did her right wrist.

Her discomfort increased. With Xavier she'd often—always—felt anxious about what he had planned, but never unsafe. Why was this different? She'd known Nathan far longer.

He stared down his nose at her. "Okay, slut." His voice was rougher. Meaner. "You're going to take what I give you, and I don't want any back talk from you. Nod if you understand."

She nodded, but being called names made her more uncomfortable than if someone had poured ants down her clothes. Too many memories lingered of her father's screaming.

He unlaced her bustier and tossed it on the floor. His hands were cruel, squeezing and pinching her nipples. "Look at me, bitch." He pinched her hard enough to make her eyes water.

"Nathan," she whispered. "This—"

"Fucking bitch." He slapped her breast. As the sting tore through her, she tried to pull away. The cuffs dug into her wrists, hurting her arms. Her breast hurt. This was pain with no arousal.

"Nathan, no."

"You don't talk without permission." When his voice rose, fear skittered up her spine with tiny claws. He grabbed her hair so hard the skin around her eyes felt tight, and with the other hand touched her between her legs. He pushed a finger roughly inside. "Slut, you're not even wet."

When he raised his hand again, she couldn't stand it. "No. I don't want this. Let me down."

"Fat fucking chance. I've wanted you on one of these since—"

"Red," she said firmly. "The safe word is *red*, and I'm using it."

To her disbelief he put his hand over her mouth. "No, you can't ruin it again. Time after time you—"

Sliding toward a morass of terror, she bit him. *Hard.*

As he jerked away, she yelled, "Red." Took a breath. "Red, red, red."

"You cunt." His face darkened to an ugly color. "If you—"

"What's the problem here?" Xavier's deep, controlled voice wrapped around her like a blanket of safety.

As he stopped beside Nathan, she halted the painful tearing at the cuffs. Her heart started to slow.

Simon approached from the right, Logan from the left, but Xavier took up the entire room. The world.

"Xavier." Nathan stepped back hastily. "It's not what it seems. This is my girlfriend."

The anger in Xavier's eyes turned cold. Then his expression went unreadable. "I hadn't realized you were involved."

"For months. She still needs some work getting into the right headspace, keeps wanting to back out, you know?"

The assessing look swept over her. "I hadn't noticed her trying to back out at the club."

Nathan stared. "She did scenes at Dark Haven? With other Doms?"

"Yes." Xavier met her gaze finally. Although the chill in his eyes dug into her skin, his voice stayed level. "Abigail, you used the safe word. That means the scene is over. Is that what you intended?"

Absolutely. "Yes, my liege."

Even as Nathan made a protesting sound, Simon stepped around him and unlocked the handcuffs. Didn't it figure that the security expert kept master keys in his pocket? She stared at his dark head, unable to look at Nathan…or Xavier.

When she was free, her knees threatened to buckle. Simon gripped her arm, steadying her. "Thank you," she whispered and stepped away, rubbing her wrists. She'd have nasty bruises in the morning.

As she tried to figure out what to say, a submissive in a thong and stiletto heels dropped to her knees. "Master Nathan." The round-cheeked brunette from Dark Haven looked like a college student. "I'm sorry I'm late. Your slut is here to serve you in any way you want. My mouth, my ass, my pussy are yours, sir."

Abby stared. Up until the night before he left, she and Nathan had been going together. Exclusive. Hadn't they?

But the young woman knelt with her face only an inch from Nathan's crotch…and the guilty flush flooding Nathan's face was unmistakable.

A knife sliced into Abby's chest, pushing deep. Hurting. He'd lied to her. He'd cheated on her. As the pieces of her trust dropped to the ground, she wanted to scream at him.

No. Don't fight. No yelling. She took a breath. Let it out. Took another. Refused to look at Xavier. "Good-bye, Nathan." She turned away from him and picked up her bustier.

"That's it? You blow the scene and that's it?" Nathan reached for her.

She stepped around him.

"Fine. And good riddance, slut," Nathan said, and she heard the cold rage.

That was what had attracted her—that he'd never turn into a monster like her father. She'd been a fool.

His voice rose, not a shout, but loud enough to be heard through the room. "Now that I think about it, I bet you're not in the club to play, are you, Professor Bern? Are these people part of your research?"

She froze. How did he know? *Oh no, no, no.*

His eyes widened as if he were surprised at her reaction. He jutted his head forward. "That paper you wanted to do on BDSM? Did you let them know you're studying them like guinea pigs and planning to expose them in a scientific journal for everyone to read?"

The entire room went silent. People turned. Their stares bit into her like piranha, taking chunks of meat with every breath.

The silence lasted and lasted.

"Abigail," Xavier said, "is that true?"

She tried to thread a lace through the hole of her bustier, but her fingers were numb. Shaking.

"Look at me." He didn't raise his voice, but the power in the command jerked her head up as if he'd pulled her hair. "Were you studying the members of the club?"

She nodded. *But they're not guinea pigs, not to me. I'm one of—*

"Explain to me." The muscles of his jaw were so rigid his words came out clipped.

Her mouth was too dry to speak. She'd never been able to talk. Not if someone was mad at her. And she'd never seen anyone as angry as Xavier. Her insides curled up, waiting for the screams, the yells, the curses.

She yanked her gaze away as Logan said to Nathan, "Your ability to overlook a submissive's use of her safe word—no matter the circumstances—ends your chance to play here." He jerked his head toward the door.

Nathan backed away, gave her a nasty look, and left, trailed by the brunette. His *slut*.

"Talk to me, Abby." Xavier paused, and his voice grew colder. "Or is it Professor Bern?"

She nodded and tried—tried to get words out. He needed to understand. Couldn't speak. Screams and curses filled her ears, pounding on her brain.

He waited as a minute passed. Two. "All right. Perhaps this is best," he said finally. "I am too angry to speak to you now, and perhaps you need time to think." Each word was measured and even and so, so cold.

Ice couldn't shield her from the knifelike words.

"In the morning I'll explain the legal ramifications of attempting to publish anything about the club or its members. I suggest you be available."

I'd never give names. The paper should help, not hurt. She shut her eyes and pulled in a deep breath. *Will not cry. Will not cry.* The weight of disapproval made her legs unsteady.

When she raised her head, it was to meet Logan's steely eyes. "You aren't welcome in here. Stay in your cabin until Xavier comes for you."

Nothing came to her lips. She nodded and concentrated on walking across the room without looking at anything. Anyone. Her coat was upstairs, but she couldn't—couldn't stop. As she reached the front, her shoulders shook as she tried to muffle the sobs welling from deep inside.

She pulled open the door and stepped into the cold.

FURY BOILING IN his veins, Xavier watched the lodge door close behind Abby. Her shoulders had been shaking, and the realization she was crying felt like a kick to his gut.

He couldn't possibly pity her. She'd betrayed him, lied to him, lied to her friends, and put the club members at risk.

Yet his instincts urged him to go after her. To comfort her.

Absolutely not. He rubbed his face, feeling as if he'd aged a decade in the last few minutes. "That was unexpected."

Logan's gaze was on the door as well. "Yeah. Dammit."

"I wouldn't have thought it of her," Simon said. Rona walked over, and he pulled her close. "She seemed to have more character."

Almost everyone in the room was staring. Whispers began to sprout like weeds.

"So I thought. I made Dark Haven private to prevent this kind of problem." Xavier pressed his lips together as anger spiked again. This had the potential to destroy the entire club. "Now I know why she was always watching the other scenes."

"I'd noticed that," Simon said.

"Did you give her a chance to explain?" Rona's face was pale. Worried.

"I asked. She wouldn't talk." Xavier frowned. Most people would have been spilling excuses, justifications. Instead she'd closed in. He'd seen that behavior from her before.

He shook his head. Her guilt had been written plain in her expression.

Yet he had a hard time believing the softhearted submissive would deliberately hurt anyone. Not just her friends, but anyone at all. He met Rona's eyes. "I'll give her another chance to explain tomorrow—when we're both calmer."

"Want to have a beer and talk it over?" Logan asked.

"That might be wise." Simon's face was dark with concern.

"Thank you, no. I need to think for a while."

Chapter Fifteen

Hours of *thinking* had only increased Xavier's frustration. The cabin was too small to pace properly, and he hadn't been able to sleep. As dawn lit the sky, he laced up his running shoes. He needed to run off his anger before talking with Abby.

The air held a frosty bite that cleared his head, and the forest closed around him with a bottomless quiet a city dweller could never experience.

The beginning of the trail rose so steeply he had to scramble up it like a cliff. But once at the top, the well-groomed path flattened into a series of gentle switchbacks. His stride lengthened, and he broke into a jog.

As the first rays of the sun slanted through the trees, he moved into a steady run, warming and loosening muscles knotted since the evening had turned into a disaster.

He'd have sworn the little fluff was incapable of deliberately hurting someone. Yet she must have known a person would be at risk, socially or professionally, if their membership in a BDSM club became known. Even more damning, she hadn't defended herself at all. Her expression had revealed her guilt, and Nathan's accusation had held no taste of a lie.

Yes, she'd been doing research in his club.

He growled. The members were under his protection, and he had a responsibility to ensure their privacy. He obviously hadn't done enough.

When his friend Zachary had recommended a personal interview for every applicant, Xavier had thought the idea excessive. Now he knew—a background check wasn't adequate. Abby's information hadn't raised any flags. On her first day, he hadn't been searching for lies, and he'd assumed her nervousness was simply because she was new.

After a glance at the rising sun, he turned back toward the lodge.

She'd told him she taught reading. Nathan called her *Professor*. Xavier had been blind. But he needed to hear her out, needed more from her than silence. Why hadn't she talked to him? She'd given him nothing.

As the tree canopy blotted out the sun, the forest turned cold and shadowy. They had *nothing*.

Less than that. Slowing, he approached a curve on the trail. Her first day when he'd asked if she had a significant other, she'd lied. That was as much of a betrayal as her research.

Xavier's pace increased, fueled by the hurt that refused to diminish. Rounding the curve, he broke into a run and—

The trail ended. White rock hung over darkness. The *cliff*.

With a grunt of anger, he dug in his heels.

Going too fast. The loose pine needles and bark provided no traction. He skidded. His foot hit a buried stone, and pain shot up his leg as his ankle twisted.

He went off the trail at the steepest part.

* * * *

Abby had been awake all night.

Dawn came. The light through the curtains brightened.

The morning passed. Crying hadn't helped. She still couldn't think of what to do. Her ability to be logical had been destroyed under the avalanche of emotion. Every argument and reason kept dissolving with the memory of Xavier's cold face. Cold, but she'd seen the flash of betrayal in his eyes before anger had covered it.

She knew, oh, she knew, what that kind of pain felt like. And she'd caused his.

Whenever she'd wrenched her thoughts from Xavier, she'd remember the disbelieving stares around her. Her new friends—women who'd laughed with her, helped her dress, teased her about Xavier—she'd betrayed them as well.

Why hadn't she realized how they would feel? She'd never have started. No paper—no job—was worth hurting people, even if they hadn't been her friends. Somehow she needed to explain, to reassure them her paper didn't include anything identifying. They undoubtedly believed the subject was about sex and perversions, not the family they'd created.

But she hadn't been able to tell them. Xavier had looked so...angry...and her cowardly body had simply frozen.

Dressed in jeans and a flannel shirt, she sat on the bed, arms wrapped around her knees, unable to summon up the willpower to move. *I hurt my friends. Xavier.* The pain of that was unbearable.

With the windows closed, drapes drawn, she listened as cars fired up and retreated down the road. Xavier didn't come. No one came.

Sluggishly she rose, her joints aching like a ninety-year-old's. Her muscles complained of yesterday's war games and a long night of not moving. She drank a glass of water in the tiny bathroom. Coffee, breakfast, tea, everything was at the main lodge, and she wouldn't go there. Ever.

Maybe she was supposed to get herself home? But surely someone would tell her that. She'd actually prefer to take a bus. Returning to San Francisco with Simon and Rona, spending hours in their silent company, would be a nightmare.

She climbed back on the bed, pushed her glasses up, and stared at the wall. At one point she'd started to calculate the mean and median number of holes in an average log.

Had Nathan left?

Do I care? She tried to find grief or sadness—even anger—but her emotions felt as if a bulldozer had flattened them. He had a "slut" at the club. How long had he enjoyed both of them? She gritted her teeth. At least Dark Haven had checked her for diseases. Who knew she'd be grateful?

Why hadn't she seen through Nathan? The signs had been there. He belonged to a BDSM club. He'd wanted to add more kink to their sex life but hadn't invited her to join. They never had a date on a Friday night. She'd been blind.

How had he figured out she was doing research? Her teeth gritted together as she realized that he hadn't guessed. He'd just thrown out the accusation to be vindictive. Unfortunately, he'd been right.

Noise burst into the cabin as someone pounded on the door. *Xavier.*

Her heart thumped so hard it probably cracked ribs. She froze for a minute, and in that interval he pounded again. The sound was a blatant indication that their talk wouldn't go well.

She pulled open the door. "I'm sor—"

Not Xavier. Logan stood on the doorstep. His face was so cold that the scarred-up dog behind him looked friendlier. "I'm taking you to town. Get your things."

"But—"

His expression didn't encourage questions.

"Right."

So Xavier had decided not to talk to her. Her hopes crumbled like winter leaves. She grabbed her purse and turned to get her bag, but Logan had already picked it up and waited by the door.

They walked to the parking area, and she climbed into his pickup truck.

Silence.

By the time the truck turned onto the larger highway toward Bear Flat, Abby's hands had curled into fists. This was unbearable. She pulled in a breath. "I'm sorry."

"Yeah." She felt the weight of his gaze. "I'm disappointed in you."

Was this what being flayed alive felt like? She stared at her hands. The roughness of his voice made it clear she'd hurt him. Hurt Becca. *Reassure him about the paper*. "I need to explain."

"I'm not going to discuss this with you, Abby. Not until you've talked with Xavier."

An interminable amount of time later, he drove into the tiny town of Bear Flat and parked. As she slid out of the truck, he plucked her bag out of the back and stowed it in a familiar-looking SUV. *Please, don't let that be Xavier's car.*

"Where's Simon?" Abby asked faintly, dread growing in her belly.

"They left a couple of hours ago." Logan's hard mouth curled slightly. "Xavier needs someone to drive him, and since he wants to talk with you alone, you got your ass drafted.

"Needs… Did he get drunk or something?"

Logan nudged her onto the boardwalk.

But they walked past the police station. The next building's window displayed BEAR FLAT MEDICAL CLINIC in black lettering.

Xavier was hurt? She grabbed Logan's arm and yanked him to a stop. "You tell me what happened. Right now!"

"He fell off a cliff."

* * * *

In an exam room, Xavier sat in a wheelchair and tried to ignore the pain. His ankle throbbed, his head hammered, and his shoulder persisted in sending burning stabs through the joint. He'd have appreciated some consistency in the texture and timing of the various hurts, but no such luck.

The clinic life went on around him. A phone ringing. A baby crying. From the room across the hall came the doctor's voice trying to reassure a child.

The tinkling sound of the front door was followed by footsteps. Xavier looked up.

Logan entered the room, followed by Abby. Her eyes widened, and the color drained from her cheeks. "You look terrible."

Despite the pain and his anger at her, he felt a hint of amusement.

Logan snorted. "You should have seen him when he was covered in blood." He gave Xavier a glance. "I didn't realize you could swear like that. Rona appreciated you switching to French."

Abby clasped her hands as if terrified to touch him. "How badly are you hurt?" Her short hair was flying everywhere, and behind her glasses, her eyes were red and swollen.

How could he be furious and still want to comfort her? "Nothing major."

"That kind of depends on your definition of *major*." Dressed in medical scrubs, Summer cast Abby an unfriendly look.

A hint of hurt appeared before Abby's expression chilled into that of a marble statue. "If I'm driving, tell me what I need to know for the trip." Her voice was as frozen as her face.

"The doctor reset his dislocated shoulder. He needs to keep the sling on. Sprained ankle. Keep it in the brace." Summer glanced at Xavier and added, "No weight on it for three days. Then a cane or crutches." She turned back to Abby. "Right now he can't use crutches because of the shoulder, so...wheelchair."

Abby nodded. “Go on.”

“Ice packs for the shoulder and ankle for twenty minutes at a time. Keep his leg elevated. He received a heavy pain medication earlier. When it wears off, ibuprofen should work. Got it?”

Xavier frowned. He’d never been talked around like this. Then again, his brain wasn’t tracking well.

“Yes.” Abby tilted her head coolly. “Thank you.”

“Let’s go, then,” Logan said. He stepped behind the wheelchair and pushed.

The boardwalk of rough wood planks almost did Xavier in. He clenched his jaw as pain stabbed through his shoulder with every bump.

When Logan opened the back door to the SUV, Xavier shook his head. “I’m not—”

“Summer’s orders. She wants that ankle elevated for a while.” Logan lowered his voice. “And you don’t want to talk with Abby until the morphine clears your system.”

Good advice should be heeded. Xavier held his hand out. “Thank you for the help.”

“Least we could do.”

“Give that dog of yours a steak for finding me.”

Logan grinned. “Becca was cooking bacon for him when we left.”

With a grunt Xavier tried to get to his feet. Logan put a hand under his good arm and lifted. The assistance was needed—and not appreciated.

As blood rushed into Xavier’s injured ankle, the pain felt like someone had turned a burner to high. His shoulder screamed with every movement, but compared to the feeling when dislocated, this was nothing. Clumsily he pivoted and slid into the backseat.

When Logan fastened Xavier's seat belt as if he were a child, Xavier managed to keep from punching him and settled for a deadly look. Logan laughed and closed the door.

Smothering a groan, Xavier settled against it.

On the other side of the car, Summer leaned in to put a pillow under his leg. She put an ice pack over the ankle and handed him another for his shoulder. As Abby climbed into the driver's seat, the nurse frowned at her. "Ignore the crankiness and do what I told you. Doms make the worst patients."

Abby nodded, glanced at him, and started the engine.

Xavier realized he didn't know if she was a good driver. After a second he closed his eyes. He didn't have the energy to care.

* * * *

Xavier woke when Abby pulled in to a gas station.

"Here." He held out a credit card.

She ignored him, filled the tank, and disappeared into the store.

By the time she returned, he'd managed to maneuver himself out of the car and into the front seat. Eventually—maybe—his ankle and shoulder would stop feeling as if they were about to explode.

She opened the driver's door and saw him. "Why aren't you in the back?"

"I'm awake. It's time to talk."

Gaze averted, she got in. In silence she drove onto Highway 120 toward San Francisco. After a minute she put the sack into his lap. "Ice. And ibuprofen. And water."

"Thank you, Abby," he said softly, watching the pink climb into her cheeks. He suppressed a sigh. She'd lied to him, spied on his club members, cheated on her boyfriend, and he wanted to comfort her. *You're an idiot, Leduc.*

He washed the ibuprofen down with water. "Tell me about your research."

"The university is doing cutbacks. I needed a publication on my record—fast—and BDSM interested me."

Because of Nathan, undoubtedly.

"To get it published in time, I have to submit the paper before July twenty-ninth." Her hands clenched and eased. "I'm writing an ethnography essay—basically my observations of what goes on." Behind her oversize glasses, her gray eyes flickered toward him and back to the road. "I wasn't taking names or talking about anything intimate or kinky. I wrote about the social interactions in the club, comparing the dynamics to that of a family."

"Personal descriptions?"

"Just gender and what position they fill in a relationship and how they fit into the club—and the hierarchy. As the owner, you could possibly be identified. No one else."

The hard knot in Xavier's gut began to unwind. Not an exposé. She didn't plan to out the members. She couldn't lie to him if he was watching for it, and she wasn't lying now.

"I want you to think back to the first scene we did." He waited until she nodded. "You were embarrassed, Abby. You felt exposed, even though others around us were also doing scenes. How would you have felt if you realized someone was studying you like a research monkey?"

Pink flowed up her neck and into her face. He'd never known anyone who blushed so often—or so beautifully.

"Answer me."

"I would have...have left." Her gaze stayed on the road, but her fingers tightened on the steering wheel. A car passed them. A logging truck rumbled past on the other side. "I didn't think writing about a social network could possibly hurt anyone or put them at risk. And the lifestyle wouldn't welcome a sociologist, but I hoped my paper would help BDSM be more accepted. I wanted to show the honesty and communication. The caring. I thought it would be good for the community."

Wanting to help. Yes, she might have started the project because she needed the paper, but in a uniquely Abby way she'd ended up trying to help. Xavier's anger kept seeping away. "Go on."

"People weren't in a bedroom—they were in a club, doing intimate performances right out in public. So how could it be wrong to observe? That's what I thought." Her eyes gleamed with tears. "But I saw the reactions last night. And Summer's today. I should have realized that, to the members, they're not in public but inside their family. I was blind."

She bit her lip. "Or maybe I didn't want to see it."

For someone so intelligent, that was a difficult acknowledgment. "You probably didn't."

Her voice dropped. "I can't think of how to make it right."

True repentance. Xavier took a slow breath, fighting the way she softened his heart. The research was only the first of her offenses. The taste of the second was bitter. "You and Nathan are lovers? Involved?"

"*For months,*" Nathan had said.

"We were during the spring." Her laugh held a doleful note. "He broke up with me before he left for Maine. The day before I came to the club."

Before I ever saw her. Another hard ball in his chest loosened. "Did you join because of him? Partly?"

Her lips trembled as she nodded. "I thought if I learned more, maybe we could make it work. Maybe I'd be comfortable with what he wanted."

She hadn't appeared *comfortable* last night.

"I'm a moron," she said under her breath.

"Why do you say that?"

"We had a committed relationship. Monogamous. We'd agreed. But that girl last night knew him. He'd been...with...her before, hadn't he?" She glanced at him.

"If you're asking if their scenes included sex, then yes." Xavier rubbed his shoulder and winced at the pain. "So the first day at the club, you told me the truth when you said no significant other."

"Of course. I wouldn't lie." Dismay filled her face. "You thought I had. Last night you believed I'd cheated on Nathan with you." She stared straight at the highway, blinking away tears. Slowly her chin firmed.

She hadn't lied to him. The rush of relief was unsettling. He might tell himself that it was because he hadn't misread her personality, but he knew better. "I'm pleased to know you weren't cheating, Abby. More relieved than I like."

"I don't particularly care." She blinked her eyes hard. "I'm no concern of yours."

He shifted in his seat to study her. Her jaw was tight, her eyes haunted. Nathan Kemp had damaged her ego—*and so did I.* Her self-confidence in relationships had been fragile to begin with.

Unfortunately he wasn't the Dom to put things right. She needed someone who could commit to her. That someone wasn't him, and the thought of doing her further harm was more than he could bear. She'd already decided to break off any relationship with him. This was obviously the right time for her to return to her own life.

* * * *

"Nice place," Abby said, staring at the golden and tan Mediterranean-style home. How could Xavier's club possibly provide enough income to afford a Tiburon mansion overlooking the bay?

His lips twitched. "Thank you."

The door to a three-car garage slid up, and she pulled in.

Without waiting for her, Xavier got out. With his sprained ankle off the ground, he held on to the car door as she unpacked the light wheelchair and wheeled it over.

"I appreciate the chauffeur service, Abby. Come in, and I'll call you a taxi," he said. When he tried to wheel up the incline into the house, she realized he couldn't use his right arm—and a wheelchair required both. As he used his uninjured foot to assist, the muscles on his jaw grew tighter. He was hurting and too stubborn to ask her for help.

The big bad Dom would normally expect a submissive to serve him…but she wasn't his. The knowledge was demoralizing. Painful. He might have forgiven her to some degree, but what they'd started… That was gone. He'd undoubtedly written her off as a total loser.

Which was good. She'd given up on men, right? Jaw clenched, she pushed the wheelchair up the ramp into the house.

They entered a tall foyer with red-gold hardwood flooring. The walls held the creamy warmth of the exterior. Stairs curved up to an inside balcony.

"In there, please." He pointed, and she wheeled him across the wide space into a living room. The subtle colors of the beige walls and carpet and white leather furniture were a quiet frame for the stunning view of Angel Island and San Francisco across the bay.

"How beautiful."

"Thank you." When he pulled out his cell phone and punched a button, she realized he had a taxi service on speed dial. Maybe for his club members? Or maybe he sent all his women home this way.

She wasn't one of them, though, was she? Odd how depression could darken the sunlight streaming through the glass. As she walked to the window, her brows drew together. With a two-story house, the master bedroom was probably upstairs. How would he get up there?

Not my problem. The couch looked comfortable, and he was an adult. But when the taxi service chirped a busy signal, her mouth overruled her mind. "Who will you call to stay with you?"

"I'll manage, thank you." His black eyes held no emotion. He punched a redial into the phone.

"You can't. You need someone here to help you."

"It's not your problem, Abigail." His mouth flattened. *Busy signal. Redial.*

"I bet you've got ibuprofen upstairs in your master bath. Your clothes will be up there. But you can't get up the stairs, can you? You certainly can't cook, balancing on one leg and using one hand."

"That's enough," he snapped. His anger came through clearly. *Busy. Redial.*

Fear turned the pale walls an ugly red, and her heart banged against her rib cage, knocking her back a step. *He's furious. Don't make him yell. Just stop.*

He'd manage. He'd be fine.

He *wouldn't.*

"You need someone to help you." She snatched the phone out of his hand. "I'm staying the night, so deal with it. Y-yell at me if you want to, but I'm s-staying." Her shoulders knotted. She braced her legs, preparing for the screams. The names. Nausea twisted her stomach.

His mouth opened...and closed. He leaned back. His gaze traveled from the phone in her tight grip upward in a comprehensive sweep to linger on her face. "If I can't get out of this chair, Abby, why are you afraid of me?"

She blinked.

The anger was gone from his voice as if it had never occurred. Resting his elbow on the chair arm, he cupped his chin in his hand and watched her.

"I'm not afraid."

"Really?" His gaze didn't waver. "Apparently you continue to have difficulty identifying your emotions. Are your muscles tight? Hands sweaty?"

She resisted the urge to rub her palms on her jeans. "This is—"

"Abby."

"Fine. Yes."

"Your eyes are wide. Is your breathing fast or slow?"

She was panting. Had retreated a step. "Okay. I'm scared." Which seemed really stupid.

"Do you think I'd hurt you?"

"No! No, you wouldn't."

"Then *what* are you afraid of?" As his voice rose, she flinched. His eyes narrowed. "Who used to yell at you, Abby?"

"That isn't—"

An eyebrow rose slightly in the ominous signal of a Dom growing impatient.

She was far more submissive than she'd thought, because the answer slid from her as if greased. "My father."

His finger stroked the beard stubble on his jaw. "Was he abusive?"

"It wasn't like that." She walked to the window, needing space. A view. An escape from those penetrating eyes. "He had cancer. A brain tumor. We didn't know—he wasn't diagnosed until a year or two later."

A gull soared over the ferryboat churning across the choppy waves toward Pier Thirty-Nine. Her father had loved to visit the wharf, but then the bustling became more than he could tolerate. "If he got excited at all, he'd burst into a rage. For so long, we didn't understand why. We thought we'd made him mad, and Mom would cry."

"Just you and your mother?"

"Um-hmm." The backyard had a wide stone patio with a pool and hot tub. Grassy stretches extended on each side like wings. Farther out, the land rolled downhill. "Xavier, it's not imp—"

"What happened after he was diagnosed? Did it get better?"

"Of c-course." At last they'd known *why*. And his berserk screaming fits had been far better than the blankness that eventually consumed his personality. Before the cancer, her father had been an even-tempered, brilliant archeologist. Near the end, in his few moments of lucidity, he couldn't bear what he'd become. "*My death will be a blessing, baby. A gift.*" He'd patted her hand. And then he'd cried.

A flicker drew her attention to where a hummingbird visited a bright globe hanging from a tree branch. In the next tree, two sparrows perched on a stained-glass feeder. Life, big and small, went on. And Mr. Oh-So-Stern My Liege fed the birds?

"Come here." That note again, the one that said he expected her to obey.

She turned.

His hand was out. Open. Waiting. And very warm when his fingers folded around hers. "How did you and your mother cope?"

Looking down at him, she made a noise that should have been a laugh but didn't sound like anything funny. "Very carefully. For a long time, as long as he didn't get upset, he did well. He never hurt us, just yelled. Called us names." She shrugged.

"So you did everything you could to keep him calm, didn't you?"

The understanding in his expression made her eyes burn. “Where’s your ibuprofen?”

“This is why you freeze up when you think someone will yell.” He held her trapped for another minute. “But you risked my temper because you were worried about me.” A corner of his mouth edged up; his eyes filled with tenderness. “Your courage wins the battle, little fluff. I have a bottle of ibuprofen upstairs in the master bathroom.”

He hadn’t yelled, had actually complimented her for being rude. She ran up the stairs, feeling as if she’d been staggering and found her balance. Her throat was tight.

He’d called her his favorite name again.

Chapter Sixteen

That evening in the guest bath, Xavier scratched his cheek, grimacing at the day-old beard growth. At least Abby hadn't offered to shave him.

Determined little submissive. If he hadn't had a downstairs bedroom, she'd have insisted on helping him up the stairs—and been flattened, trying to save him.

Maybe he should put in an elevator. A man couldn't predict accidents.

With frustrating slowness, he cleaned up, then used his foot and good arm to wheel himself into the bedroom. Lowering his ankle made it swell into a throbbing balloon.

He transferred to the bed, grateful that his shoulder had died down to a dull ache. With a grunt of pain, he took off the sling and his shirt.

"Whoa." Holding a serving tray, Abby stood in the doorway and stared at him. "You look as if someone beat on you with a club."

He glanced down. Scrapes everywhere. A jagged slice from something sharp ran across his upper pectoral. Bruises made black shadows on his dark skin. "Better me than you. With your delicate skin, you'd look like a patchwork quilt."

Her throaty laugh was a treat. After calling her tenants to babysit the puppies another night, she'd been a solemn owl during supper.

"Here's your ibuprofen." She set the tray down and handed him a couple of pills and a glass of water. As he sipped, she cleaned his scrapes and very, very gently dabbed antibiotic ointment on each.

"I'm not going to break."

"I don't want you to hurt." Her voice was soft with a resolve that shook him. "Stand up, and I'll get your pants off."

He'd often commanded slaves to unclothe him, but when he actually needed the service, the pleasure turned sour. Jaw clenched against a growl, he rose, balanced on one foot, and pushed his jeans down. After he sat, she knelt in front of him to pull them off.

Another change. Usually if he had a woman on her knees in front of him, he had something better for her to do.

"Lie back," she ordered. Her serious tone lightened his mood. As he complied she primly covered him with a sheet before arranging a pillow under his leg.

"Do you enjoy having me under your command?" he asked.

She laughed.

"Do you?"

Her hand came to rest on his lower leg like a bird ready to fly at the least movement. "I..." Her delightful mind engaged and hummed.

"Go on."

"Not really. I just like seeing you comfortable."

"Knowing you fixed it all?" When she absently stroked circles over his skin, he realized he wasn't completely overwhelmed by pain.

"Sounds rather pompous, doesn't it?"

No, it sounded like the glow a service submissive got from helping others. When he'd seen her contentment in feeding the pups, he should have recognized the trait. He frowned. Her father's behavior must have traumatized a child who wanted only to please. "You like helping."

"Of course. Doesn't everyone?"

"Not…quite. Think about after an orgasm. You're closer to your partner; everything in the world feels right."

Her cheeks turned pink. "And?"

"Some submissives feel that way when they meet the needs of others." He reached down to take her hand. "Is that how you feel now?"

"Um. I suppose. I never noticed before, but yes."

A submissive's satisfaction was increased when serving her Master. Only he wasn't, shouldn't be. Didn't want to be. *Don't lie to yourself, Leduc.*

If he let her go now, she'd disappear from his life. He'd thought that would be the best choice for both of them. Now he was beginning to wonder. "Your relationship with Nathan is over, correct?"

"Oh, definitely." Perhaps realizing what his question implied, she tried to pull her hand away.

"Little fluff, you stubbornly inserted yourself into my life, even when I was angry. What happens now that I'm not angry?"

"I…don't know." Eyes the gray of the city fog met his. "I don't want another relationship. Not for a long, long time."

He understood. Time must pass before the feeling of being betrayed would lessen. For both of them. And yet… "During the chess game, we'd reached an agreement."

"That was before."

Before the disaster. She wanted to be with him. But she didn't know him well, and she'd been hurt. How brave was the little professor?

"Besides, in a day or so you won't need me," she said.

He studied her. "You believe I want you here only because I'm injured?" Nathan had really damaged her self-confidence.

"Well…yes." Her gaze was straight and level.

Again he was pleased he hadn't misread her honesty; although in order to keep the peace, she buried matters she should share. They'd work on the problem.

"Lie down here." He patted his chest. Her expression turned wary as she registered his shift from friendly to dominant. But she wanted this, even if she didn't recognize it.

"It'll hurt your ankle."

His frown stopped further protests. His leg was angled to one side with his ankle safely cushioned on a pillow. He took her hand and pulled her down on top of him. As she gave in and snuggled against him, her legs between his, he wrapped his good arm around her.

Yes, he wanted her to stay. "Let's discuss this." He rubbed his chin on the top of her silky hair. She was as cuddly as her puppies. "Can you share why you think I don't want more from you than servitude?"

"Aren't discussions supposed to be two-sided?"

"Yes, they are." He grinned. Intelligent women were amazingly sexy. He laid his palm on the curve between her shoulder and neck, resting his thumb on her carotid artery. A little fast. "I'll let you start so I can answer your concerns."

Her huff held exasperation and a touch of anxiety. She remained silent for a minute. "First, you don't like me much after finding out about the research. Second, you were angry about Nathan. You thought I'd lied to you. Third, I hear the women you bring here are impeccably trained slaves. Fourth, I'm not glamorous or gorgeous enough for you. Fifth, we're not alike at all. I'm middle-class. And a nerd."

She was delightful. He kept his chin on her head, not wanting her feelings hurt if she saw him smile. "Nice and orderly. First, I understand why you infiltrated my club—your fear of being laid off and to find out more about BDSM." For someone who didn't deserve her. "Since the end is so close, I'm inclined to let you continue…under certain conditions."

She jerked in surprise. "Really?"

"*If* I read and approve of the paper. And if you make amends to the club members. I'd have to announce what you were doing, so those who feel uncomfortable can stay away."

"But you'd do that?"

"Ah…" Yes, he should warn her. "Abby, you've seen submissives punished. How much does this matter to you?"

Her soft body tensed. He heard her swallow. "What would I have to do?"

"I won't share that with you until the time comes."

Another swallow.

"Okay," she whispered. "I need to finish my research—and to apologize to people."

"Excellent. I'll have something to look forward to."

Her under-the-breath, "Oh, good," made him chuckle.

"Second, I was angry about Nathan. But he lied. You didn't. At this point I'm simply sorry that he hurt you."

She pulled in a shuddering breath and buried her head in his shoulder. Her job at risk, her lover cheating on her. Poor professor. His desire to make her world right surprised him, not in the existence, but in the intensity.

"Third, I do invite trained slaves here, both for my enjoyment and because I need to know them to find them the best Master."

Her head lifted. "You help slaves without Masters because of Catherine, don't you? Because she was so lost."

The ache of grief had softened, not died. "Yes. That's why."

"I thought the slaves served *you*, not another Master."

"When they're here, they do. In any way I ask."

"Oh." She'd stiffened in his arms.

"But I prefer a Dominant/submissive relationship to Master/slave, Abby."

She didn't relax. A little insecurity in a submissive wasn't a bad thing, but her doubts shouldn't be whether the Dominant cared. Time to direct that uneasiness into a different channel. "Sit up and straddle me. Then unbutton your shirt."

Her eyes widened.

No, I'm not an easy man. He waited.

Biting her lip, she pushed up and rested her weight on his hips. Button by button she opened her flannel shirt. Such creamy skin.

"Pretty bra, but it's in my way. Open it."

Her breathing increased as she undid the front latch.

"Very good." With his left hand, he pushed her arms to the sides and pulled open her shirt. Her nipples had contracted into pale pink buds. "You have beautiful breasts, little fluff. I enjoy looking at them."

He also enjoyed the tiny shiver that ran through her. Rather than touching her as expected, he continued. "What was four again?"

Her pale brows drew together; she'd forgotten their discussion. "Um. Glamorous."

"Ah. And gorgeous." *Women.* At least men usually worried only if their dicks were big enough. Females worried about everything: hips, chest, hair, fingers. He'd heard one woman fret over the shape of her fingernails. "Ninety-nine percent of glamour is from the clothing and makeup." Although he dated flashy women for social functions—mostly for the effect on other men—he rarely asked them out more than three or four times. But that number was irrelevant; the point was that Abby felt insecure. "Now, I wouldn't call you gorgeous."

"No, I'm not."

"But you are lovely."

"I'm what?" Surprise chased across her expression.

"We'll use my definitions," he said, striving for a properly pompous professorial tone. "Gorgeous indicates a surface beauty. Loveliness is a gestalt of personality and appearance, both required." He smiled. "One of my earliest lovers was a French woman. Older, with wrinkles. Sagging skin and breasts. Big nose. Not gorgeous. But she had confidence, kindness, and a joyful sexuality that couldn't be resisted. Wherever she went, men followed as if on a leash. Me included."

Abby's gray eyes lit as if the sun had risen behind morning clouds.

"Now there," he murmured. "When you smile, you have the same appeal." He stroked his finger down her cheek. "You're like a luminous moon fairy, and added to that is your sweetness and intelligence. You're lovely, Abby."

Her face was confused. Vulnerable.

"Didn't Nathan ever tell you that?" *Oh, bad, Leduc.* Not the time to bring up former lovers.

Color rolled into her cheeks. "I've been called pretty." A hint of pain crossed her face. "My stepsister is...gorgeous...and she could take a man away from me with a snap of her fingers."

And obviously had. Life wasn't always fair. "If that was her typical behavior, I daresay she lost them as quickly."

She gave a husky chuckle. "I guess she did."

"You delight me, Abby." Xavier curled his fingers over her nape and drew her down. He kissed her gently. Her instant response never failed to please him.

When he released her, she pushed back up to stare at him. Her fluffy hair fell over her cheeks.

"Last concern, you think we're not alike at all." A kiss. "If you're a nerd, and I'm the opposite, does that mean you believe I'm stupid?"

She inhaled sharply, spotting the insult. He let her see the disapproval in his eyes.

"No. Of course not. That's not what I meant."

"We're both smart, then?" he asked. She was trapped. Why men needed to hunt the forests, he'd never understood. Not when there was so much better sport at home.

"Yes."

"Mmmmh." He touched her chin. "If I told you I came from a redneck working family, would you tell me I wasn't good enough for you? Because your family has more money?"

"No. That isn't it."

Tenderhearted little fluff. "Then I lack any understanding of your last point."

She glared at him. "You're definitely not stupid."

He grinned and set his hand back on her neck. "Now it's my turn, isn't it?"

He felt her pulse pick up. "Yes, I believe so."

"Hmm. One, I like you, Abigail. I like your intelligence, your laugh, your willingness to care for puppies and grumpy Doms, your wayward hair, and the way your mind works."

Her eyes were wide now as she drank in his words like a plant at the end of a drought.

"Two, as a Dom I look for a certain personality in a submissive." He ran his finger over her lower lip, feeling the tiny quiver, so quickly controlled. "You love to help, to make people—and puppies—happy. But you don't surrender to every man walking in the door. Not even Nathan." He smiled at her. "It seems you've reserved your submission for me, and I value that.

"Three, you enjoy a fair amount of erotic pain, but you're not a masochist. You don't have any hard limits that would bother me, and as far as I've found, you don't want something I can't provide."

Her eyes kept getting wider.

"Four, I liked having you in my home today, even though I'm not at my best. I'd like you to be here longer, so I can treat you"—he tugged her nipple firmly enough that her back arched and her eyes dilated—"a bit rougher."

He pulled her down for a long, wet kiss. "I can't think of a number five. Do you have anything you want to counter with?"

"I… No."

"Then we'll simply see how it goes. Stay here with me, Abby."

"As a slave?"

"No, little fluff. As a sexual submissive." He grinned when a shiver ran through her. "Your life is your own." He rubbed his knuckles over her smooth cheek. "I just get to rule it now and then." He waited.

"I'll stay. My liege."

"Excellent. Go clean up. Then come back here."

She shook her head. "It's not a good idea. I might bump your leg."

"You'll sleep with me." He pointed at the bathroom. "There are spare toothbrushes and such in the drawers."

As she slid off the bed, he studied her face. The worry was gone, leaving peace behind. She wanted his control as much as he wanted to exert it. And although terrified of altercations, she'd dared his displeasure for his own good. She was a bundle of contradictions, wasn't she?

She returned, face pink from scrubbing.

"Clothes off."

Her fingers shook as she removed her shirt. After setting her glasses on the bedside table, she flipped the light switch to put the room in darkness before stripping the rest of the way.

"Did you acquire something I haven't seen before?"

"That's not the point. Can I sleep in one of your T-shirts?"

"No, you may not." No submissive wore clothes in his bed.

With a grumbling mutter, she carefully crawled in beside him. Ignoring her attempt to keep a distance, he pulled her closer. His immobility made him want to curse—moving her would have been easier with two arms.

Her body stayed stiff and motionless for a minute, and then she relaxed with a disgruntled sound. "Are you really all right?"

"Sore and irritated, but tomorrow will be better." He tightened his arm around her. "Thank you for your care, Abby."

She rubbed her cheek on his shoulder. "You're welcome."

He thought about something and sighed. “I assume I’m getting five puppies as interim boarders?”

Her laugh lifted his heart.

Yes, it felt right to have her snuggled close as the quiet of the night surrounded them.

Chapter Seventeen

Trying not to gawk, Abby stopped at the lobby desk in the building where Xavier's office was located.

Phone to her ear, the receptionist smiled and held up a finger to wait.

Not a problem. Abby turned in a circle to admire the two-story foyer. Rather than a typical ultrasleek modern design, the lobby had long planters of foliage taking advantage of the light streaming in from the all-glass front. The massive desk was a beautiful curve of dark wood that matched that of the inner balcony railing above. The fragrance of pastries and coffee came from an espresso shop to one side.

"Can I help you?" the receptionist asked, setting down the phone.

"I'm here to see Xavier Leduc. Could you tell me what office he's in?"

"Do you have an appointment?" The older woman wore a dark-red suit, her hair and makeup impeccable.

"No. Not exactly."

The woman frowned at Abby's jeans and green hoodie. "Miss, if you want to fill out a job application, then you need office one hundred, right over there." She pointed to a glass-fronted office across the wide foyer. "Just go inside, and someone will help you."

"Thank you, but I'm not looking for a job. I'm picking Xavier up."

Short and squat, the woman reminded Abby of a bulldog. Fully as stubborn too. "Mr. Leduc doesn't—"

"I'm sorry. I don't want to cause problems for you. But he *is* expecting me. Please just let him know that Abigail is here."

Her stubbornness won out. "Of course, miss. If you'll wait over there, I'll ring his admin."

As Abby took a well-cushioned chair in a beautifully appointed waiting area, she frowned. Why would the owner of a BDSM club need an admin? Or an office in this fancy building for that matter. Then again, considering his home, the club must be making some pretty good money. Or maybe he had another business as well?

Honestly, though, he could have left word so she didn't have to fight off territorial bulldogs.

As she picked up a magazine, she glanced at the reception desk. The woman had summoned a security guard. *For heaven's sake.*

"She says she's picking up Mr. Leduc," Ms. Bulldog said in a low tone.

Abby looked down before the guard turned. He made a laughing sound. "She's sure nothing like his usual lady friends."

"Exactly. I'm calling Mrs. Benton now. Can you show her out when his admin tells me she's never heard of her?" Clicking sounds. "Yes, Mrs. Benton, I have an Abigail here saying she's supposed to pick up Mr.— Excuse me? Send her up if she wouldn't mind?" The bulldog actually sputtered.

Abby smothered a grin. *Okay, Xavier, you're forgiven all the nasty thoughts.*

"Miss?"

She looked up. The security guard smiled politely. Respectfully. "I'll escort you up."

The guard used a locked elevator at the end of the elevator banks. When he punched the highest button, Abby's stomach roiled like she'd chugged a soda.

She swallowed. "Does this building have a name? I didn't see a sign."

"Nah. Something smashed it in the last storm, and the new one isn't finished yet. *Leduc Industries*, it's called."

"The whole building?" *Oh, this isn't good.* Whether it felt like stalking or not, she should have googled the man. She felt like thumping her head against the elevator door. "How many Leducs are there?"

The door slid open silently, and the guard stepped out with her. The creamy carpet was thick enough to drown in, and the statuary looked much like what was in Xavier's home.

"How many?" He gave her a startled look "Just the one."

Abby closed her eyes and pulled in a breath. *Don't be a moron—Xavier is the same man.* He hadn't changed because she learned he had a bit more money than a club owner did. A whole lot more money. *Don't get all weird.* Even as she told herself that, she wished she'd worn something nicer than jeans, running shoes, and a hooded sweatshirt.

"You must be Dr. Bern." The brunette woman rose from behind the desk. Her brown eyes were surprisingly welcoming. “I’m Mrs. Benton, Mr. Leduc’s administrative assistant. Let me show you the way.”

But it wasn’t necessary. An office door opened, and Xavier wheeled himself out. Or tried to. The plush carpet wasn’t wheelchair friendly, especially when he couldn’t use both arms. He smiled a welcome, but the muscles of his face were tight, his cheekbones stark, and his color almost gray. “Abby, I’m—”

“You didn’t take any pain meds, did you? Or use ice packs.” She glared. “Or let anyone help you.”

He looked taken aback for a second, then burst into laughter. The admin and guard seemed appalled.

“Abby, you are a wonder.” He held his hand out. As his fingers closed around hers, she realized she’d automatically crossed the room. The man could command her without a word.

“And you’re too stubborn for words,” she said under her breath. She turned. “Mrs. Benton, could you get him a glass of water?”

“Of course.” The woman studied Abby. “You mentioned ice packs. I can contrive one of sorts, if you’d like?”

No wonder Xavier had her. “Two, if you could? That would be wonderful.”

After giving Xavier a deferential nod, the guard popped back into the elevator.

As Abby searched her purse for ibuprofen, Xavier chuckled. “You, little fluff, are fully as stubborn as I am. If you don’t mind waiting for about ten minutes, I have one last call to finish.”

“No problem.”

"You can come in with me or wait out here, wherever you're more comfortable."

Wait in the reception area? Not a chance. When he tried to turn his wheelchair, she gave a snort of exasperation and pushed him back into his office.

"Nice place you have." From the waist up, two whole walls were glass, opening to a spectacular view of the city. His desk was gleaming walnut with matching chairs in front. A dark leather couch and chairs sat off to one side. She approved of the huge painting of a French café. She'd had a glass of wine there last time she'd been in Paris.

"Thank you." He smiled at her. "Did you get the pups settled in?"

"Moved and fed and sleeping." Since his office chair had been pushed into a corner, Abby maneuvered Xavier behind his desk. With a frown of concern, she raised the foot part of the wheelchair to elevate his leg. "Your ankle is swollen again."

"Is it?" Laughter in his eyes, he ran a finger over her scowling lips.

"It's not funny, you—"

"Maybe these will help." Mrs. Benton handed Xavier the water. Abby received two plastic bags filled with ice.

"Thank you very much." Abby gave the admin a smile and Xavier another frown. After positioning the packs, she retreated to the couch while Xavier took his pills and made his phone call.

A minute later Mrs. Benton brought a pile of magazines and a tray with a cup and tiny pot of tea, sugar, and lemon slices. "When the receptionist downstairs called up, Mr. Leduc mentioned you enjoy tea with lemon."

He'd not only thought about her comfort, but remembered what she liked. The knowledge made her feel fuzzy and warm.

Then again, considering he knew her so well, how badly would that come back to bite her at the club? Her insides clenched as she remembered the plan for Friday—punishment at Dark Haven.

No point in imagining herself into hysterics, though. She picked up a magazine, leafed through the pages, and eavesdropped on his conversation.

He was trying to get a woman into some kind of a job, but her reading skills weren't up to the employer's qualifications. In fact, the woman sounded functionally illiterate.

With a growl of frustration, Xavier ended the conversation.

"What's wrong?" Abby asked.

He rubbed his face, looking tired. "Rona took an interest in a patient in her hospital and wanted us to find her a job. She's had recent surgery. Unfortunately she has no skills and can't read. It's not looking good."

I am so confused. "Who's *us*, and what exactly do you do here?"

He glanced at her, then smiled. "We never discussed my occupation, did we?" He leaned back, making the wheelchair look like a throne. *My liege, indeed.* "Leduc Industries owns a variety of businesses. I prefer to acquire hotels, cleaning and landscaping services, food prep—places that can employ women who are down on their luck, like those who are newly divorced or support themselves and their children."

Amazing. "But how can you screen for that kind of background?"

He grinned. “A nonprofit organization, Stella’s Employment Services, has the first few floors of the building. They handle applications, training, and referrals. Their applicants are encouraged to keep learning, to move up and out, going on to better jobs and better lives.”

“Don’t tell me—you own the employment service as well? Isn’t that rather altruistic for a hard-nosed businessman.”

He gave her a Gallic shrug. “I saw the struggle my mother went through to find a job after my father divorced her. The employment market isn’t friendly to the unskilled.”

A light was beginning to dawn. “What was your mother’s name?”

“Clever professor.” His lips quirked up. “Her name was Stella.”

First he was the owner of a kink club, then a big-shot CEO, and now a tenderhearted man running a charity because of his mother. She felt dizzy. Intimidating on the outside, but inside? This was the man who’d insisted on helping her feed puppies. Who let a little boy check out his long braid. Who let a punished submissive cry on his shoulder.

“I haven’t run into the literacy problem before.” His frown turned to concern. “Women must fill out applications in the office. I didn’t realize the restriction might be a problem, but someone who couldn’t read wouldn’t even apply.”

“’Fraid not. Around twenty to thirty million Americans lack the reading ability to fill out a job application.”

He eyed her. "The professor checks out statistics on literacy?"

"I told you I teach reading. That's why I couldn't attend the club's classes."

Elbow on the side arm of the chair, he rubbed a finger over his lips. "Well, Professor Bern, at the time I assumed you were a grade-school teacher. Teaching subjects like reading, writing, and arithmetic."

How mixed up could things have gotten? "I volunteer for a local literacy project, teaching women to read." She smiled. "The program is booked solid, but I'm allowed some leeway. Want me to add your person to my class?"

"You're full of surprises."

"Back at you, my liege. You might have mentioned you do more than own a BDSM club."

"True." His gaze heated. "We have a lot of...exploring...yet to do." Giving her that imperial stare, he crooked a finger at her.

Her pulse started to speed. When she reached his chair, he tangled his fingers in her hair and pulled her down for a long, hot kiss. As her head spun, she braced herself on the arms of his chair.

He gave a rumbling sound of satisfaction. "Keep your hands right there." His deep voice had roughened. He released her hair and slid his hand under her shirt. By tugging her bra upward, he freed one breast to fondle. His gaze on her face, he rolled a nipple between his fingers.

She pulled in a hard breath, caught his exotic scent, and felt the dampness growing between her legs.

"I have plans for you, little fluff," he murmured. "Let's go home."

After straightening her clothing, she wheeled him out. When they reached Mrs. Benton's desk, the woman bade him a polite good night before turning to Abby. "He said a power chair wouldn't fit in a car, but there's no law against keeping one here. I've ordered one, and he'll use it, even if only for a few more days." She shook her head. "I have two teenage boys, and I know the drill for injuries: ice, elevate, and pain meds. Tomorrow I'll ignore his growling and take better care of him."

"You're a brave woman, Mrs. Benton. Thank you," Abby said sincerely.

As the elevator doors closed, Xavier frowned. "Now you're corrupting my staff. I'll need two hands to beat you adequately, but be assured I'm keeping count."

After a second of worry, she relaxed because the look in his eyes wasn't one of anger, but...something else.

Two could play at this game. She set her hands on the arms of his wheelchair. "Considering what you plan to do at home, you should be more polite, Mr. Leduc. You might need someone to do all the work."

His eyes narrowed, and his hand fisted the front of her hoodie. "You're correct—about someone working. As I recall, you have some lessons coming in the fine art of sucking."

Her mouth dropped open, and he released her hair to trace a line around it. "Yes. My cock between those pretty lips."

The elevator door slid open.

As she pushed his wheelchair past the bulldog receptionist and the guard, she could feel the wetness between her legs.

Chapter Eighteen

I don't want to do this. Abby was shaking with fear. As Xavier limped into Dark Haven, she wanted to stop him and tell him that she changed her mind.

At the reception desk Lindsey handed a waiting Dom a bright-green wristband and looked over with a smile. She spotted Abby, and her face turned cold.

Abby closed her eyes and swallowed down tears.

"Good evening, Lindsey," Xavier said.

"Good evening, my liege."

In the locker area, Xavier took Abby's coat and hung it up, leaving her naked except for her glasses.

She stopped at the door to the main room. *I forgot to put on my big-girl panties.* "Wait."

"No, pet." He pushed her inside.

She tried a calming breath. It didn't work.

"Stay brave." He led the way across the room.

Staying a step behind him, she focused on the backs of his boots. The temperature took a decided drop as whispers whipped around her like sleet, stinging her skin.

He climbed the stairs to the left-hand stage, leaning heavily on his cane.

She hesitated. *I'd really prefer to stay down here, thank you very much.* He glanced back, motioned, and she followed. Clasping her numb hands in front of her, she stared at her bare feet.

"If I might have your attention." Xavier's voice held no emotion. He wasn't gloating about her punishment. If anything, his attitude was sympathetic—although inflexible.

Someone at the bar cut the music to the dance floor, and silence spilled across the room.

"I posted on the members' Web site and sent you all an e-mail about Abigail's research. By doing her fieldwork here without my knowledge or the consent of the members, she has broken club rules...as well as the unspoken ethics of our community."

The angry murmuring was in agreement. Guilt washed through Abby again.

"However, I read the ethnography essay as well as the notes she kept. She presents our community in a good light. No names appear. Dark Haven isn't mentioned by name or location. Members are not described. No scene descriptions are used. Basically she's looking at the club dynamics in an interesting way, like an extended family, showing the social network, the interactions, and the hierarchy."

The crowd was silent.

"Since I'm at the top of that hierarchy, I rather enjoyed it."

Mild laughter.

"If she survives tonight and still wishes to be a member of this club, I've given her permission to finish her research here tomorrow and next weekend. I'll post a sign in the reception area and send an announcement to the members, so you can stay away if you wish. Once the paper is finished, a copy will be available online for anyone interested, and concerns can be addressed before she sends it to the journal for publication. Questions so far?"

"What do you mean if she survives tonight?" A woman's voice, strong and self-assured.

"I'm speaking of her punishment, Angela. It's divided into two parts, and the members who were wronged are invited to participate."

That started a murmur of approval.

Abby bit her lip. Xavier hadn't told her what he planned.

"Are you talking blood sports, Xavier?" DeVries's rough voice was all too recognizable, and Abby shivered. Blood? She'd have stepped back, but her feet were frozen to the floor.

"No blood. Sorry," Xavier said.

"Well, now I'm really disappointed." The Enforcer's voice didn't match his words—he didn't sound upset.

"Members present on the same nights as Abby should have received a green band," Xavier said. "Abigail's first session is on the spanking bench. Any Dom or *submissive* can trade me their green band and administer one swat with the paddle."

Abby felt a tremor run through her and stiffened her spine. *It's just pain.*

"She'll get a short recess. Then, since she was 'observing' people, Abigail will be blindfolded and hooked up to the fucking machine. Any Dom can exchange the band for one minute with the controls. I'll monitor and stop the machine before she can orgasm. At the end of that time you'll see—and undoubtedly hear—her climax. Since she observed yours, you may now observe hers."

Applause broke out.

Oh no, absolutely no. She wrapped her arms around herself as her whole body shook.

"When her punishment ends, she will apologize, and then, as we do for a properly penitent submissive, we forgive her. Questions or complaints?"

Murmuring.

"Sounds quite fair, Xavier," a Dom called.

"Thanks for letting us participate in her punishment," another said. "We know you didn't have to do that."

Xavier's boots appeared in front of Abby. His calloused hand cupped her chin. "Look at me."

She lifted her eyes to his dark ones.

He studied her for a minute, then nodded. As he ran his thumb along her jawline, the simple caress made her shudder in her loneliness. "Follow me downstairs."

In the dungeon he guided her to lie facedown on what they called a sawhorse. It resembled a warped picnic table with the tabletop only the width of a torso. The leather was cold under her belly, adding to her frozen feeling. Her breasts hung on either side of the narrow board. Padded benches supported her knees and lower legs and forearms.

Xavier put wrist cuffs on her and secured her arms and legs, adding another strap over her lower back. Her bottom stuck out over the end. She tried to move, couldn't, and her fear grew. *It's pain. I can handle pain.* They'd hit her only on her butt.

He took an incredibly wide paddle from his toy bag. When he laid the weapon on her back, she shivered at the cold hardness of it. She turned away from the room, then realized the wall in this section was mirrored. Her face would be visible, no matter what. Her breathing hitched, and nausea roiled inside her.

"Do you feel as if you're on display, pet?" Xavier asked, squeezing her shoulder. How could she be so desperately grateful for his touch?

"Yes," she whispered. *I don't want to do this. I want to go home. I wish I'd never met you people.*

ANY LINGERING ANGER at her had died the minute the little fluff had followed him into the club. A submissive who took responsibility for her own actions was one to be cherished. Xavier went down on one knee so his face was level with hers. Leaning in to keep his words for her alone, he shared his body warmth. "You're being very brave, Abby. I'm proud of you."

Her eyes sheened with tears, and his heart ached. She was a true submissive; her Dom's approval overshadowed everything else.

"*Red* is still your safe word, but using it means the punishment is at an end—as is your membership here."

She nodded.

"If you feel more than pain or embarrassment, as in muscles cramping, dizziness, sickness, your hands or feet going numb, then use *yellow*, and we'll see what's up. Do you understand? Say it aloud."

"*Yellow* means you'll check on me. *Red* means I"—her face twisted—"I lose my membership, but the punishment will stop."

He saw her determination to see it through. “Good. Abby, I’ll be here the entire time, never more than two or three feet away. You’re mine, little fluff, and I won’t leave you.”

Her tears spilled. “Thank you, my liege.”

They were both going to hurt before this was over. With a silent sigh, he pulled her glasses off and set them at her fingertips where she could touch them. “Let’s begin. Remember, if you keep your muscles relaxed, it won’t hurt as much.”

Her huffed laugh, and the look she gave him—*easy for you to say*—lightened his heart. He ruffled her hair and moved to one side.

Despite the cluster of people standing around, no one stepped forward until Simon gave an exasperated snort. He handed Xavier a green band, picked up the paddle, and dealt Abby a mildly stinging swat across both cheeks.

Abby jerked slightly but didn’t make a sound.

“I forgive you, pet.” After handing the paddle to another Dom, Simon asked Xavier in a low voice, “Will she last?”

“She’s more stubborn than you’d think.”

“How about you?”

Xavier wanted to kill every single person who looked as if they’d pick up the paddle. “I want to protect her. Instead I’m the one who arranged to give her pain.”

“I know the feeling.” Simon squeezed his shoulder. “But she needs forgiveness from more than just you. Her pleasure in the friendships she made here was obvious, and she’ll be able to recover them now. You know that, or you wouldn’t have included the members.”

"I do know, but your approval helps."

"I also noticed you picked a paddle so big that even deVries couldn't do any damage."

Very true. Xavier gave him a half smile. The large size of the paddle would spread the impact over a wider area. She'd hurt after this, but the pain would be superficial.

Time dragged.

He accepted several more green bands from Dominants in closed relationships and from submissives. The Doms usually administered a blow just over the edge of painful. Exactly what he considered appropriate.

Unless they were switches, submissives rarely struck another person, and their blows varied widely. Most gave Abby a light tap, their sympathy obvious. Seeing her in tears had dispelled their anger, even before they picked up the paddle. However, a few appeared openly vindictive and hit much harder.

"Your turn, ladies." Simon said, pushing his wife and Lindsey toward Xavier.

Xavier glanced at Abby. Silently suffering—silently breaking his heart. Hands in fists, the little fluff had her eyes closed. At least she wouldn't know her friends were here.

Lindsey administered a tap that barely touched Abby's skin, more of a caress than a blow. Openly sobbing, she threw the paddle at Simon and ran.

Simon picked up the paddle and held it out to Rona.

She pushed it back, then yanked the green band off her wrist. "Abby's already crying, you bastards. What more do you want—blood?" After throwing the band on the floor, Rona gave Xavier a deadly look and walked away.

Yes, he'd always liked Simon's wife.

OW, OW, OW. The first few hits hadn't been bad, but the pain had built up until now even the mild swats hurt. Her whole bottom burned. She'd tried to loosen her muscles at first, but that battle was lost. Tears leaked from her closed eyes and pooled on the leather under her cheek.

Then she received a blow so hard it rocked the sawhorse. A fireball of pain burst through her, and she screamed. It hurt. *Hurt.* She started crying and couldn't stop.

"Greta, stay right there." Xavier's voice sounded like ice.

A second later he bent down beside Abby. His hand stroked her forearm. "She was out of line. She'll learn manners, but that doesn't help you now."

His sympathy and anger did, though. It really did. She pulled in a shuddering breath.

With a paper towel he wiped her eyes and held it to her nose. "Blow, pet."

Too miserable to resist the command, she complied...and felt better. When she squinted at the mirror, the reflection showed the blurry figure of Greta, a pretty, large-boned woman in a chain dress. The submissive had made nasty remarks about Xavier spending so much time with Abby.

With one hand on Abby's shoulder, Xavier straightened and leaned on his cane. Greta stared at the floor as he said icily, "This is punishment, not an exercise in sadism."

"I'm sorry, my liege. I had no idea it was too hard."

Sure, you didn't. If Abby could have stood…

"I see. Well, we all have to learn sometime. Master deVries, would you mind giving Greta five swats at the appropriate level for punishing an unknown submissive. Finish with five at the same strength Greta used on Abby. I'm sure, next time, she'll know the difference."

"My pleasure," deVries said smoothly.

"B-b-but…" Greta stuttered in shock and tried to retreat.

Had she never been taken to task for her behavior? Then again, her unpleasant personality might be why she didn't have a Master.

Smiling slightly, deVries grabbed Greta's long hair and wrapped it around his fist before dragging her toward the prayer benches in the center of the room.

"Next up, please," Xavier said.

Abby closed her eyes again. A minute passed. The next person administered a tentative tap as if terrified she'd be a candidate for a deVries lesson. The following few swats hurt—oh, they definitely hurt—but none came close to Greta's.

Then nothing happened. As minutes passed Abby breathed slowly, trying to deal with the burning of her skin.

"You're done, pet."

She jumped. *Done?* Relief rushed through her.

As Xavier moved closer, she pulled at the restraints. "Let me out." *Now, now, now.*

"Shhh." He ran a hand down her back in a soothing stroke. "I'm going to rub some cream on your very red ass. You'll still have bruising, but this will help."

"I want free."

"No." His smile flickered. "This will hurt, Abby. And I have enough scrapes from cliff diving. I don't need more dealt out by a pretty little submissive."

I can't take it.

As he stroked the cool ointment over her tender skin, stinging flared from even his light touch. She yanked on the restraints, harder and harder.

"Abby, if you don't stop, I'll swat you myself."

She froze.

"Good girl. You were punished, pet, and this is what happens afterward." He continued, not missing a spot.

Every inch of her bottom throbbed and burned.

"Done." He tossed the tube into his bag. After undoing her straps, he slid her glasses back on, then lifted her to her feet and looked her over.

She bet she just looked wonderful—dressed in wrist cuffs and glasses, red-eyed and covered in sweat. After a moment of dizziness, she found her balance.

When he wrapped a blanket around her, she realized her damp skin was chilling.

"With your permission, I'll clean up, my liege." Dixon stood a few feet away with paper towels and a spray bottle. His face was white. "So you can… Uh, I left water beside the couch." When Abby tried to smile at him, his eyes filled with tears.

"That was thoughtful, Dixon. Thank you." After claiming his cane, Xavier put an arm around her waist and guided her to a couch. Cane or not, he was still steadier than she was.

Keeping her wrist in his hand, he sat down and reclined against the arm with his injured leg beside the back cushions. He tugged her down onto his lap.

As his jeans scraped her bottom, pain flared, and she moaned. She hurt—hurt worse than she ever remembered. Why was she here? These people didn't like her. They never would.

Xavier gathered her close, sliding farther down on the couch so she sprawled on top of him with no weight on her butt.

She struggled to get up.

With a firm hand he tucked her head against his shoulder. "Settle a bit, little fluff. You had a hard time."

Her eyes blurred with tears as her body obeyed him. She closed her hand on the material of his shirt, hanging on tightly. People had hit her. Even the ones she'd thought were friends. Hurting her on purpose. She couldn't keep the question back. "Why were they so *mean*?"

He laid his hand on her neck and curved his long fingers over her nape. His thumb stroked her cheek. "Abby..."

A sob ripped up through her tight throat, and she tried to choke it down. More came, and she buried her head against him and cried. She was guilty, and they'd hit her and she'd deserved it. Only she thought some were her friends. They'd humiliated her. And it hurt. It *hurt.*

"That's right," he murmured, his arm tightening. "Let it out now. I'm proud of you, Abby."

By the time she finished, his shirt was soaked with her tears, and her eyes were even puffier than before. Her throat was raw, yet she felt...different. Cleaner. Lighter. "Thank you," she whispered.

He half laughed. "You're very welcome." He kissed the top of her head. "Bottling everything up isn't good, and you do it more than most, pet." As he wiped the tears from her face, she was grateful he'd instructed her not to wear makeup.

"I guess."

"You asked a question." He was silent a second. "Most lifestylers believe a suitable punishment and true repentance can clear damage done to a relationship so the wound doesn't fester. They're the ones who swatted you hard enough to sting, but not more. A few of the submissives..." The sound under her ear was almost a growl. "I think some might be envious of the attention you get."

"From you," she whispered.

"Yes." He moved his hand and stroked up and down her bare back. "I'm afraid so, and I regret that you suffered more because of it."

Like from nasty Greta. Then again, that sub wouldn't be comfortable sitting any sooner than Abby. DeVries wasn't known for gentleness. "It wasn't your fault."

He kissed her lightly before continuing, "Finally, those who know you well usually gave you swats so light as to be laughable. I doubt you even felt Lindsey's. A few, like Rona, handed over their bands and didn't take a turn. Simon said Dixon cut his into confetti and left it all over the reception desk."

She realized her eyes had been closed for much of the punishment. "Really?" An aching knot inside her loosened, allowing a real breath.

"Yes, pet." He reached around her to open a water and put it in her hands. "Drink that."

The cool water tasted better than anything she'd ever had in her life. She guzzled half the bottle before taking a breath.

He chuckled and settled himself more comfortably. "Now relax."

As the world moved on without her, she watched her thoughts float by and listened to the lazy *lubb-dupp* of his heart. Each breath he took lifted his chest, like a boat rocking on a quiet lake. People conversed nearby, and the rhythm of the dungeon continued with moans, the sounds of whips, floggers, paddles, and a scream or two.

Eventually the world snapped into place as if someone had changed the focus on a camera, sharpening the image. Her fingers tightened on his shirt.

"You ready for the next part?" Xavier asked.

"No." She pulled in a breath. "But I'll never be."

"Are you sure you want to continue? There's nothing forcing you to stay a member of the club, Abby."

"I know." She lifted her head, wondering if she could explain to him...if she even understood it herself. "I want to be able to come here, and not only for my research."

"Go on." His gaze stayed on her face.

"I've made friends here, and they're...open. Relaxed about life and involved in more than academics and social activities. I like them, and I don't want to lose them."

"That makes sense."

She faltered out the last part. "If I use their point of view, I see it's fair to make me experience being watched, like what I did to them." A cold ball of ice grew in her belly as she thought of the machine. "But I hate it, and I might hate you."

“It’s a risk.” His expression showed he meant it seriously, and he realized what this could do to their—whatever they had. “But if I gave you a meaningless, easy punishment, you’d continue to feel guilty. And I’d feel unhappy that I let the members down because of you. A D/s relationship can’t survive long with those kinds of emotions.” He kissed her forehead. “Let’s get this over with before you stew yourself into a puddle.”

No. No no no.

Chapter Nineteen

Could the little fluff last? Mouth tight, Xavier led Abby to the center of the dungeon, past the stairs. From the dismay on her face, she'd hoped her punishment would occur in a corner or a private theme room.

When she spotted the ominous-looking red machine with two dildos, her eyes went wide and scared.

He arranged her on her back on the hip-high gynecological table and turned her head so he was all she saw. "You can do this. Some submissives beg for this as a reward for good behavior."

"They can have my turn, my liege. No problem."

A woman who could be sarcastic despite her fear was a treasure. "You're very generous, pet." Smiling, he lifted her legs onto the padded knee supports and pulled her hips down until her ass hung slightly over the table's end. After adjusting her feet in the soft stirrups, he tightened straps over her ankles and thighs. He moved the supports even farther apart so the blonde curls of her pussy were exposed completely. She gave a convulsive shiver.

Working his way up, he cinched a strap above her mound and another below her breasts, removing any chance of wiggling out of the position he'd put her in. He checked that her wrist cuffs weren't affecting her circulation or nerves and clipped them to D rings beside her thighs.

Even as the members started to gather, Abby's gaze stayed on his face as if he were a lifeline. He pulled in a breath. This wasn't going to be easy for either of them, but they had to do it. This would be his punishment as well for not questioning a new applicant more carefully.

As Xavier walked to the head of the table, Abby obviously saw the audience, and her body turned rigid. Although she'd enjoyed the camaraderie of the club, she wasn't an exhibitionist—which made this a most appropriate punishment.

But she didn't need to suffer quite so much. He picked up a blindfold.

LET ME OUT of here! Abby bit back the scream as more and more people crowded around her. Her legs were strapped down and pulled wide apart, exposing everything to their stares. Somehow her eyes wouldn't close to blot them out. She couldn't—

"You'll do better with this." Xavier removed her glasses, laying them beside her fingers, then blindfolded her. "You'll know the people are here, but you don't need to see them," he said quietly.

Thank you. I think. She wasn't sure the darkness was better.

His hand ran down her arm, then her leg as he moved to the foot of the table. "I'm going to insert the dildos now, pet. The first is small, since you're not used to anal play."

She gasped as something pressed against her anus. A flare of stretching pain made her stiffen as it breached the ring of muscle and slickly slid in.

"Abby, I'll adjust the machine so nothing can go too far." He patted her thigh. "You're already in for a long ride. No need to scare you further."

He pushed the other dildo into her vagina. The thing wasn't huge but filled her completely. Gritting her teeth against protests, she tried to wiggle away and realized her lower half was immobilized.

I don't like this. She swallowed, then stiffened again as something settled over her mound. Soft and squishy and cool, it pressed right against her clit as Xavier secured it with straps around her legs.

Someone asked a question in a low voice, and Xavier answered, "Since this will last awhile, soft is better. Irritating her clit right away would take the fun out of it."

Thanks a lot.

He chuckled. "Look at that face. Is a little submissive displeased with her punishment?"

People laughed.

He rubbed her shoulder, and it was scary how much she craved his touch. "I don't want any portion of your body to feel neglected, so I'll add these."

A hard circle slid around her right breast; then she felt a gentle squeeze as if a mouth were sucking on her nipple. Her back arched up. The cold device vibrated erratically, but the suction continued. He did the other breast, and she shivered.

"You're ready to go, pet. Remember—*red* and *yellow* for safe words." He raised his voice. "Doms, your green band gives you one minute at the controls. Be warned, though. She isn't allowed to climax until the end, so if she gets close, I'll use the foot pedal to halt the action, and you'll lose your remaining time."

General laughter.

"I'll take the first shot," a gruff voice said.

Silence, and Abby started to panic. Xavier had left her here with all these men, at their mercy. "Yellow. Please, yellow."

A hand closed over hers. "Little fluff, what's wrong?"

He's still here. "Don't go. Please." Tears burned her eyes. "I can do it, but don't leave me."

He kissed her lightly. "Abby, I'd never leave you. I'll sit beside you the entire time, but...you can't see me, can you? Hmm." She heard the scrape of a chair, the rustle of his clothing as he sat. "Here you go." He opened her fist and closed her fingers over something soft and thick.

He'd put his braid in her hand.

"Will that help?"

The feeling of drowning in panic receded; she had her life preserver. "Yes, my liege. Thank you." *So, so much.*

"You're very welcome. And Abby, if you feel someone touch you, it's me. I'm the only one who gets to touch. Do you understand?"

"Yes, sir." A tenseness inside her relaxed slightly.

"The machine might be uncomfortable at times, but we're going to keep you lubed up. Tell me if you start to feel dry. *Yellow* again. Clear?"

"Yes, sir."

"Fire away, Garrett."

The dildo slid into her pussy. In, out—slick and firm as the one in her anus started to move, much more slowly. The thing over her clit buzzed softly, vibrating, only she wasn't in the least interested.

Coldness trickled between her legs. Someone had squeezed more lube on her, making the dildos penetrate with soft, slurpy noises.

"Fuck, that's hot," she heard.

"Speed it up, Garrett," a man urged.

She squeezed her eyes shut, despite the blindfold, wishing she could shut out the sounds of the people as well.

As if he knew her thoughts, Xavier said, "I took away your vision, but I want you to hear them talking about you, Abby. Part of this is to show you the difference between playing in a friendly…family…or performing like a zoo animal. A lab specimen. Do you understand?"

"Yes, my liege." Tears dampened the blindfold.

She heard him sigh quietly. A few seconds later, he said, "Next up. Who has a green band?"

The vibrator sped up, bumping all the sides of her clit, making her jolt. Her body woke, and a wave of heat ran over her. The dildo in her pussy increased in speed, hammering into her. Her muscles tightened as arousal blasted through her, as she felt her insides begin to—

"Next." Rustling.

The vibrations on her clit decreased, right when she was beginning to enjoy it. The dildo in her pussy slowed as well, but somehow went deeper with each thrust, and the one in her anus kicked alive—fast and hard. Her hips tried to rise, her legs pulling in, trying to escape the strange sensations. More, less, *something.*

"Next."

The clit vibrator sped up. The dildo in her vagina went shallower, faster. Angled differently, it rubbed over a sensitive spot inside her. Pressure built as she started to reach the precipice. She was going to come—needed to come. *Closer, closer.*

Everything stopped.

Laughter burst out around her, and through the haze of frustration, she heard people razzing whoever had been at the controls.

A fine perspiration broke out over her body.

Time ticked by with nothing happening. A minute. Two. Her arousal faded, leaving her cold inside. How could she have almost orgasmed in front of everyone?

"Time to rev it back up, girl." DeVries's voice was as rough as sandpaper. The dildos came to life, and he varied everything, playing the controls like a master. He increased the speed on the vibrator, then the dildo in her pussy, then the anal thing, one-two-three, like a waltz of arousal.

Her need soared, and her breathing increased. As Abby's climax approached, deVries snorted, and the one-two-three dance changed. Everything slowed, leaving her burning. His laugh was that of a sadist.

Another Dom took his place, then another…

They blurred; it all blurred except the feelings in her body. Xavier stopped the machine again, two more times, and at the last one she groaned, hanging right on the edge, everything throbbing. Both dildos pulled out of her.

Xavier removed his braid from her hand.

"No. No, please. Don't leave."

"Shhh." His hand stroked her cheek. "I'm not going anywhere, Abby. I'm going to change things out."

The suction thing came off, and her nipples throbbed.

"Beautiful."

"Look at how red they are against her white skin."

"They're huge. Maybe I'll get some for my girl."

"Pretty, aren't they?" Xavier said, running his finger in a circle around each areola.

His finger circled again, only this time with something cool. The scent was familiar, the feeling familiar. Peppermint. Her nipples began to tingle and burn. She tried to move—couldn't. There was no escape.

He trailed his fingers down her stomach, then checked each restraint. "Any numbness or tingling, Abby?" he asked.

"No, sir."

Something scraped. His clothing brushed the insides of her thighs. He left the straps around her legs but removed the soft thing from her clit.

Cool air washed over her tight, throbbing nub, making her gasp.

"That's one wide-awake clit," someone said.

"Gorgeous pussy. I see why he let her keep the hair." General agreement.

He fastened something new over her, squashy but harder than the first.

A larger dildo slid into her vagina. "Hmm. Might as well make it fun," Xavier said and pulled it out, then pushed in one even bigger. It went farther as well, all the way to her cervix, and that didn't feel good at all. She tried to squirm, making noises.

It receded slightly but remained inside her.

More noises, and she heard the chuckling around her. *God, what is he planning?* A dildo pressed against her anus. It felt huge. She made a helpless sound, and he stopped. "It's about the size of two fingers, Abby. You can take this."

After a moment she managed to relax her muscles, and it slid in. Stretching her. Burning. Her muscles tensed, tried to move. Got nowhere.

"Looks about right." He removed the dildos. When he slid them back in, they were even slicker than before. "Gentlemen, she's all yours. Same rules about not letting her come."

When he tucked his braid into her hand again, a sweet ache filled her heart. He'd remembered. God, she lov—

"Since she had a break, I'll start slow," someone said. "Y'all can push her closer during your turns."

The vibrator over her clit came to life with a blast, and she jerked, trying to sit up. But then it was dialed down. Only, this setting had a strange vibration, coming in slow waves before stopping entirely. The dildo in her pussy pushed in and out, stretching her. With the bigger thing in her butt, everything felt too tight. Too full.

"Time." Xavier said.

"Let's have some fun now." The man's voice was older, experienced. The clit device jumped into a harsh vibration. And stopped. On, off. The pussy dildo increased, slowly but surely, as if being fed caffeine, yet the one in her anus slowed.

"Next," Xavier said.

This Dom slowed the vibrator but somehow made the vibrations harder. He stopped the dildo in her pussy, leaving it in and full, but drove the one in her anus to a hammering speed.

She couldn't think as everything in her surged upward, heading straight for a climax, and nothing was going to—

It all stopped.

"Nooo." She struggled against the straps, furious and ready to cry.

People were laughing. How could they laugh?

Nothing moved as the seconds ticked away, and she...she hurt. Embarrassment was losing out to the need to come. Her hand fisted so tightly around Xavier's braid that her fingers ached. Her lower half felt swollen and tight and hurting, and her abused nipples burned.

"Next," Xavier said.

Two more Doms took their turns, sending her up and down, bringing her close, letting her go back down, playing her like a computer game.

Sweat trickled between her breasts, under the blindfold. Her muscles ached, close to cramping from straining against the straps. Her mouth was dry from panting. She wanted to cry.

"No more?" Xavier asked.

"Looks like that's it," someone said. "I'd be happy to take another turn."

The Doms laughed, agreeing, as she lay shaking. The dildos were inside her, and her inner muscles quivered around them, trying to get them to move.

"Abigail, would you like to come?"

Oh please. "I hate you," she whispered.

He kissed her. "I know, little fluff. That's not what I asked."

He was going to make her say it, and she tried not to. Didn't want to, but her endurance was gone. "Yes."

Under the blindfold, her eyes squeezed shut. “Yes, my liege.”

“Very good.”

To her shock, rather than starting the machine, he peeled the vibrator off.

Air rushed over her clit, teasing her hardness, making her throb worse. “Nooo.”

“Shhh.”

She felt the brush of his suit against her outer thigh.

He patted her leg, stroking gently. “Trust me.”

I don’t want to. But she had no choice. No defenses.

The machine started again. The dildo in her vagina seemed angled differently. Its short strokes ruthlessly rubbed against…the sensitive place inside her. She felt as if she needed to pee, and yet the feeling increased like an expanding balloon. Her exhausted muscles strained upward, needing more, the feeling worse than ever, encompassing all of her, and she couldn’t… A despairing groan escaped her. *Please, please…*

Fingers touched her labia, opening her widely, and suddenly her clit was engulfed in heat. Wetness. When Xavier’s hand gripped her right buttock, pain flared at the same time his tongue rubbed directly on top of her clit. Everything inside her contracted, tighter and tighter, and nothing could possibly stop the glorious inevitability. Like champagne, pleasure burst out, flowing over the top of the container of her body, and sensations streamed outward so forcefully that her back arched. She could hear her own jerking screams.

Every spasm sent exquisite pleasure through her, and with each one she wanted more.

He gave her more in a deep, pulling suction that sent her over again with a wailing sound. Her legs jerked in the restraints; her hips tried to buck. Even when it was almost pain and not pleasure, she craved for it not to stop.

But he pulled back and blew a stream of cool air over her clit that made her clench.

As everything halted, she lay limp and panting, hearing only the roaring in her ears, feeling her heart pounding at her rib cage. Her muscles had deflated like leaky balloons until she couldn't move.

Xavier slid the dildos out, leaving her empty and aching inside. One by one, the straps were removed. He wiped her breasts off. Finally he removed the blindfold, and the first thing she saw was his hard face. It held no expression, but his eyes were readable—approval and worry and unhappiness.

Her arm didn't want to move, but she reached up to touch his cheek. "Are you okay?"

He flattened his palm over her hand, and slowly his lips curved. "You're one of the sweetest submissives I've ever known."

He kissed her fingers and helped her sit up. Her head spun for a minute, and she shivered as the sweat on her body cooled. Her bottom burned like fire, her insides throbbed with a dull ache, yet her bones still sang a song of satisfaction.

When he slid her glasses onto her nose, she saw all the people ringed around the table and almost begged for the blindfold again.

Xavier lifted her to her feet and steadied her. Closing his hand around hers, he leaned on his cane. "Kneel, Abigail."

She needed his hand as her rubbery legs gave out halfway down.

No one spoke as she knelt before them, naked and vulnerable and cold.

“Do you have something to say to the members, little fluff?” Xavier’s voice was…kind, the chill from earlier gone. “Look at them now.”

She raised her gaze, meeting their eyes, and tried to remember the speech she’d crafted to ask forgiveness. Couldn’t. Tears started without warning. Her shoulders shook. “I’m sorry.”

She pulled in a breath and tried again. “Please—” The words weren’t there, only the feelings. “I’m s-sorry.” She felt her tears dripping onto her breasts.

“That’s as repentant as they come,” said deVries. “I forgive you, girl.” The roughness of his voice was the softest caress she’d ever received.

The others followed. “Forgiven.”

“Apology accepted.”

“She took it like a trooper.”

“Clean slate, pet.” The voices murmured a song of forgiveness, and the cold spot inside her filled with warmth as she heard the approval in the music.

Slowly the people filtered away, leaving Lindsey and Simon and Rona.

Rona gave her a smile that didn’t need words to show her forgiveness.

Lindsey glanced at Xavier and got a nod. She curled Abby’s limp hand around a bottle of water. The squeeze on her shoulder said it all.

Simon touched her hair lightly and handed Xavier a blanket.

Xavier pulled her to her feet and wrapped her up. “Your evening is over, little fluff. Let’s go home.”

* * * *

Unwilling to leave his exhausted submissive alone, Xavier tucked her under a soft throw on the downstairs couch while he dealt with the puppies. Finally weaned, they jostled each other getting to the trencher of mushy food. The sounds of contented lapping and snuffling filled his home as he cleaned the messes and put down new paper. Abby planned to take them outside tomorrow and let them get accustomed to grass under their paws.

Once finished, he pulled Abby onto his lap. She didn’t rouse except to moan when her sore ass rubbed over his jeans. She’d have trouble sitting for a while.

His smile faded as he thought of Greta, who’d used the chance to vent her spleen. He’d have to keep an eye on her. A warped submissive could be as destructive to a club as a bad Dom, turning a supportive atmosphere into emotional hash. It was another reason he’d lengthened the application process, closer to that of the BDSM club he’d visited in Florida. Of course, he had no intention of making Dark Haven as exclusive and expensive as the Shadowlands. The local lifestylers here came from all walks of life.

In the wading pool two puppies engaged in a tug-of-war with a piece of knotted rope. Another jumped in and used its needle-sharp milk teeth on a sibling, netting a loud squeak.

Abby opened her eyes. “What?” She tried to sit up and hissed as the movement rubbed her abused ass.

“Relax, pet. It’s just puppy wars.” As his members had earlier, the pups returned to playing happily, all transgressions forgiven. Although he and Abby needed to discuss the night, he'd achieved his goal, and she was back in the good graces of the club.

He'd also lost the last sense of betrayal that he'd harbored.

As her brows drew together, he traced one delicate, silky arch with his fingertip. "Why are you holding me?" she asked.

"Because I wanted to."

Her lips quirked. "Arrogant Dom."

"That's right." He smiled into her eyes. "Now that you're awake, I want to check you over." Despite her grip, he pulled open the blanket. Her nipples had a few red splotches from the suction machine. Good thing he'd set it to low. Smiling at her squirms, he pushed her legs apart and inspected her clit. Still swollen but improving.

"On your feet." He helped her rise and then slapped her legs lightly. "Open for me."

Her mouth dropped open—he hadn't shown her much dominance outside the bedroom. Then she complied. Watching her face, he ran a finger around her entrance and pushed in, past the puffy tissues. She winced. Withdrawing, he glanced at his finger. No blood. "How sore are you?"

"Not bad." Her face flushed. "I still can't believe you used a…a machine on me."

He laughed and turned her around so her back was to him. "Bend over, hands on your ankles, knees bent."

She didn't move.

He lowered his voice. "Now, pet."

She complied quickly. Good little submissive. She had a bruise across the right buttock, probably from the higher percentage of right-handed people wielding the paddle, and her ass cheeks were red and slightly swollen. They would heal.

Parting her sore buttocks, he ignored her whimper. Her asshole was red, but again had incurred no damage. "Looks good, but you're going to be sore for a day or so." He rose and helped her straighten. "There are ice packs in the freezer. Use them."

"Yes, sir." To his surprise she leaned into him, her forehead pressed against his shoulder.

He wrapped his arms around her. "What?"

"Did you like seeing me...? The machine and the other men?"

He rocked her. It was the same question he'd intended to ask her.

Odd that few subs or slaves ever asked him if he enjoyed something. Perhaps they thought a Dom never did anything he didn't like. But that wasn't true. A D/s relationship was a two-way street. His subs occasionally had to do what they didn't like. So did he, if the submissive needed it.

"I enjoy showing you off," he said. "It's a competitive male trait: *see the pretty submissive I have.*"

His little professor snorted. "Testosterone-ridden animals."

"I like smacking your tender, round ass. I enjoy seeing other Doms paddling their submissives. I *didn't* like them paddling *you.*" He rubbed his chin over her hair, trying to explain. "Part is protectiveness. No one should hurt you. Although I'm the one who arranged the punishment, I found it difficult to see you in tears."

She didn't speak, but her arms came around him.

"Part of it's territorial. You're mine, and I rarely let anyone touch what's mine. For the fucking machine, I've rewarded submissives with it before, and I'd enjoy using it on you if I was at the controls."

"Huh."

But he'd let others do that, and guilt still hung like a cloud over him. "I'm sorry, Abby. This was the only way I thought might mend your relationship with the members. I could have punished you in front of them, but they needed to participate in order to forgive you."

"I understood that."

He waited for more and only received silence. "Tell me how you felt."

She stiffened.

Her defenses had risen. Regretting the necessity, but not about to let her hide from him, he administered a stinging swat to one very tender area.

Her outraged squeak made him grin.

He really did enjoy the feel of a round ass under his hand. "Answer me. Honestly."

When she didn't answer, he lifted his hand again.

"I *hated* being paddled and having those…people…using stuff on me. I don't know if I'd like the machine if you did it, but I didn't like *them*."

"Good girl. Why didn't you answer me the first time?"

She gave him a disbelieving stare. "More questions?"

"You're a forthright person, unless you're afraid someone will yell at you. Did you think I'd get angry at your answer?"

Her gaze dropped, and she bit her lip. "Not angry."

"What did Nathan do when you told him something he didn't want to hear?"

He might have missed the tiny flinch, except she was plastered against him. "Nathan was open-minded about anything except intimate things."

"I see. And?"

"If I didn't like something, he acted as if I'd insulted his…dick. He'd get cold. Sarcastic."

"Ah." One of those who believed *I'm a Dom. I can do no wrong*. "Abby, if I ask you a question, I want a truthful answer, even if I don't like it. Trust me. I'll be angrier if you aren't honest. Is that clear?"

On his shoulder her head moved up and down.

"As long as we're speaking of intimate things, I noticed you're on the pill. Since our medical tests are both clean, do you have any objection to me not using a condom?"

"All right." Her shoulders tensed. "But if there's anyone else…"

The thought of her being with another man was unpalatable, but she'd posed a fair question. "Use a condom with the other person. And then I will also, until the testing is repeated."

"Good."

His mouth tightened. She hadn't made any objections about the possibility that there would be others for either of them. Well…that was good.

The sound of her stomach growling diverted him. "You didn't eat much today, did you?" Too nervous. "Let's go get you some soup." He smiled down into her big gray eyes. "We'll eat in the media room, and this once you can even pick the movie."

Her mouth rounded up, giving him a hint of the dimple at the corner of her mouth. “I feel a real need for a chick flick.”

He chuckled. “Vengeful little pet.” As she headed into the media room, tucking the blanket around herself, he watched in admiration. Another submissive might have spent the night in his arms weeping. The professor had more stamina and guts than he'd realized.

And a vicious sense of humor. If she picked something like *Runaway Bride*, he'd make her suffer.

Chapter Twenty

As the chimes rang through Xavier's house, Abby hurried to open the door. Yesterday she'd asked Rona over. Forgiven or not, Abby feared she'd damaged their friendship. She swung the door wide. "Hi—"

"Hey," Lindsey said from where she stood beside Rona. "I asked if I could tag along." Her smile was tentative. "I don't want to lose you."

With a huge sigh Abby hugged them both. "Thank you for coming." She blinked back happy tears.

"Don't you start leaking, or I will too." Lindsey's eyes reddened.

"Right." Abby motioned. "Come on in. I made éclairs so we can get a sugar high." As she entered the living room, the puppies started to whine.

Lindsey spotted the tiny heads peeking over the edge of the wading pool. "Oh my blessed Jesus, look at them." She dropped to her knees beside the pool.

As her streaky brown hair fell forward, the puppies took it as an invitation to play, jumping and trying to grab the curls. She laughed and lifted Tippy. "Aren't you just the sweetest baby?" she crooned, cuddling the brown ball of fur.

"Want a dog?" Abby asked.

"More than I can say, but I just signed a lease for a new apartment." She wiggled her eyebrows hopefully. "I'm moving in a week, if y'all feel like carting boxes around."

"No couches or beds to carry?" Rona asked. She crouched beside Lindsey and picked up Freckles.

"No. Where I'm living now was furnished, so I'm fixin' to buy furniture for my new place. Finally."

Abby joined the other two on the floor. Blackie's tail wagged furiously. "Hey, snookums." Puppy breath and a deadly fast tiny tongue and squirms and wiggles. "You are the sweetest baby."

"Oh, they all are." Lindsey chose Blondie. "Isn't it going to break your heart to let them go?"

"It's hard," Abby admitted, smiling down into soft black eyes. "It's worse when one grabs you, like this one." She planted a kiss on his fuzzy nose. "Maybe it's because his eyes are the same shade as Xavier's."

Rona laughed, then gave Abby a keen look. "If you're falling for a puppy because of a resemblance, I'd say you're also falling for the man. And you are living here now, aren't you?"

"I'm not falling. Absolutely not." The thought sent a chill into her stomach. "I'm just here because I wanted to know about the Dominant/submissive stuff, and he needed help around the house. That's all."

"The sacrifices a woman makes. You probably don't even like him, huh?" Rona said in a dry voice.

"Fine. I like him." Oh heavens, she really did. She looked up to see understanding expressions on both faces. "More than I'm comfortable with, especially after Nathan. Being around him is like being on a roller coaster. He comes in, and I feel all bubbly inside. When he uses that

Dom voice, the bottom drops out of my stomach and my knees go weak."

Rona laughed. "I know what you mean."

"I wish I did." Lindsey sighed. "I had the loverly bubbles when I first got married—for a little while, at least. I've had that sinking feeling from a few of the Doms. Never both together." Lindsey cuddled Blondie close. "So you don't figure Xavier is permanent?"

"Get real. He's *my liege.* Rich, powerful, gorgeous. I teach college students, trip when kneeling, and my butt's so big I could use it for a serving tray."

Rona raised her eyebrows. "Xavier lets you run yourself down like that?"

"Ah." Abby flushed. "No." The last time she'd complained she had a fat ass, he'd given her one of those frowns and then…

"Oooo, Missy Red-Face. Tell us what happened," Lindsey demanded.

"He simply said he liked my ass." Abby gave in to the expectant expressions. "And if I called it fat again, he'd turn it a pretty pink." Then he'd stripped off her jeans and shown her exactly what he meant. The feeling of being over his knees, of his hard hand on her bare bottom, had been so humiliating and so…intimate…that she'd never be able to explain it. "He seems to think he needs to help me overcome stuff. Like I have some horrible background."

"Did he really put it like that?" Rona asked.

"Well. No."

Rona gave her a smug look. "I didn't think so. He obviously likes the way you look—and who you are. Honey, he's happier than I've ever seen him."

Really? Abby realized Blackie had squirmed out of her arms and was exploring. Tiny and defenseless…yet so brave. His ears were forward, his body eager for what experiences the world had to offer.

When did I turn into such a coward that I'm scared to leave my own wading pool?

XAVIER OPENED THE door to the sound of laughter and had to smile. Simon had mentioned Abby'd invited Rona over, and that Rona had been delighted. Now he knew why she'd been nervous today.

But the little professor hadn't told him. That was a disappointment. Anything that affected her emotionally should be shared with her Dom, but she kept herself so guarded that it worried him.

Then again, neither of them had been in this kind of awkward situation before. The slaves he brought home had always known there was a time limit and they'd leave once he found them the right Master.

He and Abby had set no time limits. Neither of them wanted anything serious. Not at this point. She was learning how to please him; he was learning her vulnerabilities and where he could help her become stronger. That was enough for now.

The door to the patio was open, and the women and puppies were outside in the patchy sunshine. As he headed past the living room toward his study, he saw the iced tea glasses on the coffee table and a plate with éclairs. The rope the pups used for tug-of-war lay on the floor next to Abby's sandals. Not clutter, but signs that someone lived here.

He turned in a circle, realizing the house felt alive.

Catherine had loved the Old West and had decorated with rugged, dark furniture, rough tables, Western paintings, and crafts. The style hadn't quite matched the building's elegant lines, but neither of them had cared. When she'd died, he couldn't stand seeing her favorite furniture, and a decorator had changed everything over to a light, contemporary look.

He hadn't realized how cold the house was until pieces from Abby's home appeared. Her plants had been rescued when she found she didn't get back often enough to water them. A giant schefflera in a hand-painted ceramic pot brightened one corner. Ferns in wrought iron stands softened the foyer. Parsley, chives, and thyme were in small terra-cotta pots on a kitchen windowsill.

Now every time she went to her duplex she returned with touches of convenience and beauty. A glazed earthenware bowl was on the dining room table, filled with fruit. A dark-red porcelain stand held umbrellas by the front door.

Apparently her archeologist father had taken his family with him on digs, and after graduating, she'd used his life insurance money to travel overseas every summer, shipping home whatever delighted her. Tapestry pillows from Belgium, as comfortable as they were bright, were in the corners of the sofa and chairs. An Italian cashmere throw lay over the back of a chair.

He walked into his study and smiled at the rounded lines of the Middle Eastern leather ottoman she'd brought over, hoping he'd keep his ankle up on it.

She was quite the traveler. Would she enjoy having company this year?

* * * *

Abby tried to snuggle down into the covers, but Xavier's hands ran up her body. Firm, confident, and unstoppable. A hard cock pressed against her stomach. He was awake.

"Don't want to get up." It couldn't be much past dawn. All weekend she'd frantically worked to finish analyzing her observations. She still had more literature searches to do and only ten days until she had to submit the article. And now her time would be filled with end-of-term school matters—exams, essays, projects—and handing in the students' grades.

A low chuckle sounded in her ear as he stroked her breasts. "But you're going to anyway."

Her nipples tightened to hard peaks; warmth flowed downward. She looked up into his molten dark eyes, saw the line of his determined jaw, and went from sleepy to wet and aroused. How did he do that?

He kissed her shoulder and bit it.

The sharp pain woke her completely. Excited her completely. At least until he set her onto her hands and knees and slid into her from the rear.

My liege's favorite position. Because he didn't want to see her face. Because he didn't want to remember she wasn't his beloved Catherine. Her resentment was followed by a wave of unhappiness, and her hands clenched. She buried her face in the pillow…so he wouldn't have to look at her.

He stopped moving. "What's wrong, Abby?"

Not a thing except I'm not your dead wife. "Nothing." She kept her hips up and available to him, even though her interest had died the minute he'd flipped her over. "Keep going."

"Nothing?" His voice had turned to clipped ice.

Her body stiffened. He was angry.

As if to prove the point he pulled out and rolled her over. His mouth was tight, his face cold. "I dislike lies, pet."

She flinched. Her hands made an abortive gesture toward covering her ears, to keep her from hearing him yell. Only…she'd never heard him yell.

He swung a leg over her, straddling her—an appallingly efficient way to pin her down. "Look at me, Abby." Although the hardness was gone from his expression, the displeasure remained. His long black hair swung loose as he leaned over her.

As she met his shadowed eyes, her heartbeat echoed through her hollow chest. The Tin Man should have been grateful for the emptiness; hearts only caused pain.

"In vanilla relationships, honesty is important. In BDSM, it's essential. Even with as much experience as I have, I'm not a mind reader." His accent came through clearly, making him sound almost like a stranger. He touched her chin with one finger. "What are you feeling?"

"Nothing." She felt her emotions trying to pull back inside to safety.

Another sigh. "What does your stomach feel like?"

Didn't he ever give up? "Tight."

"Chest?"

"Tighter."

He lifted her hand to show her the fist she'd made and then ran a finger over her compressed lips. "One more time, what are you feeling?"

"I'm mad." Everything inside her flinched in anticipation of his response.

"There we go. Was that so difficult?" He eyed her and answered his own question. "Apparently it was. How do you manage if you can't tell someone you're upset? Say it again—like you mean it—and add who you're mad at."

She stared at him. "What?"

"You heard me. Now." No anger in his voice. No expression: not warm, not cold. The emotions here were all hers.

Her stomach churned. Considering he was sitting on her, she wasn't going to be able to run. "I'm angry." She managed to add a little force…enough to terrify a mouse. What was wrong with her?

He lifted his eyebrows.

"At you." It came out just past a whisper.

No yelling. "Again."

"I'm angry at you."

"You sound as if you're giving me month-old stock market news. Again."

Insulted, she scowled at him. "I'm *angry* at you."

A smile flickered on his lips. "Very good, pet. Again—and this time tell me why."

No. She felt herself try to retreat into the mattress.

"It doesn't help to know you're mad at me if you don't say why." He had a jaw like granite to go with his obstinate nature. "Now, Abby."

"I'm angry at you." Okay, those words came easier. Louder. The next, not so much. "For…for…" Her fingernails dug into her palms. "For turning me over."

His brows drew together not in anger, but confusion. "You don't like that position? I thought…" His eyes narrowed. "You have no trouble saying when I go too deep. Or if nipple clamps are too tight. That you hate the cane. Why would you have a problem telling me this? What am I missing?"

She felt an embarrassed flush rise into her cheeks. "It's nothing."

He pried her hand open and kissed the knuckles. "If you knew I was unhappy, how would you react if I wouldn't tell you why?"

Her mouth opened. Closed. She'd feel horrible. Her imagination would offer up every possible thing she might have done wrong. She'd be afraid to do anything for fear of making his unhappiness worse.

She had discovered a heady freedom with Xavier because he didn't hide his feelings. If he disliked a movie or a food or...anything, really...he'd tell her. Or he'd bargain with her, trading something he didn't enjoy—a chick flick—for equal time doing something he preferred and she didn't, which was how she'd ended up playing pool last night.

He wanted the same honesty from her. Deserved it. Her lips quivered. "I... It hurts that you don't want to look at my face. That you see hers. And—"

"Hers?" He looked utterly baffled. "Catherine's? You think I turned you over because of that?"

He was making her sound stupid. Furious, she yanked her hand away from his and pushed at his shoulders. Shoving her hips up, she tried to buck him off.

He leaned forward and pinned her wrists beside her head.

"*Tu es stultior quam asinus.*" Oh, she didn't have words to say how she loathed him.

"I'm dumber than an ass?" Laughter lit his eyes before disappearing. "Perhaps so, since I imagined everything except this reason." He kissed her gently. "That first night with you—the reason I left so quickly was because I *didn't* see her face, just yours, and it worried me how much pleasure I received from watching you. That has never changed, little fluff."

Oh. Her eyes stung with tears.

"I still have things to work through from losing her, but I don't think of Catherine when I'm with you, Abby." He frowned. "You still need work on vocalizing your emotions, though."

She shook her head. "Nothing like getting yourself a damaged submissive. Maybe you should—"

"Damaged?" He stroked her cheek, his calloused hand strong. Dependable. "Hardly. You're an incredibly strong woman, Professor. But no one grows up without collecting some emotional wounds and then creating defenses around them. At this point in time, yours mostly focus on anger and mine on losing Catherine."

She lay still beneath him. He'd called her strong. Not damaged. "You Doms love to fix things, don't you? Even people."

"Ah, you've figured us out." His fingers laced with hers, although he still kept her pinned against the mattress. "Doms have defenses too, you know." He considered. "A scene for you—a sub—is like lancing an abscess. Opening it. Applying healing ointment."

Painful example, but…yes, she could see that. "And Doms?"

He rubbed his beard-roughened cheek against hers. "Tending a sub's needs fills something in a Dom, balances him so he is able to look deeper into himself. You're the crutches after spraining an ankle."

The thought of helping Xavier, of being his balance, felt good. The relationship wasn't all one-sided, and he wasn't perfect. "Then why did you want to have sex like…"

"Why did I turn you over?" His eyes crinkled. "We both have to go to work today, and I plan to fuck you first." He released her hands and cupped her breasts. "And I *really* want to play with all my favorite pieces at the same time. Doggy style allows that." He gave her a lethal smile. "You, pet, get off much quicker when I can reach your clit."

She felt her cheeks heat. "Well."

"It's that simple, but I'm glad we talked." He moved down to lick her breast, then sucked on the nipple hard enough to make her toes curl. "However, if you want face-to-face, and I want my hands free, you'll have to do the work this morning." Gripping her waist, he rolled them over in bed, positioning her to straddle his hips. Her pussy rubbed against his cock.

She leaned forward to run her hands over his chest. So smooth with hard, contoured muscles beneath the skin. His flat nipples were dark and tantalizing. His stomach was like a washboard where she could travel the ridges. Moving back onto his thighs, she delighted in how the skin strained over his erection. Tracing a fat vein with her finger made his cock bob. He wanted her. She cupped his balls, always surprised at how heavy they were.

Wiggling her way back up, she rose to take him in, but he shook his head. *Uh-oh.* His face had taken on that Dom look. How could he be on his back and still radiate enough authority to make her insides quake? She swallowed.

"Lift up and off of me."

She obeyed.

When her pussy was off his cock and in the air, he pushed her legs farther apart, opening her. "Hands locked behind your back. Eyes on mine. Don't move. Don't speak."

With his gaze fixed on her face, he reached down and touched her, sliding his finger over her clit. His touch was enough to send heat rushing through her. Eyes half-lidded, he watched her as he pushed his finger into her vagina, then slid it up to the nub of nerves. Circling, teasing. She felt herself swell and harden as the pressure grew inside her.

He traced lines up and down her labia and around her entrance before returning to her clit.

As she trembled, his hard finger rubbed her, demanding her response. He brought her to the edge, over and over, until his intent eyes and touch blurred the surroundings, until her need filled her world.

Finally…finally, when her legs were shaking uncontrollably, he held his cock up to her pussy. His finger never stopped circling her clit, drawing her to the very point and holding her there. "Down. Now."

Her trembling legs gave out, and she dropped onto his shaft even as he pushed up with his hips, sliding in with one hard thrust.

Swollen tissues stretched; nerves fired. Her back arched as everything—*everything*—gathered inside. His calloused fingers bracketed her swollen clit, teasing both sides at once. The cascade burst, flowing in massive waves outward, shaking her convulsively and flooding her with pleasure.

While he was deep inside her, joined in the most intimate way possible, he reached up and cupped her cheek. Even as she realized his gaze hadn't once moved from her face, he said softly, "I see you, Abby. Never think otherwise."

Chapter Twenty-One

On Tuesday afternoon Abby hugged her mother and Grace and motioned them into Xavier's house.

"What a beautiful home," her mother said, turning in a circle. "I love the stonework everywhere."

"It's pretty, isn't it? Grace, the puppies are outside." Unsettled at having her family in Xavier's place, Abby led the way to the long stretch of patio in the back.

"Hey, you can see the Golden Gate and Angel Island." Grace slowed long enough to check out the bay before making a quick dash to the puppies.

"It's a spectacular view at night." Abby followed her sister to the small "kennel" that Xavier had contrived on the side lawn. The babies liked being outside when the weather was nice.

The fog had cleared, and sunlight sparkled off the waves far below. The scent of the dark-red roses mingled with the brine in the air and charged Abby with energy. Or maybe it was the way Xavier had woken her early in the morning, with sweet kisses and slow sex.

He'd told her that "rough sex" was for other times and places, and mornings should be loving. Of course, he wasn't prepared to let her sleep either. Sex might be leisurely, but it was also determined. Burrowing back into the covers sure hadn't worked. A shiver of heat ran through her at the memory of his firm grip as he'd clipped her wrist cuffs to the headboard. Now she knew why he made her wear cuffs to bed.

When she'd demanded that he leave her alone, he'd tilted her chin up, staring into her eyes as he thrust—*slid*—into her easily. Smiling, he murmured that if he ever found her not aroused, then he'd let her sleep. Since just the sound of his voice made her wet, she had a feeling that sexless mornings were a thing of the past.

"This place is amazing. I didn't realize a professor made this kind of money," her mother said.

Abby winced. Today—or soon—she needed to tell Mom that she and Nathan had broken up. And that the house belonged to Xavier.

Thank goodness, he wasn't home today.

Her mother settled on the edge of the patio and picked a happy puppy out of the pen. As it wiggled and licked to express its delight, she laughed and looked at Abby. "You and Nathan must be getting along very well if he's keeping your puppies. Or are you living here?"

"Ah..."

"She's living here—but not with Nathan."

Abby spun.

Xavier stood in the doorway. He'd taken his suit coat off and loosened his tie, looking fully at home as he walked outside.

"You must be Abby's mother." He leaned down to shake hands. "Xavier Leduc."

Even her mother wasn't immune to his devastating smile, and she smiled back. "Carolyn."

"Leduc Industries?" Grace asked. When Xavier nodded, she gave him a wide grin. "I invested in your company in my economics class. You made me a lot of fake money."

Xavier laughed. "I'm pleased to hear it."

Her mother shot Abby a look that said she had some major explaining to do.

I should have hauled the puppies over to Mom's. Her parents and Grace had—thankfully—been on vacation since the Fourth of July. How was she supposed to explain what had happened? Let alone how she'd ended up living with Xavier?

She glanced at him and realized he was watching her, his eyes slightly narrowed. She pulled on her professorial cloak of confidence and told him, "Grace talked my parents into letting her have a puppy. After doing research on cockapoos, she thinks she wants one."

His smile was a caress. "Sounds like intelligence runs in your family."

"Well, just the half that came from Mom," Grace said. "Good manners too, for that matter."

"Grace!" Her mother straightened.

Scowling, Grace walked away.

But Abby had seen the tears. She made a motion to her mother to stay put and followed.

Holding a puppy, Grace stood with her back to the patio and stared at the bay.

Abby put an arm around her. "What's up, sweetie?"

"Janae. She's such a bitch."

Not good. Grace never swore. "What did she do?"

"I'm dating Matthew." Grace flushed. "You met him last year when you came to the basketball game. He brought you a soda, right?"

Long and lanky with an attempted mustache, he'd been both smart and courteous. "I remember."

"Well, I asked him over when we got back yesterday. We were going to watch the new *Men in Black*. Only, Janae came over." The scornful, hurt expression looked wrong on Grace's freckled face. "She…she made a play for Matthew."

Abby stared, an ugly feeling arising. "She's thirteen years older than you two."

"Yeah, well, that didn't seem to matter." Grace nuzzled the top of the puppy's head. "Matthew was, like, weirded out. She was all over him, touching and everything." Grace batted her eyes in one of Janae's flirtatious mannerisms and said in Janae's coo, "*Oh, Matthew, does basketball give you shoulders like that?*"

Abby closed her eyes. She remembered too well how effective her stepsister's techniques were. Abby's few boyfriends had fallen quickly. "Where were Mom and Dad?"

"Outside on the deck." Grace sighed. "I thought about telling them, but Mom wouldn't do anything. And Dad thinks Janae's his sweet little girl, and she'd make it look like I was just jealous."

"I'm not sure what to tell you." Abby's method of hiding her head in the sand hadn't solved anything. Yet the thought of confronting Janae—or anyone—made her insides shrivel into a hard ball.

"It's okay." Grace's mouth firmed. "I know Mom tells us not to rock the boat and to always be polite. But I don't think that's the answer."

Not for Abby's little sister. Mom might have raised her to be polite, but Grace was the daughter of a CEO who'd never backed down from a fight. "I'm afraid you'll have to find your own answer."

"I guess I can *politely* warn the guy that Janae has slept with so many men she probably has every disease in the books."

Abby sputtered a laugh and hugged her.

XAVIER HAD EXCUSED himself to change into jeans and a casual shirt. For a few minutes he watched Abby with her sister from the upstairs window. The two had inherited their mother's big eyes, dainty eyebrows, straight nose, and plump lower lip. Grace's reddish-blonde hair and freckled skin came from her mother, and probably her long legs from her father. A very pretty girl. A troubled one.

But whatever had happened, Abby would help her feel better. His submissive had a comforting personality. But not a forthcoming one. He frowned. She hadn't told her mother about breaking up with Nathan or moving in with Xavier. That was annoying.

They'd have a chat about her silence tonight. Meantime, he intended to get to know her family.

As he walked out on the patio, Grace and Abby had returned to the fur balls. The girl's spirits appeared back to normal as she tried to decide on a puppy.

Xavier grinned at Abby's descriptions. "Blackie is male and headstrong and stubborn," Abby said.

And her favorite, he knew. His as well—the pup had more personality than many humans.

"Blondie is female and sweet. Tippy"—Abby touched the brown one with a black tip on his tail—"male and a wussy. Freckles is male and just plain funny, always carousing and wanting to play. Tiny is female and very shy."

"You couldn't find better names than that?" Grace looked outraged.

"The people who adopt them will give them real names. These are just for identification for me and Xavier."

Her mother smiled at him. "You help her?"

"I've been drafted into late-night feedings, cleaning pens, and washing off paws, yes." And wouldn't give up a minute of it. He gave Abby a look that drew her to his side, then felt her stiffen when he asked, "Would you two care to join us for supper? We're competing for the best French dish. It's my turn tonight."

A couple of hours later he'd decided Abby had a delightful mother and sister. They'd insisted on helping in the kitchen and deliberately dropped tidbits about Abby—how she'd graduated high school at sixteen, done her doctoral thesis at twenty-two. How she'd used her father's life insurance money to travel to a new country each summer in a unique way of memorializing the special times she'd shared with him. Their pride in her was as obvious as her love for them. He was a bit envious of their closeness.

As they dined, Grace peppered him with questions about his past and his business, finally confessing she wanted to be a reporter. She'd be a fine one. At least he'd managed to keep the fact that he owned a BDSM club out of the conversation.

After the meal, he and Grace fed the puppies while Carolyn and Abby cleaned up the kitchen. As he returned with the water dish, he heard Carolyn ask Abby, "Are you going to invite him to the party this Friday, dear?"

Silence. "Um, no."

"Why not? I'd like Harold to meet him. He seems to be a very nice man."

"He is that, but no, Mom. I'm coming alone. I'll be able to help you out with refreshments without worrying about a guest."

Xavier frowned. The little fluff didn't do dishonesty well, and he could hear the lie in her voice. Why?

"But..." The pause stretched out until Carolyn said, "All right, honey. It's your choice, of course."

* * * *

Xavier stood in a downtown hotel ballroom the next day, nodding to people he knew, occasionally joining in conversations, and concealing his boredom. Although he attended many events supporting single mothers, he didn't find charity benefits particularly interesting. In the past, for business and community affairs, he had brought a date to have someone to talk with.

A shame Abby had been buried with grading exams. Her company would have enlivened the evening.

His glass of water stopped partway to his lips. Have her here? She was already staying in his home, serving as staff at his club, and starting a literacy class at Stella's. She'd blurred the lines he'd drawn for years, and now he wanted to add her to his social life?

He needed to think about that.

"Xavier." As an older woman approached, he smiled, grateful for the diversion.

"Mrs. Abernathy, it's good to see you."

"It's wonderful to have you here." Attired in a silver gown that matched her hair, Mrs. Abernathy took his hands. "I appreciate the funding your business has given us over the years."

"It's a worthy cause. A lot of the women coming into Stella's have been helped by you."

"I hope that can continue." Mrs. Abernathy spoke for a few minutes about how the recession had decreased donations to the shelters, yet the number of women needing help had drastically increased.

Xavier listened with a frown. Much as he wanted to help, the corporation's charitable budget already exceeded the board's comfort level.

After an affectionate pat on his hand, Mrs. Abernathy responded to a hail from another guest and bustled away.

"Xavier."

He turned to see someone he knew.

"How nice to see you." She took his hand and went on tiptoes to kiss his cheek. Janae Edgerton was a strikingly beautiful woman with waving, dark-brown hair and dark eyes to match.

"Janae, how have you been?" Something looked different, he thought. Ah. Since he'd seen her last, the medical profession had endowed her with fuller lips and *Playboy*-sized breasts. Being a man, he could appreciate the effect, although he preferred the feel of real breasts. "I don't recall that a charitable event was your usual hunting ground."

She gave him a smile that he knew left most men dropping in her wake. "It's not. But I remembered this was one of your favorite groups."

"And?" Wariness made the question clipped. They'd dated a few times several years ago. As usual, Xavier had disengaged and moved on to the next, although she'd wanted to continue.

"One of my father's favorite charities folded, and he's looking for a replacement. I thought if you met him, you could convince him this would be a worthier cause than preserving some wetland down south." She gave him a flirtatious smile.

He frowned. "I'm merely a contributor. Mrs. Abernathy—"

She shrugged. "Daddy doesn't deal well with women."

"I see." Mrs. Abernathy had convinced him of the urgency for new funding. It would be a shame to lose a donation for something as trivial as a gender bias. "I'd be pleased to speak with him. Will you introduce us?"

"Oh, he's not here. He doesn't attend these things."

Xavier put his hands behind his back and waited patiently for her to come to the point.

"He's giving a party on Friday, and there should be time for you to meet him. He respects people in his…social class." Her appreciative gaze ran over him.

Although Janae had made a vivacious companion and served the purpose of eye candy quite well, he'd never wanted more. Even without his disinclination for vanilla sex. Was this a contrivance to get him to start dating her again? "You want me to attend a party on Friday."

She undoubtedly saw he intended to refuse and added hastily, "Just for an hour. Long enough to talk with Daddy. At nine?"

He didn't have plans for Friday. Abby would be at her parents' party—the one she didn't want him to attend. Dark Haven could survive without him. He had no reason not to obtain a new funding source for Mrs. Abernathy.

But he preferred Janae not make any false assumptions. This would not be a date. "If you give me the address, I'll swing by. For an hour."

Her smile was brilliant. "Perfect. In fact, I'll meet you outside the house so you don't have to search for me." She hastily scribbled down the address.

He turned the paper over in his hand. She'd gone to some work for this. "Thank you, Janae. This is thoughtful of you."

"Not a problem." She kissed him on the cheek, her breasts pressing into his arm, and then strolled away, hips rolling.

As Xavier dismissed her from his mind, he wondered if he could slip out early. Abby should be out from under her test papers by now, and he had a craving to hold her soft little body on his lap.

* * * *

Taking a deep breath of the fresh morning air, Abby stretched her sore neck and shoulder muscles. She shouldn't be out here. She had exams and projects to check, grades to hand in, and her own essay to finish. But eating breakfast on the patio had been a temptation she couldn't resist…especially since Xavier had surprised her with eggs Benedict.

Normally they'd cook together—unless they were competing—but he'd known she was falling behind.

She checked her watch. "You're going to be late to work."

"There's a benefit to being the boss. Mrs. Benton will handle any problems until I get in." He glanced at the clouds in the west. "I wanted to grab some sunshine before it disappears."

The wind had started to pick up, whipping Abby's long batik caftan against her body.

He eyed her. "You wearing anything under that?"

Uh-oh. "Behave yourself. Some of us have to work."

He sipped his coffee, his gaze lingering on where the soft fabric outlined her breasts.

"Men really do think about sex all the time." She frowned. "In a D/s relationship, what happens if you want sex and I don't?"

"I win, pet." A crease appeared in his cheek. "But if I don't make you crave to be fucked, then I'm a poor excuse for a Dom."

Guess that makes him an awesome Dom. She flushed, remembering how quickly he could get her to that craving state. "Then for other stuff—who chooses what chores to do, where to go, the decorating…? There *are* other things besides sex, you know."

His smile disappeared. "I hope you're not teaching your students such a foul lie."

She choked on her tea. "Wouldn't that be an interesting topic? *It all comes down to sex.*" She'd definitely have the attention of every student in her class. "But seriously…"

"You've been here awhile. Is what we're doing not working for you?"

"I keep waiting for you to order me to kneel or say I have to do all the cooking and cleaning."

In the bright light of morning, she could see the laughter in his black eyes. He was dressed for the office in a long-sleeved, cream-colored shirt, but the top buttons were open, giving tantalizing glimpses of his tanned, muscular chest.

She yanked her gaze away. Maybe he was right, and it really was all about sex.

"If you were a slave, then those orders would be reasonable—and expected. However, a Dominant and his submissive usually work out between them how far his dominance extends." His eyes glinted. "There might be times I will have you kneel...simply because I like the way you look at my feet. And how your expression and body change when you do."

Her bones turned soft as she saw the stern set of his jaw and the utter confidence in his posture. "What if I don't want to?" she managed.

"But you do, Abby." He closed his fingers around her hand, firmly enough that she knew she couldn't pull away. He trapped her gaze as well as he said softly, "And if it was inconvenient or uncomfortable, you'd still obey, because it would please me."

She would. The knowledge was frightening and heady at the same time.

"But later, if something truly bothered you, then you'd tell me. And we would adjust the boundaries."

"That sounds workable." But awfully vague. She frowned. "What are the boundaries now?"

"I don't interfere in your work, relatives, friends, what you wear outside the house, or what you do when you're not with me. Your finances and possessions are your own."

Well, that left her a lot of leeway.

"Inside the house or the club…or if we're somewhere together, I assume command since we haven't set any boundaries. So just because I don't care to choose your clothing or ask for service now doesn't mean that will continue." His smile grew. "In fact, I considered telling you to take off your caftan so I could enjoy the sight of you in the sunlight."

She felt heat filling her cheeks with color.

"But I won't because you have work, and the minute you stripped, I'd have you bent over the table."

Her entire lower half tingled, danced, and screamed, *Yes, yes, yes*. She pulled in a breath and kicked her brain into gear. He'd settled her fears on how far his control would extend and created a whole new set of worries. But she was more curious than afraid. "Okay. But what if I just absolutely can't…?"

"Can't do something I order?" His gaze softened, and he squeezed her hand. "You have your safe word, pet. It works as well in the home—or anywhere—as it does in the club."

She hated when he understood her worries so well. Even if it did make her feel all squishy inside.

On the other hand, maybe she needed to test some of those boundaries.

When he set his cup down and reached for the platter in the middle, she snatched the last piece of Canadian bacon off the plate before he could…and was rewarded with a dark frown. "So sorry, lord and master, but you snooze, you lose."

XAVIER TAPPED HIS fingers on the table. She would definitely pay for her theft. "That, my little fluff, is called bratty behavior."

Her chewing stopped for all of one second before the smirk reappeared. Yes, she was starting to be able to read him, now that her fear of his anger had decreased. "Do I get a funishment, then?"

"This is a serious crime." He stretched his legs out, enjoying the warmth of the sun. "I'll think of something nasty. Perhaps painful as well. Tonight, I believe. Or maybe at the club tomorrow."

Ah, her gaze held a tiny hint of anxiety. Perfect.

Then he frowned. "Didn't you mention being gone this weekend?" Would she invite him?

She blinked. "Oh, right. Yes, I have a party to attend on Friday night. It's at my parents' house for their anniversary." She went no further. Extended no invitation.

He didn't like the uncomfortable feeling that invaded his chest. Apparently, even after she'd had time to think, she didn't want him to meet the rest of her family. Or her friends. His hand tightened on the cup. Then he set it down slowly enough that it made no sound.

"How about you? Are you going to the club?" Abby asked.

He'd hoped to be with her, but come to think of it, he had an appointment to meet Janae Edgerton's father. Mrs. Abernathy would definitely owe him a favor.

"I'll—" He stopped. Abby had mentioned his *gorgeous and glamorous* women. Telling her that he was joining one at a party would make her more insecure. "I'll probably stop by Dark Haven."

Chapter Twenty-Two

The day had turned gloomy in the way only San Francisco could. A rare summer storm had blown in from the ocean. Rain ran in long streams down the windshield, resembling the tears Abby refused to shed. Her hands were clenched tightly in her lap. *I didn't want to let them go*. Her heart ached, and each beat made the hurt worse. *I wasn't ready.*

The phone call from the rescue organization had taken her by surprise.

Xavier took one hand from the steering wheel to stroke her arm. "The woman said they'd get good homes. They're careful about who gets to adopt, and the pups will be safer than if they returned to the shelter."

"I know. At least Grace took Blondie." She blinked hard. "Thank you for coming with me." It was good that he had, actually. Her mind wouldn't have been on driving. "I didn't realize turning them in would be this hard." It never had hurt so much before.

He rubbed his knuckles over her cheek. "I daresay you probably smothered the pain before. You're quite good at hiding your emotions from yourself." The corner of his mouth tipped up slightly. "Or you were."

"I think I'd rather they stay smothered," she whispered as he drove into the garage.

She didn't wait for him to open her door but hurried up the ramp into the house. All she wanted was a place to hide away so she could cry.

Unyielding hands closed on her shoulders and turned her around. He pulled her into his arms, cradling her head against his shoulder. "Let go, Abby. Don't be ashamed of crying."

"B-but it hurts." Blackie had watched her leave, confusion in his dark eyes. *I want him back*. She tried to push away and got nowhere, and as if the struggle had destroyed the last of her walls, the sobs tore through her, hurting her chest, shattering the peace of the quiet house. The icy ball around her heart started to melt.

He held her close, a mountain against the storm of her tears. Solid. Immovable. His warmth seeped into her; his breathing never faltered.

When she'd finished and only shuddering breaths remained, he kissed the top of her head. "You're shivering. Come." He took her hand and pulled her out to the right side of the patio, past the swimming pool. As he uncovered the stone-encircled hot tub, steam rose from the surface.

"I just want to—"

"Hide. I know." He stripped her, ignoring her protests. As if she were blind, he guided her into the tub, keeping a hand on her until she sat down. The heat penetrated her skin, moving deep into her bones and melting the last of the coldness.

With a sigh she leaned back and watched him undress as thin tendrils of steam lifted around her. His darkly tanned body was beautiful, and her gaze lingered on the line of muscles that indented his thighs and his tight buttocks.

He caught her watching, and the concern in his face eased as he took a seat next to her.

"I'm okay now. Thank you." She shouldn't have let herself get so attached, except at first she'd considered keeping one of the puppies. *Keeping Blackie.* But when she'd moved in with Xavier, she'd known it couldn't happen. His beautiful landscape would have to be fenced, his antiques would be chewed on and carpets peed on. And they weren't really together, not permanently. He wouldn't change his whole home for a summer lover.

The woman said she had prospective homes for all of the babies. They'd be fine. They would.

As the erratic rain started again, cold drops pattered on her face and made tiny ripples on the surface of the water. Silently Xavier picked up her hand and kissed her fingers. He wasn't trying to seduce her, but merely comforting her.

"You're a nice man."

His laugh sounded surprised, but the deep, rich sound filled the hollows inside her.

They sat in silence for a few minutes, and then Xavier told her about his day. Sharing without being asked, as if he knew she needed a diversion.

He wasn't a man to talk of himself, which seemed funny, for she was the same way. But they were both extremely good at quizzing another person. She hadn't realized how one-sided her conversations with Nathan had been, perhaps because they'd discussed other matters—politics, academics, society. But although he'd shared his day's activities, he'd never asked about hers. She hadn't noticed the lack before, not until Xavier.

"Marilee said to tell you thank you."

Abby frowned. "She's not leaving my class, is she? She's progressing incredibly fast, but she's not ready—"

"No, pet." Xavier moved closer, putting his arm behind her back. "But she now reads well enough to get hired. One of my friends owns a pastry shop on Market Street."

"Really?" Happiness for the woman welled up inside her. Then she frowned. "How? Surely she can't sound everything out yet, and—"

"Her placement counselor took her in to practice everything she'd have to read."

Abby gave him a suspicious look.

"Yes, I leaned on my friend a little, but Marilee is intelligent. I think she'll be excellent at the job. It'll serve until you teach her enough to train for something challenging."

She snuggled into his side. All of this because he'd seen his mother's suffering. "You always expect them to move on. Isn't the turnover rather taxing for Leduc Industries?"

"Mmm." He rubbed his cheek against hers, the slight abrasion of his day-old whiskers like a spark igniting dry kindling. "The managers know I expect the women to make something more of their lives. Minimum-wage jobs have a high turnover no matter what, but our women are highly motivated. They show up on time, work hard, and learn quickly. My managers are happy."

"That's very cool."

"I'm a nice man, remember." A crease appeared in his cheek as heat grew in his eyes. "Nice men must be rewarded, or they'll turn to evil." His hand closed in her hair, trapping her as he fondled her breasts and tugged lightly on her nipples.

“We can’t have that.” Her voice came out breathy.

“No. We can’t.” He curled her hand around his cock, moving it up and down. When he pinched her nipple, heat flared inside her, and her fingers tightened involuntarily. He laughed.

“Kneel up, Abby, sideways on the seat.” She pulled her legs under her and faced him. The water was at her waist, the air cool against her heated skin. Her nipples bunched.

When he set her hands on his arms, she stroked his biceps, enjoying how his wet skin stretched tautly over rock-hard muscles.

He cupped her breasts, pressed them together, and sucked on one nipple. He grinned when she squeaked, ran his tongue around the peak before sucking on the other. Back and forth.

The rhythm sank into her bones, flowed down to her lower half, and woke her core to a molten arousal. Each pulse of his mouth increased her need until she ached for more. Her fingers locked on to his shoulders, her nails digging into his velvety skin.

How could she get him to touch her pussy? Her aching clit? Trying to direct Xavier was like attempting to steer a bulldozer from under the treads.

His amused gaze met hers. Oh, he knew full well what he was doing to her. “Turn around now.” He gripped her around the waist, facing her outward.

In the thick fog, the lights from the Golden Gate appeared and disappeared like hovering fireflies. “Hands forward.” She put her arms onto the coolness of the stone surface around the tub, feeling the cold rain spattering on her shoulders. He rose behind her, reaching for the concrete statue of a sea monster near the edge. From a concealed compartment in its scaly side, he removed lengths of hard, narrow plastic and a pair of heavy scissors.

"You're going to use zip ties on me?" She stared at him in disbelief.

"Mmmhmm. They work nicely in damp areas like hot tubs and pools." He tightened one plastic strip over her wrist and one of his fingers. Her anticipation—and anxiety—increased with the staccato sound the zip ties made. After slipping his finger out and checking that the tie was loose enough, he did her left wrist. The cool plastic heated quickly over her skin.

He hooked the bracelets together with a third, then pulled her arms forward so he could slip the band under one of the monster's hook-like claws.

The restraint forced her to lean over the side of the hot tub, and the edge dug into her breasts. "Ow, that hurts."

"Sorry, pet." With an arm around her waist, he lifted her up and arranged her so her breasts rested on the cold stone.

"What are you—"

A quick pinch on her nipple silenced her. He pulled two wide canvas straps from the compartment. Reaching under the water, he put one strap around her right lower thigh and hooked the ends to something, securing her leg. He did the same on her left, tightening the strap until it pulled her legs apart.

"Now that's a pretty sight. A kneeling submissive restrained to a monster, legs wide open so her cunt is available…for anything I want to do." He ran his hands up and down her torso, then leaned forward to fondle her breasts until they were swollen and tight. Cold rain hammered her arms and head as he tugged lightly on her nipples. He rolled the peaks between his fingers until she was panting with the combination of pain and pleasure. His cock rubbed in the crack of her butt, teasing her.

When she yanked futilely on the restraints, he leaned his chest against her back and whispered in her ear, "It's a shame you can't fight, isn't it?"

Her lower half felt as if it had reached the temperature of the water and kept rising. "I changed my mind," she muttered. "You're not nice at all."

Laughing, he reached underwater to play with the hot-tub jets. Sheltering her pussy with one hand, he adjusted the output until…

When he lifted his hand, a driving stream of water hit her clit.

"Oh no." The high, hard velocity shoved her straight toward a climax.

"You're right. That's far too quick," he murmured and rotated the face of the jet. The pressure decreased to that of a firm finger and the flow oscillated in circles, like a showerhead massager. "Good." He patted her shoulder. "Stay put, pet."

She struggled for a moment, trying to shift toward or away from the stream of water, and got nowhere. The undersides of her breasts scraped on the stone edge, adding an erotic touch of pain. As the pulsing circled her clit, pressure built within her. More and more. She looked for Xavier and saw him sitting on the side, his hand fisted over his thick shaft that glistened with lube. He didn't move, simply enjoyed the show.

"You…" He was going to leave her here?

The jets of water took no notice, tapping and rubbing her clit. Everything inside her gathered.

He smiled as her climax approached, impossibly inevitable. "Look at me, Abigail."

His dark eyes held hers as the tide crested inside her and swept outward, shaking her body in waves of pleasure. Her eyes closed with the shudders of the aftermath.

She stiffened when Xavier's body pressed against her from behind. Momentarily cool against her heated flesh, his hand covered her pussy and blocked the jets from her now sensitive clit. "I do like watching you come," he murmured in her ear.

With one hard thrust he entered her, thick and long. Her insides spasmed around the penetration, sending shock waves of pleasure tingling along sensitized nerves. He reached forward to the jet and did something, but his hand still covered her pussy.

"I'd say hang on, but the restraints remove that option." He nibbled on her earlobe as he pulled back and slammed into her again. "There are times I like taking you this way," he whispered, "knowing you can't do anything to stop me. Your body is mine to play with—mine to fuck." Each word was emphasized by a thrust of his cock, and she felt arousal and need beginning again.

"I can watch you orgasm without me." With his free hand, he fondled her breasts, pinching the tips to make her insides clench. "But there's nothing like your cunt battering at my cock when you come.

"Come again." His hand on her pussy shifted, so his fingers V'd around her clit, pulling the folds back to expose it. To hold it in place. The jet struck in heavy pulses right on the top.

"Aaaaah!" Goaded unbearably, her body went rigid. His hand didn't move as he hammered into her from behind, timing his thrusts to match the pulses of the jet, so the sensations merged. *Too much.* Too overwhelming.

She tipped over the edge in an avalanche of pleasure, shuddering and shaking. Her cries echoed off the pavement, and he laughed, then made a wonderful guttural sound as he pushed deep and let himself go.

By the time her heart stopped hammering her ribs into kindling and she could take a slow breath, he'd turned off the jet, snipped her zip ties, and unstrapped her legs. When she sat on the bench, tiny bubbles rose from below and tickled her overly sensitive pussy, making her squirm.

He laughed and turned her to face him. "Straddle me, pet."

Settling her knees on each side of his thighs, he slid forward and pulled her down on his still-hard cock.

"I thought you came?"

"And I certainly enjoyed it." He cupped her jawline, holding her for his kiss, long and lingering. "I wanted to be inside you for a while yet," he murmured and kissed her again.

She felt him softening within her core. With his arms around her, his thighs between her knees, his tongue in her mouth, she felt twined with him in so many ways she wasn't sure where he started and she finished.

He released her and leaned her against his shoulder.

Absently she unraveled his braid so she could enjoy the feeling of his loose hair over her fingers, her shoulders. "I should start supper. It's my turn."

His heart beat an even rhythm as he stroked her shoulders with firm hands. "Relax for a bit, Abby. You've had a hard day."

He took such care with her. As emotions swept through her, irresistible as any she'd had, the words were out before she could recall them. "I love you. So much. I—" She froze and choked. *What have I done?*

His hand stopped in the middle of a stroke, then continued on. He didn't speak.

She couldn't stand the silence. "Have I ruined everything? What—"

"I didn't quite expect this, Abby. I don't know."

Obviously not. Had she really expected to hear, *I love you too?* Her jaw tightened. "Well, what do you feel like? Is your stomach tight? Heart hammering? Throat closed?"

He snorted. "Sassy submissive." He gripped her shoulders and pushed her back to look at her. His expression was unreadable, his eyes not cold but...distant. "Give me a day to think, and then we'll talk. Can you do that?"

"Sure." She wanted to tear herself away. To run and hide like a little girl. But he pulled her forward, and his arms closed around her.

"I care, Abby. Never doubt that."

Uh-huh. He cared about everyone in the club. That wasn't the same. But...life hadn't gone out of its way to give her what she wanted—especially when it came to relationships. Look at Nathan, and at all the guys who preferred Janae to her. Maybe she just wasn't enough.

She settled into Xavier's embrace, and the feeling of his arms holding her close, so strong and firm, so everything she'd always wanted, gave her the most bittersweet feeling she'd ever known.

Chapter Twenty-Three

Xavier started the weekend early and drove out to his small ranch near Bodega Bay on Friday. The ranch hands were pleased to see him and filled with news of the horses. After admiring the two new mares, he saddled a horse and went for a ride. The sun was hot and the scent of ocean heavy in the air. He'd forgotten how much he enjoyed being here.

Loosening the reins slightly, he rocked the horse into an easy canter over the rolling grasslands. His freed hair whipped over his shoulders, dispelling the memories for a moment. At one time he and Catherine had visited every weekend to enjoy being out of the city—and to visit her rescued mustangs.

He smiled slightly. Abby had the same nurturing spirit.

At the highest point on the ranch, he dismounted and stood on the bluff, watching the distant ocean. This had been their spot. Catherine had called it her place to settle and get her head on straight.

She'd died down there at the ranch house.

Up here was where he'd buried her ashes.

"Well, Catherine." Over the years he'd felt her presence here. Perhaps his imagination, perhaps not.

Last night, when Abby had said she loved him, he'd realized he still hadn't resolved his feelings for Catherine. He wasn't able to offer all of himself, and that wasn't fair to Abby.

With a sigh, he settled beside Catherine's stone marker. BELOVED WIFE.

"You were that," he said. "My beloved slave and beloved partner as well." He leaned against the tree that sheltered her. "You died so quickly. I never got a chance to tell you good-bye."

She'd driven up to see a new foal, staying by herself in the ranch house. The two ranch hands had found her the next morning, already gone. The doctors insisted her death happened quickly—a ruptured aortic aneurysm. Nothing would have saved her.

The reasons didn't matter. He should have been there for her.

"I came to say good-bye, Cat." He traced a circle in the dirt. "I'm ready—and I know you're saying, *About time.* Abby's a lovely woman with as big a heart as yours."

A red-tailed hawk circled overhead. Far below, gulls dived at the water.

He hadn't thought he'd ever arrive at a time when he wanted to open his heart again. Yet here he was. His chest ached as if the horse had kicked him.

"I'll always love you, little slave. I didn't think I could care for someone else as deeply, but she's taken hold." He pulled in a breath and admitted it to himself. To the world. "I really do love her."

The words struck him, ran through him, shocked him. So he said them again. "I love her. Abigail Bern." He gazed out at the land rolling down to the ocean. Somehow he'd found a trail he hadn't anticipated.

Yet life wasn't a nice flat plain, as he'd believed in his youth, but hills and valleys, corners and switchbacks and cliffs. "Wish me well, Cat."

* * * *

On Friday night, taking a moment from the party, Abby checked herself in the bathroom mirror. Not too shabby. Her new gown was a light lavender. The halter top style was perfect for her breasts, and the fuller skirt slenderized her hips. She'd pulled the sides of her hair back in tiny French braids to show off her silver earrings.

No necklace, though. She traced a curve over the hollow of her neck. How would it feel to have a silver choker? One like Rona wore?

That wasn't going to happen, was it? Why had she blurted her feelings out? The memory of Xavier's reaction darkened her mood like the atmosphere before a storm. She glowered at herself in the mirror. If he didn't want to hear about emotions, then why did he keep hammering at her to express them?

What did she get in return? Politeness. *I love him, and he wants to* think *about it.*

Plastering a smile on her face, she walked into the crowded living room filled with Harold's business associates, Mom's friends, people from the charities they supported, neighbors, and older friends.

Her mother spotted her. "Your idea to put twinkling lights in the trees was brilliant. It's so romantic out there that people are dancing already."

"The band sounds great." Every anniversary, Harold gave a party to celebrate "*finding the most wonderful woman in the world.*" Over time the number of guests had tripled, but the feeling of love never changed.

"I'm glad you came, dear." Her mom hesitated. "Is there anything wrong?"

"Nope. Happy anniversary, Mom." Abby gave her a quick hug and released her as more people entered the room. The hum of conversation increased.

After checking the bathrooms and living rooms for messes, Abby wandered out to the wide patio and smiled. The lights might be romantic, but Mom and Harold were even more so, waltzing to Anne Murray's "Can I Have this Dance?"

Swaying to the music, Abby sighed. She'd never danced with Xavier. She had a feeling she never would. Why had she ever opened her mouth?

"They look good together, don't they?" Grace stopped behind her, grinning when her father gave a hearty laugh and kissed their mother right on the lips.

"Makes you believe in love, doesn't it?" Abby asked lightly. The ocean breeze whispered over her bare arms. Thank goodness she hadn't invited Xavier to the party. It would have been horrible to see him so distant. To know the "talk" was coming.

"A couple of the guys asked about you, by the way," Grace said. She nodded toward a man with a goatee.

Abby looked. His hair was receding, but when he met her gaze, his eyes were sharp and intelligent.

"The other one works in Dad's company. Dad called him brilliant, and I figured you might like him." Grace grinned. "I know you prefer smart men—and he's cute—and he asked what your name is."

Abby gave her a wry smile. "That's only because Janae hasn't arrived."

"Oh." Grace's face hardened. "I hope she doesn't come."

Uh-oh. Abby squeezed Grace's hand. "Is she still trying for Matthew?"

"He avoids her." Grace blinked back tears. "I'm glad she doesn't live here. She used to ignore me, but now she smiles and cuts me to pieces."

Abby took a slow breath. "I think..." She hesitated, then went ahead. "I think it's because you're a woman now and getting more beautiful by the day. All of a sudden you're competition."

"Get real." Grace sputtered a laugh. "Like I'm anything like—"

"Remember Snow White? When the mirror told the stepmother that she was no longer the 'fairest in the land,' she tried to kill Snow White."

"So my half sister's trying to slaughter me with insults." Grace snorted. "She can *try*."

Abby's worry eased. Nothing kept Grace down for long.

"Is that why she's nasty to you? You're competition?" Grace said. "But—"

But Abby wasn't any challenge when it came to men. "She was an only child. Before me." Abby tilted her head toward Harold. "She got used to being the center of attention, and that's what she has to be. With Harold, in classrooms, with men."

"So it's not *personal*, huh? Hey, it's wicked cool to think I'm competition." She tapped Abby's knuckles with hers and headed off toward her teenage friends. Her shoulders were back and her hips swinging with a new assurance.

Abby caught her mother's glance and smiled. *Thanks, Mom. Although you stuck me with a bitch of a stepsister, this one makes it all worthwhile.*

Her mom smiled back.

Half an hour later Abby had turned down dates from the two men—although she seriously considered getting their numbers. What would Xavier do if she informed him he had to wear a condom again because she'd indulged herself with another man?

He might say they weren't committed, but she had a feeling he'd be upset.

Unfortunately she didn't want anyone else. Dutifully she did another check of the rooms, swung by the kitchen to remind them to take drinks to the tiny band, then returned to the patio. She took a seat at a linen-covered table with a sigh of relief. Her feet were killing her. Why didn't men have to suffer the torture of high heels?

Harold's laugh boomed out as he and her mother chatted with the neighbors. The younger business associates had settled by the food, arguing about capital gains taxes. Having talked the band into something livelier, the teen set was dancing. At a nearby table, some women discussed day-care issues. The party was rolling along well.

And she missed Xavier with an ache that continued to grow.

In fact, she swore she heard his voice. *Nice imagination you have, Abby.* But… She tilted her head. That was his laugh, deep and resonant, coming from inside the house. Had Mom invited him after all?

Had he come to be with her? The surge of joy was almost frightening. Smiling, she started toward the patio door.

Janae stepped out. Her dark-red dress must have been sprayed on, and set off full breasts she hadn't possessed a few years ago.

When Xavier followed her out, Janae turned and snuggled against him.

Abby's breath caught in her throat.

Xavier said something, and Janae looked up at him with the same slow smile she'd used to conquer man after man. He laughed and walked with her across the patio.

He hadn't even seen Abby. Hadn't looked for her.

Abby couldn't move. The pain was too much, spilling out onto the ground, and every beat of her mangled heart added to the pool. *He didn't come here for me.* Janae had taken him away, just as she had every other man Abby had liked.

Even worse, they looked so comfortable together that Abby knew Xavier had been dating her. *And fucking me.* She blinked back tears until Janae flicked a glance over, and the gloating showed in her eyes.

Icy armor slid over Abby's skin, settling in place as if it had never gone away. As if she'd never left herself open to being wounded. But the defense arrived too late. The pain was already lodged deep in her chest, pounding from inside against the barrier.

They would never, ever know how much they'd hurt her. She pulled in a breath and forced her hands to unclench.

Janae reached up to plant a kiss on Xavier's lips and then walked with him over to her parents. With a shocked expression, her mother looked at Abby.

I'm going to be sick.

As Harold shook hands with Xavier, Janae sauntered over to Abby. "Did you see my eye candy?" Janae's laugh was so loud and false that several people turned to look.

"Yes." Insult after insult rose to the surface of her mind, and she pushed them down. *Don't start a fight. Be cold. Be ice.* Abby took a step back.

Janae grabbed her arm. "You gonna run? Go hide?"

"I'm not interested in talking with you." Abby tried to pull her arm away.

"Oh, did fat nerd-girl get her feelings hurt? Did you actually think he might be interested in you?" Another laugh. "Nathan—yes, *your oh-so-kinky* Nathan—told me Xavier's habits are common knowledge. He keeps several women: a smart one for business. A gorgeous one to date. And a slave to fuck… Oh, that would be *you*."

Nathan? Janae had sex with Nathan too? But the blow had little impact under the avalanche of pain.

Dixon had warned her Xavier wouldn't be serious. She hadn't listened. She'd lied to herself. She'd been a moron. But seeing him with Janae was intolerable.

She yanked her arm away, and Janae's long fingernails tore her skin. Turning, she ran into something immovable. Hard. *Xavier.*

TRYING TO UNDERSTAND what he'd heard, Xavier caught his little sub as she stumbled.

When she looked up at him, her pale skin was the white of snow and her gray eyes frozen. She took a step back, shoving his hand away. "Don't. Touch. Me." Her smooth voice held no expression, no heat. She'd retreated from him before, but never like this.

"Abby," he said. "This isn't—"

"Red, Xavier. Red, red, red." The cold mask of her face never changed as she used the safe word that ended a scene.

She turned and ran, and he could almost hear the ice shattering.

"Abby!"

Janae grabbed Xavier's arm, holding him back. "You're with me, remember?" Her smile grew.

Xavier stared down, seeing the vindictiveness in her eyes. "You're her stepsister, aren't you? And you set this up to hurt Abby. With her soft heart, I doubt she's ever done anything to you."

Janae's face twisted. "You don't—"

"No, I don't. But I recognize a self-centered woman who hurts everyone around her." He peeled away her hand like removing a slug from his shoe, strode through the house and out the front door.

"Can I help you, sir?" The valet hurried over.

"Abby. Has she—"

The uniformed man pointed toward red taillights speeding away. She must have parked near the door rather than in the lot.

Janae had set him up like a patsy, just to get her claws in Abby. And he'd fallen for it. Rage simmered in his guts, but guilt—and worry—overwhelmed it.

He hit speed dial on his phone, calling her cell. *No answer*. He left a message on it and then at her house. "I'm sorry, Abby. We need to talk. Call me."

Although knowing she wouldn't return to his house, he went there anyway. Hoping. He had to check. Yes, her clothing was still in the dresser.

Back out into the cold. *How could I have screwed up so fatally?*

She wasn't at her duplex. As he stared at the blank windows, his jaw was so tight his teeth made grinding noises. Where was she? Driving? Hurt? She might be crying. Wouldn't be careful. Could have an accident.

He called the emergency rooms. All of them. Called in a favor and had a friend check the police reports.

Nothing.

What the hell had he done? Last night she'd said she loved him. As if in answer, he'd taken her stepsister to her parents' party.

He punched in another number. Simon said she hadn't called.

She wasn't at her office at the university.

Xavier drove to Dark Haven, where Lindsey's number was in the files. Abby hadn't called her. Wasn't there.

How could he get her to believe he wanted to be with her? Only her.

What about her parents? Harold Edgerton's number was listed. He punched it in. Grace called him several names, the nicest of which was *slimy scumsucker*, but finally admitted Abby wasn't there.

Back to Mill Valley. He parked on the road and stared at the empty parking spot and the black windows. She hadn't returned to her duplex.

He let his head fall back. Let his anger loose…

Goddamn motherfucking son of a bitch. If—when—he found her, he was going to turn her ass a rosy red, after he fucking apologized for a fucking eternity. He had been a fucking gullible idiot. Janae would regret hurting Abby—yes, she definitely would—but he was the one who'd done the damage.

He scrubbed his hands over his face and pulled in a breath. Pulled back his control.

He stuck a message to her door. Put more messages on every voice mail she owned. "Abby, I'm sorry. I love you. Call me."

When he gave up and returned home, the house was too quiet. No Abby. No warmth. His world had been hollowed to emptiness in one night.

He'd ripped her heart out and stomped on it—that was how she must feel. The knowledge that he'd caused her such pain—even if he hadn't intended to—sliced through him, leaving agony behind.

How could he fix this? He needed to *fix* it.

* * * *

At the vista point at the end of Point Lobos, Abby watched the starlight on the Pacific Ocean. No moon at all. Waves broke over the rocky cliffs below, covering up the noise from the city. *Lands End.* It seemed the place to be right now. Ships had wrecked here off the rocky coast, unable to navigate the waters. Much like her attempt at a relationship.

Or maybe it hadn't even been a relationship.

What was wrong with her that she wasn't enough for a man? First Nathan, then Xavier. The damp air swirling up the cliffs chilled her tear-dampened face.

"I don't get it," she whispered to the dark trees. "He acted as if he liked me. He wanted me to live with him." *And stupid me, I fell in love with him.*

But who wouldn't? Along with that hard-edged domination, he was tender and loving and protective.

Janae had called her a slave, just someone for him to fuck. Abby rested her chin on her knees as her hair whipped around her face. *If all he wanted was a slave, then why did he cook me breakfast yesterday? And hold me when I cried?*

He'd said over and over that he didn't want a slave. He wanted someone to talk with at supper, to trounce at billiards, and to play tag with in the swimming pool. He'd said he enjoyed arguing with her.

"I'm not a slave," she muttered, feeling the familiar anger and frustration at her stepsister. The waves below slapped into the rocks. Her hand shook with the need to slap Janae's face.

But violence wouldn't change the truth.

Just like all her men, Xavier preferred Janae. *I wasn't even good enough to date.* He'd never taken her anywhere. Not even to a movie.

She swiped her arm over her wet cheeks. He'd been loving and sweet last night…until she said she loved him.

"*Give me a day to think,*" he'd said. And then he took Janae out. To dance with. To introduce to his friends and be introduced in turn. To Mom and Harold's party.

She'd done his introduction to Mom and Grace wrong. *It should have been: "Mom, this is Janae's date and my Master who keeps me around to fuck."*

Year after year Janae left her feeling inadequate. But she'd never felt like the dregs at the bottom of a teapot before. The mournful sound of a boat coming in wafted over the water. The air had cooled, and she was still in her gown. It would be stained from sitting on a rock. *I never want to see it again.*

I never want to see Xavier again.

As she stood, her stiff muscles ached, and she shivered, chilled inside and out. What should she do now? Her clothes were at his house.

Xavier would want to talk. If she didn't return to his place, he'd show up at hers. He might not love her, but he never abandoned his responsibilities. He'd want to make sure she was all right.

Well, she wasn't. And she didn't particularly care what he thought.

Discedere ad inferos, my liege. *Go to hell.*

Chapter Twenty-Four

Xavier parked in front of Abby's duplex. It was Wednesday, and her car wasn't there. *Still.* He'd driven by several times a day—and night—and as far as he could tell she hadn't returned home since the party last Saturday. Her summer classes had concluded as of last week. She wasn't at the university. He'd stuck another note on her door.

At the volunteer center she'd called in and handed over her beloved literacy class to a different instructor for "a while." He scrubbed his face, scowling at the scrape of stubble. He needed to shave.

He'd left messages everywhere.

But she was alive. The last time he'd called her parents' home, her mother had informed him that Abby was fine, then hung up on him. That didn't sound fine.

He closed his eyes. How could he make things right if he couldn't find her? Talk with her? He huffed a laugh. He couldn't even send her the old standby, flowers, to get his foot in the door.

With a sigh he turned his car around and headed home.

An SUV sat in his driveway, and his front door stood open. His spirits lifted like a wind had filled the sails. The car wasn't Abby's, but no one else had a key to his house. She was here. He started to pull in beside the vehicle.

No. "No more running, little fluff." He parked his car directly behind the SUV, thwarting any chance of her escaping him.

Hopes rising, he strode up to the house.

Rona stepped out and almost dropped a suitcase at the sight of him. "Xavier." Her face turned an interesting color of red.

"Are you robbing me, Rona?"

"I... We... I wasn't expecting you."

"Is Abby inside?"

After a second she regained her self-possession in the way that so delighted Simon. Her chin rose. "No, we're not stealing from you, and Abby isn't here."

From her stubborn expression, she'd dispensed as much information as he would get. He heard someone pattering down the inside stairs and after a second realized they weren't his little sub's footsteps. She really wasn't here. His optimism drained away, leaving him exhausted.

Lindsey trotted out the door and stopped short with a startled huff of air. "Oh."

"Tell me where Abby is." He put an edge of command into the order.

"She's—" Her mouth closed, and her expression matched Rona's. "Sorry, sir. I'm just a moving girl and sure not going to poke my nose into something that's none of my business." From the hostility in her face, she'd definitely taken sides.

Xavier tamped down his anger. He'd hurt Abby badly, and she had a right to protect herself. He shouldn't be surprised she'd found some staunch defenders. His little fluff had the knack of winning hearts, even if she didn't realize it.

Lindsey made a wide detour around him and put the suitcase in the car. With a dismissive look, Rona followed.

He had half a mind to tell them never to set foot in Dark Haven again, but they hadn't broken club rules. Rona hadn't even disobeyed Simon, since their D/s relationship didn't extend to certain areas—like who Rona had for friends.

Xavier wanted the same kind of flexible arrangement with Abby—if he could ever figure out how to find her.

After opening her car door, Rona glared at him. "Xavier, please move your car."

"In a minute." From the unfriendly stares bouncing off his hide, he'd have no success pleading his case with them. And that discussion should happen between him and Abby. "Will you ask her to call me?"

Rona shook her head. "She doesn't want to hear about you or from you."

Then she'd probably never listened to the voice mails he'd left. "You will take two messages to her from me." His voice came out hard, and they both took a step back. "Her research project is due tomorrow, but the deal was that I'd read the final draft."

Lindsey looked at him in dismay. "But—"

"The first message is—I'll accept Simon's judgment as an adequate substitute."

Relief crossed Rona's face. "That's kind of you. She's been worried."

The little fluff wouldn't believe any admission of love. Not at this point. What would work to lure her to him? "The second message is simply this: I was wrong."

Both women looked startled.

He attempted to smile. "I won't try to track her, *if* you promise you'll convey just that."

Lindsey still looked more ready to spit in his face than take the message, but the streaky-haired Texan had fled a brutal divorce.

He looked at Rona instead.

She finally nodded. "Okay. You've got your two messages."

* * * *

Abby took her suitcase and swung it onto the bed in Lindsey's guest room. "Thanks, Rona."

"You're welcome. However, the price is that you join us for some wine, Ms. Hermit." Rona gave her a mother's formidable frown.

I don't want to leave this room. But she needed to. She'd hidden like a wounded lion in a cave. "I haven't been very sociable, have I?"

"Quite understandable, but it's time to rejoin the world. Now."

"Are you sure that Simon is the dominant one in your marriage?"

"Most definitely." Rona smiled smugly from the doorway. "But everywhere else? I *rule*."

As the door closed, Abby laughed, probably her first one in days.

She washed her face in cool water, then followed the sound of voices down the narrow hallway, through the almost bare living room, and onto the balcony. Lindsey's new apartment was on the eighth floor with a pretty view of the city. The two women sat at a tiny café table. Lindsey had propped her bare feet on the wrought iron railing. Her deep-red toenails shimmered with glittering stars.

Not having toenails that could compete, Abby chose a chair behind the table and poured herself a glass of wine. "Mmmm." The merlot was smooth and fruity. "Very nice."

"It's one of my favorites. When I took a group tour of the Napa Valley, I fetched back a few bottles for my wine cellar." Lindsey grinned. "Poor me. My cellar is only a wooden rack in the hall closet, but it's a start."

"I've visited wineries, but since I drove, I had to stop after a drink or two," Abby said, making an effort to share in the conversation. "A tour would be smart."

Rona nodded. "That's true. Maybe we should book a weekend and go enjoy ourselves."

"I—" Abby started to refuse and stopped at the sight of Lindsey's hopeful eyes. The streaky-haired brunette had moved from Dallas to escape a horrible marriage, but she'd grown up in Texas, and her family and friends were all there. How sad to go from an abundance of relatives and friends to none. "I'd love to try a tour." Especially since she didn't have the heart to go on her usual vacation abroad. "I've got almost a month before school starts. Sign me up."

Much like Grace, Lindsey showed every emotion—and now she glowed. "Shoot, the three of us? Those wineries won't know what hit them."

Odd how making someone else happy could lift a person's spirits. Abby's smile seemed to fit on her face again. She raised her glass to toast, and there was nothing there. "How did I drink that so fast?"

Rona filled the glass. "You're not driving, so who cares?" She poured some into Lindsey's glass. "Neither are you." After opening a new bottle of wine, she filled her own. "And you two are going to steer me into a taxi. Simon wanted to pick me up, but he might well share the address with Xavier. Men are totally untrustworthy that way."

"I appreciate it." Abby said. No, the mention of Xavier's name had not sent tremors through her body. It *hadn't.*

"To friends." Rona raised her glass and clinked it against the other two. "It's nice to have more women in the lifestyle, and even nicer that you're a few years past drinking age."

Abby winced, remembering Nathan's young "slut." She should have punched him. Making a hard fist, she nodded. She really should have, even if she'd have hidden under a table when he yelled.

She gulped more wine. As it started to buzz in her head, she remembered she'd skipped lunch. Actually she'd missed quite a few meals, enough that her jeans were loose. Excellent diet—the *Xavier Plan.*

"So." Rona's blue-green eyes turned serious. "Xavier showed up at the house."

"What?"

"I saw him and almost had a conniption fit." Lindsey wiped mock sweat away. "If the invincible Rona hadn't been there, I might have buckled. He's scarier than a pissed-off wolverine."

Despite the pain of thinking of him, Abby snorted. "More like Count Dracula."

"True." Lindsey tilted her head. "Did you ever listen to those messages he's left you?"

"Uh-uh. I delete them right away." *Because I'd cave in and listen otherwise.*

"Impressive willpower," Rona said. "Well, I'll blurt this out quick. He said he'll accept Simon as his proxy for reading your research article."

Abby's mouth dropped open. "Really?" As her spine turned to jelly, she sagged. "That's…that's nice of him. I'll give you the papers before you leave."

"His second message was to say '*I was wrong.*'"

"Rona!" Abby shoved away from the table, making it rock, and put her hands over her ears. "I won't hear this."

Rona caught her wine glass before it hit the floor. And just looked at Abby. Patiently.

"I can't believe I worked so hard not to…" She lowered her hands. "What does that mean—he was wrong?"

Rona winked at Lindsey. "I don't know. He knew I wouldn't bring you a big explanation or apology."

"*I was wrong.*" Xavier had actually said that. He was so rarely wrong.

But he had been once. At the club. He'd cuddled her and apologized. "*I'm sorry, Abby. The remote wasn't a good choice for you. I thought it would teach you to listen to your body without putting you on display. I never intended that you should feel abandoned.*"

When he was wrong, he admitted it. And if he said something, he meant it.

"We weren't exclusive, you know." Abby swirled the wine in her glass.

"You agreed to that?" Lindsey sounded shocked. "I know some of the subs do, but you?"

"After Nathan, I wasn't interested in getting involved with anyone. And Xavier and I both agreed. Only, then, when I was living with him…I didn't think he'd still go out with someone else."

Rona squeezed the bridge of her nose. "I'm surprised, actually. He's very up-front about having more than one woman. I think if he'd continued to date other people, he would have told you."

"Blind, deaf, and dumb—that's me." Abby stared at the skyline. The setting sun turned the Bay Bridge to a fantasy and sparkled on the water. "We talked about his wife once. He said she was his whole world."

Rona nodded. "Simon said while Xavier was turning Leduc Industries into the powerhouse it is, Catherine was beside him all the way. His admin, his submissive, and his wife. He hasn't taken anyone seriously since."

"Yeah. So it seems."

Rona's hand closed over Abby's. "Until now, Abby. Until you."

Tears swam in her eyes. "Sure. That's why he went out with my stepsister."

"'*I was wrong*,' remember?" Lindsey leaned back in her chair. "Now I only started going to the club a month before you, but he…" She paused. "He looked more alive after you came. Like you woke him up or something."

"You need to think about this," Rona said.

"Sure." *Not gonna happen.*

"Dropping the subject of idiot males, what about your stepsister?"

Abby gave Rona a frown. "What about her?"

"Are you going to let her continue to step on you?" Rona took a meditative sip of wine. "You said she's done this to you before?"

Abby snorted. "Every single boyfriend I ever had."

"Exactly. But Abby, what did you do to deter her?" Rona tilted her head. "Do you enjoy pain that much? If you're a masochist, I know some sadists at the club who–"

"No, I'm not a masochist! Just how was I supposed to stop her?"

"Oh please," Lindsey said. "If one of my sisters had shown up with my guy, there'd have been hair-pulling, name-calling, and serious screaming."

Abby managed to close her mouth. Screaming?

"Now, that said, we battled out the no-poaching-on-a-sister rules when we first got tits," Lindsey continued. "But if you always let her shove your face in the mud without a good catfight, then…"

"I…" Abby stared at the table. *Keep your voice down. Never start a fight. Don't argue; just agree.* All those behaviors she'd learned because of her father. She couldn't upset him, so she'd retreated. But Daddy was gone, and living a life without altercation wasn't natural. It hadn't been his fault, but… *He's dead, and I haven't moved on.*

"Does it seem like you can hear her thinking?" Lindsey whispered.

So when Xavier had shown up with Janae, she'd run. Not knocked Janae on her ass or grabbed Xavier's lapels and asked him why he'd do such a thing to her.

Because... Her mouth dropped open. Because he wouldn't. She stared as the lights of the city flickered on in the evening dusk. Xavier would never deliberately hurt her like that—not anyone, but certainly not her. And his face had held sheer shock and then anger, but not at her.

Janae had conned him somehow.

"Abby?"

Abby held up her hand. "Wait. I'm having an epiphany here."

"Sounds mighty painful," Lindsey muttered, getting a snort from Rona.

"My assertive skills are screwed up," Abby stated.

"That's an epiphany?" Lindsey scowled. "No, sister, an epiphany is when God hauls his big ass out of the clouds and smacks you over the head."

Abby giggled and drained her glass. "Today you and Rona did the thumping."

"Oh Crom." Rona made a grab for Abby's glass and failed. "Have you had anything to eat today?"

"Nope." Abby poured herself more. "And my head's going to hurt tomorrow. But—trust me—Janae's head will blow off her shoulders by the time I get through with her." She held her glass up. "But first I have to deal with Mr. *I-Was-Wrong* Leduc."

Two glasses clinked against hers in a unanimous toast.

Chapter Twenty-Five

Abby almost cried when she walked into Dark Haven and the familiar scents and sounds surrounded her. She'd missed this place.

"Abby?" Dixon stood behind the reception desk...which was covered in papers again. "*Abby*!" He scurried around the desk and dropped to his knees, hands clenched in front of his chest. "Tell me you're coming back. Puh-leeeze." The puppy-dog eyes he gave her would have melted the hardest resolve.

And his joy at seeing her lifted her heart enough that she could smile. "I'm not sure yet. We'll see."

After rising, he hooked his fingers in his chain-mail shirt and eyed her clothing—a black vinyl dress that buttoned up to her chin. High, black vinyl boots. "Fantastic Domme outfit. Armed for battle?"

"Absolutely." Almost what she'd worn the first time she'd met Xavier, only this time with even more coverage. Confrontations were too one-sided if one opponent was clad in only a corset and thong.

"Go on in, sweetie. Make sure to come back and let me know what happens. Or..." As Abby headed for the door, she heard the beep of the touch phone. "Gina, my peachie-poo. Can you take over the desk? I have something to watch."

Inside the main room, two Doms were setting up the left stage for a suspension demonstration. A few people were dancing. At the tables, people socialized and negotiated the terms before going to play.

No Xavier.

The stairs to the dungeon had grown much, much steeper, or maybe her wobbling legs affected her perception. She passed the first scene area where Angela was cleaning up the cross, her sub bundled in a blanket on the floor.

Heart rate increasing, Abby walked across the room. Past a flogging. Past the spanking benches in the center. A man in a cock-and-ball torture scene groaned continually. Screams came from a genital needle play on the other side.

Still no Xavier.

To her disgust she spotted Nathan instead. What was he doing here? His young, chipmunk-faced submissive knelt beside the sex swing as he checked the chains. His leather bag lay on a bench nearby.

"Nathan," Abby called. As she walked past the bench, she grabbed a short cane from his toy bag.

He turned, shocked. "I can't believe they let you in."

"Well, I'm surprised they didn't cancel *your* membership."

"If I'd been in Dark Haven rather than Serenity, I'd have been pitched out." His face twisted with anger. "Because of you, I'm on club probation. I had to take the beginner's class."

Oooh, bet that hurt. Nonetheless, it didn't make up for the rest of his crimes. She whipped the cane in a vicious backhand. It hit his right thigh with a loud smack.

Although his jeans must have dissipated the effect somewhat, he gave a satisfying yelp.

"That's for saying we were in a committed relationship all spring while you were screwing around with your toy here."

He took a step back. "What the hell?"

"And you fucked my stepsister, didn't you?"

His eyes shifted as his face turned red.

Oh, he had. She sliced through the air, and the cane slapped his left thigh.

"Dammit!" He tried to grab the cane.

"You're pitiful, Nathan. You should master yourself before you try to master someone else."

"You slut." His eyes were infuriated as he lunged forward.

"Fun's over." Xavier stepped between them. Ignoring both Nathan and Abby, he frowned at the kneeling girl.

Abby's heart broke at the girl's betrayed expression.

"Kirsty," Xavier said. "Did you know he was with Abby last spring?"

Tears welled as she shook her head.

Xavier's cold stare made Nathan back up a step. "Kemp, you give the club—and the lifestyle—a bad name. I'm canceling your membership. Your dues will be refunded."

He glanced at Tyrol, the biggest submissive on staff...or anywhere, actually. Built like a sumo wrestler, the man would kneel only to a Domme. "Tyrol, please see Kemp out."

"By your command, my liege." Towering over Nathan, Tyrol motioned for him to pack up his toy bag. A female staff member put her arm around Kirsty and led her away.

Xavier closed a hand around Abby's wrist.

She yanked free and tried to ignore the surge of desire his touch induced. The way her body betrayed her roused her anger again. Turning to face him, she gave him a hard shove that pushed him back all of six inches.

His brows drew together.

"You're no better than Nathan, my lie—*Xavier*." She raised her chin. "Did you know Janae was my stepsister? Did you care?"

His chiseled face stayed expressionless as he stared at her so intently she almost backed up. "You want to discuss this here?"

She saw people moving closer to the show. Planting her feet, she crossed her arms over her chest, imitating his stance. When a corner of his mouth tipped up, she would have kicked him—except her legs were shaking too hard. "Sure. You like being an exhibit, right?"

One eyebrow rose. "All right, Abby. For your orderly mind: First, I didn't know she was any relation to you. Second, I didn't know it was your parents' party. Third, it wasn't a date. She said Harold was looking for a new charity and that she'd introduce us. I met her in front of the house."

Pursuing a donor. That would be like him. But this was more than just a mix-up. She didn't move.

His lips tightened. "I totally missed how well she manipulated me." He touched her shoulder.

She slapped his hand away. He hadn't known Janae was her stepsister. Light was filling her. But she was still furious. "You looked far too comfortable to have just met her."

"We had about four dates several years ago. That's how she knew me."

"She dumped you?"

"No, Abby. I never dated any woman more than a few times."

Dated. He'd used the past tense. And he hadn't wanted to continue seeing Janae. *He wants me and not Janae?*

"So your '*I was wrong*' message was just you *conning* me?" Sure it was. He didn't see that he'd done anything wrong. Disappointment felt like a raw wound inside her. *"How about you? Are you going to the club?"* she'd asked him, and he'd agreed, not saying anything about Janae. She took a step back. Away from him.

"No, Abby. I *was* wrong." He met her eyes, and for a moment, just a moment, she saw the seething emotions under all that control. "I should have told you that I planned to meet Janae. When you asked me what I was doing, I didn't give you the complete truth."

Her feet had frozen to the floor. He knew. He knew the omission had hurt her almost as badly as seeing him with Janae. "But why?" she whispered.

"Partly because I remembered what you'd said about gorgeous and glamorous women." Then he gave her a rueful look. "And because you didn't want me with you at your party."

Her mouth dropped open. She'd hurt his feelings? Then she glared. "You always make me—"

"Share your feelings. And I didn't."

She was so, so mad. She smacked the cane across the outside of his thigh.

As gasps sounded around the dungeon, he snatched the cane and tossed it onto a chair. "Now that wasn't smart."

Oh heavens, what did I do? Horrified at her action, she raised her hand to push him away. "Just s-stay away from me. I—"

"Never." He grabbed her hand and yanked her off balance. His fingers closed around her upper arms in an unbreakable grip.

SHE WAS HERE. *Finally.* Xavier's heart felt overfull.

The little fluff who constantly repressed her emotions was definitely expressing them now. Her gray eyes flashed with silver, and her cheeks had flushed red. "Let me go!"

"Oh, I don't think so." He tucked her wrists into one hand and caressed her cheek with the other. "You wouldn't be here if you didn't care, Abby."

"I don't." She glared at him, so full of life she almost glowed.

"You do." He kissed the pouting lips lightly. "And I'm going to keep you."

Her eyes widened, and he felt a momentary hesitation in her struggles.

"I'm sorry, Abby. I was wrong not to share. And I was exceedingly slow to realize how I feel about you," he said gently. "That's what I did last Friday—I said good-bye to Catherine and told her I had found someone to love." He cupped her cheek in his hand, feeling as if he'd caught a butterfly. "I love you, Abby."

"You don't. You can't."

He slid his hand down to her neck, enjoying the pounding of her pulse. "I do and I can." He pulled the ring from his pocket and slid it on her finger before she realized what he was doing. Excited whispers erupted from the onlookers.

Abby didn't move.

As Xavier stepped back, he took a slow breath. She might be fully in the moment, but so was he, and if she didn't agree, she was going to break his heart.

Her hand turned over as she stared at the diamond, then him. "You gave me a ring." Her dazed expression was delightful, much like how she looked after an orgasm.

He planned to put that look on her face often in the years to come. "Marry me, Abby."

Her mind clicked into gear, making him smile. "So I'll be the *home* woman. Don't you need another woman or two for your club and for society?"

"You've already filled all those roles. I wasn't ready to admit it. " He couldn't stay so far away. Slowly he folded her into his arms until her soft breasts pressed against him.

"You don't want commitment."

"I don't want anyone but you. There will be no one but you." The words came out almost a growl. "And there will be no one for you but me. That's commitment."

When she leaned into him, the impossible coil of worry in his chest eased. "Marry me, Abby."

"But..."

"You need me, little fluff—and I really do need you."

Her breath was a slow exhale, and she rubbed her face on his shoulder, snuggling in. "I'm not ready."

He laughed. "No one ever is."

"You'll hurt me." Her arms came around his waist in a sweet embrace. "I'll probably hurt you too."

He rubbed his cheek in her hair, floral and spice, trying to hear her mind working. It was, he knew. "I daresay."

Her arms tightened. "But I'll love you even more. Yes, I'll marry you."

The rush of relief and joy took his breath away. Cheering filled the room, reminding him of where they were. But the people at Dark Haven were family. With a sense of coming home, he tipped Abby's chin up and kissed her, slow and deep, staking his possession.

When he pulled away, she frowned.

"What?"

"I really liked hitting you. And yelling at you."

Laughter came from those surrounding them.

Apparently his marriage with Abby wouldn't be as peaceful as he'd envisioned. Could she be any more perfect? His smile grew. "You've caused enough trouble, pet. And since you're now mine, it's my job to see that you don't cause any more."

UH-OH. THE look in his eyes was one she recognized. Abby tried to step back, but he seized the front of her dress.

"I dislike seeing overdressed submissives," he said mildly. He hooked his fingers between the buttons and yanked. Buttons pinged off the equipment as he ripped the front open. He spun her around and pulled the dress off completely.

Cheers drowned out her gasp. She stood there, naked but for a thong and her high-heeled boots. Heat flared in her face. Where had all these people come from? Her hands flew up to cover her breasts, although she knew better.

"Hands down." His dark eyes heated as he watched her force her arms straight, and then he walked around her. "Pretty little submissive, don't you think, my friends?"

The chorus of agreement sent more heat to her cheeks. Why, oh why, did she have to fall for a Dom who gathered a crowd wherever he went? Yet being with him and hearing the dark edge to his voice filled her with joy.

He stepped up behind her, pressing his body against hers, reaching around to cup her breasts and fondle them until arousal overcame her embarrassment.

He slid his hand between her legs. "Very nice, pet." She knew she was wet from the rumble of pleasure in his voice. "Now there's only one thing lacking in your attire."

"W-what's that?"

For a minute, without speaking, he rolled her nipples, sending a sizzle of desire straight to her core. "I believe a submissive should be glowing before she's collared," he whispered into her ear.

Before she could react, he put a boot between her feet and nudged her legs apart so he could slide his hand under her thong. So he could slick his fingers and rub her clit firmly. He curled his right arm around her, caging her against his chest, before closing his fingers over her left nipple. Pinching and teasing. Unable to escape, she strained against his hold. Her head fell back against his shoulder, her eyes closing as he stimulated her expertly, mercilessly.

"You're mine to play with, Abigail," he said, pushing a finger inside her and making her jerk. "Mine to display, and I enjoy showing off your beautiful breasts." He pinched her nipple, and she inhaled as the heat kept rising. "I like sharing how lovely you are when you come."

"You'd share me?" She tried to move.

She was yanked back as his hands formed restraints harder than steel. "If anyone ever *touches* you, I'll break every one of his fingers. Is that clear?"

"Yes, my liege." She swallowed past a dry throat and forced out her own demand. "And if any woman puts her hands on you, I'll cane you both."

"Absolutely." His cheek rubbed hers as he murmured, "I'm yours as much as you are mine, Abby."

"Okay." All her muscles went limp, and she relaxed against him, knowing he would hold her safe.

"There, that's right. That's what I wanted." His body was a wall of strength behind her. Something cool brushed against her neck before he held it up in front of her face.

She touched it with light fingertips. Much like the thick, golden choker that Rona wore, this was a single band of shining silver.

"We're not in a Master and slave relationship." His voice was husky and as tender as she'd ever heard it. "But I've seen the way you look at Rona's collar. So, little fluff, this shows you belong to me. No matter what we work out as to how far my control over you extends, that will never change."

Her bones were melting right into the floor. Could a person have too much joy?

"Do you accept my collar, Abby?"

"Yes, oh yes. Yes, please."

The muted pleasure of the crowd added to her own. She tilted her chin up and heard him mutter, "Do you know how much I love you?" The cold smoothness of metal surrounded her throat.

Yes, maybe she did.

Chapter Twenty-Six

In his study, Xavier looked up at the sound of the front door. As his spirits lifted, he grinned and rose. The house felt as if it came alive when she returned home. He spotted her as she sped through the living room, obviously looking for him. Her face was so lit with happiness that his question seemed almost irrelevant. "How did it go, Professor?"

"I got the job." She danced across the room and twirled in a way that sent lascivious thoughts rising. Put her in silks and—

"Starting this spring, I'm back in the tenure track."

No wonder she was dancing. "Congratulations." He lifted her in the air, smiling up. "You'll be an excellent asset to them."

He rather thought the small college had realized what a treasure they were acquiring. He knew—he'd made a point of visiting her university and reading her glowing evaluations and commendations. This was one professor who possessed not only solid teaching skills, but a sincerity that drew in the students and a brilliance that illuminated the most boring subject. "I'm proud of you, Professor Bern."

Her small hands framed his face as she leaned down to kiss him. He'd been surprised at the difference the engagement—and collaring—had made in her behavior toward him. Much of her reserve had been due to insecurity. He would do his best to ensure she'd never again doubt how much he loved her.

He lowered her until her feet touched the floor, then tugged her hair back so he could deepen the kiss and enjoy the way her body melted against him.

Arousal hummed in his blood when he finally lifted his head and surveyed what he intended for his afternoon treat. Her eyes shone with love, her face was flushed, her lips were wet and reddened. Yes, he'd definitely start with those lips around his cock.

She shook her head as if to clear it. "So what do we need to do to get ready? When are the caterers coming? Are—"

"It's barely past noon. The caterers will arrive around six to set up. The cleaning service was in this morning, as was the yard service." As was the moving service he'd hired for one special room.

He gave her a long look that made her flush even more. "Being female, you'll probably need an hour to bathe and dress. That leaves four hours during which I'll require your exclusive attention."

Her eyes widened, and she took a step back. "Xavier, I don't really—"

"Yes. Really." Bending, he set his shoulder against her stomach and straightened. As he wrapped an arm over her kicking legs, her little fists pounded his back, but he felt her laughing uncontrollably.

"Beast. We're having a party. We can't have sex now. Are you insane?" She yanked on his loose hair.

Insanely happy.

He slapped her ass hard enough to make her squeak and started up the stairs, pleased his ankle didn't even twinge. In contrast his cock was trying to throb through his pants. "Abby, be silent or I'll gag you. And I'll enjoy it." In fact, that wasn't a bad notion.

She gave him one last thump on his back and then stayed quiet as he headed down the hall to one of the guest bedrooms. He opened the door and set her on her feet.

AS HER BLOOD returned to where it belonged, Abby had a second of dizziness and a longer one of disorientation. She was in Xavier's house, but this was *her* bedroom. She turned in a circle, taking in the heavy, cinnamon-colored draperies, the king-size four-poster with the intricate Moroccan carvings, her Oriental carpets.

The contemporary room had been transformed into an Arabian Nights fantasy—*hers*. "What have you done?"

The corner of his mouth lifted, and she realized that with his dark coloring, long black hair, and black eyes, he looked far too much like someone out of her fantasy.

His expression changed. Cold face, hot gaze. "English women—they never know when to be silent. But I didn't steal you from your caravan to listen to you chatter."

Her eyes widened as she realized he wasn't in jeans, but worn leather pants. His white shirt made him look even darker, and...was that a sheathed knife buckled to his belt? She retreated a step, her heart beginning to hammer.

"Ah, she's quiet now." He circled her slowly, making her feel like a quail chick face-to-face with a bobcat. He brushed his hand through her hair. “I have a fondness for women touched by moonlight,” he murmured. “With hair soft as the silks that I will have you wearing.”

“Xavier—”

He gripped her hair and yanked her head back. “Is this how you address your Master?” he asked, his voice harsh. “Shall I put red stripes up and down your fair skin?”

Shocked, she shook her head frantically. Her mouth had gone dry, her breathing catching over and over.

“Better.” He cupped her chin, his thumb and finger pressing against her jaw mercilessly. His gaze was just as merciless. “If you do everything I say, I will be pleased with you.” His voice dropped, and so did the pit of her stomach when he whispered, “Do not risk my displeasure, English.”

This is Xavier. This is my fiancé. The reassurances weren’t working, not when he jerked her suit jacket off and threw it in the corner. He looked at her shirt and growled, “Remove that.”

Her fingers fumbled at the buttons, finally getting it open. One yank and it joined the coat. He circled again, and the cool feel of the air made goose bumps rise on her arms.

He stopped in front of her and frowned at her bra. “Disgusting device to keep a man from touching as he pleases.” When he unsheathed his knife, the blade far too long and sharp, a squeak escaped her, and she staggered back.

“Stand still,” he hissed. He fisted her hair, bringing her to a sudden stop. Cold metal touched her stomach, and she whimpered. The smooth blade slid under the front of her bra. A tug and it had sliced through the fabric. Very, very sharp.

"Xa—"

He shook his head slowly, holding her gaze with his.

I don't like knives. No no no. The cool metal was warming…against her skin…as it slid down the inner side of one breast.

"Don't annoy me, English, or I'll discover if your blood is as red as your skin is white." The flat of the knife caressed one breast, then the other, turned and scraped over the top as if shaving. Sharp as a razor. "Do you wish to remove your skirt…or shall I?" he asked softly.

"Me," she whispered, barely able to breath until the blade lifted and he stepped back.

She unzipped the dignified straight skirt, shoving it to the ground, following with the panty hose before he could ask. He watched silently, a slight curve to his hard lips.

The light filtering through the heavy drapes shadowed his face and lent an ominous, reddish cast to the room. He studied her for a second before his hand closed over her throat in a light grip, holding but not—quite—cutting off her air. As the blade rested on her cheek, he leaned forward, his face only an inch from hers. His black eyes stared into her wide ones. "Tell me you're going to please your Master, English."

Afraid to even move, she said through stiff lips, "Yes. Master."

He stepped away, leaving her shivering. "I thought so. Put your forehead on the carpet, your ass in the air. Show me what I risked my life to kidnap."

A flush ran through her in a long stream of heat. Swallowing hard, she knelt, put her face to the soft Oriental rug, and lifted her hips.

He didn't speak, his gaze like a weight running over her skin. She heard the thump of his boots. Music started slowly, Loreena McKennitt's lushly romantic *An Ancient Muse* album. Candlelight sent flickering shadows over the floor.

She heard him opening his leathers. "Up, English. Let's see if your mouth is as soft as it looks."

She pushed back onto her knees.

Emerging from trimmed, black pubic hair, his cock was rigid with engorged veins running up to the thick head. When she reached out, he slapped her hands. "You do not touch me without permission."

Growling under his breath, he took a silk scarf from her trunk at the foot of the bed and bound her wrists behind her back.

With a grunt of satisfaction, he stood in front of her again. His hand behind her head drew her face toward his cock. "Take me."

Her heart kicked up faster as she opened her mouth, and he pushed inside. She licked frantically, inhaling his dark, musky fragrance, tasting the first salty drop on the head.

Using her hair to move her, he ordered, "Suck" or "Lick" when the notion hit him. She swirled her tongue around him obediently, then, defying his hold, pulled back to suck only on the head.

"I don't think so." Fisting both hands in her hair, he pushed deeper into her throat, setting off her gag reflex. "Take it, English. You can and you will." He pulled back, waited a second, did it again.

Her eyes teared as she fought the restraints, fought his hold, and with every failure, lost more of her sense of control over anything.

Her muscles went slack as she surrendered, giving him everything, letting him move her as he would. Push her to do more.

"Better. You have much to learn, English." He pulled out and released her.

She dropped down, her bottom on her feet, shaking uncontrollably. Yet...she could feel the wetness slicking her upper thighs. The desire to have him inside her was a pounding need. She swallowed, tasting him on her tongue, the most potent and frightening of aphrodisiacs.

"Face to the carpet," he snapped. She complied.

With the sharp sound of leather on skin, pain flared over her right butt check. Her yelp filled the room. Trembling, she waited for more as the burn remained, throbbing and yet erotic. Shockingly erotic. She raised her head slightly.

He tossed a leather strap onto the trunk. "Next time you will do better, yes?"

"Yes, Master," she whispered. Anxiety over what he'd do next shivered through her, yet she needed him so badly that her core burned as painfully as her bottom.

He bent and smoothed his hand over the sore flesh. "Pretty round ass. Tempting a man to savagery. To do as he pleases." His merciless hand on her hip held her still as he pressed his fingers to her pussy, tracing the wetness. "So...the woman wants a man to take her?"

In a smooth move he lifted her up and tossed her on the bed on her side, intimidating her with his cruel strength. With her arms still tied behind her, she struggled to sit up. He'd done his leathers back up, the bulge blatant. Straining to be free.

She'd done that. Staring at him, she tensed in a mixture of fear and anticipation. He'd take her, and he wouldn't be gentle. Her nipples bunched, and her pussy felt as if it swelled even as she waited.

He untied her hands and pushed her onto her back. Without a word, he shoved a pillow under her bottom to raise her hips, then wrapped silk around her ankle, over and over, forming the softest of cuffs. He tied it loosely to the bottom post.

When he grasped her other leg, fear flared, and she tried to pull away. His powerful hand gripped her tighter, and he easily lashed that ankle down as well. He positioned her arms next to her sides, keeping her still with a deadly look from his black eyes. After tying one end of a silk scarf to the left headboard post, he tied the other end to her left wrist, then repeated the process on the right.

What kind of bondage was that? Her arms were almost completely loose.

Amusement glinted in his eyes as she lifted her arms. Slowly, deliberately, he wrapped silk around each thigh just above the knee, making thigh cuffs.

He bent her left leg, pulling it out toward the side of the bed, and then tied her wrist cuff to her thigh cuff. Her hand flattened over her knee. He did the same on the other leg.

She stared up into dark unreadable eyes, and his lips curled in a hard smile. His hand pressed between her breasts, making her nipples contract harder. "You like being bound, English. Thus I will do it so well that you cannot move from my attentions. From any pain I choose to give you."

Her heart thudded hard against his palm, and his laugh was as dark as his gaze. At each of the four posts, he tightened the silks until nothing moved. Her legs, tied to her wrists, couldn't pull down, and her arms couldn't pull up, and her knees were bent and splayed out, leaving her open to anything he wanted to do.

He watched her struggle for a while, and the slight curve of his mouth and amusement in his eyes said he enjoyed seeing her helpless.

Her breathing was close to panting; she wasn't so sure she liked it at all.

When he walked over to an armoire against the wall, she stiffened. That wasn't her furniture. He took something out. It looked like a fat dildo at first. Then he turned it and lubricated a second, smaller shaft. A double dildo. Her jaw dropped as she realized it would go in both her pussy and anus.

He leaned forward and put the larger dildo against her pussy, sliding it in an inch. She squeaked as the other shaft pushed against her anus. "No, no, I don't want that."

"I didn't ask." With a few rocking movements, he pressed the shaft through the ring of muscles and slid both dildos all the way in with one hard penetration.

Her anus burned and throbbed. Her pussy felt stretched and full. When he flipped a switch, both shafts vibrated together, making her clench around them. As her excitement flared, she squirmed helplessly.

"This keeps you occupied until I make you silent." His mouth turned down in disgust. "Mouthy English women."

He picked something up that had been lying on the quilt. "You will remember these?" He held up the nipple clamps from her first day at Dark Haven. A fine chain dangled between them.

Her eyes widened. Oh no—her breasts were already swollen and aching.

Ignoring her attempts to move, he attached one. Tightened it until it bit into her. She waited for him to ask for a number, for how badly it hurt.

He didn't ask. Her breath thickened in her throat as he moved to her other breast. Pinching, pinching. She was panting when he stopped.

Testing, he gave the chain a tug. She sucked in a breath at the painful pull on each nipple. "Very good." His smile didn't reassure her at all as he set a small lead weight on her chest. A woven rope had been tied to the ring on it.

Xavier glanced up.

Oh heavens. A chain crossed from the top of the left head post to the top of the right bottom post. "What is—"

He tossed the end of the rope over the high chain.

The vibrations in her pussy and anus never stopped. Her clit throbbed frantically as her need grew.

She stared as he pulled on the rope, lifting the metal ball until it swung in the air.

"This will teach you to keep your mouth closed"—his eyes glinted—"unless I have use for it." He pressed a midsection of the rope between her teeth, letting the tail end lie on her chest. "Bite."

When he let go, the weight on the other end pulled against her hold.

This wasn't so bad. If she opened her mouth, the weight would drop onto her stomach. It weighed less than a kiwi.

But then he took the tail end lying on her chest and tied it to the thin chain between the nipple clamps. Holding on to the rope, he glanced at her. "Let go."

No, I don't think so. She shook her head, saw the ruthless look in his eyes, and opened her jaw.

He played the rope out slowly. As the weight descended, the chain between her breasts rose and tugged on the clamps until it felt as if fingernails were pulling her nipples upward. Her back arched as she tried to relieve the pressure. "Noooo."

"Yes." He pulled on the rope, lifting the weight until the chain between the clamps lay slack again. Then he offered her the section of the rope she'd been holding before—the one just above where it tied to the breast clamps.

As she closed her teeth on the rope, she felt the weight swinging on the other end, and she groaned as she understood what he'd done.

"Yes. Your teeth hold the weight now. If you open your mouth and release the rope, the nipple clamp chain will get the weight." His smile was cruel. "It might hurt a bit."

No. No no no. Her jaws locked on to the rope.

"Next time I will add a clit clamp." He surveyed his work with satisfaction—and arousal. "But I intend something else for that pink English clit today."

She inhaled through her nose as too many sensations swept over her: the biting of the clamps, the vibrations in her pussy and anus. Her swollen clit throbbed.

He put a knee on the bed, looking down at her. “Pretty pale woman, tied up and open for me to use.” He cupped one breast with a gentle touch that contrasted with the burning pinch of the clamp. Leaning forward, he teased the metal with his tongue, wetting the compressed peak, then blowing a stream of air to cool the burn…only the pain didn’t go away. His mouth worked the other one as he fondled her full breasts. Playing with her as the vibrations went on and on.

She couldn’t move, couldn’t speak, and the feeling of helplessness filled her. She couldn’t do anything. Her mind circled, drifting farther and farther away, as the overwhelming sensations shook her body.

Chuckling, he nipped her soft stomach.

She started to gasp, felt the rope move, and her teeth gritted down.

He stroked over her open thighs as he checked her leg and wrist restraints. “You’re quite helpless, English. How does it feel?”

With the rope in her mouth, she couldn’t answer.

XAVIER SMILED. SUCH big gray eyes. She watched him like a mouse facing a hungry owl. *Lovely*. He pulled out a small flogger. The three short strands were made of very soft leather. It could feel like a massage…or a harder flick of the wrist could impart a sting. Perfect for tender areas.

He dangled the flogger over her, giving her the scent of leather, trailing the ends down her neck, her shoulder, between her breasts and back up. When he moved lower, the muscles of her stomach quivered.

She shivered as he teased over the creases between her cunt and thighs. With her pussy stuffed full and her legs splayed, her clit was beautifully exposed—a fat, glistening pink pearl. They hadn't done much pain play, and he looked forward to her reactions when the flogger hit her most sensitive bits.

As she fully realized her vulnerability, her breasts heaved and wobbled with her fast breathing. Half fear—and, judging from the slickness around the dildos, half anticipation.

He flicked the miniflogger over her legs very, very gently. Then faster. He set up a rhythm of whispering caresses, up one leg, down the other and back up, over her stomach to the undersides of her breasts, avoiding the clamps and rope. He played her sweetly until her breathing deepened. Her hips started making urgent gyrations as the sensations added to those of the vibrator, pushing past her barriers.

The flogger roved over her hips and thighs. This time he added a bite of pain as he followed the same map, up over her stomach to her breasts. Her skin took on a flush, reddening under the increased flogging.

Her eyes drooped to half-lidded as she started losing track of her surroundings under the storm of sensation.

Flogging in an even pattern, he moved back down her stomach. He struck her inner thighs lightly, the outer legs harder, harder, and heard her pulling in air through her nose. Down and back up.

Her clit appeared almost inflamed with need. Laying the flogger to one side, he set his knee on the bed between her spread legs and ran his tongue all around the tiny nub.

The sound she made sent a rush through him as every dominant instinct in him surged up, needing more. His cock hardened unbearably. He continued the slow circles until she was as close to panting as a person with a rope in her mouth could get. Her hips lifted the inch he'd permitted, over and over.

Was there anything more satisfying in the world than this? Smiling, he took her whole clit into his mouth, rubbing one side, the other, sucking and licking without pause—and sent her over.

Her hips bucked against the restraints as she screamed and climaxed. Another, higher scream sounded when the weight dropped two inches to yank her nipples upward.

Oh yes. He'd never tire of hearing the noises she made when she came. Chuckling, he reached up and took the weight off her nipples. "Foolish English female. Don't damage my property." He tucked the rope back in her mouth.

Her teeth bit down, although her eyes were almost glazed.

Rising, he picked up the tiny flogger and started on the same pattern, knowing her body was anxiously preparing for the sensations. That sense of anticipation in a submissive was exactly what every Dom hoped for.

Up her left leg, down, and up again, over to her right, down and up her stomach. Harder this time, so the undersides of her breasts had tiny red marks. Tears gleamed in her eyes even as her cheeks and lips pinkened with arousal.

Up and down, slowly he worked his way toward her clit. It had been soft after her climax but was now slick and straining out of its hood. Moving up her inner thighs, he lightened the strikes, stopping short of her groin.

Building and building her anticipation.

PAINFULLY NIBBLED TO death. Abby wanted to glare at him but didn't dare. This time the flogger that had felt so wonderful was dealing out tiny, stinging bites everywhere it struck. He moved over her body quickly, keeping the blows light enough that the pain was right on the edge—and everything he did increased her need.

He flogged up her inner legs, stopping before he reached her crotch and moving back down her outer thighs. Her clit hurt as if each flogging journey pushed more blood into it. No longer a nub—it felt as if it had swollen to the size of a mushroom.

The pattern changed, and the flogger struck the inside calf of her left leg, the inside of her right. Left, right. Each blow sank into her clit in throbbing bursts as he moved upward in an inevitable path. Her hips rose, straining uncontrollably toward the torture.

Please, please, please.

He reached her lower thighs.

Upper thighs.

Oh no, oh no. She tensed.

Without pausing, the three strands flicked onto her clit. *Right on top,* over and over and over, in exquisite pain. Pleasure.

An orgasm blasted through her, a massive upheaval of pleasure, churning with noise and boiling into her veins. Her back arched, her neck arched, and she screamed.

The rope slipped. The weight dropped.

"Aaaaah." Her nipples flared with pain, and her insides clenched, sending another blast of brutal pleasure exploding outward.

Over the roaring in her ears, she heard a pleased laugh. He tugged the double dildo out, leaving her clenching on emptiness.

Xavier pressed his cock to her pussy and thrust. One hard, shocking thrust. She groaned as he stretched her almost past bearing, painful and yet the most intense of pleasures.

He tightened his hands on her hips, and then he stopped.

She met his laughing gaze as he unclipped the weight and tossed it on the floor. The chain between the clamps dropped like a cool blessing on her breasts. He stretched forward. His chest rubbed over the clamps, over her so-tender nipples, and made her hiss.

She glared at him. "You're despicable."

The white of his grin appeared in his dark face, before his expression changed. "Are you speaking to me, foolish English woman?" The threat was thick in every word, and she tensed.

With his cock deep inside her and his weight holding her to the bed, he curved one hand over her throat, pressing until she had a moment of panic.

"Don't speak." Braced on one arm, he leaned down and took her mouth, controlling the kiss. Controlling her. His hand around her neck enforced her helplessness. Her mind spun, her body melting beneath his.

Lifting his head, he started to thrust, hard and fast. With his hand on her throat adding a terrifying restraint, he trapped her gaze with his as he hammered into her. His hair fell onto her shoulders, curtaining her in silky black.

He felt good—so wonderfully good. His weight, his control, his cock. Her eyes pooled with tears as she stared up at him, letting him see what he wanted, take what he wanted.

Giving a low sound, he kissed her, gently this time, drawing it out until she felt as loved as she did controlled.

He nipped her chin and started over again. Faster and slower, and now, every few thrusts, he twisted and ground his pelvis over her clit, bringing her back into need as if she'd never climaxed at all.

"I like you restrained, little fluff," he said, rocking against her clit. "You're wide open. Can't move." The sun lines at the corners of his eyes crinkled. "You have to take whatever I want to give you." He sped up again, and her core throbbed in time with his thrusts.

Her body gathered, nerve endings screaming for release.

"All you can do is offer yourself for my pleasure." Another circle and she felt the inevitable tightening of her body around his cock.

He whispered, "And to come when I want you to."

The pressure grew unbearable, teetered for a moment. Then a tidal wave of sensation crashed over the rocks, taking her senses with it, filling her with pleasure. She bucked under him as he came inside her. He pressed deep into her, his pelvis on her clit, and she spasmed around him again and again.

Eventually she managed to open her eyes. Her heart still thudded against her ribs, trying to batter free. Sweat trickled between her breasts, down the creases of her legs. He'd released her throat and was teasing her hair with his fingers. Waiting for her to recover.

She licked salt from her lips, feeling how swollen they were from his cock, his kisses. As the room blurred back into focus, she stared around at her harem room—the seraglio.

He must have taken one look at the style and known what kind of fantasies she had. Then he'd not only given her what she wanted but had pushed until she had no control, and it was more, more than she'd ever dreamed. "Your English woman thanks you," she whispered. "I think."

"You're very welcome." He nipped her chin. "Next time, English, you will learn to show your gratitude properly."

"I love you." *So, so much.*

He nuzzled the curve of her neck and kissed up her jaw. "That's a good start."

Chapter Twenty-Seven

As laughter and conversation burbled behind her, Abby stood near the pool and looked out at the night. Across the dark water of the bay, San Francisco sparkled like a fairyland.

"Xavier's home is perfect for parties, isn't it?" Her mother stopped beside her. "You look happy, sweetie."

"I am." Abby turned, smiling at how their guests spilled out of the house and onto the long, wide patio. "You know, I never thought life would take a turn like this. Last spring it seemed as if my path was all laid out, nice and straight."

"Sometimes the curves lead you to the best places." Her mother smiled. "To a very nice man and… I forgot to ask. How did the university take your resignation?"

"They weren't happy with me. Apparently I wasn't even on the list to be laid off. Go figure." She smiled, already anticipating the new school year. "I think, for me, smaller will be better. I'll have time to actually enjoy teaching, and I'm having fun planning my new courses for this spring."

"You always enjoyed a challenge," her mother said. "At least intellectual ones."

Abby grimaced at the qualification. "True. Social challenges? Not so much."

"I think you sell yourself short, honey. You have quite a crowd here."

Let's not talk about where I met them, okay? She glanced around. Not far away, Simon and Rona, Lindsey, deVries, and Dixon were enjoying the view.

At a table with some of the Dark Haven members were the two Hunt brothers, Virgil Masterson, and their wives. They'd driven over from Bear Flat and would stay in the guest rooms tonight. Apparently Xavier had told them of Abby's explanations and punishment—they'd all given her affectionate hugs. Her teary eyes had set off the other women, making the Doms laugh.

Hopefully they'd stay for a few days. She knew Xavier planned to convince Becca and Logan to remain until after the baby was born. To his mind, a medical clinic wasn't safe enough for a first birth.

Her mother had followed her gaze. "You have a wonderful group of friends."

"She does, doesn't she?" Xavier tucked an arm around Abby, running his palm down the open back of her gown, then taking her gloved hand. "We've managed an interesting blend." He nodded at the knot of professors talking with teachers from the literacy program. The BDSM group knew many of the animal shelter staff, as well as Xavier's business friends. Their Tiburon neighbors were chatting with counselors from Stella's Employment Services. "A few drinks and they'll mix it up even more."

"I'm afraid there aren't many youngsters here, though. Good thing Grace brought Matthew." Abby glanced over at her little sister and saw her glaring at someone inside the house.

Abby turned. *Janae.* "What's she doing here? I didn't invite her."

Her mother frowned. "Neither did I, but Harold probably told her."

Yeah, Janae was ballsy enough to show up, just to spoil the night. A chill swept over Abby.

Her stepsister looked spectacular. Men turned their heads, their gazes following her through the room. She stopped and did a slow turn. Her ice-blue gown glittered with rhinestones and showed off her dark hair and tan. Cut extremely low in front and back, her dress revealed every curve.

"I don't want her here," Abby said, a sense of hopelessness filling her. "But if I tell her to leave, she'll cause a scene."

Xavier's hand closed on Abby's nape in a hard grip. His black gaze showed his annoyance, even as his lips curled in an easy smile. "Quite a few of us are used to scenes and screaming and tears, you know."

In fact, Dark Haven was filled with such things. She choked on a laugh.

"More to the point, I see no reason why we should tolerate her presence. Go get rid of her."

Her mother gasped. "But… You'll make Abby do it?"

"Carolyn, normally I would take out the trash, but it's time for Abby to indulge in…" He ran a finger down Abby's cheek. "What did you say Lindsey called it? *Catfights*?"

"That's what it'll be." Her boast to Lindsey and Rona about taking care of Janae seemed foolish now. Dread weighted Abby's chest as she tried to muster some internal resolve. And oddly enough, found a bit of courage. "Okay. I'm going in. Cover me."

"Always."

As Abby crossed the patio into the house, out of the corner of her eye she saw Xavier look around. Just as when he ruled the club, the Dark Haven members were aware of him. He tilted his head toward the living room, and they flowed in that direction.

Wouldn't help much, though.

A smirk on her glossy red lips, Janae watched her approach. "About time. I could use a drink."

"I'm sorry, Janae, but you weren't invited. Please leave."

"Oh dear." Janae's voice rose. "Are you still upset that Xavier took me to Daddy's party?"

"No." Abby lifted her chin. "I know what you pulled to get him there."

"Like I needed to do anything? If you can't keep a man, it's hardly my fault."

That hurt. Abby sucked in a breath, wanting to retreat. Then she caught Xavier's gaze. He stood a few feet behind Janae, arms crossed over his chest. *Participate in life. Tackle it head-on.* "Oh, it's definitely your fault, considering you've fucked every guy who was interested in me." She forced a laugh. "From high school on. Aren't you getting tired of this?"

Janae's color rose, turning her tanned face a dark purple. "You bitch. You lie. I've never had to offer anything, and I wouldn't want your disgusting men. I—"

"Is that why you offered to fuck my boyfriend?" Grace pushed through the gathering crowd, Matthew in tow. "Don't you think a high school junior is a little young for you? Oh, wait—isn't that called being a pedophile?"

Whoa, talk about getting backup.

Janae made a sound like a boiling teapot and fled.

Abby stared. *She ran. She really ran.*

"You know, that was icy fun. Thanks!" Grace held her knuckles out for Abby to bump.

As Abby complied, she realized her fingers were numb. "Fun. Right." She cleared her throat. "You might want to talk with your dad now, though."

Standing beside their mother, Harold looked as if he'd been run over by a truck. He stared at the door, then Grace and Abby.

Her mother's face was pale, but she gave Abby and Grace a nod of approval.

"Jeez, Grace," Matthew muttered. "I didn't mind the show, but I'm not that young."

Abby heard Xavier muffle a laugh, and her spirits lifted. Nothing seemed to upset him, and wasn't that a lovely thing to know? She stepped into his arms, sure of her welcome.

"Very nice job, pet," he murmured in her ear. "I'm proud of you."

She grinned up. "You know, so am I."

"Now that you've cleaned out the dregs, we should get the party moving." Xavier gave her a hard kiss and then stepped to her side, his arm around her. His voice rose. "As long as we have you conveniently gathered in this room…" He waited for the laughter to die down. "We want to share our happiness with you." After tugging Abby's glove off, he lifted her left hand so the engagement ring showed. "Abby has consented to be my wife."

Grace's scream of delight was almost drowned out by the cheering and whistles filling the room. Abby was smothered in her little sister's hug, surfacing only long enough to be grabbed by her mother. She looked up for a moment to see Xavier receiving congratulations from those who hadn't yet heard.

After a few minutes he raised his hand again. "I tried to decide what to get her for an engagement present."

Abby stiffened. If he brought out a paddle or flogger in front of her mother, she'd deck him.

"I wanted something expensive, of course. And elegant. However, after I decided on the perfect gift, Virgil informed me that he actually started the tradition." He tilted his head toward the man from Bear Flat.

What tradition? Abby glanced at the women. Summer frowned before delight bloomed on her face.

The front door swung open, and with a wide grin Dixon strutted in, carrying a picnic basket covered with a red-checked cloth.

We're going on a picnic?

Xavier reached into the basket and pulled out a furry puppy. Totally black. Its ears flopped half over. It stared at her with eyes as dark as Xavier's.

As she closed her hands around the tiny body, the puppy whined, frantically squirming to get closer. "Blackie. You got me Blackie." Tears spilled over as happiness welled inside her. She choked, remembering his lead-in. "Expensive and elegant?"

People around them burst out laughing. As Blackie bathed her chin with tiny licks, Abby stared up at the one man who knew exactly what she'd love most. But...what had he done? "He'll dig up the grass."

"That's what a lawn service is for."

"He'll chew your boots."

"That's what shoe stores are for."

"He'll wake you up in the night to go outside."

His grin flashed. "That's what a wife is for."

Laughing, she leaned against him. As the puppy tried to choose which neck to lick first, Xavier's arms closed around her.

"I continue to have difficulty identifying my emotions, my liege," she whispered, nestling in.

"Tell me."

She stood on tiptoe to murmur in his ear. "I'm warm all over like I'm wrapped in a fuzzy quilt. Relaxed and bouncy at the same time. As bubbly as if my heart drank a glass of champagne. What do you think?"

"I think you feel what I do, little Professor." She felt his lips curve against her hair. "*Loved.*"

Cherise Sinclair

Now everyone thinks summer romances never go anywhere, right? Well…that's not always true.

I met my dearheart when vacationing in the Caribbean. Now I won't say it was love at first sight. Actually, since he was standing over me, enjoying the view down my swimsuit top, I might even have been a tad peeved—as well as attracted. But although our time together there was less than two days, and although we lived in opposite sides of the country, love can't be corralled by time or space.

We've now been married for many, many years. (And he still looks down my swimsuit tops.)

Nowadays, I live in the west with this obnoxious, beloved husband, two children, and various animals, including three cats who rule the household. I'm a gardener, and I love nurturing small plants until they're big and healthy and productive…and ripping defenseless weeds out by the roots when I'm angry. I enjoy thunderstorms, playing Scrabble and Risk, and being a soccer mom. My favorite way to spend an evening is curled up on a couch next to the master of my heart, watching the fire, reading, and…well…if you're reading this book, you obviously know what else happens in front of fires. :)

—*Cherise*

Visit Cherise Sinclair on the web at http://www.cherisesinclair.com

Loose Id® Titles by Cherise Sinclair

Available in digital format and print from your favorite retailer

Master of the Abyss
Master of the Mountain
My Liege of Dark Haven
The Dom's Dungeon
The Starlight Rite

* * * *

The MASTERS OF THE SHADOWLANDS Series
Club Shadowlands
Dark Citadel
Breaking Free
Lean on Me
Make Me, Sir
To Command and Collar

* * * *

"Simon Says: Mine"
Part of the anthology *Doms of Dark Haven*
With Sierra Cartwright and Belinda McBride

* * * *

"Welcome to the Dark Side"
Part of the anthology *Doms of Dark Haven 2: Western Night*
With Sierra Cartwright and Belinda McBride

CPSIA information can be obtained at www.ICGtesting.com
Printed in the USA
BVOW010119080113

309973BV00001B/70/P

9 781623 001254